To Cook a Squirrel

A novel by
Betty Rae McCormack

To my beloved friend [...]! Enjoy!! God bless and keep you and [...]!! Blessings!!!! Betty Rae McCormack

Portland, Oregon

MT. HOOD PRESS

This book is dedicated to my beloved husband Wendell. I miss him every day.

Chapter 1

HARRY FEARS THE WORST

In the winter of 1948, the Reverend Harry Petersen strode purposefully through the village of Prairie Meadows, Wisconsin. As he drew near the home of Bill Collins, his most prominent and articulate parishioner, he slackened his pace. Confronting Bill, the acknowledged leader of the Prairie Meadows Church, was no small matter, for Harry knew that Collins could make or break his ministry. From the beginning of their friendship last year, Harry had relied on Collins' guidance and encouragement. Over fragrant coffee and home-cooked meals he had shared his problems with Bill and his out-spoken wife, Jane. To him, becoming a minister of the Gospel and marrying his sweetheart, Babs, was a dream come true. Furthermore, securing a post in scenic Wisconsin where he could hunt and fish on his days off, was an added delight. Not even the trials of poverty had discouraged him, for Harry was certain that God had called him to serve in central Wisconsin.

During his first year as pastor, Harry had visited in the homes of the people, delivered sermons, conducted weddings and funerals and organized the business of his three churches. The farmers and townspeople were responding favorably to his pastoral leadership, when unaccountably, Bill Collins' behavior toward him had abruptly changed.

Crossing the street, Harry flushed and shook his head, recalling last Sunday's service at the Prairie Meadows Church. After Harry had announced his sermon topic, Bill Collins rose up from his pew at the front of the sanctuary, deliberately donned his hat and coat, and stalked out of the church. With remarkable poise, the fledgling minister had continued to lead the worship service, but his heart was heavy. Without the support of his friend Bill, he felt bereft, lonely, and close to despair.

Swallowing hard, as he made his way toward Collins' home, he racked his brain again in bewilderment. What had he done or said to offend Bill Collins?

Thinking back, he remembered last year arriving at Bill's house, after his first Sunday as a ministerial candidate, having conducted the services and preaching to the congregations of the Prairie Meadows, Sterling, and Rosebud Churches. Bill was there on the porch welcoming the young candidate.

Feeling tired from preaching three sermons and meeting crowds of people, Harry began to ascend the steps of the home, looking forward with both fear and joy to dinner with the Collins,' Prairie Meadows's foremost lay family. Suddenly, his progress was halted by an indignant screech! "M E E O O W!" proclaimed their outraged tabby cat, as Harry's right foot landed squarely on her tail. Harry hastily moved up, clumsily stumbling over a floral arrangement in the corner.

"Poor Mandy," said Bill's daughter, picking up her offended pet, "He didn't mean anything, baby," she murmured as she scanned Harry's ample frame.

"Mandy thinks she owns the steps," said Bill. He introduced his daughter Carrie and son-in-law, Doug, and invited him inside. Immediately, Bill had waved him to a comfortable chair in the living room.

"You and Doug have a lot in common, since you're attending seminary and Doug's a senior at Wisconsin University in Madison."

Exhausted, Harry sank thankfully into a large overstuffed chair. Glancing around, he noticed the casual maple furniture and the matching davenport and chair. The living/dining area had a comfortable appearance.

"Welcome to Prairie Meadows, Rev. Petersen. Doug, can't you see that he's tired? Get off that ottoman and let him put his feet up!" ordered Jane with a scowl on her pale face, as she tied an apron over her simple brown skirt, preparing to fix dinner.

"Yes, my mother-in-law," answered Doug, getting up, shoving the ottoman in Harry's direction, and pulling out a dining room chair for himself.

Observing the sulky expression on Doug's sensitive face as he bent over the Sunday newspaper, the young minister tried awkwardly to return the ottoman,

"That's okay, Doug. I don't need it."

"Keep it," advised his host, Bill, looking over at Harry, his rimless glasses pushed up on his balding head. "Stretch out, while Jane rustles up our Sunday dinner. Doug, you don't mind, do you?"

"Nope," returned Doug, studying the sports section of the *Milwaukee Journal*.

"You remember the names of all the people in the three churches, don't you, Harry?" teased daughter, Carrie, arching her dark eyebrows, her brown eyes twinkling.

"Afraid not," he responded with a dry laugh.

"Too bad if you don't. Our last minister was a genius at recalling names," warned the girl.

"Good for him," replied Harry, stretching his legs.

"Be sure to notice Mrs. Blodgett, anyway," she persisted.

"How can I remember everyone?" he asked irritably.

"It's easy to spot Mrs. Blodgett. She always wears purple and loves fancy hats."

"And she's usually with Jane, plotting ways to make money," added Bill.

"Are you talking about me?" asked Jane, as she brought in the silverware. "Set the table, Carrie."

"Yes, you and Doris Blodgett and the activities of the Busy Bees," replied Bill, looking up from the headlines.

"We have a lot of fun putting on dinners and raising money at rummage and cake sales. Carrie, when you finish, come in and stir the gravy for me!"

Harry frowned.

"Seriously, Bill, if the churches call me as pastor, I'll have to remember people's names, won't I?"

"Not all, right away, Harry," answered Bill, putting down the JOURNAL. "It'd be nice if you recall a few, like Tim Woods. Tim's father, the Reverend Woods, was pastor here years ago."

"Did you mention the Rankins, Dad?" asked Carrie, setting the butter and cranberry sauce on the table.

"Oh, yes, he's in business like me, an accountant, and she's very stylish, and active in our church and the Busy Bees."

"She's usually on the wrong side of the argument when we're deciding what to do, but you have to give her credit, Lola Rankin's no dummy," pronounced Jane, bringing in mashed potatoes and gravy. "Come on, you men, before the food gets cold! Harry, with your long legs, I'm going to put you at the end of the table. The rest of you, sit anywhere."

Doug moved a chair toward the end of the table, and Harry sat down, but missed the seat, landing on the floor.

"What's the matter with me," fretted Harry to himself. "This has been a disaster."

"Oh," said Bill, "I'll give you a hand, " helping him up.

When everyone was seated, Bill offered a prayer of thanks, and everyone began to eat.

"The food is delicious, Mrs. Collins," exclaimed Harry, hoping to redeem himself. "Chicken is my favorite."

"Call me Jane, Harry. Carrie, take the biscuits out of the oven and bring them to the table, will you?"

"What about the other churches, Dad?" asked Carrie, getting up. "Who are the really important members?"

"In Sterling, you'll get to know Ed Wells. He's Sunday School Superintendent, and real cranky," answered Jane, passing the green beans.

"I don't know too many at Rosebud," mused Bill, helping himself to the gravy.

4

"Oh, Bill, you've met the Rosses, that heavy-set couple that work a farm north of town," said Jane, buttering a biscuit. "Pass the biscuits, Doug."

Doug took two biscuits and handed the basket to Harry.

"Oh, that's right," replied Bill. "And there's that lady who's been married several times, what's her name, Jane?"

"Oh, you mean that redhead, Mrs. Knight. Yes, she gets around."

"Speaking of names," said Harry, "what do you call your black lab who likes to hang around the dinner table?"

"Oh, he's The Enforcer! Keeps order around here," said Bill.

A lover of animals, Harry decided to win over one member of the family and offered The Enforcer part of his biscuit. Immediately the dog loped to the corner to finish it off.

"Harry, we never feed our pets at the table," advised Bill. "The vet told us that's a no-no."

"Strike three," said Harry to himself, glancing at The Enforcer, who was licking his chops.

"Boy, you can pack it away," observed Carrie, as she cleared the empty serving dishes. "I see where you get that extra weight, Harry."

"Everything is so good!" he confessed.

"You're not through yet! Here comes dessert!" jeered Doug, as Jane handed Harry a piece of apple pie. "You're getting first cabin treatment, Rev."

"Don't pay any attention to Doug. He's just a sociology major, and what do they know!" quipped Jane.

Bill patted his plump stomach.

"Doug's right! We hardly ever have pie."

"I'm honored, Mrs. Collins."

"Well, young man," Jane had answered, "if you're going to be our pastor, we want you to be on our side."

"With Dad and Mom in your corner, Rev., you're sure to be called by the Prairie Meadows Church," pronounced Carrie.

"I'll have a lot to tell Babs when I get back to seminary tonight. If this parish calls me to be their minister, she'll love these friendly people," Harry thought.

Carrie's prediction came true. In the spring of 1947, with the active support of Bill Collins, the three churches had asked Harry to become their preacher.

Reflecting on that happier day, when Bill and he were of the same mind, Harry passed by the Methodist parsonage and crossed the street to the Collins' bungalow. Seeing Bill's red Dodge sedan in the driveway, Harry concluded that he was home. As he approached, he heard a radio on in the living room.

"I have to find out what's eating Bill," said Harry to himself.

Squaring his shoulders, he went up to the door. With hope and dread in his heart, he knocked.

Chapter 2

PRAIRIE MEADOWS PUTS OUT THE WELCOME MAT

The streets around the Prairie Meadows Community Church were buzzing with activity as women came and went, bringing linen, decorations, flowers, and food in pans and covered dishes. While children played hopscotch and tag, a large, black labrador retriever loped here and there among them. Babs watched a tall, gray-haired man supervise a crew of men who were hauling tables from the cellar, up the church steps, and into the church proper. Some lugged sawhorses and tabletops, others, stands of various sizes. Finally, the tall man carried a large coffeemaker up the steps, pausing for a moment in front of the church doors.

The bustling activity on this hot humid day in August 1947 was preparation for the gala potluck dinner in honor of Prairie Meadows' young minister and his bride. Presiding over the entire affair was a woman in her fifties with a loud voice who appeared in the church doorway from time to time, giving instructions. From the parsonage across the street, the bride watched the goings-on, as she dressed for the occasion. As six o'clock drew nearer, she began to fidget.

"Harry, I'm scared. I won't know what to say to these people. I'll forget their names. You've been here six months, and you know them and what they're like, but I don't know anybody! Do I look all right? Will they like me?"

"Of course they'll love you. How could they not? You look beautiful, Babs." Drawing her close, he kissed her.

Wearing the new navy blue, double-breasted suit he'd picked out for their wedding trip with a red tie and matching handkerchief in his breast pocket, to Babs, Harry looked like a winner.

"Just wait till I plan his meals," she said to herself. "He'll take off those extra pounds in no time, and he'll look even better!"

She stroked his wavy, brown hair.

"Sweetheart, tell me, who's the lady telling everybody what to do?"

"That's Mrs. Collins. She's head of the women's society and plays the piano for church. You met her husband, Bill, when he stopped by last night to welcome you."

"Oh, yes. Did he used to be a minister?"

"Right. Now he owns property in town, and he's involved in some businesses. He and his cousin run Collins' Auto Shop off Main Street."

Babs glanced out the window again.

"I see so many older people. Are there any young couples in the church, Harry?"

"Not many. The soil around here is sandy. Potatoes and onions are the main crops."

"Young couples don't like to raise potatoes or onions?"

"The problem is that potatoes and onions don't bring in much money. Yesterday, you noticed a lot of the buildings around here look rundown. People just can't afford paint. There's no industry around here. After kids graduate from high school, they find jobs elsewhere. But there's a few young farm families around, and I've been calling on them."

Hearing a knock at the front door, Harry answered it. It was the tall man in charge of setting up tables. About seventy, he had an air of authority, and when he spoke, his gray eyes twinkled, and his smile was warm.

"Reverend, I need to use the phone. The cord on one of the coffee makers is broken, and I need to let the missus know to bring an extra I have around the house. This must be your wife, huh?"

"Babs, I'd like to introduce Fred Young. He's chairman of the trustees and the man who, at first, drove me around to preach at the other two churches in this parish."

"That was kind of you."

"Glad to help out. Besides, I'm kind of slow, and by the time I heard his sermon the third time, I could understand what he was saying."

After a quick phone call, Fred returned to the church.

At 5:45, Harry, always punctual, was ready to leave.

"My hair's a mess!" wailed Babs. "I thought I had fifteen more minutes!"

"As pastor, I go early to welcome people," he explained patiently.

"I'll hurry."

In the living room Harry began to pace back and forth.

Suddenly, an old man, short, with a bald head and a calculating eye, appeared from the kitchen. He said with a smirk,

"Waiting for the missus, Rev.?"

"Yes, Mac."

"The ladies have been working hard on your welcome party, Rev."

Before ducking out the front door, he confided,

"They can hardly wait to meet the minister's wife!"

At 5:59, she emerged from the bedroom, her gray suit spotless, wearing a wide-brimmed, black hat with a lavish, aqua feather, and carrying long, black, kid gloves with an aqua-colored hankie tucked into her spacious, black bag. Harry's impatience melted at the dazzling sight of his lover with her brown eyes and long, shining dark hair.

"Do I look all right, Dear?" she asked, with a shy smile.

Before he could answer, Babs took one more look at the people arriving at the church.

"Harry, a lot of the women are wearing hats, but none of them seem to be wearing gloves."

"I don't expect to see anyone wearing gloves. It's August. Who wears gloves in August?"

Harry suppressed a sigh as she stood uncertainly in the middle of the drab living room. After one more glance out the window, and another at her prized kid gloves, she darted back into the bedroom and returned without them.

"Promise you won't tell my Mom that I went to the official, welcoming dinner without my new gloves?"

He nodded, and summoning her courage, Babs walked out the back door and across the street with Harry. Pick-ups and cars were parked for blocks around the church. People were carrying covered dishes, and everyone was staring at her. Climbing the church steps, they entered the social hall.

"You must be the minister's wife," said the woman in charge. "I'm Jane Collins."

Wearing a beige dress with a green belt and navy blue shoes with her salt and pepper hair twisted into a casual bun, Mrs. Collins seemed indifferent about her appearance. Babs wondered if she were over-dressed.

"Hello, Mrs. Collins," she replied.

"How do you like our weather? Is it much different from California?" asked the older woman.

"Today is pretty warm—"

Harry broke in as other people were arriving,

"Honey, I'd like to have you meet Mrs. Lola Rankin. My very first wedding was marrying her older son and his bride. And this is Dan, her younger son. He's in our youth group."

Babs turned to greet the newcomers.

"Glad to meet you both. Dan, what grade are you in school?"

"I'm a freshman, Mrs. Petersen," answered Dan, his blue eyes shy and earnest.

"We are so happy to meet you. May I call you Babs?" asked Mrs. Rankin, extending her free hand.

"Yes, please do," she said, as they shook hands warmly.

Lola was wearing a smart-looking, green linen suit with a white, frilly blouse showing at her neck. She had on a yellow hat and carried a hound's-tooth bag for their utensils, while Dan carried a larger package.

Mrs. Collins grabbed the package.

"About time you were getting here, Lola! You know we have to cut the pies before we can sit down for dinner!"

Babs heard some of the women chuckling. Father Kelly of the Our Lady Catholic Church had accepted their invitation for dinner.

He had asked them to seat him in the social hall, rather than in the worship area. In setting up the tables for a crowd, the folding walls were expanded, and Father Kelly ended up in the sanctuary. He, however, did not ask to be moved.

"I wonder if that was an accident or a power move," thought Babs, when she heard about it.

Across the room, she noticed a family of five. The man with curly hair looked intelligent and thoughtful. No, Babs reasoned, he looked sad, or did he merely look resigned? His wife, holding a baby, wore her dark hair in braids wound around her head. Their two daughters were also in braids, wearing gingham dresses matching their mother's. All were standing together quietly except for the older daughter, about nine years old, who was circulating around the room and talking to everybody.

"With a little style," Babs thought, "They could all shine."

"That's Tim and Pricilla Woods. Tim's dad was pastor here years ago. Tim's a beekeeper and farmer, and Pricilla is handy with the needle. She makes all their clothes. Look at Margie, saying hello to everybody."

Young, blond, and out-going, the speaker had noticed Babs gazing at the family.

"I'm Alberta Smith," she went on. "My husband is in the milk delivery business, and we live a couple of blocks south of here."

"Hello, Mrs. Smith," replied Babs, responding to Alberta's warm spirit and her pageboy hairstyle.

"Please call me Alberta.

Just then, nine-year-old Margie took Bab's hand and led her across the room.

"You're the Reverend's new wife, aren't you? I'm Margie Woods, and here's my Dad and Mom," announced the girl.

"Welcome to Prairie Meadows, Mrs. Petersen," said Pricilla, glancing at her husband, who simply nodded.

"Oh, Mrs. Petersen, I want meet you," called a woman from across the room. She was dressed in purple and wearing an elaborate hat of artificial flowers and bows, and her short ample figure was draped in a longish skirt trimmed with purple lace. As she drew closer, her shrewd, brown eyes moved from Harry, greeting the people, to Babs in her trousseau finery.

"Here comes Mrs. Blodgett, treasurer of our women's group," Pricilla said.

"Yes, I keep the books for the Busy Bees," she acknowledged. "Mrs. Petersen, my nephew lives in Redlands, California. They have their own beautiful swimming pool. You're from California? Does your family have a swimming pool?"

She leaned forward to hear Babs' reply.

"No. They live near San Francisco where it's much cooler than in Redlands."

"What does your father do?" pursued Mrs. Blodgett.

Suddenly Mrs. Collins tapped Babs on the shoulder.

"Where are your dishes, cups, and silverware?" she asked. "Didn't Harry tell you that this was a potluck? We didn't expect you to bring food, but you are supposed to bring your own dishes!"

Blushing, she turned in confusion to go for their things, when Fred Young's wife, spoke up,

"That's all right, Babs. I'm Thelma Young, and we have plenty of extra dishes. Here, I'll set your places here at the head table."

"Thank you, Mrs. Young," she replied gratefully.

At the front of the hall, Bill Collins was calling for attention. After singing the Doxology, the congregation bowed their heads as Harry completed the blessing.

At the table, Babs looked around the room, noticing a tiny older couple.

"That's Mac and Rita Barker. She's the church treasurer, and he's the resident miser. They say he hasn't paid any income tax for years. They live just a block from the church," confided Alberta.

After dinner, several people from the church and community welcomed the minister and his wife. Pat Riley of the Prairie Meadows Business and Professional Men's Association spoke first, followed by Jim Barry, editor of the local weekly newspaper, *The Banner*. Blond Alberta Smith represented the PTA, and Sunday School Superintendent, Jane Collins, each gave a short speech. Bob Rennik, their mailman, spoke for the postmaster.

"There won't be as much mail for me to deliver, now that you are both here in Prairie Meadows. The reverend got a lot of letters from California. In fact, our postmaster claims that because of the love letters going back and forth between Wisconsin and California this summer, Prairie Meadows may qualify for a higher classification."

Babs's face was red when the mailman sat down, but stealing a glance at Harry, she saw that he was not in the least embarrassed.

In the absence of the Methodist and Pentecostal ministers, who had sent their regrets, Father Kelly brought good wishes from the clergy.

"Welcome, to Prairie Meadows, Reverend and Mrs. Petersen," he concluded. "Our village is blessed to have you both in our community."

Later that night as she brushed her hair, Babs thought about all the people she had met who, from now on, would be part of her life. Fred and Thelma Young were the salt of the earth. Little Mrs. Rita Barker, the treasurer, was nice lady, while her husband, Mac, was a character. Alberta Smith and Lola Rankin and her son, Dan, seemed like friends already. But not that nosy Mrs. Blodgett!

Babs couldn't help wondering about the bookkeeper/ farmer, Tim Woods. An air of mystery seemed to surround Tim. A minister's son, he was obviously a poor man, cold and distant, but his daughter Margie was as friendly as could be. Had he always been so reserved?

As Harry came into the bedroom, Babs recalled Mrs. Collins's brusque manner.

"It was scary but nice, meeting all the people from Prairie Meadows, but I wonder, why did Mrs. Collins scold me in front of all the people?"

Harry, on the other hand, was thinking about preparing his weekly message. It was Wednesday, only three days left to write his sermon. So little time. He failed to hear what Babs said.

Chapter 3

COMPANY COMING

A piercing sound split the air.

"Harry, wake up, the phone is ringing!" cried Babs.

"Whuh--whuh--" he muttered, fumbling to wake up.

Scrambling out of bed, she dashed into the dinette, answering the phone on the sixth ring.

"Hello. Is Rev. Petersen there?"

The man's voice on the line was gruff.

"Yes."

"Ed Wells of Sterling here. My son, Harvey, had an accident. Let me speak to the minister."

"Oh, I'm sorry," replied Babs, handing the phone to Harry beside her.

"It's Ed Wells," she said.

"Hello, Ed. What happened? . . . Harvey fell?"

Harry frowned.

"I see. . . Is he hurt bad?. . . I'll meet you at the hospital. . . . Yes, I'll leave right away. . .Tell Clara I'll pray for him," added Harry, returning the phone to the wall hook.

"What happened, Harry?"

"Harvey slipped and fell in the barn. He's lost blood, probably broke his arm, and is in a lot of pain. His wife Clara is driving him to the hospital. The doctor is meeting them at St. Michael's Hospital in Stevens Point. Clara asked for prayers for Harvey."

"Will you have time for a cup of coffee?"

"No, I have to go. I'll get coffee at the hospital."

Following him into the bedroom as he dressed, she asked, "Is it serious?"

"They don't know. They're meeting his doctor there."

"I hope he'll be all right. Honey, when Harvey is badly hurt, it's selfish of me to say, but with your mother and dad arriving tomorrow, I'm nervous about entertaining them when I'm just learning how to cook and keep house."

Reaching for his suit coat, Harry kissed her.

"I'm sorry to dash off, but Harvey and Clara need me. Don't worry. My parents love you, and they'll help, you'll see!"

She watched by the kitchen door, as Harry drove off in their 1941 Chevy.

Putting on the coffee to perk, she recalled the recent bridal shower given them by the Sterling Church, the second largest in Harry's three-church parish.

"Clara was the one who presented us with that hand-made quilt from the ladies of Sterling. She looks so delicate. I remember Harvey, a big man. I hope he'll be all right."

After breakfast, washing their flowered dishes, which she'd purchased with money from Harry's family and friends, her face clouded at the prospect of her in-laws' visit. She'd enjoyed being in their home but felt defensive about entertaining them in the dingy parsonage. The kitchen, dinette, and living room walls were a depressing, soiled blue, and the hall, two bedrooms, and bath, a grimy gray. With no closet doors, their bedrooms looked messy. The guest room stood empty, save for a decrepit scratched double bed bravely covered with the quilt from the Sterling Women's Missionary Society.

On a previous visit, Harry's parents, finding no curtains on the parsonage windows, had purchased paper drapes for the living room and guest room. Worn brown shades were on the other windows. It was not the setting Babs had dreamed of for entertaining her husband's family.

Laying her concerns aside, she made a list of jobs to be done. She had fixed a gelatin salad and put it in the cool basement to harden, cleaned the bathroom and kitchen, and was dusting the living room, when Harry returned from Stevens Point.

"How is Harvey, and what happened to him?" she asked, pausing next to the davenport with the carpet sweeper, as Harry checked through their mail.

"While he was milking, he slipped on the edge of the gutter and fell against the stanchion, broke his arm and punctured himself on a nail. He bled quite a bit, and Dr. Sutherland said that he'll have some pain, but he's going to be all right."

"Thank goodness for that!"

"Harvey is lucky that his dad can take over the milking for a few days," said Harry, settling into his chair.

"Guess what? Alberta came by today. She wants to give us these two black kittens," said Babs, showing Harry a basket containing two round balls of fur.

"Would you like to keep them?" he asked.

"They would be company for me, so far away from home. What shall we call them?

Harry shrugged.

Babs carefully put the kittens back in the basket.

"Have you had anything to eat today?" she asked, preparing to wield the carpet sweeper.

"Yes, Clara insisted on buying my lunch."

"Good!" she said, going after the dust in the carpet.

Finished with the sweeper, Babs sat down for a moment. Harry looked at his wife sympathetically.

"Do you feel you're ready for my parents' visit?"

"I'm getting there. I have to stir up a yellow cake for dessert."

"I thought you were making chocolate," he said tossing aside some ads.

"It's too complicated. I was reading through my cookbooks, and yellow cake is easier to make. Maybe next time I'll try chocolate."

"Any phone calls?" he asked, opening the phone bill.

"Yes. Pat Riley from the Businessmen's Club called to invite you to their weekly luncheon meeting at the Rocket Cafe next Tuesday."

"I was wondering when they'd ask me. Now that I'm an old married man, they're going to take me in," he said, with a grin.

"Old married man indeed! How about a hug from my favorite minister?"

"Ah, I like this," he said, drawing her down into his easy chair.

She caressed his cheek and was covering his face with kisses, when suddenly, she stiffened.

"Listen."

They could hear the faint sound of footsteps in the kitchen, and a diminutive old man with bushy white hair, red cheeks, and inquisitive, blue eyes, rounded the corner of the kitchen into the dinette. Fingering his overall suspenders, he smiled first at Harry and then at Babs, as she leaped up from the chair.

"Hello, Rev. and Mrs. Petersen, do you remember me? I'm your neighbor, Henry Perkins. You met me and my daughter, Nell, at your welcome party."

As he spoke, Henry was heading toward the front door.

"Uh, hello, Mr. Perkins," answered Babs in confusion.

"Just call me Henry!" he said, opening the front door and backing out, still smiling as he closed the door.

"At least he's friendly. I forgot to tell you, Mike and Claudia Morgan from Sterling stopped by with two bushel baskets full of tomatoes--one for us, and one for his brother, Eben. Is Eben a redhead? Didn't I meet Eben and Marcia Morgan?"

"Yes, Eben has red hair and is senior deacon of the Prairie Meadows congregation," he answered.

"Honey, the fresh tomatoes are tasty. But without a refrigerator I don't know what to do with them all."

"Mrs. Jones from Sterling predicted we'd be getting some tomatoes. She gave me a canning kettle, a recipe book, and some jars and lids. They're all in the basement. I used to help my mom with canning. If you want, we could put up some tomatoes."

"I've never canned, but I'm willing to try. I hate to waste food."

That evening Babs rinsed out the jars, while Harry assembled the new lids and salt and began to fill the canning kettle with hot water. As they worked together, Babs was pleased, for the tomatoes would be a delicious addition to any meal. Besides that, their very own canned goods would make pretty gifts. By the end of the evening, fourteen quarts of tomatoes, canned in sparkling glass, graced the counter in the kitchen.

"According to the book, if the lids have sealed, they will sing if I tap them with a spoon," said Babs, gently tapping. To her delight, all but three jars apparently sealed immediately.

In the living room, Harry was reading an impressive-looking

book on Egyptian archaeology. Laying the book aside, he opened his arms as Babs came in.

"Come here, darling. Don't work so hard. Mother and Dad are looking forward to being with us. They won't be critical."

She relaxed in his lap.

"I guess you're right, but I'd like their visit to be perfect."

"They enjoy driving north into Wisconsin, and they love you. We'll have a good time."

After a while, Babs got up and went into their bedroom, emerging soon in a pink nightie and carrying a small bag.

"What do you have there, Babs?"

"Pink socks."

"What for?"

"My hair."

"Your hair?" Harry looked puzzled.

"Yes, pink is a good color on me, so I told my friends that after I was married, I'd put up my hair at night in pink socks."

She was dampening her hair, rolling it into curls, and tying them with the socks.

"When my girlfriends gave me a shower, the first package I opened were these socks. How do you like them?"

As she turned her head, her curls in pink socks bobbed from side to side.

"You look good to me, no matter what you have on."

"Really? A girl worries about how she'll look, going to bed with no make-up on and wearing curlers. Do fellows worry about things like that?"

"No. I just made sure I had a couple of new pairs of pajamas. Had to buy extra talls."

"No fuss, huh? You guys are lucky," she replied.

"I certainly am lucky!" he said, watching her appreciatively as she put up the last curl.

"Harry, I have the menus for the weekend planned. For dinner tomorrow, do you think your mother and dad would enjoy pork chops served with stewed tomatoes?"

Chapter 4

MONEY: ROOT OF ALL KINDS OF EVIL

"This tastes pretty good," said Babs, sampling her casserole before shoving it into the oven.

Last week, Mrs. Ethel Jones had invited them over for dinner on the evening of the business meeting at the Sterling Church. She had been surprised when Babs had asked for her main dish recipe, for she made it with whatever she had on hand. However, since her minister's wife had been persistent, she had written out a list of ingredients.

Babs liked the flavor, and noticed that Harry had relished it. Besides, since it was made with tomatoes and hamburger, it would be inexpensive to make.

"My biggest jobs are learning to cook and staying within the budget," she reminded herself.

Yesterday, armed with Mrs. Jones' recipe, she had purchased the onion, ground meat, spaghetti, a can of red beans, and seasonings. Today, adding her home-canned tomatoes, she had painstakingly prepared the dish. It was a bit soupy—next time she would drain the spaghetti more thoroughly—but not bad.

She wished that she had known that recipe last weekend for Mel and Louise's visit. She found his parents weren't critical of the food she fixed. Once she'd gotten over the stress of entertaining, she enjoyed hearing about their adventures when Harry was a teen-ager and they, city people, had farmed in northern Wisconsin. Shortly after they had arrived, Mel went into the kitchen to put coffee on for everyone.

"You really made Dad feel at home, Babs," said Harry later. "Maxine and my brother, Lefty, have been married for ten years, but I never saw my father put on the coffee pot at their house."

These thoughts were going through her head as she prepared Sunday dinner. At 11:30, Babs knew that Harry was beginning to preach his sermon at Sterling. With the table set, the individual salads prepared, and the casserole baking in the oven, Babs sat down at the piano and began to run through a Beethoven sonata. Harry loved to hear her play Beethoven.

Harry had told her that on a visit at the prosperous Morgan farm in Sterling, he'd admired their fine upright piano. Their daughter had taken piano lessons when she was young, but now she lived in Milwaukee, and no one played the piano. When Claudia and Mike found out that Babs was a pianist, they offered to lend the instrument to Harry.

Harry said that shortly after that, four men in overalls arrived in a Chevy truck to deliver the handsome walnut piano. Mike and his friends had pushed and shoved it from the truck, along the cement path in front of the parsonage, up three steps, through the front door and into the living room, installing it against the wall opposite the bay window. When Harry brought her home to the Prairie Meadows parsonage, the first thing she saw was the beautiful piano. Touching the shining instrument, Babs acknowledged that the Lord *does* provide.

As she finished the sonata, she heard the back door slam, and Harry came in, tired and hungry, with two sermons under his belt.

"It's nippy out there today! Boy, dinner smells good," he said giving her a kiss.

He noticed a salad at each place.

"Oh, we're going to have salad first."

"And I want you to dish up our casserole after that."

Harry wrinkled his nose but reluctantly went along with her serving arrangements.

"Honey, was my sermon was okay this morning?" he asked as he sat down at the table.

"Harry, I think you did a great job," she answered as she poured a glass of milk for each of them. "I noticed that Mrs. Blodgett was hanging on your every word as you described how Jesus loved Zacheus, even though he'd gotten rich in his job as a crooked tax collector."

"Do you think the illustration warning us against using God's money for ourselves instead of giving it for His work was interesting?"

"Yes. But I felt guilty that we use part of our tithe to make our car installment," she said, starting down the basement stairs with the milk.

Harry waited until she was back in the kitchen.

"Dear, the car is for the Lord's work. We must have one; without it, I can't call on people or build the church."

As they were finishing dinner, they saw Rita Barker coming up the walk. As usual, her white hair was braided into a precise knot, and she was wearing a worn green coat and gloves with holes in the thumbs.

"Every Sunday she delivers my salary from the Prairie Meadows congregation," noted Harry going to the front door.

"Here you are, Pastor," she said, handing him a used envelope with twenty dollars in it. "I didn't want to keep you waiting. I have to get back 'cause I have a chicken in the oven."

"Thank you, Mrs. Barker," he said as he closed the front door after her.

"It's funny receiving the actual church offering," mused the minister, as he sat down in his easy chair and opened the envelope. It held two fives and six one-dollar bills, three fifty-cent pieces, nine quarters, a dime, two nickels, and five pennies.

"Not many members are tithing," Babs remarked.

"No, I don't think they are used to the concept of giving one tenth of their earnings for the Lord's work. But when Fred Young heard that I was giving a dollar to the Prairie Meadows Church, he decided that he'd raise his giving to a dollar, also."

"You didn't tell him that we gave to each of the churches?"

"He didn't care what we gave to Sterling and Rosebud. But he didn't like the idea of his minister giving more to his church that he did!"

"He and Thelma are darlings, aren't they?"

As Harry settled into his chair, Babs brought in steaming cups of coffee and took her place on the sofa.

"I'm really concerned about our money situation, Harry. We have that car payment, the utilities, gasoline, and food to buy. There's nothing left for clothes, furnishings or emergencies. And you've been charging stuff at Collins' garage. I hate that."

"Don't forget that $10.50 a month for the set of encyclopedia I bought when I was in seminary," added Harry.

"Encyclopedia!" exploded Babs. "You never told me about that! $10.50 for an encyclopedia! How could you buy that when we are so pinched for money?"

"I didn't know what I'd be making when I became a minister. The salesman said it was a must for me and my future family."

"What a great salesman!" she sniffed, glaring at her husband over the rim of her scalloped cup. "I've been thinking. I'd like to put our money into jars on the closet shelf. We could have one for car, gas, coal, utilities—"

"And encyclopedia."

"And encyclopedia," she added, scornfully. "And that reminds me, why do we have a private phone, Harry? No one else around here has one. It costs more!"

"The people feel that the pastor should not use a party line. Anyone on the line can pick up the phone and listen to the conversations."

"Well, that's great! They should at least pay the difference between a party line and a private one."

Babs went in search of bottles and returned with six-pint jars, canning labels, and a pen. With a flourish, she printed Car, Gas, Fuel, Utilities, Encyclopedia (with a dirty look at Harry), and Washing Machine.

"We can't forget the wringer washing machine that we're buying from Mrs. Blodgett, Harry."

"With all this talk about our obligations, it's lucky I already bought the tickets for the Cal-Wisconsin football game in Madison next week," he answered.

"I'm glad we're going, Harry!"

Babs was looking forward to the game. She hadn't attended one for two years. Unfortunately, Coach Stub Allison had the reputation of sending his men straight through the line. Even so, she hoped that they'd see some fancy passing from Cal's team.

"Honey," said Harry as he was looking over the jars, "there is some good news about our finances."

"What's that?"

"You know Bill Collins works for the Red Cross?"

"Yes."

"He wants me in charge of the blood bank program for this area. They don't pay a salary, but by charging twenty-five cents a mile, I should come out ahead."

"Oh, that's wonderful. I hate getting behind."

With that, she started to distribute the money into the Car and Utilities jars. Since Sterling paid by check, and Rosebud, the smallest church of the three, would pay that evening, the rest of the jars could wait. Resuming her place on the sofa, she looked across at Harry.

"Harry, what did you spill on your tie? "

"I spilled?"

"Yes, probably your dinner. Gorgeous, that reminds me, didn't you like what I fixed?"

"Of course. It was delicious!"

"At Mrs. Jones,' you had three helpings of the casserole. Why did you have only two helpings of mine?"

Chapter 5

SETTLING IN

They woke to a world in white. A soft layer of snow lay across the fields. It was an early storm, dazzling, crisp, and cold.

Harry sipped his hot coffee and looked out the dinette window at a fresh, clean world. Leaving his empty cup on the table, he donned his winter coat, snowcap, and gloves.

"I have a funeral at Rosebud, and after that, I'll be making some pastoral calls. I want to see Mr. Davis and Mr. James, two elderly, Rosebud residents," he said, kissing Babs and slamming the back door on his way out.

Babs had plenty of work lined up. Yesterday, she had dampened the ironing and wrapped it in a tea towel, the way her mother did. As she fed the kittens and cleaned up the dishes and kitchen, she was dreading the task ahead. While her mom in California, using her mangle, sat down to press her clothes, Babs had to iron standing up, and it took forever, for example, to finish one of Harry's white shirts. Every week she had at least five. How glad she was when she'd ironed the hard stuff and got to handkerchiefs.

Persistence pays, however, and two hours later, Babs was ironing hankies. She felt proud as she hung her blouses and his shirts in the closet.

Sitting in Harry's chair and putting her aching feet on the ottoman, she welcomed Blacky One and Blacky Two into her lap.

"You little guys follow me wherever I go, don't you?" she told the kittens. "I'm taking it easy now, but after lunch, I have to shop."

That afternoon, Babs walked home from the village stores carrying two large grocery bags. In the clear, cold air, the dark, bare trees contrasted with the bright, crusty snow. She heard the crunch of her stadium boots and felt the resistance of the snow, as she made a path across the smooth fields toward the parsonage.

With a blanket of snow on the roof, their cottage looked attractive. One could not tell that the structure had almost no insulation and lacked amenities such as doors on the closets. Mac Barker had built the house for his son and daughter-in-law. After the young family left to farm in North Dakota, he had sold the place to the Prairie Meadows Church, undoubtedly securing a good price for it.

Shifting the heavy grocery bags, she felt that she'd made some good purchases. Prairie Meadows boasted three food stores. The IGA, run by Pat Riley, a member of Father Kelly's flock, often had the best prices. Down the street was the Prairie Meadows Market, owned by Bob Clark and his family, loosely connected with the Methodist Church. Further on was the Friendly Market where Gary Lewis worked. Since Gary was a kind person and a tenor in their church choir, Babs felt most at home shopping there, where Gary would answer her questions about how to prepare meat, or tell her what produce was at a reasonable price for Wisconsin.

Living on thirty-six dollars a week was a real challenge. Babs tried to plan dinners, so that the main dish cost fifty cents or less. The tuna recipe she had found in the Boston Cookbook and painstakingly prepared with cream sauce and peas topped with crumbs and cheese, had not made a hit. It was a pity that Harry disliked tuna. Tonight, with veal cutlets on sale, she would fix them the way Gary suggested, and she was hoping that Harry would relish them.

She quickened her pace, remembering that she had purchased coffee on sale, and she wanted to get it into the Hills Brothers can.

Harry insisted on Hills Brothers coffee, and he wanted it, not weak, not medium, but strong. Babs knew Harry preferred Hills Brothers Coffee, but she thought that if she could deceive him, she could save some money by buying a cheaper brand.

Last evening, Harry had rebelled against carving the meat.

"I don't feel at home the way you do things. At our house, my mother always sliced the meat ahead of time, put it on a platter. She'd put the vegetables, potatoes and salad in bowls, and we'd pass the food around."

"My mother always served dinner in three courses," said Babs.

"Three courses? Every night?" yelled Harry.

"When Mother called us to dinner, there'd be an individual salad at each place. Sometimes she served crackers, too. After we had our salads, she'd clear the table and put the plates in front of Dad and bring on the meat on a platter and potatoes and the vegetables in bowls for Dad to serve."

"That's too much fuss!"

"After we finished that, she'd bring in the dessert along with the dishes, and she'd serve us cake or pudding or whatever."

"Fancy! Fancy! This is our home, not a palace! Besides, it's easier for everybody to help themselves."

"It's not fancy. People like to be served."

"I don't like it! To me, it's a lot of fuss. And by the way, while we're on the subject, I like gravy with my meat. I wish you'd fix gravy for us."

"Gravy, now there's a lot of fuss!" she said. "It's hard to make, and besides, you are putting on weight!"

"I am not! Here's how I feel: I want gravy for dinner. My dad never had to carve the meat at the table, and I don't want to do it either!" said Harry taking his plate to the sink and slamming the door on his way upstairs to the study.

Babs cleared the table in a huff, muttering to herself about stubborn Danes. She was not only angry, but she was also surprised. She knew that married couples had disagreements, but here they were—arguing about gravy, and how to serve the meals.

"Passing things—that's what you do at a picnic," she said to herself. "When I got married, I assumed that I would decide how to arrange the table," thought Babs. "Arguing is stupid, but I don't know what to do."

Arriving home, she hurriedly transferred the cheaper coffee into the proper can and put things away. She had left the meat in the cool basement and was coming up the steps, when Mac appeared in the kitchen. Babs was startled every time either Mac or Henry Perkins showed up in the parsonage. She tried to remember to lock the doors, but this afternoon, she'd forgotten. Mac made a silent tour of the kitchen, dinette, and living room and let himself out the front door.

Locking up after him, she began to prepare dinner. Along with the cutlets she was frying, she fixed boiled potatoes, canned peas and carrots, and waldorf salad. Lettuce at twenty-five cents a head she had passed up, but she had indulged in the extravagance of a few walnuts to go with the apples and celery in the salad. For dessert, she made chocolate pudding, garnished with a bit of coconut, and served it in the small crystal bowls from her Aunt Ann.

With the tablecloth of autumn colors, individual salads prepared, and the main dish about done, she had time to arrange chrysanthemums from the garden in a flat blue vase, a wedding present from her friend, Mary. Babs was pleased with her dinner preparations. Everything was ready, but where was Harry?

Turning the dinner on the stove very low, she curled up on the couch to read *Screwtape Letters* by C.S. Lewis. As it got darker and darker, she began to worry. Harry had never been this late making home visits. She got up and paced the living room, looking out the window, but seeing no one. When her neighbor, Nell Perkins, phoned to ask her to play the piano at the next Busy Bee meeting, she said she would, silently wondering how Jane Collins would react, since Jane was usually at the piano.

"Nell, Harry isn't home yet, and I'm getting anxious,"

"It is getting late, isn't it?" Nell's comforting voice answered. "He's probably run into somebody who needs to talk to him. If he isn't home by eight, give me a call, and we'll get on it, Babs."

Somehow reassured, she hung up and fed the hungry kittens.

"I'm starved, too!" she said to herself.

Finally, at ten minutes to eight, she sat down and began to eat her salad. Hearing a familiar step at the back door, she ran to Harry and flung her arms around him.

Harry savored this unexpected enthusiasm.

"Darling, where were you? I was getting so scared and hungry! What happened?"

Harry looked down at his bride with her dark hair and the luminous brown eyes that always melted him. Seeing her pale, anxious face, he felt contrite.

"I'm fine, Honey. After the funeral, I saw Mr. Davis, and Mr. James asked me to stop by at his son's farm nearby. Young Dick James had just bought a new (for him—it's used) tractor, and he wanted to show it to me."

"But Harry, it's been dark for two hours! How could you even see the tractor? I was getting so frightened! I fixed a special dinner for you, but it's all dried up now! You must be hungry! I'm famished! And look, I'm using the tablecloth your Mom gave us, and see, I fixed a centerpiece for our table. Doesn't it look nice?"

As she spoke, she led him into the dinette, where Harry saw two places set "just so" with the new tablecloth and flowers, and an apple salad at each place. She'd remembered that he liked waldorf salad! Harry drew her close and began to kiss away her tears.

"I'll have a little salad with you. I'm not really hungry."

"Not hungry? How come?" she asked, as she sat down, beginning to eat in earnest.

"Well," he answered, tasting the salad, "by the time Dick James had taken me out in his fields on the tractor, it was getting dark, and we were all hungry, and Mrs. James absolutely insisted that I stay for dinner. They had just slaughtered a heifer. Boy, what a great meal!!"

Instantly, he knew he was in trouble. Babs was struggling to learn how to cook, and he'd admired another woman's repast!

Tears rolling down her cheeks, she flounced out of the dinette,

"Couldn't you even call me on the phone, Harry?"

Later that evening, as Babs ate a cold dinner, Harry apologized, agreeing never to miss a meal without letting her know.

"The Jameses don't have a phone. For months I was here alone, and I just didn't think."

"You'd better think next time, Gorgeous, or you'll really be in trouble! Taste this veal cutlet. Do you like the way I fixed it?"

Harry took a bite of the cutlet. Chewing on the dry morsel, he said,

"It has a good flavor. Too bad I missed out on it."

That night, in bed, before turning off the light, Harry looked at her thoughtfully.

"I know your way of serving means a lot to you, as mine does to me. Why don't we do it your way one night and mine the next? That way, each of us can feel really at home."

Caressing his wavy, brown hair, she whispered,

"What a wonderful idea, Gorgeous!"

Chapter 6

TRYING TIMES

The man at the front door was dressed in shabby blue jeans, a faded yellow shirt, and a brown sweater with holes at the elbows. Standing on the parsonage steps, with an apologetic air, he fumbled with his worn suspenders and scraped the cement porch with the toe of his dirty left boot. The minister waited patiently, for the fellow seemed reluctant to speak.

"You see, Rev, I've been out of work for a spell, and I haven't eaten in two days. I just got word that my mother in Milwaukee is real bad off. I'd sure like to see her. But I don't have a dime. I hate like blazes to bother anyone, but I heard that you and your wife were real nice people. Now, if you could just lend me $35, I'll mail it back to you when I get to my family."

"What's your name?"

"Bob Smith's my name, Rev."

"Wait here, Bob, and I'll see what we can do."

Harry closed the door and went to find Babs. He found her sitting on the bed, weeping. Still in her nightie, innocent of make-up, her hair in tangles, she was clutching a letter from her mother.

"What did she say this time?" asked Harry angrily.

He had noticed that Babs was reduced to helpless frustration whenever a white envelope outlined in navy blue arrived in their mailbox. At first, he was happy to see a letter from California in Ruth Walker's precise handwriting. However, observing the anxiety in Babs' eyes as she read the notes from home, Harry wished that Ruth would not write so often. On the other hand, if Babs received no word from her mom and dad, she became anxious. A no-win situation, he thought.

"Harry, I wrote to her about the Cal-Wisconsin football game and my shock at seeing all the women wearing the New Look, where skirts are now halfway between ankle and knee. I told her that my lovely trousseau with skirts barely covering my knees is completely out-dated."

Harry sat down next to her on the bed and put his arms around her.

"And what did she say to that?"

"She wrote, 'You've made your bed. Now you can lie in it. We did our part. It's up to Harry to buy you new clothes.'"

Babs sighed.

"We will have to get you some new things, Dear," he admitted.

"You know we can't afford new clothes, Harry. Did you see the bill for filling our coal bin?" she asked, reproachfully.

Harry frowned and changed the subject.

"Oh, that reminds me, Babs. I'm sending in the reservation for the Wisconsin church conference in Green Bay. Bill Collins said we should go. Delegates stay in people's homes, they give us breakfast, and churches give us expense money for gas and meals."

"I'll come, if you don't mind if my skirts are too short. At I. Magnin's, they let the skirts down as far as they would go. I can't lengthen them anymore."

Harry kissed her.

"You'll be the prettiest woman there, no matter what you're wearing!"

Ignoring his compliment, she continued,

"Besides that, she said I should buy a new winter coat for the icy weather in Wisconsin."

"She's full of advice, isn't she?"

"She asked if I'd written to our family doctor, to thank him and his wife for the lovely crystal vase they gave us. Finally, she said that her friends keep asking her if we received their wedding presents. She wants me to finish writing my thank-you notes."

"You're always writing thank-you's. Why can't she leave you alone?" he responded angrily.

"Yes, but Mother wants me to be perfect."

Her eyes filled with tears.

"Darling," he said, "to me, you are perfect."

He drew her close, kissing her eyes and lips.

She cuddled in his arms.

"Harry, I love you," she smiled, pushing him away, blowing her nose, and wiping her eyes.

She continued more hopefully.

"We have that lovely piano. I've decided to give piano lessons. I can teach some children who might not have lessons otherwise, and we can sure use the money."

"Yes, we can. Oh, that reminds me, there's some one at the door."

"Mac Barker or Henry Perkins, I suppose?"

"No, a man who hasn't eaten for a couple of days, plus he needs to get to Milwaukee," Harry reported.

"I'll pack him a lunch. I was going to boil some eggs to make sandwiches. But what about getting him to Milwaukee? We can't take him."

"He says that a bus ticket is $35, and he'll pay us back."

"He will? I hope so. We have about half a tankful of gasoline. Should we take some money out of our gas fund, Harry?"

Some time later, Harry appeared at the front door with a sack lunch and an envelope. Inside the envelope was a 3 by 5 card with Harry's name and address along with $35 in cash.

"Thank you so much, Rev. People told me you were real nice people. I'll pay you back when I get to Milwaukee."

With a final, slight smile, he left.

They never heard from him.

Chapter 7

BABS GETS THE FLU

Harry was concerned. Mornings, with fall in the air, he'd go down to the furnace, shake down the ashes from the last night's fire, dispose of them, add coal, and open the draft, so that the heat would circulate through the house. Usually, Babs bounced right out of bed and had the breakfast underway by the time he'd shaved and was ready for his coffee. Yesterday and today, however, she had remained in bed, dozing fitfully. He'd made his own coffee, and it wasn't as good as usual.

This morning he had a Red Cross meeting in Waupaca. Since Father Kelly was on the Red Cross Board, Harry had arranged to pick him up. Checking the bedroom, he saw his wife still lying between the white sheets. After a while, she opened her eyes.

"Do you suppose I have the flu? I have a terrible headache and my tummy is upset."

Coming over to the bed, he touched her forehead.

"I don't think you have a fever. Did you, by any chance, get a letter from your mother yesterday?" he asked.

"What is that supposed to mean?" she asked, her voice rising.

"Sometimes she upsets you," he responded, lamely.

"No, I didn't get a letter from my mother!"

Summoning as much dignity as she could muster, Babs rose and started toward the bathroom. Weak and pale, she took a couple of steps, and sank back down on the bed.

"Honey," he said, "I'm sorry you don't feel well. Don't worry about breakfast for me. I'll just have a piece of toast."

"Thanks," she said, looking relieved as she lay back among the pillows. "And, Harry, would you feed the kittens?"

"Yes," he answered, without enthusiasm.

He peeked into the bedroom before leaving and saw she was sleeping. On the way to Waupaca, he stopped to pick up Father Kelly.

"I hope you are enjoying our fall weather. I realize this climate is colder than California. How's your wife?" asked the priest as he got in the car.

"She's been fine. Except for the last two days."

"I have a proposition for you, Reverend Petersen. We have a brand new Hammond organ. I understand your wife is an organist."

"Yes, she is."

"It costs almost nothing to run an electronic organ, and it's good for them to be played. I'd like to invite your wife to come over and practice at Our Lady's. I can show her how the drawbars work. Has she ever played a Hammond?"

"I don't know."

"Keep it mind. We like to help where we can."

"Thanks, Father Kelly."

On the way home from the meeting, the young minister was thinking about the challenging goals that Bill Collins and the committee had set up for the blood bank program, and wondering if he could possibly achieve them. As he stopped to let Father Kelly off by the Catholic Church, the priest, observing his anxiety, patted his arm, gently reminding him,

"We have to have faith, my brother."

At lunch, Harry told Babs about the Red Cross blood program and Father Kelly's invitation.

"Isn't that kind of him, Harry? I'd love to practice on the organ. I played a Hammond once at a friend's wedding. No one was around to tell me about the draw-bars, and I was pretty confused."

"Father Kelly will show you."

"He's thoughtful, isn't he?"

"Yes. By the way, are you planning to attend the Busy Bees meeting this afternoon?"

"Yes, the meeting is at 2:00, and I seem to be feeling better. They are working on the rummage sale, and every one is needed. Harry, I want to take five dollars out of the gas fund to pay Mrs. Blodgett for the wringer washing machine. She's asking only $50 for it, and I know she's wondering why we haven't paid anything yet."

"Sounds like a good idea, Dear," he answered starting upstairs to the study.

Bringing her sewing basket into the living room, Babs began to mend Harry's socks. Soon she saw little Mrs. Barker arrive at the church. She was wearing an old-fashioned navy blue dress and jacket. With her white hair in a precise braid, and the dark clothing, she looked tinier than ever.

Arriving next were Doris Blodgett, dressed in burgundy, with her neighbor, Nancy Addison. According to Alberta, Mrs. Blodgett loved to handle the money during rummage sales and actually seemed to caress the cup of change, which she always held tightly in her hands.

As for Nancy Addison, Doris had spread the word around the village that Nancy had gone through all her savings and was now on public assistance. Unaware of the gossip, Mrs. Addison always had a bright smile for everyone. Today, her red dress was accented by a colorful scarf around her slender shoulders. Babs had heard that, as Sunshine Chairman of the Busy Bees, Nancy sent cards to those who were sick, had babies, or suffered the loss of a loved one. Selecting every card with care, she wrote with bright blue ink in a pretty script. People told Babs they were cheered by Nancy's messages.

Pulling the mended sock off the darning egg, Babs noticed Mac and Henry Perkins standing in front of the church, looking across at the parsonage.

"I must be sure to lock the door when I leave," she said to herself.

Slipping a sweater on over her white blouse, she found her purse, and walked across the street, as her neighbor, Nell Perkins, arrived carrying a cookie tin. Nell's red hair was streaked with grey, and she gave the younger woman an encouraging smile.

"Are you beginning to remember people's names, Babs?"

"Some of them, Nell. Now, that lady in the print dress coming our way with two children is Mrs. Woods, isn't she?"

"Yes, Pricilla Woods, Tim's second wife."

"I met the family at our reception, and Margie comes by for a visit sometimes. Pricilla seems like a quiet woman."

"Yes. She's not at all like Tim's first wife, Jessica. Excuse me, I must hurry because I'm on the refreshment committee today."

Babs would have liked to hear more about Jessica, but Nell had already disappeared into the church. As Pricilla approached, Babs noticed that she and her younger daughter were wearing the same print dresses they had worn at the reception. With her olive complexion and her dark hair in braids, Pricilla was carrying a baby dressed in blue.

"What a darling baby boy," she said, pausing on the church steps to greet Pricilla. The toddler was shy, but Babs got a beautiful smile out of the baby.

"His name is Tom, after my husband's father," answered Pricilla.

The Busy Bees met in the "parlor" next to the sanctuary. At the welcome reception for Babs and Harry, the wall had been slid back to accommodate a big crowd. Today, the wall was in its usual place, making an attractive, if old-fashioned looking, social hall. Alberta Smith, her long, blond hair arranged in her usual pageboy, came forward with a smile to remind Babs that she'd promised to play the hymns for the song service before the business meeting.

"I'll be glad to play the piano, Alberta," said Babs.

Mrs. Blodgett eyed the minister's wife in her calculating way.

"Before we start, we are going to have to wash a lot of dishes and silverware getting things ready for the sale. Nancy was supposed to bring dishtowels, but she forgot. Would you run back and give Jane Collins some of yours?"

"Sure. How many do you need?"

"Four should be enough."

When Babs returned with the tea towels, Mrs. Collins laughed.

"Oh, look, girls, Babs brought over her fanciest, embroidered towels! Here's one with a kitten, one with a dog, a swan, and this one has a girl in a sunbonnet!"

Babs flushed.

"Jane, she's a new bride. I'll bet all of her tea towels are embroidered," said Thelma Young who had just walked in. "They're lovely. I especially like the girl in the sunbonnet, Babs."

The minister's wife thanked Thelma with her eyes.

At dinner that evening, Harry talked about his progress with the blood bank program, as he enjoyed Babs' tossed salad.

"I've lined up workers in Sterling, Plainfield, and Wild Rose. Bill Collins congratulated me on what I'd done."

Looking at his plate suspiciously he asked,

"What do you call this?"

"It's my favorite vegetable. Artichoke!"

Wrinkling his nose, he watched to see how Babs ate the peculiar plant.

"How was the Busy Bees meeting?" he asked.

"We washed a lot of things, and they set the dates for the bake sale and the rummage sale. But, Harry, I don't really enjoy their meetings. The women depend on Mrs. Collins to decide everything. She'll be visiting Carrie, her daughter, Saturday, and even Thelma Young said she didn't know how they could manage without Mrs. Collins to tell them what to charge for the cakes and everything."

"Sounds like she makes all the decisions."

"You're right, and she loves it! By the way, after the meeting, I stopped at the Catholic Church to make arrangements to practice the organ. Guess what? I saw the first person in our village wearing the New Look!"

"You mean long skirts?"

"Yes, she had a long skirt, a wide hat, and sexy pumps!"

"Do I know her?"

"It's that very attractive lady, Mrs. Adrianne Downing. She's in the Culture Club, and her husband is principal of Prairie High School."

"Oh, I know her husband, Phil Downing. We got to talking over coffee at Wilkerson's Malt Shop. He said that when the people of Our Lady Church got word that Father Kelly was being transferred from Prairie Meadows, they were upset. Phil and a group of men went up to Green Bay and talked with the bishop."

"They must have been persuasive; he is still here."

"Yes he is. And by the way, I'm thankful you're feeling better. I hope you're over that flu."

Harry's relief was short-lived, for, in the morning, he woke up to the sound of Babs throwing up in the bathroom.

"This flu is hanging on. You need to see a doctor," he said.

Babs, to the contrary, didn't think it was the flu. She recalled their weekend at the church convention in Green Bay, and their romp on the bed with the squeaky springs. She said to herself,

"We must not have been as careful as we thought!"

Chapter 8

UPS AND DOWNS

"Can you find middle C? Look at the black keys. Do they help you find where C is?"

Pamela shyly raised her beautiful eyes and shook her head, "No," and sat, waiting for Babs to help her. With her curly, blonde hair and rosy cheeks, she was a little beauty, a helpless little beauty. Babs tried again.

"Do you see two black keys here and three black keys there?"

Focusing her green eyes on the keyboard, Pamela nodded.

"Remember I said that C is just below either the two black or the three black keys. Which is it?"

Pamela pointed to the three blacks.

"Now that was a good try, Pamela, but C is below the two black ones. Where do you think middle C is?"

Harry walked into the kitchen in time to hear Babs say,

"Very good, Pamela. Now place your fingers on the keyboard."

Harry had been surprised that, as soon as Babs let people know that she was available to give piano lessons, five pupils had signed up: three little girls, a boy, and Pat Rice, a single woman in her thirties.

All were making good progress, except Pamela, whose parents, Margaret and Bob Clark, owned the Prairie Meadows Market. The talk of the village was that the Clarks had planned to have four children—Pamela being their fourth—but after a night of drunken celebration, Margaret found she was again pregnant. People said that she was having a difficult time adjusting to the coming "blessed event."

Eager for her children to have all the advantages, Margaret had brought Pamela to the parsonage to arrange for piano lessons. Margaret had said that she dreamed of beautiful Pamela, seated at the piano, fluttering her gorgeous, long lashes, and playing a romantic sonata. Unfortunately, to date, Pamela had showed no interest in making music. Aware that the child's talents possibly lay in another direction, Babs was, nevertheless, doing her best to interest Pamela in the piano.

That night as they got ready for bed, Harry said, "Do you remember that Edith Murray is coming over tomorrow at 10:00?"

"Edith Murray?"

"The wallpaper woman."

"Oh, yes. She's bringing over books of wallpaper, and I get to choose a pattern for each room. I'm thrilled to get away from all this dirty-blue paint."

"I'm glad you'll have the chance to pick out what you want, " he said, crawling between the sheets and kissing her cheek.

"I'm glad, too," she said quietly. "I'm very glad."

"You look so serious. What's on your mind?"

"Harry, I may have some important news."

Stroking his hair, she observed him closely.

"If it's true, Harry, we'll never be the same."

"Never be the same? That sounds grim. What do you mean?"

"Nothing bad. It's. . . it's . . . I think we're going to have a baby."

"A baby," he said, throwing off the covers and sitting up. "A baby? What makes you think that?"

"I thought at first I was sick, a bad cold, or the flu. But I don't have a cough or a fever, and I always feel better as the day wears on."

Tears welled up in her eyes, and she took his hand.

"A baby? You a mother? Me a father? I can hardly believe it!" he said.

"I was getting suspicious, and then I missed my period."

"You did? Wow! Babs, what a responsibility! I hope I'm up to it. You'll be a wonderful mother."

"I don't know. I'm still learning how to cook, keep a house, manage a budget, be a minister's wife, and now maybe a baby is on the way. I'm happy, but I'm scared."

Harry took her in his arms and kissed her tenderly.

"We'll be parents together. We'll help each other. And God will help us. 'Ask and you shall receive,' the Bible says."

She stroked his face and cuddled close.

"Tell me, Babs, how do you feel about having a baby so soon?"

"At first, I was frustrated. We'd planned to take a year to get adjusted to one another and the responsibilities of being married. Having the baby now changes everything."

"I wanted a family, but not the first year," he said.

"I'll get a lecture from my mom, but I can take it."

"I'm concerned about supporting a family. We don't have enough to get by, and now there'll be another mouth to feed."

"Not right away, dear. The women in our family always nurse their babies. I intend to nurse our little one."

Snuggling close, they talked on, finally falling asleep wrapped in one another's arms.

The next morning Harry got up and made the coffee and brought her a cup.

"This is for the little mother. Now, do you remember that I planned to go deer-hunting around Thanksgiving?"

"Yes. I hope no one takes a shot at you—"

"I will be very careful, and I have something here—"

"For me? A surprise?"

"No, sorry, not a surprise. When I'm in the woods, by law, I have to wear orange. I bought this orange cloth for you to sew on my hunting jacket."

"That looks like a lot of work."

"I'm a big guy."

"I hate sewing, but, for you, I'll stitch this ugly cloth onto your jacket. That color reminds me of an orange and brown sweater that I used to have. Mom got mad when I refused to wear it."

After breakfast, Babs got out her mending basket, ready to begin her struggle with the jacket.

"I don't have any orange thread, so I'll use this tan which matches your jacket," she said, threading her needle. "By the way, did you get to see the Graham family?"

"Yes. The whole family wants to be baptized and join the church. I'm starting a membership class, which they plan to attend. Nancy Addison wants to come, and I'm hoping that Dick and Mrs. James from Rosebud will also come to the class. Bill Collins looked surprised when I told him about it."

"Oh, that reminds me, Freda called to tell me that they have a phone now, and she asked us to come to dinner at their farm on Friday."

"Who is Freda?"

"Freda is Dick James' wife. She not just Mrs. James. You need to pay attention to the wives' names, Harry."

"You're right, Babs. Just so long as I don't pay too much attention to the wives, huh?"

"Rascal!" she said, in mock distain.

Friday afternoon was Babs' first appointment with the doctor in Stevens Point. After giving her a preliminary exam, and a test to determine if she were pregnant, Dr. William Sutherland spoke to them at length, sharing how scientists for years had assumed that nausea in pregnant women was emotionally based. Recent tests, however, had revealed physiological factors which accounted for morning sickness. Next he gave Babs a diet to follow: two servings of proteins each day, a quart of milk or milk-substitutes, and lots of fruits and vegetables as well as grains. As the visit drew to a close, he said,

"I am a Lutheran. Since I value the work of pastors, and they are apt to be underpaid, there will be no charge my services."

Shocked and greatly relieved, Harry finally stammered:

"Thank you so much, Dr. Sutherland. I can't tell you how much this means to us."

Suddenly, with Dr. Sutherland's generosity, the future looked brighter to Harry. As he drove home, he felt that if Babs were indeed expecting, somehow, they could handle the cost and their new responsibilities.

Before they left for dinner at Dick and Freda's, Harry recalled that James' had a piano. While Babs picked a bouquet of chrysanthemums from the garden, he slipped his violin and a few hymnals into the car. When Freda opened her door, two shining faces greeted her with flowers, a violin, and joy.

After serving an ample farm dinner, Freda got out her cello to begin their impromptu concert. Harry tuned up his violin, Dick and his father and the children sang, and Babs accompanied on the piano. What a wonderful evening they spent!

Their harmony seemed especially sweet on one of Harry's favorite hymns, *All the Way My Savior Leads Me*.

Chapter 9

BITTERSWEET

Today, Harry faced making two calls at St. Michael's Hospital in Stevens Point. Both patients were from Sterling—one, a joy, the other, a pain. The first was Mrs. Jones, who earned a minimal salary waiting on people at the feed store. Often she would press five dollars into Harry's hand. Aware of her modest circumstances, he was reluctant to accept money from her.

"Pastor," she'd say, "I can't be in the front lines of God's army, but let me have a part in the battle."

Harry noticed that when he felt at the end of his rope, Mrs. Jones would often surprise him with a gift.

Thinking about what lay ahead of him, he sat down at the breakfast table, ready to enjoy a really good cup of coffee. He smiled as Babs came with the coffee pot.

"Thank you, Babs," he said.

After sampling the weak brew, he exploded.

"This isn't real coffee! It's got no zip, no taste! What's happened to the Hills Bros coffeemakers? Can't they manufacture a decent product anymore?"

Babs looked startled.

"Is this fresh coffee? Did you buy it around here?"

"I got it at the Friendly Market on Main Street."

"I'm going to speak to Gary, no, the owner. Hills Bros has really gone down hill."

"Harry, you don't need to speak to Gary, or the owner, or the people at Hills Bros."

"Why not? I'm their customer."

"It's my fault Harry. I've been so worried about money, and Hills Bros is expensive coffee. When another brand went on sale, I bought it."

"I've been making coffee some mornings. This stuff came right out of the Hills Bros can!"

"That's because I put that coffee in the Hills Bros can, hoping you wouldn't notice, and we could save some money."

"I don't feel like breakfast this morning," he said, stalking out and getting into the car.

Reflecting on his wife's deceit, he quoted Matthew 10:36 to himself, "A man's foes shall be they of his own house." Not ready to face Ed Wells without a decent cup of coffee, he drove to Main Street, parked his 1941 Chevrolet in front of Wilkerson's Drug and Malt Shop, and sat at the counter.

Diana, blonde waitress and clerk, was pleased to see the tall young minister and welcomed him in her friendly manner when he entered. During the six months when Harry was a bachelor in Prairie Meadows, he had often dropped by for coffee. They had had a lot of good talks. But, now that he was married, Diana hardly ever saw him. His wife seemed rather uppity—not nearly as friendly as Reverend Petersen. Thank God, Catholics like herself didn't have to put up with clergyman's wives. At least, not officially.

Diana chuckled over a parish joke. This year, her mom and a group of ladies from the church had gone over to Father Kelly's to give the parsonage its annual spring-cleaning. As a prank, one of the women had hidden the broom. Weeks passed, and Father Kelly's housekeeper, Mary, had complained that she couldn't find the broom anywhere. Finally, she purchased a new one. The ladies were laughing because the broom had been hidden in Mary's bed. Diana shared the attitude of the parish, which was:

"Oh, well, what's the harm? Father Kelly is a wonderful priest. He's just human."

Diana noticed that the Rev. Petersen was very quiet this morning. His mind must be on other things, she thought, as he had his usual—two cups of strong, black coffee and a large dish of vanilla ice cream. Diana was disappointed when he merely paid his bill, left a tip, nodded a brief thanks, and walked out.

At the hospital, Harry saw Ethel Jones first. They talked a while.

"Pastor, will you read my favorite passage from the Bible, Psalm 100?" she asked.

"Of course, I will," he answered, looking through his Bible. "It's a good thought for today."

Make a joyful noise unto the Lord, all ye lands!
Serve the Lord with gladness!
Come into His presence with singing!

As he read the ancient poetry, he was fortified by its message and reassured by Ethel's strong faith in God. After they prayed the Lord's Prayer, he left her bedside refreshed. Walking down the hall to the men's surgical section, he braced himself to deal with Ed Wells.

Wells had been Sunday School Superintendent at the Sterling Church for years. He loved to get up in front of the Sunday School and rant and rave against wicked practices such as smoking, drinking, attending movies, dancing, and playing cards. He warned that these pastimes were of the devil, and must be shunned.

People had grown weary of his tirades. Consequently, a few weeks ago, during the election of officers, Clara Wells, his own daughter-in-law, had been elected Sunday School Superintendent in his place. The Education Committee of the Sterling Church had hoped that Ed would accept the beautiful Schofield Reference Bible they presented to him and retire gracefully.

Not Ed! Instead, he continued venting his anger. Tenderhearted Clara had phoned the pastor for help. When Harry had come by his home to visit, Ed had exploded angrily:

"You're just here to have a good time at our expense! You became a preacher, so that you could come and eat our chicken dinners! And you don't really preach the Gospel! You're just a cog in the denomination's machine! We want the Old Time Gospel, and you only preach what they tell you to!"

Babs had smiled when he'd told her what Ed had said.

"With Bill Collins advising you to preach about modern heroes, and Ed Wells complaining that you don't preach the Old Gospel, you must be striking a good balance."

With Ed now in the hospital recovering from a hernia operation, Harry hoped to bring comfort to the invalid. Since clergy were free come and go at any hour, Harry usually dropped in before visiting hours, so that he could listen and talk, read the Bible, and pray, if appropriate.

Harry, therefore, walked into Ed's hospital room, unannounced. There was Ed, sitting up in bed with a contented smile on his face and smoking a big, black cigar. Ed quickly drew the cigar under the covers. Harry, innocent as could be, stood by the bed, politely inquiring about Ed's surgery and his family. When it appeared that his pastor had all the time in the world, Ed, red-faced, finally drew the big cigar out from under the covers.

"I'm sorry, Pastor, that you see me here smoking a cigar. I don't know what to say, I'm ashamed as can be."

Gone was the rigid and righteous Pharisee who scathingly condemned his fellows, and in his place was a normal, if flustered, human being.

With the air cleared, Harry was able to offer a prayer for Ed's continued recovery. After talking a while, the men exchanged a smile and a handshake. As he left, Harry was happy that the visit he had dreaded had turned out well. Turning the car homeward, he experienced a warm glow. Times like these made him thankful that he had answered God's call to the Gospel ministry.

"Problems can be solved, and people are wonderful to work with," he said to himself. He pictured Ed, less abrasive, putting his talents to work in the Sterling Church.

In the midst of his euphoria, Harry perceived a fly in the ointment. He sighed. Certain self-righteous feelings that he had been cherishing this morning had to go. He saw, to his chagrin, that even over an important matter like good coffee, a man must forgive his wife. Harry felt that, coming down from a mountaintop experience, he had banged his ego on Reality. Painful!

Again, he sighed. As he drew closer to Prairie Meadows, however, he thought of Babs, and the self-righteous anger he had been cherishing, subsided. He knew that when he asked her forgiveness, she would smile, tears might fall, and he would feel her loving arms around him.

"I've been selfish and greedy. I don't deserve His grace, but God's been good to me. I have a lovely wife. I'm a fortunate man, a fortunate man indeed."

Chapter 10

LEARNING THE ROPES

Babs lay on the davenport in the living room, looking up at the ceiling. The ceiling looked so tidy! Not an article out of place! Not a thing! Just the ceiling and the tops of the walls. However, as soon as she let her eyes drift downward, she saw utter confusion. Harry's chair was piled with sweaters, books, newspapers, Red Cross papers, and orange peels.

On the piano were hymnals, piano music, and an assortment of dirty glasses, cups and dishes. On the sofa she saw more sweaters, a radio, her manicure set, and half-finished flannelgraph figures. Newspapers, clothing, Bibles, and other books were scattered over the window seat. So few pieces of furniture, but all stacked with stuff! It was discouraging, especially to a woman in her second month of pregnancy, experiencing morning sickness.

Apparently she and Harry were slobs. She hadn't realized that she was a messy person. Hadn't her Mother and Dad's home been neat? Her own room had been tidy. How did that happen? Was it because her mother picked up after her all time? Harry's mom was neat as could be. Had she been straightening up after him? Whatever the cause, everything was in confusion, and it appeared to Babs that it was up to her to get things in order.

It was hard to know where to begin. One of her mother's most often repeated warnings was:

"There's a right way to do everything!"

The ominous tone of Mother's voice suggested that it was hard to find the right way, and that Babs would probably fail to recognize it. Should she miss, her effort would be wasted, since she had tried to do it the wrong way.

Another oft-quoted piece of advice, from the Scripture, was:

"Man looketh on the outward appearance."

(Ruth always left out the rest of I Samuel 16:7: "but the Lord looketh on the heart.")

Sometimes, Babs' mother had talked about her own girlhood. Ruth's father had judged any young man who came to call on one of his daughters by whether he had thoroughly polished the heels of his shoes. Heels without polish clearly indicated that the young man was either lazy, incompetent, or both.

Accordingly, if Babs' hairstyle, her choice of dress or accessories, or her appearance in general displeased Ruth, she heard the familiar quote. Babs was placating her tummy by lying on the davenport, but she knew she had to get up and start picking up the room. It seemed that she might miss the "right way," but since appearance was so important, she'd better try anyway.

Lying there, unaware that her mother's teachings were at the root of her feelings of inadequacy, Babs studied the furnishings in the parsonage. In the living room was a large, dingy, over-stuffed chair with ottoman, the faded, brown davenport she was lying on, a borrowed, upright piano, and on the window set, twin lamps. Before they married, at an auction, Harry had purchased the lamps, a kitchen stove, and their living room pieces. One of the lamps, which the auctioneer had held up for Harry to see, was in good shape, but later, he found the twin had been broken and clumsily mended.

The other rooms were sparsely furnished by the Prairie Meadows congregation. A scuffed wooden table and three dilapidated wooden chairs, on loan from Gary Lewis, occupied the dinette. In their bedroom was a brass double bed, a fourth worn kitchen chair, and an old walnut dresser. The drawers of the scratched bureau were heavy with a handle missing. (Babs often lost her temper when she tried to pull out the drawer.) In the front bedroom was an old walnut double bed. The small closet had a few shallow shelves. Without a door on any closet, it was hard to maintain a neat appearance. This was some dream house!

Coming home from the Prairie Meadows Business and Professional Men's Association breakfast, Harry found his wife on the davenport in tears. Learning the reason, he kissed her and started picking up. He grabbed his brown sweater, her navy blue one, two of her hats, and three books on the prophets. Unencumbered by the thought that he might not be doing it the "right way," Harry was speedy. Babs, finding courage as the armchair was being cleared, started picking up papers and magazines. She made a neat stack of recent magazines, and took the newspapers to the basement. In no time, the room was orderly. She saw that with a little dusting and flowers arranged in vases on the window ledge and window seat, the room would pass.

"Thanks, Harry. Do you think that Bill Collins and his wife would like meat loaf tonight?"

"Oh, is this the night they are coming to dinner?"

"Yes."

"You make a good meat loaf. What else are you having?"

"I thought I would fix baked potatoes, scalloped corn, tossed salad, and tapioca pudding."

"The kind of pudding my mother makes?"

"Yes. She gave me the recipe."

"Good."

With that, Harry mounted the steps to his study, and Babs went to the kitchen. As she began to fix the pudding, she could hear his typewriter as he pounded out the minutes of the Business Association.

That evening, the Collins' arrived a few minutes early. While dinner was baking, the wrestling of the black kittens amused them. Bill watched them for a while and observed,

"Look at them. They're nip and tuck, aren't they?"

"Nip and Tuck!" repeated Babs excitedly. "That's what we'll call them! Mr. Collins, you named our cats."

Bill grinned with pleasure.

Although the dinner wasn't done on time, the meatloaf and potatoes were good. Afterwards, Mrs. Collins insisted on helping with the dishes—she washed, so that Babs could put away. The men, in the living room, talked about the blood bank campaign. Over dishes, Mrs. Collins inquired about their wedding in California.

Later, as they were talking about their marriage service, Harry and Babs brought down their wedding presents, which were packed away in Harry's study. Jane's eyes opened wide as she looked at many fine trays, including a pair of silver ones, a number of costly cake plates, English bone china teacups, vases, several pairs of cream and sugars, occasional dishes, silver bowls, candlesticks, and salt and pepper shakers, and finally, twelve place settings of sterling silver emerging from the packing boxes. While Bill admired their gifts, especially taken with the silver candlesticks, she had scarcely a word to say.

"You remember our daughter, Carrie, and her husband, Doug, Harry?" asked Collins, putting down a vase.

"Yes, of course, Bill. How are they?"

"They're both fine. Doug has been hitting the books hard and expects to pull A's at Madison. He's no dummy."

"Has he decided what to do after graduating?"

"He's decided that he wants to go into the ministry and has applied to McCormack Seminary in Chicago," said Mrs. Collins.

"That's wonderful!" exclaimed Harry.

"I don't know. I never pictured Carrie as a minister's wife," she answered, shaking her head.

"Please give them our congratulations and best wishes on their decision."

"Actually, it's Doug's idea. Carrie is not enthusiastic about it. He'll never make any money as a minister," she sniffed.

"Now, Jane, Doug is smart and determined. If anyone can get ahead in his profession, Doug can," reasoned her husband.

After they left, Harry studied his list of Red Cross blood donors, and Babs stretched out again on the davenport.

"I'm so tired by the time dinner is over, I wish people would not insist on helping me do the dishes," she complained.

"That's the way people are, Honey. Look at it this way, your dishes are done and put away. Isn't that great?"

"I guess so."

In a few minutes, Babs reluctantly got up and started re-wrapping the wedding gifts to be taken upstairs.

"This room looked pretty good until we got out all our gifts and your Red Cross stuff," she said. "When you are through with that blood bank folder, will you put it on the stairs to take it up to the study tomorrow morning? I'm putting the coffee cups in the sink right now."

Returning from the kitchen, she said,

"Harry, look up at the ceiling. When you look at the room from that angle, isn't our house as neat as a pin?"

Chapter 11

THE HUNTER

Thanksgiving was just around the corner. It had always been Babs' favorite holiday. Each year, she looked forward to attending a united service with other churches and enjoying a delicious turkey dinner with her father's side of the family. She loved the joyful songs of the season. It would be different this year: Harry would go deer hunting.

As she stood in the dinette, ironing his white shirts, her thoughts were punctuated by the sounds of a small, wooden spool hitting the legs of the ironing board as Nip and Tuck scampered after it. Finished with the ironing, she hung up the garments.

"I'm lucky to have you two little guys for company," she remarked.

Harry loved to hunt. Bringing home squirrels and pheasants that he'd shot, he had shown her how he dressed out the meat. He'd taught her how to cook it. In the case of squirrel, he would soak it in salt water overnight. After that, the water would be drained, and the game put in the slow cooker where it would be steamed for a long time. Potatoes and vegetables could be added after a while.

Pheasants, on the other hand, could be roasted in the oven. She found a recipe for Brown Sauce to go with the game, and what a great dinner they had! Babs appreciated the savings as much as the taste!

It was Thanksgiving time, and here she was in the living room, sewing orange patches on his huge jacket! For once, she wished she had married a small man. She had sewn bright cloth on both sides of the front, but the back seemed to go on forever!

And there was Harry outside, talking to an attractive shapely brunette. Margie Woods, fifth grader and purveyor of the neighborhood news, referred to that person as the "milk lady." Was Harry telling her to leave more milk? This was a long conversation. Babs had stitched two sides of the enormous square patch on the back, and they were still talking. Rolling her big, brown eyes at him, Milk Lady smiled coyly. They were laughing! What was funny?

It wasn't funny to Babs as she painstakingly drew her needle back and forth through the thick, unyielding jacket. She should let him do this himself! That would show him!

Threading her needle again, she noticed that Harry was standing very close and talking earnestly to the young woman. Babs didn't know what Harry was thinking, but she understood that flirt! Harry had told her how her own brown eyes had melted his heart, and here he was, talking for an hour and a half in freezing weather with a brown-eyed beauty! How could he be taken in like that?

Adding to her chagrin, passers-by stared at the couple. Mac Barker strolled along, taking in the scene. Mailman, Bob Rennik, tipped his hat, as he walked his route. Returning from town, bag of groceries in hand, neighbor, Henry Perkins, greeted them. Babs groaned when Mrs. Blodgett, probably on her way to Mrs. Collins,' swept by the front of the church, gazing fixedly on them from across the street. Babs was thankful, at least, that since it was a school morning, Margie wouldn't see them.

Babs decided to take a break. Laying down the jacket and going to the piano, she started playing a Beethoven sonata. Finding her fingers out of practice, she started doing arpeggios, scales, and finger exercises that Mrs. St. John had taught her years before.

"Oh," said Harry as he entered the room, "You're doing some serious practicing. Great."

"See what else I'm doing," she answered, pointing to the jacket, which covered half the sofa.

"I see. You're working on my hunting outfit."

"It's not my favorite job."

"Thanks, Honey," answered her husband, as he opened the door and walked up to his study.

Later, at lunch, he noticed Babs looking unhappy and asked what was wrong.

"Oh, dear, you know me. I can't find my purse. I've looked everywhere—the living room, our bedroom, the kitchen, dinette. I even checked the bathroom and the basement and searched the car. I can't find it anywhere."

Tears started down her cheeks.

"Do you remember where you had it last?"

"I had it when we were calling on Alberta and Art and the kids yesterday. I showed her some pictures of my mom and dad. The pictures were in the purse."

"Do you remember having the purse when we left?"

"I'm not sure."

"Let's call Alberta and see if she's seen your purse. Is it the black one?"

"Yes. I was wearing my black pumps and carrying the matching purse."

"Why don't you call her right now?"

"I hate to disturb her. I don't know why I do these things. Losing things is the curse of my life, Harry!"

"Don't berate yourself. Go ahead and call her."

As she made the phone call, Harry began methodically to search the house. Babs' losing things was a familiar pattern. He had found her glasses in the pillows of the davenport. Her hairbrush had fallen behind the dresser. Ruth Walker's letter had been located under a pile of papers on the window seat. Her mittens had found their way under the front seat of their car. The other day, Gary Lewis had phoned from the Friendly Market to let her know that she'd left her wallet by the cash register. Each time she lost something, she felt guilty.

It was clear to Harry that his mother-in-law had nagged and fussed at Babs, to no good. He had noticed that she seemed more likely to misplace her belongings when she felt under pressure. Was she feeling pushed now? He couldn't think of a reason.

He could see when she returned to the living room that she had not located the purse. He decided to check the car for himself. There between the passenger seat and the door, he found the handbag. What joy he saw in her face when she saw it!

"Thanks so much, Harry." she said, giving him a grateful hug.

"That's what husbands are for," he answered, gently kissing her.

"Honey, is something special coming up?" he asked.

"I don't know. Oh, Sunday is the annual meeting of the church, and we are having your Executive Supervisor, Dr. Miller, here for dinner after church."

"Oh, I see," he said, "that's right. Have you decided what to serve?"

"I'd like to serve an oven roast—you know, put the vegetables in with the beef. But, I have trouble getting things done on time," she complained.

"I'm going to call the utility company. Tim Woods says they'll come out and check the temperature of our oven, free."

"Oh, would they? I'd like that. Nothing I put in the oven gets done when it's supposed to."

"If they don't make it before Sunday, try turning the heat up higher for Dr. Miller, okay?"

"What a great idea, Gorgeous. I always assumed that the oven was accurate. I figured I was making some mistake in preparing the food."

It was time out for a little hugging and kissing. After a while, she paused and looked directly into his blue eyes,

"Harry, may I ask you a question?"

"Shoot."

"What were you and the "milk lady" talking about for an hour and a half this morning?

Chapter 12

THANKSGIVING WITH THE GALVINS

It was a cold, gloomy morning, as Harry, rifle and deer tags in hand and wearing his orange visor and warm jacket covered with large orange patches, bent to whisper goodbye to his wife in bed. Drowsy as she was, Babs caught the purposeful gleam in the eye of the hunter. After he had kissed her, she snuggled down again among the blankets and pillows. From her cozy nest, she couldn't figure out why Harry, who hated to get up in the morning, would, nevertheless, leap out of bed at dawn to go to a fire or to hunt deer.

Shortly after they were married, sirens wailed around midnight, and Harry was up in a flash putting on his pants. Sleepy and bewildered, Babs surveyed that bundle of energy, her husband.

"Want to see what's happening? It's a two-alarm fire and might be interesting."

Hating to miss anything, she struggled into her blue slacks and sweater. Moments later, they were driving through the darkness at a breakneck pace. To her amazement, other cars and pick-ups were on the road, driving in the same direction.

"Does everybody around here go to fires in the middle of the night?" she had asked.

"Some are volunteer firemen, and they'd better go!"

"Do you suppose it's a house?"

"It could be a house, a farm building, or even a business."

It was a barn. Apparently a spark had ignited the straw, and the barn was ablaze. Across the farmyard, Jim Barry of *The Banner* and tenor, Gary Lewis, worked the water pump. The volunteers labored for an hour and a half, before getting the fire under control. The barn was a total loss, but the livestock and the other buildings were spared. Gary said, "Too bad about the barn, but at least we saved the homestead."

The farmer's wife looked vaguely familiar. Babs saw several children huddled on the porch in their bathrobes. Oh, it couldn't be. Yes, it was! Pamela! The farm belonged to Margaret Clark and her husband, Bob, who owned the Prairie Meadows Market.

Apparently many business people owned small farms. Babs had assumed that farmers owned tractors. On the contrary, since it took a large spread to support a tractor, many kept horses to pull their equipment. On that early morning, as the fire trucks pulled out of the driveway, Babs gave a sympathetic hug to Pamela and Margaret before she left.

After that brief sally into the chilly, dark night, Babs occasionally went to the fires, but more often stayed in bed. Wisconsin nights were freezing! Writing to her mother she explained,

"On an icy Wisconsin night, I love my warm bed!"

On this morning, she woke up, ready to celebrate Thanksgiving Day. Slipping into her bathrobe and turning on the radio to classical music, she walked around the house, occasionally touching the bright, new wallpaper that she had picked out.

Last week, Edith Murray had come by with several books of wallpaper, and Babs had chosen paper for the dinette, two bedrooms, the hall, and the living room. She had a promise from Harry that, since the Busy Bees offered to pay for the paint, he would paint the kitchen later on.

"I have so much to be thankful for!" she thought. "Besides living in a bright and cheery house, Harry and I won't be alone for the holiday."

Harry and Babs had been invited to Thanksgiving dinner with the Galvins. Dr. Galvin, a Methodist minister, and his wife, Isabel, had selected for their retirement an attractive home across the street from the Collins. When the local Methodist Church had discovered that there was a minister in their midst, they had immediately applied to the Conference to secure him as their pastor. After some thought, he had accepted the challenge. While Edgar had guided large congregations in Fond du Lac, Milwaukee, and Green Bay, it would a new experience for him to take charge of a small country church. His wife, however, announced that SHE had definitely retired. People were not to count on her for anything except attending worship services!

A warm friendship had developed between the older couple and Harry and Babs. Harry sometimes went to the older man for advice. Said the Methodist minister,

"I don't see how you get along without a District Superintendent. I couldn't have managed without my D.S."

When Babs had heard that remark, she had replied:

"The Lord knew we needed some help, and He sent us you."

Babs enjoyed Dr. Galvin and loved talking to Isabel, a minister's wife who held strong opinions on every subject.

When Isabel had learned that neither their son's nor daughter's families would be with them for Thanksgiving, they had invited the Petersens to join them. Babs had insisted on bringing a tomato aspic salad—putting it outside on the back porch for a while, so that it would harden. In addition, she prepared whole cranberry sauce, the way her dad liked it.

That evening, at six o'clock, Harry the hunter, and Babs arrived at the Galvin's.

"Where's the venison you were going to bring us?" Edgar inquired when he answered the door.

"Don't mind the big tease," laughed Isabel from her easy chair in the living room.

"I saw three deer. Two were does and the buck was too far away. Next year, I'll be more lucky!"

"Sure, sure, Harry. Come along and tell me what you think of this pamphlet on stewardship," declared Edgar, leading the way to his study.

"You know that 'stewardship' is 'minister talk' for raising money, don't you?" exclaimed Isabel. "Tell me, how do you like your new wall paper?"

"You heard about that already? Who told you?"

"My neighbor, Mrs. Collins. She has a big mouth. I guess the Busy Bees have a big bill now?"

"They do?"

"She said the women were totally surprised at how expensive the paper was. Did they give you any guidelines for your selection?"

"No. Nobody even mentioned money. They said for me to pick out what I liked, so I did."

"The ladies realize that this is the first time you ever selected wall paper. They kind of expected the woman who showed the samples—"

"Edith Murray—"

"They expected her to let you know the prices of the different patterns. And she didn't?"

"Not a word! Oh, am I in trouble with the Busy Bees?"

"Don't worry. The ladies will get over it. They should have had a committee to work with you."

While Isabel attended to last minute preparations, Babs filled the crystal goblets with ice water, silently admiring the Spode China, the silver utensils, and the tasteful arrangement of chrysanthemums in the center of the table.

After setting tomato aspic salads at each place, Isabel called the men to the table. Edgar said grace, and they began to eat. Following the salad course, the hostess brought in the turkey on a silver platter, setting it in front of Edgar to carve. He served the meat and dressing with style, and Babs, next to him, assisted by adding mashed potatoes and vegetables to each plate. Isabel passed piping hot rolls, delicious gravy, and Babs' cranberries.

"This is just like home!" exclaimed Babs.

Harry's eyes were on Dr. Galvin, as he expertly carved the turkey, seeing that everyone got a helping of light and dark meat, as well as stuffing. The younger man noticed, too, that Edgar was enjoying his role as provider.

After clearing the table, Isabel served pumpkin pie and hot coffee. Turning to Harry she asked, "Did you know that the whole Collins clan is in town for the holiday?"

"Bill mentioned to me that daughter, Carrie, and son-in-law, Doug, would be home," answered Harry.

"Have you talked to Jane lately about the family?" Isabel inquired.

"Some," answered Babs.

"Doug will graduate in January, and has been accepted at a Chicago theological seminary. I guess he heard the call to the ministry," responded Edgar.

"Jane said she was floored. He's so self-centered," said Isabel.

"I surely wish him the best," said Harry.

"Sounds like you don't see him as a threat to your job," kidded Edgar, pushing back his empty plate and taking a sip of coffee.

"Hardly," returned Harry, dismissing the thought.

That night as they were retiring, Babs confided,

"I didn't realize that I was selecting expensive wall paper patterns, Harry."

"Don't worry. The ladies understand."

"I don't want to be a burden."

"You're not a burden," he replied, admiring her full figure under her white satin nightie. "The parsonage really looks much better. They will end up being proud of how it looks."

"I hope so," she said, twisting her final curl and tying it with the last pink sock. "By the way, did you enjoy being in the woods this morning?"

"Yes, it was a thrill. I stood on a stump near a deer trail. I didn't move a muscle. I saw lots of squirrels, a rabbit, and three deer."

"Did you like the lunch I'd packed?"

"Very good."

Harry paused, re-living his day in the wild. Babs folded back the spread, preparing to slip between the sheets.

"Harry, wasn't that a delicious Thanksgiving dinner?"

"It sure was. Her mashed potatoes, gravy, and pumpkin pie were almost as good as my grandma's."

"Did you notice how Edgar carved the turkey?"

"Yes, you know, I liked the way he did it."

In view of all their arguments about serving food, Babs recognized that she had received one more blessing to thank God for tonight, Harry had enjoyed a dinner served in courses.

Chapter 13

PREPARING FOR THE HOLIDAYS

"Babs, I don't have time to hunt for a tree to cut for Christmas! Anyway, it wouldn't look as nice as a commercial tree!"

"Maybe not, but we're going to be with your family for Christmas. None of your old friends or family will see our tree."

"I'm tied up with extra holiday worship services. Besides that, since Clara Wells' sister, Mrs. Rigsby, wants to be baptized in a river rather than in the baptistery in the church, I must find a suitable spot for her."

"Isn't the river frozen now?"

"Yes, it is. I have to locate a level spot on the bank where her family can stand, where I can break through the ice, so that she and I can wade in."

Babs shivered and drew her sweater close around her.

"Break through the ice! I'm glad I wasn't called to be a minister!"

"I feel really pushed, and you're asking me to go out and cut a tree," he complained.

"You look tired, Honey. You got up and went to that fire last night, didn't you? What time was it when you finally got home?"

"Oh, around 3:30 am I didn't check my watch."

"I know you're busy, Harry. But think of cutting a tree as a present to me. Remember, we have had a lot of extra expenses during the holiday season. I think it's extravagant to buy a tree, when you can cut one in the wild."

Harry wrinkled his nose, gave her a hasty kiss, and left, carrying the last group of twenty-five Christmas cards which Babs had created. He groaned at her parting words:

"We may have to have scrambled eggs a couple of times this week to make up for this extra postage expense!"

Backing out the car, he expertly drove their blue Chevrolet through the icy streets. He was both annoyed with his wife, and feeling guilty over his reluctance to fuss with mailing cards and cutting a tree. He had to admit that she had done the lion's share of getting ready for the holidays. He'd seen her pouring over catalogs looking for appropriate gifts, he'd heard her exclaim when the Five and Dime Store had a sale on gift-wrappings, and he'd seen a growing array of gaily wrapped presents stacked in the corner of the guest room.

Besides that, she had spent many evenings drawing and coloring their cards. At last, she had completed and mailed fifty cards with the theme—"Warm greetings from under our snow-packed roof." While the cards looked fine to him, she wasn't satisfied with their appearance but sent them off anyway with personal notes to everyone

When more greetings came from people they knew, she had made twenty-five more. Twenty-five more three-cent stamps were an unexpected burden on their fragile budget.

As he stopped at the corner to let Margie Woods and her little sister cross the street, his thoughts turned toward his church family. Christmas seemed to be a stressful period for many of his parishioners. In fact, he wondered if people weren't having more problems than usual.

Take Myrtle Dodds, for example. She worked hard as a cleaning woman, and she and Herb had only his small pension and her earnings to keep them afloat. They were among the poorest in his congregations. Yet she would sometimes put a five-dollar bill in his hatband. Since their son Brad was studying for the ministry,

Myrtle seemed to sense the problems facing a young pastor. She was a jewel.

Lately, however, she complained all the time. No one could cheer her up. Yesterday, Mrs. Dodds had come over to the parsonage bringing a jar of homemade pickle relish. Standing in the parsonage kitchen and looking infinitely sad, she started whining about the date of the Busy Bees' bazaar. Babs looked bewildered, but Harry had burst out:

"What is *really* bothering you, Myrtle?"

Startled, she cried,

"My dearest friend, Edith Nichols, passed away!"

"Oh, yes. I conducted her funeral."

"It was sudden."

"Yes, it was."

Myrtle's shoulders began to shake with deep sobs.

"Out with it! What's eating at your heart, Myrtle?"

Her answer was more sobs. Her body shook and tears ran down her wrinkled cheeks. Harry drew her to him and put his arms around her. Gradually the weeping subsided. He looked into her faded blue eyes, his own blazing with intensity. Gently he repeated:

"Tell us about it, Myrtle."

Myrtle squared her shoulders and blew her nose.

"Dorothy and I have been best friends since childhood, even when she lived for a while in Wisconsin Rapids."

"She loved you, Myrtle."

"Not any more!"

"What?" asked Babs incredualously.

Myrtle wiped her eyes in despair.

"Why do you say that?" Harry had asked.

"Oh, we had a stupid argument. You know that my Herb likes to carve figures."

"He does a beautiful job."

"We have a corner shelf that Herb made years ago. It's really fancy, and I keep it in the living room."

"Yes."

Tears welled up again in the faded blue eyes.

"What about the shelf?"

"Dorothy always admired that shelf, and one day I promised her she could have it. Later, I felt that we should leave it to our son

Brad. When I told her, she clammed up and wouldn't speak to me."

"Oh, dear," Babs had murmured.

"The very next day after we talked, her car skidded on the ice and was hit by a truck. She died in the hospital, and I never had a chance to make up with her!"

Myrtle had wept as Harry and Babs held her in their arms. Time passed and prayers by each of them were offered before Myrtle began to acknowledge that one small episode could not really destroy the friendship of a lifetime.

Harry liked to remember her as she had left the house, clutching a pint of tomatoes canned by her pastor and his wife, her face a bit red from crying, but with a sparkle in her eyes, serene at last.

"Reconciliation," he said, "that's what Christmas is about. I am here to share God's love with the people around me."

As he drove down Main Street, he spotted Margaret Clark, pregnant, crossing the street in front of him. In a flash, he pictured his wife with her swelling body, listening to him as he preached, wrapping gifts for his father and mother, mending his socks, and sewing orange patches on his hunting jacket. He sighed.

"The holidays are also a time for service. I must find the time to select and cut a Christmas tree."

Chapter 14

THE BATTLE IS THE LORD'S

"A minister's wedding fees go to his wife. I like that tradition," said Babs, getting into the car.

"In a way, everything I have belongs to you, my dear," answered Harry, starting the engine.

"Everything I have is yours, too, but, with our limited means and since you have to buy books all the time, I'm glad to receive this money so that I can buy maternity clothes."

"Right," he answered, backing out into the road. "By the way, were you glad my cousin Julie and her husband Harvey dropped by this morning?"

"Yes, I'm glad they looked us up. And we'll get to see them again on Christmas Eve at your Grandma's."

"Since they missed the family reception for us in Waukegon last summer, they've been wanting to meet you."

"I didn't realize that Julie had married a minister. You and Harvey have a lot in common."

"Yes. I lent him some of my copies of *Pulpit Digest*. Like me, he's always looking for sermon illustrations."

"Yes, he said he envies older clergymen who have interesting stories to tell."

On a clear, cool day in Wisconsin, they passed by several red barns on the road to Wisconsin Rapids.

"I was amused though," Babs said.

"Amused?"

"In the kitchen, while I was fixing cinnamon toast, Julie confided that Harvey would soon learn to enjoy coffee, like the rest of the Petersen family."

"She predicted that?" he asked.

"Yes, but so far, he's holding out!"

"He is?"

"Do you notice what he was drinking?"

"No, what?"

"He asked for water or tea, so I fixed him a pot of tea!"

As they passed more small farms with dairy cattle, Babs lapsed into silence. After a while, Harry noticed that she was starting to fidget. By the time they arrived at Wisconsin Rapids, she confessed that she had a terrible headache.

"Honey, what's the problem? Is your stomach upset?"

She shook her head.

"Are you worried about spending the money? We'll be all right, you know."

"No, not money."

"What's wrong, Dear?"

"Harry, I hate to go shopping. I can hardly shop by myself!"

"Really?"

"It's dreadful," she cried, dabbing at her eyes and blowing her nose again.

By this time, Harry had found a parking place in front of a shop called, Great Expectations.

"What bothers you about it, Dear?"

"Mother always went with me when we bought clothes. I always liked one style, while she preferred another."

"That sounds pretty normal, Babs. Disagreeing with your mom bothered you?"

"Yes, it did. But that wasn't the worst of it! The dresses she liked always had big shoulder pads and huge pockets. She favored wide belts and horizontal stripes. But, when I looked in the mirror and saw myself with extra broad shoulders, I felt that I looked like a tackle on a football team."

"Did she make a big issue of her taste over yours?"

"Yes, she did. All the time. And we disagreed about colors. I liked simple outfits with bright colors like red or blue, or soft shades of pink or yellow, while she preferred orange and brown. I've always hated orange, and I don't care much for brown."

"So, what happened?"

"She would convince me that the outfits she selected looked better on me than the ones I liked. I lost confidence and decided I have no taste in clothes."

Pastor and parishioner looked at each other in silence.

"It takes courage for you to shop for yourself?"

"It sure does. I hate to make a mistake. I feel that there's a couple of dresses in the store that are the right style at the right price, but I'm afraid I won't recognize them."

"That's nonsense, Babs. There's a lot of dresses in there that would look nice on you. And we're not in a rush. Take your time."

"And to hell with the rest?"

A determined look that Harry had come to recognize was returning to her face.

"To hell with the rest!" he said.

"Harry, in a little while, will you come into the store and see what I've chosen?"

"Of course, Babs. After a while."

He watched as, gathering strength, she got out of the car, squared her shoulders, and advanced toward her ordeal. Harry knew that fellow customers and the clerks in the store saw only a bright-eyed shopper making her choices.

"But the Lord and I know the battle she's fighting," he said to himself.

And battle it was! Many dresses were tried on, viewed critically in the mirror, their price noted, and the style and practicality considered. True to his word, after a while, Harry came into the store to see the outfits she had chosen. While she modelled for him, he applauded her selections

Finally, with a radiant smile, she returned to the car with two maternity outfits. Like the Levite, Jahaziel, in II Chronicles 20, Babs believed that her battle was the Lord's.

"To hell with my fears!" she said, throwing her packages on to the back seat and sliding into the car. "We're going to Waukegon for Christmas, Harry, and I'm ready to celebrate!"

Chapter 15

GIFTS FOR THE MINISTER

"I'm glad that Barbara had to leave early," declared Jane Collins as the Busy Bees met in the church parlor. "It gives us a chance to talk about their Christmas presents."

"Yes. They need all kinds of things," said Pricilla Woods, adjusting the man's sock she was mending.

"Doris, did you get a chance to see what they have in their bedrooms?" asked Rita Barker, a sympathetic smile on her face.

Mrs. Blodgett nodded triumphantly.

"Yes, I went over to the parsonage and said I wanted to see the quilt that the Sterling ladies made for them. She hurried into the guest room and was taking it off the bed to bring it to me, but I followed right behind, so I could look around and see what they have in their bedrooms."

"Was she embarrassed?" inquired Thelma Young.

"Yes, she was. They don't have a single thing in the guest bedroom but the double bed you and Eben lent them, Marcia," answered Doris, reveling in the limelight.

"What about their bedroom? Did you see that?" inquired Jane.

"The door was open, and as I went past, I saw a brass double bed, a kitchen chair, a walnut dresser, and a wooden box at the head of their bed."

"A wooden box?"

"They use it for a bedside table," sniffed Doris.

A thoughtful silence fell over the Busy Bees. Many were recalling their own humble beginnings.

Rita broke the silence.

"I usually take the offering over to them after church. They don't have much furniture in the living room, do they?"

"No, they don't," said Jane.

"While I was there I looked around. There's a sofa, a chair and ottoman, the old rug, twin lamps on the window seat, and the piano, of course," offered Doris.

"Harry bought that stuff at an auction before they were married," remarked Jane.

"They aren't getting enough money *here* to buy anything! That's for sure!" stated Myrtle Dodds.

"They're babes in the woods! They don't know how to manage money," said Jane complacently. "Now take my daughter, Carrie. She and Doug take advantage of sales and they get along fine on their limited income."

"I feel very uncomfortable about this discussion," said Lola Rankin. "When we asked Doris to find out what the pastor and his wife needed, I didn't realize she'd have to go sneaking around."

"How else could she find out, Lola?"

"I don't know, Jane. Let's get back to the subject."

Mrs. Blodgett glared at Lola, opened her mouth, thought better of it, and settled back into her chair.

"They don't have any tables in the living room for the lamps, do they?" asked Thelma thoughtfully.

"No, and Tim says that he wonders whether one of the twin lamps works. It looks like it's been dropped and mended, and they never turn it on," said Pricilla smoothing her baby's hair.

"Maybe we should get something for the living room. What do you think?" asked Thelma, her needle poised over her embroidery.

"I'd like to give them a money tree," said Myrtle. "That way, they can get what they want."

"We have more experience behind us than they have," said Jane. "Let's decide what they really need."

"I saw a lovely crystal lamp at the furniture store in Wisconsin Rapids. I know Babs would love it," contributed Sunshine Chairman, Nancy Addison.

"Nancy, be practical. We don't have a fortune to spend on their presents," said Doris.

Lola smiled sympathetically at Nancy, who had been effectively squelched.

"I think Nancy has a good idea. They could use a pretty lamp to go with the other one," said Lola.

"Haven't we collected enough money to give them more than a lamp?" asked Myrtle.

"Yes, the money has come in real good," answered Doris, nodding complacently

"Why don't we get a couple of tables for the lamps?" said Jane. "Who wants to pick them out? Thelma, will you be on the committee? And Marcia, how about you?"

"Since I have the money, I'll help," said Doris decidedly.

"Now, all we have to do is decide when to give them their presents," said Jane.

Next Sunday morning, following morning worship, Harry's usual flight from Prairie Meadows to the Sterling Church was delayed. Bill Collins asked him to remain at the front of the church, while Fred Young ceremoniously escorted Babs to stand next to the pastor. They stood there awkwardly, while the gift committee vanished into the church parlor.

In a few minutes, Bill Collins, Fred Young, and Eben Morgan returned with two be-ribboned lamp tables and a green, ginger-jar lamp, placing them before the bewildered couple.

"Merry Christmas to you, from all of us in the Prairie Meadows congregation," announced Bill as he handed a large Christmas card to Harry.

"We hope you can find room for them somewhere in your house," said Eben, his bald head shining, as he reached up to shake the hand of his tall pastor and the pastor's wife.

"You shouldn't have done this," said Harry as he opened the envelope and read the card aloud, "'May you experience all the joys of the season. To our pastor and wife, December 1947.'"

Harry was tongue-tied. Finally, Babs leaned over and looked at the card.

"You've all signed it! What a lovely surprise! We will enjoy our new furniture. Thank you," she said.

"Yes, uh, yes, uh, thank you all, very much," replied Harry.

"And you all must come over and visit us. That way you'll be able to see how much we're enjoying these lovely, useful gifts," added the minister's wife.

Harry and Babs, having steadfastly denied themselves any new furniture, were profoundly touched at receiving the practical presents from the people.

And, as the church family watched them, many people found themselves struggling with lumps in their throats, and fumbling for their handkerchiefs. Myrtle and Herb Dodds had tears in their eyes, Doris, a self-satisfied smile, and Jane Collins' vague expression barely masked unbidden feelings of discontent.

Chapter 16

WAUKEGAN BOUND

"You're taking so darn much, Babs. We'll only be gone a few days. I can't get all this stuff in the car," said Harry, balancing a cardboard box in each hand.

"We both need changes of clothes," she explained patiently. "There's a suitcase for me and one for you, plus my make-up kit. We're taking Christmas gifts for your Mom and Dad and for your nieces. I didn't get gifts for your brother, Lefty, or his wife, Maxine."

"They don't expect gifts from us."

Harry made short work of stowing the suitcases.

"What did Margie say when you took the kittens over there?"

"She said that she'd take good care of them."

"Did you give her the cat food and their box and their bed?" persisted Babs.

"Yes. And I told her how much we usually feed them. Is that about it, Honey?"

"Just about. I locked both doors and I stopped the milk delivery. Did you check the furnace?"

"I sure did. We're ready to leave now, aren't we?" he asked hopefully.

"I guess so," she answered doubtfully as she got into the car, "but it seems like I'm forgetting something."

"Leave it for the next trip," he said cheerfully, warming up the engine of their Chevy.

Harry smiled at Babs. There beside him, she looked so cute, wearing the navy blue print dress she'd picked as one of her maternity dresses. While her pregnancy didn't show, she said her clothes already felt tight.

They were well on their way to Waupaca when she groaned and told him to turn back.

"Go back? Why?"

"I forgot something!"

"You did? Do we absolutely have to?"

"Yes. Please."

Reluctantly, he headed back toward Prairie Meadows.

"I forgot three loaves of banana bread," she said.

"What's so important about banana bread?"

"They're gifts. Whenever you visit someone, you always bring a gift—especially if you're going to a party at their house or you're staying overnight."

"My family never does that. My mother brings gifts for a shower or some one's birthday."

"Well, it's the polite thing to do."

The silence was frosty on the return trip. Reaching home, they saw Mac on the back porch peering into their kitchen.

"He's checking things out," reflected Harry.

"Sit still, Dear. I left the quick bread down in the cold basement."

Harry nodded to Mac as he listened to the news on the car radio. Finally she emerged, carrying three gaily wrapped packages. Settling into the car, she said,

"Lucky we had to come back. The water faucet in the bathroom basin was running, so I turned it off."

"Are we set now?"

"Yes, and thanks for coming back," she said, kissing him lightly on the cheek.

It was Christmas Eve Day, and, as they again set out for their three-hour journey, Harry felt profoundly contented. Christmas

Eve at Grandma Petersen's was the tradition he loved the most. After a while, Babs broke the silence.

"Tell me about your family celebration, Harry."

"Grandma makes fruit cakes every Thanksgiving and puts them away for the following year. At Christmas time, she brings out the year-old fruitcakes. She and the girls cook up a big feast with turkey with all the trimmings for all the family. Right now I can taste that good gravy, rich stuffing, and mashed potatoes."

"How many children did Grandpa and Grandma Petersen have?"

"They had ten kids, five boys and five girls, including Aunt Edith whom they adopted. My dad is the oldest son."

"At the reception I met most of them. Two of your uncles are ministers, right?'

"Yes, Marvin the second oldest son, and Arnold, the youngest."

"Three aunts live in the family home with Grandma, right?"

"Yes."

"It's kind of scary, marrying into a Danish family. While your mom and dad have given me a warm welcome, the rest of them seem to be still looking me over. Two ministers among the Petersens—what do the other guys do for a living, Harry?"

"My dad works at the steel mill, of course, along with Frances' and Mabel's husbands. Edith married a physician. Roy is an attorney, and Eric is a salesman."

"I remember Eric's wife, Amy. She's kind and gentle."

"Yes, she is, but Grandma doesn't like the fact that she's Episcopalian, and Eric joined the Episcopal Church."

"Grandma wants everyone to belong to her church, right?"

"Yes, and most do. Grandma can be stubborn. Like when her doctor told her to drink a little wine before dinner, she refused. So the doctor prescribed red wine, and my aunts paid the price of a prescription and brought it home. Only then would Grandma take her medicine."

"That's funny. What are your favorite memories of Christmas at Grandma Petersen's?"

"I can see the tall Christmas tree, brightly decorated and standing in the middle of the room with all the packages arranged under it. I can smell the coffee and the delicious food, especially the spicy pumpkin pies. I remember hearing Grandma and

Grandpa and my dad and my uncles and aunts singing Christmas carols in Danish, as they walked around the tree."

Harry paused, and Babs could see tears flowing down his cheeks.

Catching a glimpse of the sign, "Waukegan City Limits," Babs whispered excitedly,

"Just think, Harry, we should be at Grandma's in fifteen minutes!"

Chapter 17

WINTER GOSSIP AND
THE CULTURE CLUB

"I understand you attended the Culture Club, Babs."

"Yes, I played the piano for them one evening."

"Good for you. It's good for us ministers' wives to belong to a group outside of the church."

Isabel stirred her tea.

"Do you think so, Mrs. Galvin?"

"Yes, I do. It broadens our outlook. I don't go out as often as I did, but I enjoy hearing the latest. What village talk have you heard, Babs?"

"Pamela Clark told me that she wants a little brother."

"Pamela Clark? Not Bob and Margaret's daughter?" asked Isabel, her eyes twinkling.

"Yes, Margaret's daughter," answered Babs, checking the oven.

"So Pamela is excited about the baby? Oh, poor Margaret. They belong to our Methodist Church, you know. I guess she was about ready to leave Bob when she found out she was expecting again."

"They worked things out, I guess," answered Babs, sipping tea from her bone china teacup.

"Speaking of gossip, do you get visits from little Margie?"

"Margie Woods? I sure do. She always knows all the neighborhood news."

"The family goes to your church, don't they?" asked Isabel.

"Yes."

"One day our neighbor, Jane Collins, got to talking about the Woods family."

"She did?"

"Did you know this is his second marriage?"

"I'd heard that. I'm curious about his past."

"According to Jane, Tim, (is it Tim?) at one time was a very successful young accountant. He was married to a gorgeous young woman named Andrea. They lived in a spacious home on West Main and hobnobbed with the "high society" here in Prairie Meadows, people like the Ray Golds and the Downings."

"That's hard to imagine. Tim and his family live in a humble little place, and she makes all the clothes for herself and the children."

"According to Jane, at that time, people vied to be invited to their parties. Tim had a reputation for being witty, and Andrea loved to entertain."

Babs raised her eyebrows in surprise.

"One evening, Mrs. Galvin, when the trustees were over here for a meeting, I went into the living room to serve cake and coffee. There was a terrible smell. I could hardly stand it."

"What was it?"

"The Woods keep a cow. Harry said that Tim had manure on his boots. Can you imagine going anywhere with manure on your shoes?"

"No, I can't," answered Isabel, shaking her head. "To get back to the story, one day Andrea simply left Tim."

"Oh, no."

"After that, the Wood's home which had been so bright and attractive became dark. Tim's bookkeeping business fell off, and he began to farm in a marginal way. He never fixed the screens or painted the place. The house took on a neglected air. Finally, he sold it, and moved into the little house his father, a minister, had left him."

"How sad!"

"One Sunday, some time later, Tim showed up in church with Pricilla. There must have been a divorce, for after a while, they were married."

"You are talking about a man I've never met," responded the younger woman, "and all these years, he must have kept his anger bottled up inside!"

The sound of footsteps descending the steps was heard, and Harry and Edgar entered the dinette.

"Is dinner about ready?" asked Harry hopefully.

"Good timing. I was about to call you for dinner."

"Doesn't the table look pretty, Edgar?" asked Isabel.

"Sure does," said Edgar as they gathered around.

"You say that you sang at a funeral this afternoon? And you fixed this delicious dinner, Babs? Isn't this salmon loaf outstanding, Edgar?"

Babs looked amused as the Methodist minister finally caught the cue from his wife.

"Yes, oh, yes, it's very good, Babs. I'm glad you invited us over."

"Thank you both. I'm trying to please Harry and learn how to prepare puddings, gravy, and white sauce."

"With your mother 2,000 miles away, Babs, who is your teacher?"

"One of our wedding presents, the Eighth Edition of Fannie Farmer's Cook Book."

"Babs is doing better all the time, and she's right, I love gravy. Besides that, she uses the ricer and makes great mashed potatoes," beamed Harry.

Babs basked for a moment in their warm approval.

After a while, Edgar broke the silence.

"By the way, Harry, did you get an invitation to the week of evangelistic services at the Assembly of God Church?"

"Maybe," he replied doubtfully.

"You aren't sure?"

"Edgar, I'd just as soon forget about it. With all my obligations in this parish, I don't see how I can make it."

"Harry, I didn't mean to go all week. I just thought that we four might go together on one night to show some clergy support for their ministry here."

Harry frowned.

"You think we ought to, Edgar?"

"Couldn't hurt to encourage a fellow minister, could it?"

Harry's frown deepened, but he said nothing.

Babs began to laugh.

"Has Harry told you about his friend, Don, and the dog, Bugzy?"

"No, he hasn't," answered Edgar looking puzzled.

"Why did you bring up Bugzy, Babs?" complained Harry.

"Sounds interesting," Isabel said. "Tell us about Bugzy."

"Well," began Harry reluctantly, "when I was a kid, my friend, Don, had a fox terrier. The dog went everywhere with us. One Sunday night, as we were walking past the Assembly of God Church in Waukegan, we heard the people whooping it up. Don and I sneaked up to the door of the church, opened it, threw Bugzy in, and ran off. We could near Bugzy barking above the noise of the prayers and shouts and moans of the congregation."

Isabel chuckled. "You had no idea at that time that you'd become a pastor?"

"Absolutely not. I was pretty rebellious. My mother always figured that my kid brother, Lefty, would become a minister. As a kid, I liked baseball more than church or Sunday School."

"So here's the rebel, now the preacher! Tell us, what does Lefty do?" asked Edgar.

"He's a carpenter. Darn good one, too."

As they enjoyed an after dinner cup of coffee, Isabel looked around the parsonage living room, where Nip rested contentedly in Babs' lap, and Tuck purred loudly in Harry's. She cherished their friendship with the young couple, but couldn't help noticing how the elegant English bone china teacups contrasted with their sparse and shabby furniture.

As the Galvins were leaving, Harry shook hands with Edgar,

"I'll think about going to a service at the Assembly of God Church with you, okay?"

"Whatever you decide. Isabel and I do plan to go one night."

Since Isabel had not insisted on helping with the dishes, Babs and Harry worked together cleaning up.

"You didn't see today's mail, did you?" he asked.

"Singing at the funeral and preparing the meal, no, I didn't."

"Uncle Marvin answered my letter. He said that he'd be glad to conduct a week of meetings at Sterling."

"That's great, Harry."

The next day dawned, sunny and frigid. A soft snow had floated down in the night, leaving the landscape clean and sparkling in its whiteness. As she picked up the milk at the back door, Babs saw her breath in the frosty air. As usual, when the milk froze, it expanded and pushed the lid off, exposing the slender column of cream (which had risen to the top) to the air. She smiled and waved to Henry Perkins, out for his morning constitutional, and hurriedly closed the door.

Since Harry had meetings to attend and studying to do, they were getting an early start for the day. Babs had put the coffee on to perk and now measured the oatmeal and raisins into the mush kettle. She had only to squeeze the orange juice and set the table. Harry brought the loaf of bread, the colored margarine, and a jar of Thelma Young's peach jam up from the basement.

"Boy, that coffee smells good," said Harry as he closed the basement door. "That is Hills Bros. Coffee, isn't it? You aren't trying to fool me with that cheap stuff, are you?"

"It's Hills Bros., Dear. Sit down at your place and I'll pour you a cup."

Harry gave her an appreciative kiss as she brought the fragrant morning brew. Drinking a good cup of coffee was his idea of really living.

Noticing he was in a good mood, Babs decided to broach the subject of the Culture Club. Alberta had asked her to be her guest at the next meeting. It was to be held at the home of Polly Jarvis, whose husband managed the local movie theater. Polly had secured a speaker from The Boston Store in Milwaukee. Her topic was "Tips on Using Your China and Silverware in Entertaining."

Even with their beautiful wedding presents tucked away in the attic, Babs was wanted to hear the speaker. It would be nice to dress up, wear a little perfume, and be in a roomful of women where Mrs. Collins did not dominate the meeting. That woman was not in the Culture Club. Mrs. Blodgett told Babs that the group had snubbed Mrs. Collins. As a result, Doris and Jane had no use for the Culture Club. To Babs, however, one of its attractions was that she would not encounter Mrs. Collins.

At breakfast, Harry read *The Milwaukee Journal*'s most famous comic strip, "Pogo." He enjoyed the comments on the political scene from the animals in the swamp.

Harry put down the paper.

"What's on your mind, Honey? You are a hundred miles away."

"I was, I guess. I was thinking about the Culture Club."

"Oh, are they asking you to join?" he asked uneasily.

"No. But you look unhappy. Would you dislike it if they asked me?"

"I guess not."

"You've never talked about it, but I feel you really don't like my going. Why not? You're not jealous of my having other interests, are you?"

"No."

"It's hard for you to talk about this, isn't it?

"I don't know," he responded vaguely.

"We don't have time to talk now, but I'd like to know what's on your mind."

Harry finished his third cup of coffee. He gave her a hug, put on his winter coat, and walked out in the bright, crisp air. As he turned for a last look at her before he drove off, the light of the sun on his face was harsh.

Chapter 18

THE CULTURE CLUB

Babs had almost finished cutting out the young shepherd boy, David. She had glued the flannel backing on Goliath, the giant. With the backing for David prepared, she had only to glue it onto the David paper doll, and she would be ready to tell the story of David and Goliath at the Rosebud Sunday school. In reading the story of David, the young shepherd boy, she thought about the giants that the children of Rosebud faced: problems stemming from poverty, ignorance, alcoholism, and envy. She longed to tell the Sunday School pupils about the power of God's love.

Hearing a knock at the back door, she opened it, and found Myrtle and Herb Dodds, standing on the cement porch. They were smiling, and Mr. Dodds was carrying a large package.

"Come in, you two. I was about to have a cup of tea. Will you join me?"

"We can't stay, but Harry has have something to give you, Barbara. May we have tea some other time?" she asked.

"Of course. Call me Babs. What do you have there wrapped in wall-paper, Mr. Dodds?"

"Something he made for you."

"How exciting!" she cried.

"Open it right now."

"Is it a valentine?"

"Yeah, kind of a valentine," he answered shyly.

Babs took the parcel and ripped the paper off, revealing a delicately carved wooden shelf.

"Oh, Mr. Dodds, I love it. I can display some of my fancy teacups on it."

He blushed with pleasure.

"He hoped that you would find a use for it," added Myrtle.

"It belongs on that wall in the dining nook where we can see it when we eat. Now I must choose which teacups to put there. I think there's room for a pair of salt and pepper shakers, too."

"Do you like it?" he asked.

"I sure do. Thank you so much," she said, giving each a hug.

"We have to go, but we'll be back in a day or two to see how it looks in your dining room," said Myrtle as they left.

Babs stood watching the old couple, he, small and precise in his movements, she a little taller and stooped.

"How generous they are!" she marveled.

It was Valentines Day, so Babs had splurged. Dinner would be pork chops with applesauce. She had selected four small tomatoes as part of a celery and purple cabbage salad and had frosted and decorated a white layer cake with candy hearts. She would make pan gravy. With dinner underway, she chose a crystal necklace with teardrop earrings to dress up her maternity dress, dabbing Windsong perfume behind her ears and on her wrists. (Mother always said a lady used perfume for a special date). Tonight promised to be festive.

She was filing her nails when Mac appeared in the door.

"It smells good in here," he observed. "You having company or something?"

"No, just us."

"Good thing. Costs a lot of money to have people over for dinner," he said, shaking his head for emphasis. "I tell the wife that all the time. Bad habit. Costs a lot."

He shuffled over to the piano to check out the music on the rack. Pausing, he looked around.

"You have the heat up pretty high, don't you? That sure runs up the fuel bill."

"If I put on a sweater, I could turn the heat down."

Mac gave her a rare smile.

"You sure could," he said, approvingly. "Yeah, smells good," and he left, carefully closing the front door against the chilly weather.

"I've got to remember to check the doors," she said to herself, locking up after him and watching his spare bent frame, as he ambled along toward home.

She was slipping into her blue sweater when she heard Harry's step at the back door and flew to give him a hug and a kiss.

"I love this welcome," he said. "Boy, it smells good! What are we having for dinner?"

"Pork chops with gravy and applesauce! How's that?"

"Great!" he said. "And what do you suppose I have here?"

"A present? For me?"

He watched her as she tore the wrapping paper and opened the box.

"Oh, Harry, a corsage of red roses! You shouldn't have! But I love it."

"This is our special day, Babs."

"Yes, you popped the question on Valentines Day!" she said, drawing his head down and kissing him tenderly.

Releasing him, she ran to the bathroom mirror, pinned on the flowers, and stood looking, first, at the roses on her left shoulder and next, at her swelling figure in the flowered blue print.

After dinner, Harry had no meetings or appointments, and while they drank tea, they listened to classical music on the radio.

"I saw Pamela at Clark's Market. You know, after the fire in their barn, Clarks have been able to rebuild."

"Good," replied Harry. "They've had a rough time."

"I also saw Mrs. Miller, the pastor's wife at the Assembly of God Church. She looks as pale as a ghost."

"Honey, that reminds me, do you want to go one night to the Assembly of God Church? Edgar was asking me, again."

"Larry Miller's a fellow pastor of yours. Frankly, I'm curious. I've never worshipped at a Pentecostal Church."

"I guess we'll go, okay?"

She nodded.

"Harry, while we're settling some things, I have a question for you. How do you feel about my attending Culture Club meetings?"

"You have a right to go if you want to."

"We are not talking about rights. How do you feel?"

"It's okay, I guess. I like Alberta. Miss Hawk, the librarian, seems like a nice person, too."

"But something is bothering you."

Harry stirred his tea and petted Nip who was trying to play with his teaspoon.

"Maybe you feel that it will take up too much of my time?" she persisted.

"I don't suppose it would."

She was silent. Tuck approached her and jumped up on her lap. Harry scratched Nip behind the ears, and the kitten purred in appreciation. He looked over at his bride.

"Yesterday at Wilkerson's, Bill Ford and I were talking."

"About the Culture Club?"

"Yes. You know his wife, Polly. She's in the club. He was saying that they have big doings in the spring. It's a card party. The money goes for charity."

"That's right."

"I don't care for card parties."

"I know your Mom and Dad don't play cards."

"Mother used to before she married Dad. She was a regular card shark."

"She was?"

"She was a Presbyterian. They play cards."

"Why did she stop?"

"I hadn't thought about it. I guess she did because of Dad."

"That was generous of her."

"She didn't seem to miss it."

Babs poured a second cup of tea for each of them.

"Thanks, Honey. The tea is good."

Babs was silent while her husband stirred his tea.

"I was wondering, Babs, do you miss playing cards?"

"So far, I'm too busy to miss it."

"I was wondering if you joined the Culture Club, would they expect you to help out with the card party?"

"If they ask me to join, maybe I could tell them that I'd prefer to skip that project. I don't have to go, if it bothers you."

"Babs, it's your decision. I'm not going to tell you what to do."

"I know that, Harry! They may not ask me to join. But I would like to go to the next meeting."

"Go ahead, Dear, and have a good time. You may even pick up some good tips on how to entertain the Busy Bees," kidded Harry, looking relieved, after sharing his concern.

Tuck was purring in her lap, her husband was smiling, and the roses smelled sweet . . .

"I'm so lucky, Gorgeous. By the way, did you notice the beautiful shelf that Herb Dodds made for me? Would you please hang it up in the dinette?"

Chapter 19

LONG WINTER OF 1948

"I can feel little Judy kicking," said Harry, his hand on his wife's tummy.

"I'm so thankful that I'm feeling good, again!" answered Babs, as she threw the covers aside and got up.

According to Dr. Sutherland, her pregnancy was progressing well. The morning sickness that plagued her at first was over by the end of the fourth month, and her zest for living had been restored.

Harry, too, was thankful. It was unlike Babs to drag her feet in the morning, and he hated to see her feeling miserable. Once again, she was bouncing out of bed and into the kitchen to make his coffee.

Harry was, however, concerned about the mail from his mother-in-law. Since Ruth Walker was a trained nurse, her letters were full of advice on prenatal care. In addition, starting in February, she extolled the beauty of spring in the San Francisco

Bay Area, where, apparently, all the fruit trees up and down the East Bay hills were in full bloom.

"If only you were here, Barbara, to enjoy the view with me!" she wrote.

Letter in hand, Babs had looked out at the snow, which, after a warmish, windy week, had turned to dirty, heavy slush.

"When does spring come to Wisconsin?" she had asked her husband.

"Trees start to bud out about the first of May," he had answered.

Harry had been busy setting up the week of Bible study for Sterling. He had been in touch with the news editors in Stevens Point and Waupaca. The papers had carried a story and picture of Marvin and his topic: "Put On the Whole Armor of God." The young minister hoped for a good attendance, and a more out-going spirit among the church members.

He had another concern. Marvin would stay with them. While Babs was looking forward to entertaining Harry's uncle, assuming that Marvin would be supportive like Harry's Dad—after all they were brothers—Harry had his reservations. He knew that the two men were, in many ways, opposites.

It was Sunday morning. Harry looked at his watch. They had had their usual quick breakfast, and she had left to teach at the Rosebud Sunday School. Along the way, she made five stops to pick up youngsters. She had told him that two weeks ago the car had become mired in a farmyard. It had taken twenty minutes for farmer, Dick James, to dig her out.

Babs had laughed.

"They were ready for me last Sunday, and Freda held up a warning hand to tell me to avoid their farm yard and stay on the snow-plowed road. Right away, Bob and Ruthie came out and got in the car."

From that day on, she avoided snow-filled, farm driveways. Having never driven in snow before, she was fearful; yet, she persisted. Harry liked her spunk.

After taking on the Rosebud Sunday School as her project, Babs had enlisted a couple of helpers: old Mr. Davis fired up the stove, so that the church was warm; and Mrs. Fox, universally disliked for her alleged flirtations, played the piano—poorly, but faithfully. Unfortunately, Babs had found no volunteer to handle the offering, so that she was in charge of it and tried to keep the meager finances straight.

In order to teach Bible stories to children of varying ages, Babs was using figures on a flannel board. To her delight, the Sunday school was growing. Twenty-five last Sunday! Babs' face had shone when she told Harry.

He smiled as he thought about his wife's ministry. It was 9:45 am Nip and Tuck were cuddled together in his lap. Taking a last swallow of coffee, he put the kittens, still purring, into their basket in the corner of the dinette. His pulse quickened as he crossed the street, greeting his neighbors and friends as he went. This was the time of the week that he lived for!

As he entered the old-fashioned sanctuary, he heard the piano. Mrs. Collins' prelude was a laborious rendition of "Largo" by Handel, a piece that Harry despised, since his piano teacher years ago had insisted that he practice it by the hour. Never satisfying the teacher, young Harry had finally switched to the violin.

"I've got to rise above my irritation," he said to himself, "or I can't bring a message of hope today."

He noticed that his home visits were paying off, for scattered throughout the congregation, were three young families sitting in the pews with their children. On the opposite side of the sanctuary were two widows he'd become acquainted with when he'd conducted the funerals of their husbands.

He saw Herb and Myrtle Dodds, looking tired but cheerful. Behind them were Nancy Addison with a colorful scarf around her neck and Mrs. Blodgett, dressed in purple and wearing her usual look of disapproval. Peter and Elsie Wilkins, a prosperous, middle-aged couple, were seated behind Tim and Pricilla Woods and their three children. Bill Collins, as usual, sat in the front pew by himself. All were there with various needs and with different points of view.

"God, let me speak your word of kindness and love," he prayed silently.

Mrs. Collins was playing the second congregational hymn, *What a Friend We Have in Jesus*, when Babs walked in, returning from Rosebud. Instead of taking her usual spot at the back of the church, she caught Alberta's sign of invitation, and walked forward to sit with her near the front.

Harry rose to announce his topic.

"You recall that last week I preached on 'God's Forgiveness,' how we receive grace by the Savior's death on the Cross. That is only the beginning. Today we will think about forgiveness from another perspective: God's commandment that we forgive those who have hurt us."

At that moment, a loud crash was heard as a hymnal slid off a pew onto the floor. Harry caught sight of Tim Woods' pale, troubled face, as he stooped to retrieve the book.

"My topic this Sunday morning is: 'Forgiving Those Who Have Wronged Us.' "

Abruptly, Bill Collins, a haughty smile on his face, rose from the front pew, deliberately donned his overcoat, stalked down the center aisle and out the front door. The people stared open-mouthed at the one-man parade, marching toward the door. As the door slammed, the congregation turned around and stared at their young pastor.

Clearing his throat, Harry read the text from Matthew 18:21:

"Peter said to him, 'Lord, how often shall my brother sin against me, and I forgive him? As many as seven times?' And Jesus said to him, 'I do not say to you seven times, but seventy times seven.'"

"In this life," began Harry, "we are given many opportunities to forgive one another."

Chapter 20

THE TONGUE: A LITTLE MEMBER

"No tea, please. I prefer coffee."

"We usually drink tea in the evening. Would you like me to fix a pot of coffee for you, Uncle Marvin?"

"If you please," he replied.

She glanced at the appetizing plate that Harry had just served her. Since Marvin, driving up from Illinois, had taken a wrong turn, their dinner had been delayed until 7:00 pm. Babs felt ravenous, even a bit faint.

"M-m-m, it smells so good," she said to herself. Harry was occupied in serving his uncle, who looked at his plate with disfavor.

"No broccoli for me. It upsets my stomach."

Leaving her inviting serving of food, Babs rose and put on the percolator for coffee.

"Why this fuss and feathers with you serving each plate, Harry? Just put the food in serving dishes and pass it," advised their guest. "That makes a lot simpler for everyone. It's the way Luella and I do it—in fact, all of our family. Doesn't Louise slice the meat ahead of time and put it on the platter?"

"Uh huh, Marvin."

Babs returned to her seat at the table, spreading her napkin over her enlarging tummy, in anticipation of that first bite of mashed potatoes and gravy.

"You have some cream and sugar, don't you? I'm used to having cream and sugar in my coffee."

"Sorry, I forgot, Uncle Marvin. We take ours black. We have no cream—just whole milk down in the basement."

"Or, we could open some canned milk for you," added Harry, helpfully.

"No cream? I can make do with cold, whole milk."

Harry missed the appealing look she gave him before she started down the basement stairs to get the milk from the basement. Returning, she poured it into a small pitcher. By the time the coffee was ready, she had found the sugar shell, filled the sugar bowl, and had set milk and sugar on the table. Silently, she poured the coffee.

"What are you giving me? I can't drink this! It looks like weak tea! You need to use more coffee when you perk it. Is this the kind of coffee you make in your house?"

"Babs is a bride, just learning to cook, but she's doing better all the time," declared Harry defensively.

"Harry, will you make the coffee, so that Marvin gets it the way he likes? Thanks, Dear," she said, seating herself once more.

Harry was clattering around the kitchen, emptying the rejected brew and rinsing out the coffee pot.

"Bring me a mug, will you, Harry?"

"What's that, Marvin?"

"Bring me a mug, will you? These little cups don't hold enough."

Eating her cold dinner, Babs said not a word.

"You'll have to get along with a cup, Marvin. We don't have any mugs."

"No mugs? Luella and I got several as wedding gifts. Not one mug? Too bad."

Disappointed, Marvin turned his attention back to the food before him.

Finally, the meal was over. While the men retired to the living room to discuss last-minute details about the Bible study, Babs cleaned up the kitchen, groaning as she threw out a pot of strong coffee. She had been looking forward to this opportunity to get better acquainted with Harry's family. Disappointed, she resolved to make Marvin as comfortable as she could.

The next morning, dawned clear and cold. A gentle snow had fallen during the night. The beautiful new day lightened their hearts. However, with Harry making the coffee, breakfast was a little late, and Marvin became restless.

"I'd like to glance at the headlines."

"We'll get a paper in to town," replied the host.

"What, no morning paper?" he replied, surprised. "By the way, Harry, the bed in your guest room is too soft. I could hardly get to sleep last night."

"Is that right? It seemed okay when we slept in that bed."

"Luella and I like a hard mattress, better for your back. Mind if I phone Luella? She isn't feeling well."

"Go right ahead, Marvin."

As Marvin hung up the phone, Harry, with some pride, brought out *The Banner*, Prairie Meadow's weekly paper, to show the publicity given to the week of Bible studies in Sterling.

Marvin was not impressed.

"You would think, with an out-of-town speaker, they'd, at least, put it on the second page, wouldn't you? And they misspelled my name. It's Petersen—not Peterson as they have it. Couldn't they read your writing?"

"I typed it, Marvin."

"I'll put up with it. I hope the people invite a lot of their friends. It's easier to speak when the church is full," he asserted.

Babs was clearing up, as the men prepared to leave.

"Marvin, what I'm hoping is that the people of Sterling will receive a message of hope and encouragement. They will invite friends to church after they realize how much God loves them, recognize their own potential."

Marvin looked crest-fallen.

"Small group, then?"

"Could be."

The front door slammed as the two ministers left. As Babs was pouring a second cup of coffee, diluting it with hot water from the teakettle, the phone rang.

"Hi, Alberta. . . Yes, I'll go to the next Culture Club meeting with you. I want to hear what the speaker has to say about entertaining."

For the third month in a row, they wouldn't be able to give Mrs. Blodgett the payment for the washing machine. They had already spent the gasoline and utility allotment for the month.

When the coal ran out, they would have to charge again. In the winter, it cost them $300 a month to heat the house. The money she received from piano lessons and what he got for funerals was a help, but not enough to meet the bills.

About 9:00 pm, Harry and his uncle returned from the first evening of meetings. Marvin seemed animated, but Harry was quiet.

"The farmland in Sterling is a lot better than the sandy soil here in Prairie Meadows, Harry. Some of the people seem fairly prosperous. Too bad they didn't bring more people out to the service. I'm pretty tired. I think I'll take an early bath and go to bed," announced Uncle Marvin as he left the room.

Soon they heard the bath water running.

"Did we get any mail?" enquired Harry.

Opening the door to the upstairs, she handed him a parcel.

"Here's a package to you from Bill Collins."

"Looks like books. Oh, one by Norman Vincent Peale, and another author I don't know."

Harry, book in hand, left the wrappings on the floor and sat back in his chair.

"These books look interesting. I'm going over to see Bill tomorrow morning."

"You know, Harry, by stamping out of church Sunday, I think Bill Collins lost some prestige. When I was downtown today, several people came up to me and were unusually kind."

"They were?"

"Yes. They inquired about you and asked me when the baby is due."

Harry looked up from the Norman Vincent Peale book.

"What do you have there in your hand, Honey?" he asked.

"It's a mug."

"A mug?"

"Yes, I hope he likes it. It's for Uncle Marvin."

Chapter 21

CONFRONTATION

Bill Collins looked surprised when he opened the door of the small Red Cross office in his home and found a determined-looking Harry Petersen standing on the porch.

"Good afternoon, Bill," said Harry. "We need to talk."

"We do?"

"Yes, absolutely."

"If you must," answered Bill waving Harry to a seat and settling into his comfortable office chair. "Did you receive the books I sent you?"

"Yes, I did. Thank you. What I came here about is your leaving the church Sunday."

"Surprised you, did I?"

"You surprised everyone. Why did you do it?"

"Your sermons leave me cold, Harry."

"Sorry, Bill. I try to prepare helpful messages."

Bill took off his rimless glasses, surveyed them and began wiping them with a small cloth.

"Oh, I guess you try. But the week before, you had covered that doleful theme of forgiveness," he responded, holding the right lens up to the light. "Sunday morning, when you announced more 'forgiveness,' something snapped, and I just couldn't stand the thought of listening to another sermon about how helpless and ineffectual we are."

"Is that the way you see the Atonement, Bill?"

"You've got it! I hate hearing about 'forgiveness' and sin all the time. Why do you dwell on negative ideas all the time, especially since there are so many positive topics you could preach about? That's why I sent you the books: to help you look at the world in a more affirmative light."

He examined the left lens, blew on it, and wiped it, replacing his glasses on his nose. Harry was quiet for a moment.

"Bill, I'm sorry we don't see eye-to-eye. I look at forgiveness as a chance to start a new spiritual life, to grow, and be led by the Holy Spirit into a life of genuine service."

"Now I agree with you on the genuine service part; but my question is: how do we get to that point? If you would focus on courage and bravery, helping out other people, or subjects like peace of mind, or on men like Gandhi who have changed the world, I would be more enthusiastic about your leadership in my church."

"I appreciate your honesty, Bill, and I'll read the books. But do we have to agree on every point to enjoy good fellowship?"

"You are asking a lot to expect me to support you as a preacher and pastor in my church when I see you barking up the wrong tree all the time. Especially when some one else could provide the encouragement I am waiting to hear on Sunday mornings."

"Do you have someone in mind, Bill?"

"Not really. But, you know, our son-in-law, Doug, has decided to become a minister. It has crossed my mind that even a novice like him could do a better job than you have, up to now."

"Doug is a capable young man, and I'm confident that he'll do well, wherever he goes. Babs and I wish him and your daughter, Carrie, the best. But Bill, your support has meant a lot to me. Let's shake hands, and pledge to continue to working together."

Bill looked with distaste at his pastor's extended hand. He hesitated, then touched the offered hand an instant and withdrew, turning his back on the younger man. Harry stood quietly, hoping Bill would turn and smile, giving a sign that their friendship had been renewed.

He had come seeking reconciliation, but apparently, he had failed. Regretfully, he turned and left.

Chapter 22

MORE TONGUES

Nip and Tuck were crouching at the kitchen door when he got home, and scampered before him, as he entered. Babs, at the stove, saw his face, and opened her arms to give him a hug.

"Honey, you look beat. You had two funerals today, didn't you? That takes a lot out of you."

"Oh, I guess I did conduct two funerals—one at 10:00 am and another at 1:00 pm."

"You'd forgotten? What happened? You look like you've lost your best friend."

She turned off the gas under the meatballs and drew him to the living room where they sat on the shabby couch.

"In a way, I guess I have."

She waited.

"After David Brown's funeral, I went over to the Collins'. I wanted to thank him for the books and reach an understanding."

Harry sighed.

"Really? You went over there to thank him for the books? After the way he acted?"

"I tried to reach him, but I failed."

Kissing him on the forehead, she handed him the mail.

"Why don't you rest for a few minutes? Dinner is almost ready."

"Smells good. Why so early?"

"Remember, tonight we're going to the Assembly of God Church with the Galvins."

He wrinkled his nose.

"I had forgotten. I wish I hadn't said we'd go."

"Oh, it may take your mind off things you can't control."

At dinner, putting aside his disappointment, he noticed Babs looking at Herb Dodds' little shelf. Last week he'd put it up for her in the dinette. She had chosen three of her prettiest engagement teacups, along with two pairs of salt and peppers, and placed them on the ledge. Several times that day, he had caught her looking at them and smiling.

"Harry," she had said that evening, "With the bright new wall paper and that quaint shelf, isn't this room more inviting?"

Who would have predicted that, a couple of days later, Uncle Marvin would brush against the shelf, knocking off a colorful teacup and a dainty demitasse?

Marvin had covered his embarrassment by a gruff, "That's a narrow ledge. Hope those weren't valuable antiques. Sorry. Of course, I'll pay for them."

His offer had been refused. How could he know that the teacup came from her Aunt Mary, and the demitasse was a gift from her mother's closest friend? Tears came after he left the room. As she swept up the precious bits of china, she had said, "Do you believe our motto for the year: people are more important than property?"

"Of course. Don't you?"

"Yes, so why am I feeling so sad?" she had asked, beginning to dry her tears.

After Marvin's departure, Harry had re-hung the shelf. Copper candlesticks and metal bells (sturdier stuff), now adorned the shelf. To Harry, it looked as attractive as before.

Back to the present, as Harry's eye fell on the little shelf, he said, "I like the practical way you've arranged your bells and candleholders."

"Thanks, Dear."

At 7:45, Galvin's 1946 Cadillac drew up in front of the parsonage. Harry called, "They're here! Are you about ready?"

Seeing the car, Babs got excited, as they locked the door and walked to the curb.

"Dr. Galvin, I just love your automobile. Wouldn't it be fun some day to own a Cadillac? What color is it? I can't tell in the dark."

"It's black. One of our former parishioners in Fond du Lac offered to keep an eye out for a good, used Cadillac for me. He came up with this one."

"It's Edgar's latest toy, Babs. Come and sit in back with me. The men can stretch their legs up front," said Isabel.

With a crowd at the small Pentecostal Church, they had to park and walk three blocks in the dirty, melting snow. They heard an old, slightly out-of-tune piano, as they climbed the steps of the white frame church. The entrance was filled with people: men in their Sunday best suits and women in warm coats over their dresses. Some smiled shyly at the two couples.

Opening the door to the sanctuary, they saw seven ministers dressed in tight, black suits, seated on a low platform in front. The pastor, the Rev. Larry Miller, recognizing his tall colleague, called over the sound of the piano:

"Brother Petersen, so glad you came! Come here, Brother, and sit up in front with us!"

Harry pointed to the row where Babs, Isabel, and Edgar were seating themselves, and said abruptly: "I'll sit here!"

The service began with Gospel hymns, and after each song, the congregation broke out with praise and moans. "Halleluiah!" "Praise the Lord!" "Dear Jesus!"

Feeling trapped as he sat on a hard wooden folding chair, Harry hoped that all seven preachers were not scheduled to speak. One by one, the first six took part, reading a number of Scripture passages, praying, and presiding over the offering. A young couple from Stevens Point sang *His Eye Is On the Sparrow*.

Suddenly, one of the ministers in black began to speak in a language Harry did not recognize. Again, a chorus of moans and praise arose from the congregation. The sixth minister rose, and in a voice of authority, spoke:

"I was glad when they said unto me, let us go into the house of the Lord."

Praise, and moans erupted at a more intense level.

Finally, the seventh minister came forward to preach, announcing the Scripture lesson.

"Go into all the world and preach, baptizing them in the name of the Father, Son, and Holy Spirit. And lo, I am with you always."

Normally, Harry was sweltering, crammed next to a heavy-set woman, who, like himself, was sweating profusely. Besides that, his back, crushed against a rigid chair, was killing him. Edgar and Isabel showed no reaction, and Babs was still as a mouse. At last, the preacher finished his lengthy sermon and stood at the pulpit with a bowed head. Again, a voice from the rear, this time a woman's, spoke in an unknown language. After she had finished speaking, Pastor Miller's voice broke through the sounds of supplication from the people, to interpret:

"In quietness and confidence shall be your strength."

A final Gospel hymn, the benediction from the pastor, and the congregation was dismissed.

As Edgar guided the big car through the slushy streets, Isabel said nothing, but Edgar couldn't contain his frustration,

"So that's speaking in tongues! Did you see Mrs. Miller, the one who spoke from the back of the sanctuary? A woman like that annoys me to death. She's as pale as a ghost, she's a foot taller than her husband, and she always wears black! She's severe with a capital S! That woman is a hatchet-face!"

"Shall we go again tomorrow night, Edgar?" asked Babs with mock innocence.

"Not on your life!"

As the black Cadillac made its way through the frosty night toward the Community Church parsonage, Isabel broke the silence.

"In quietness and confidence,' the minister said. If indeed, God were trying to convey a message to the congregation by speaking in tongues, was any one listening?"

Chapter 23

MORE CULTURE

"This is the evening the deacons are to meet, isn't it, Pastor?"

"It sure is, Tim. Come on in. You're a little early, but that's all right."

"I'm the first, am I?" asked Tim, standing uncertainly just inside the living room door.

At that moment, Babs came into the living room, wearing her navy blue maternity suit with a pearl necklace and earrings. She paused to shake hands with the visitor.

"Good evening, Tim. You look so nice. Is that a new outfit you're wearing? And new oxfords?"

"Thanks, Babs," he answered shyly. "Yes, they're new. Pricilla likes this color on me."

"I agree with Pricilla, and your teal blue shirt looks great with the tan slacks. Very becoming!"

"Will you be here when we talk about ordaining Harry?" asked Tim.

"No. She's going to the Culture Club meeting. She'll come home and tell us country people how to behave," teased Harry.

A car stopped in front of the house.

"That's Alberta. Bye," said Babs, waving to Tim and giving Harry a kiss, before putting on her coat and hurrying out into the cold night.

"I've never seen you look so sharp, Tim. Have a seat," said Harry.

"Thanks, Pastor. I came early, hoping we'd have a moment to talk."

"No time like the present," he answered.

Tim sat down on the sofa and took a deep breath. Harry waited expectantly.

"I hardly know where to begin. Did you know I was married before?"

"Yes."

"We were both so young. I was desperately in love with Andrea. She kept me laughing all the time."

"You were happy together?"

"We were. We lived in a beautiful, big house in town, and she loved to entertain. Her best friend was Adrianne Downing, wife of the Prairie Meadows School principal. Anyway, she inspired me, and I was ready to give her the world. With Andrea, I felt I could succeed at anything."

"Your career was going well?"

"I was flying high. Then, one day, everything came crashing down," said Tim softly, pausing.

He wiped his eyes. The silence was painful.

"On our third anniversary, we had a heart-breaking argument, and I realized I was wrong and came home with a bouquet of glads and a box of chocolates. The house was dead quiet. I walked from room to room, and finally found the note she had left me. Andrea wanted a divorce."

"Tim, no! What a shock!"

"I was devastated," Tim admitted softly, taking out his handkerchief and wiping his eyes. "She was tossing me aside! I was hurt, desperate! I called Adrianne Downing, told her that my wife had left me. She didn't know what to say. We talked a while, and after I hung up, I vowed I'd never to speak of Andrea again."

Tim struggled to regain his composure.

"After that, I didn't care about a thing! I lost my big accounts, one by one. I sold my house for a song, moved into my parents' little home, which I'd been renting out. After a time, I met Pricilla. She's a wonderful person, but I was afraid to love again. I figured she'd leave me, too. Finally, we married. You know the rest, Pastor."

"Tim, where did you get the strength to tell me this?"

"Pastor, it was your second sermon on forgiveness. You were speaking right to me. Your message broke my heart!"

Tim's eyes filled with tears, and he reached for his handkerchief again.

"I knew I had to forgive Andrea and let go of my anger and ask forgiveness for my bitterness and neglect."

Harry's eyes welled up. Suddenly, Tim began to laugh.

"When I asked God to forgive me, and to help me forgive Andrea, a terrible weight slipped off my heart. It's as if I've been let out of prison! The sky is bluer, the stars are brighter, and I love my wife and family more than ever!"

"You are celebrating life?"

"I am really celebrating."

As the two men mingled tears and smiles, they heard footsteps on the porch.

"Oh, the others are arriving. You won't say anything, Pastor?"

"Not a word."

"I'll go wash up."

"Go, Tim."

Harry opened the door, greeting each man as he entered. When they were all seated, Harry spoke.

"I am so pleased that everyone of you could make it to this meeting to consider my ordination. Oh, here's our secretary. Tim, would you mind reading this communication from my seminary?"

"Look at Tim, all spruced up," remarked Gary.

"I invited Bill Collins to our meeting, but he said he couldn't make it, so we'll just go ahead," said Tim, putting on his glasses and reading a letter from Harry's divinity school.

Fred Young looked puzzled.

"Would you mind reading that note again? Gary and I are new at this deacon business. I don't understand what we're supposed to do."

Gary nodded in agreement.

"Fred, the seminary Harry graduated from is recommending that we call a council to ordain him," said Tim.

"Ordain? What's that? Isn't he already a minister?"

Tim turned to Harry.

"Yes, I am a minister. But I need to receive formal recognition of my orders. Because I'm serving this church along with Sterling and Rosebud, it's up to you to form a council and work with the other churches in our area, so that I become a regularly recognized and ordained minister."

"Our area? Does that include the churches in Stevens Point, Plainfield, Wild Rose, Sterling, and Wisconsin Rapids?"

"That's right, Eben."

"Do we have to work with Sterling? There's no problem with Rosebud; they'll go along with us. But that bunch at Sterling won't cooperate," sighed Fred.

Eben pointed to the piano. "There's some people in Sterling who like to cooperate—like my brother, Mike. He and Claudia lent that piano over there to the Rev, so the missus could play it whenever she's a mind to."

Eben looked to his pastor.

"Of course, Eben. I think the Sterling Church and the rest of us can work together."

"Some one needs to move we form a council to ordain Harry," said Tim.

Herb Dodds had been silent until now.

"I make a motion we do it," he said.

Fred and Gary turned to Eben, the senior deacon.

"I second it," said Eben.

The motion carried unanimously.

"Thank you, my friends. Now, Tim is an old hand at this, since his Dad was a minister years ago."

Tim explained the steps that must be taken for Harry's ordination. The men got excited at the prospect of helping their young pastor qualify as a full-fledged minister.

"We'll meet again to work out procedures," said Tim, sipping the coffee Harry served.

"These brownies are good," said Fred, helping himself to a second.

"Oh, I see headlights," said Gary. "Babs must be coming home.

The deacons' meeting was breaking up, as she came in, her eyes sparkling.

"Thanks for these good brownies," kidded Eben. "Or did Harry make them?"

"Do you think Harry has time to make brownies, Eben? You like them?" she asked.

"We all do," said Gary.

After the men left, Babs said,

"That speaker at Culture Club gave me some ideas that I'd like to try out."

Petting Nip and Tuck who had jumped into her lap, she noticed that Harry seemed preoccupied and asked,

"Is something on your mind?"

"They voted to go ahead with my ordination. Now I need to study. Fellow ministers and laymen will be asking me all kinds of questions."

"They will? But, you are well-informed, Harry. Do you think they will try to stump you?"

"Maybe."

"Honey, tomorrow is your day off. Remember we're going to Wisconsin Rapids."

"Do you need more maternity clothes from 'Great Expectations'?"

"No, I can get along with the two outfits I have. But we're going to get you some new shoes."

"Shoes are expensive."

"Harry, your feet hurt all the time. You need relief from the pain. And I need some relief from your crankiness."

She looked stubborn.

"Okay. Want to go after lunch?"

The next day, Harry found a pair of shoes that fit and the salesman measured his foot for necessary alterations.

"We can pick them up next week," he said turning the car toward home.

"Sorry we'll have to put off paying the garage bill at Al Collins'. Say, with all my concerns, I forgot to ask about the Culture Club meeting, last night."

"I had a good time," she said.

Harry mounted the steps to his study, and Babs began to fix his favorite tapioca pudding. Soon the six dainty, stemmed crystal goblets from her Aunt Alice were filled.

At dinner that evening, she could hardly wait for the main course to be over. Clearing the table, she brought in a tray with two goblets of pudding, and her silver cream soupspoons. Placing a dessert plate in front of Harry, she put the pudding on it and set a cream soupspoon at his right. She laid a similar setting for herself, poured tea for each of them, and sat down. Feeling really elegant, Babs picked up the soupspoon and began to eat the pudding from the goblet.

"The speaker at the Culture Club pointed out that teaspoons are properly used only for tea or coffee, while the larger cream soup spoons are correct for desserts. She reminded us that we put away our cream soup spoons and seldom use them."

Silently, Harry watched her, as she awkwardly scooped up pudding from the dainty goblet with the big cream soupspoon. After a while, he got up, went to the silver chest, selected a large serving spoon and brought it to his place at the table. While Babs was managing to get a tiny taste of pudding with each bite, Harry did her one better, and applied the large serving spoon to the tiny crystal goblet, getting nothing.

Babs watched him for a moment and then burst into laughter.

"Okay, Harry, so much for culture!"

Chapter 24

NEW BEGINNINGS

"You're gonna postpone all the baptisms until the weather warms up, aren't you? It'll take a bundle to heat enough water to baptize that crowd, Rev."

From his easy chair, Harry looked up from his book.

"Each person has made a profession of faith, Mac, and wants to be baptized. Now's the time."

"I'm a practical man, Rev. Costs real money to heat all that water! Take my advice and think about it."

Mac's bald head fairly gleamed with earnest concern.

"Okay, Mac. I'll think about it," said Harry as the slight man left, making his way down the parsonage front steps toward his home.

"Will you put off the baptisms, Harry?" asked Babs, dishtowel in hand.

Harry looked up from his book again.

"No, they are ready to follow Jesus Christ and join the church. It will be a great joy to everyone. In fact, I predict it will be the start of a warmer spirit in the Prairie Meadows Church."

"I understand, Dear, but I doubt that Mac will. By the way, don't you have a wedding this afternoon?"

"Yes, I do, at 2:00 pm."

"It's 1:30. Don't you have to leave soon?"

"No. They're coming here."

"What? Coming here? The house is a mess! Look at that stack of books and papers by your chair! There's our sweaters and stuff on the couch and my piano music and manicure set scattered around!"

"They won't notice."

Babs had grabbed a dust rag and was going over the piano, the tables, the lamps, and the wide window seat. She hastily picked up everything from the davenport and began to put things away. In her excitement, she never considered whether she was cleaning up "the right way."

"Please, Harry, help me get this place in order!" she begged.

Disturbing Nip curled up on the couch next to him, Harry got out the carpet sweeper. Over the noise, he repeated: "They won't notice."

Remembering the months of preparation for their own wedding, Babs thought that a likely story indeed! Swiftly, she hung up sweaters and coats, and put her flannel-graph material in the bedroom closet, vowing that one day, she would have a house with doors on the closets.

"Do you think they will come in by the back door? I made a cake and haven't washed the dishes, yet."

"I think they will come to the front door," he answered, clearing the end table.

"For a wedding, the beginning of their lives together, we should have flowers in the living room. The place looks shabby, but I'm glad, at least, we have pretty new wall paper," said Babs.

She set a colorful vase on the lamp table and set the Christmas cactus Thelma Young had given her on the window seat. Spreading a fresh tablecloth on the dinette table, she arranged oranges, walnuts, and apples, gifts from their parishioners, in a fruit bowl.

"A few grapes would give a nice touch, but it's not the season. There," she said. "Does the room look more festive now, Harry?"

"It sure does, Honey," he replied, as a dusty and decrepit 1938 Ford sedan drew up in front. Two couples got out. The men, in worn jackets, one in slacks, the other in faded jeans, were smoking cigarettes. One woman was wearing an ill-fitting, green sweater. The other, with a large, port-wine birthmark above her right eyebrow, wore a shapeless mustard-colored coat.

"Oh, I hope the groom is hiding a corsage," said Babs, wistfully as the quartet mounted the front steps. Gazing at the wedding party, Babs saw neither joy, nor flowers. Instead she saw a teary-eyed bride. Babs breathed a prayer for the couple as she left the living room.

Soon all were standing in front of Harry. The best man slouched, his eyes darting around the room, a cigarette dangling from his mouth.

"Extinguish your cigarette, please," said the minister in a stern voice.

The bride had shed the mustard coat and stood up in a faded, gray housedress to recite her wedding vows.

As Harry proceeded with the service in the living room, Babs, behind the closed bedroom door, tried to concentrate on her flannelgraph Sunday School lesson for the children of Rosebud. After a while, as she was cutting out the figure of Joseph the Patriarch, Harry opened the bedroom door and stood, watching her work. Walking over, he put his arms around her and kissed her, saying, "I love you. You bring so much joy into my life."

"I love you, Harry."

"Are you preparing for Sunday School?" he asked, holding her away.

"Yes, I am. The children are sweet. They love this unit on heroes of the Old Testament."

As she held up the figure of Joseph, son of Jacob, for Harry's inspection, she felt their baby move.

"And speaking of joys, our little girl is growing so fast. What a great kicker! Do you suppose she or he will be a dancer? Put your hand on my tummy. Do you feel the little feet?"

"I sure do. Is she hurting you?"

"No, but I feel more and more movement from our little darling. And that reminds me, you know, I haven't done a thing to get ready for her or him. Don't you think we should start getting some baby furniture and picking out clothes for the baby?"

"No, not yet. The shoes I'm getting blow the budget as it is. Are you ready to go to Wisconsin Rapids?"

"Just about. I can't find my reading glasses and the two greeting cards I addressed. One card was for Miss Hawk who's just been elected state president of the librarians' association, and the other was to Gladys Wilson, recovering from pneumonia."

She finally found the glasses in the back of a dresser drawer, and Harry located the cards under the newspaper on the dining table. Delighted, she started to slip the cards into the envelopes.

"Oh dear, I reversed the envelopes. It looks funny, but I can put Gladys' small card in the big envelope. What am I going to do with this big card and the little envelope?"

"All you can do is cross them both off, rewrite the addresses, and hope that they will be legible."

"Okay. They won't look very nice, but it's the thought that counts, isn't it?" she said as she got into the car.

As Harry eased the Chevy into third gear, Babs sighed and made a face.

"We couldn't pay a penny when they refilled the coal bin. That bill just keeps going up, and you had to charge more gas at Collins' station."

"I'm concerned, too. I saw an ad, which I'm going to look into. I think it will help out a lot."

"A part-time job? You said you wanted to avoid that 'cause you don't want to be known as a part-time minister. As a full-time pastor, you may get a transfer some day. So how can we survive here and prepare for the future at the same time?"

"It's a tough situation. Let me see about this."

Both were lost in their own thoughts.

"Harry, I hate to admit it, but you're right."

His appreciative, blue eyes focused on her before returning to the road ahead.

"What am I right about?"

"The wedding party. Nobody noticed how the house looked."

Chapter 25

MOVING AHEAD

"Pat, I'm so pleased at your progress on the piano. I can tell that you are practicing regularly. Children sometimes progress slowly, but you're almost through the second book."

Pat flushed at Babs's praise.

"I really do want to learn to play the piano. My mom is my biggest fan. She tells me I'm getting better all the time."

"You're almost ready to tackle hymn-playing. Since this piano course gets you all over the piano, it will be easier for you to learn how put in those little extra notes when you play a hymn."

"My church in Wild Rose wants me to substitute for their regular pianist," confided the young woman as she left.

That evening at dinner, Harry was silent.

"Are your new shoes comfortable?" she asked.

"Yes. I hardly knew I had feet today."

"Good."

Finding candy wrappers and peanut bags around the house, Babs wondered what Harry was worrying about.

"What's on your mind, Dear?" she asked, clearing the table and setting a dish of canned peaches at his place.

"You know we had meeting at Stevens Point concerning my coming ordination. The pastor there, Jim Staley, will preside at the ordination, and Tim Woods will be the clerk."

"Who else will take part?"

"I'll ask my uncles, Marvin and Arnold, and the pastors of this district."

"Will any lay-people attend?"

"Our local sister churches will elect lay delegates."

"Wow! I didn't know so many people would be involved."

"In the afternoon, delegates will be asking me questions to see if I'm a worthy candidate for ordination."

"What kind of questions?"

"Questions about my faith, my standards, my knowledge of the Bible, and theology."

"Will they put you on the spot?"

"Yes. I have an idea of what Jim is going to ask me. He was telling how he had to give an outline of the Bible for his ordination. I'll bet he's going to ask me to do that."

"So you can be prepared."

"Yes. But you never know what kind of questions people will throw at you. I hope I do okay."

"Of course you will."

Harry scratched behind Tuck's ear, and the kitten purred loudly.

"Maybe, but I'm scared."

"Do you think that Marvin and Arnold will try to stump you?"

"I expect them to be supportive."

"Will you invite Dr. Galvin to attend?"

"Good idea. I'd like him to come."

"May I be there, along with your mom and dad, when they question you?" she asked

"Sure, if you want."

"Of course. I wouldn't miss it for anything."

At 11:00 pm Harry was in bed, not sleeping, but feeling restless. Looking over at Babs, sound asleep beside him, he felt envious.

"I wish I could sleep like that," he thought. "I'm going to toss and turn all night."

Harry found himself back in high school at church camp. A pretty, blonde girl was waving to him across the campfire. Everyone was singing Gospel choruses. The girl was smiling at him.

"Smoke follows beauty!" she said, as Harry coughed.

"I've got to move. The smoke is getting worse here."

Suddenly the girl grabbed his arms and shook them. Harry coughed again.

"Wake up, Harry! There's smoke in here."

He coughed.

"There's always smoke when there's a camp fire. Settle down and let me be."

"Harry, I'm scared. Nip and Tuck just jumped up on our bed. Wake up!"

Harry coughed. Reluctantly opening his eyes, he could see that the light was on, Babs had on her bathrobe, and the air was full of smoke. Babs was coughing, too.

He found his robe and started exploring the house. Grabbing his hand, she went with him.

"The smoke doesn't seem to be coming up out of the registers. I better check the furnace. You stay here, and I'll see."

The cats were mewing.

"Put a hankie over your mouth," she said.

Harry found his flashlight and, to his surprise, the door to the basement was open. Holding a hankie over his face, he cautiously made his way down the steep stairs toward the furnace.

"The smoke is thicker," he said, choking in spite of himself. The furnace door was slightly ajar and smoke was pouring out. Harry slammed the furnace door shut and hurried back upstairs, coughing and choking.

"It looks to me like the flue is obstructed. I've turned the heat down low. We'll have to get a man over tomorrow. But we can't stay here the rest of the night."

"Where shall we go?"

"I'm sure Collins would take us in, or Galvins."

"I don't want to disturb Galvins, and I'm not comfortable with Collins," she said, putting clothes and toilet articles in a bag.

The street was dark, the temperature below freezing, and their footsteps resounded on the icy ground, as they walked to the garage, carrying their belongings and two small, black cats.

"At least, we're not coughing and choking out here," she said, laughing and shivering at the same time. "Do you know where we're going?"

"Yes, the very place. You have suggested that we get up and about earlier. This morning, we'll pay the Fred and Thelma Young an early morning call."

"Oh, Harry, we're going to visit some one, and I'm don't have a gift for the host and hostess."

"Well, just this once, I won't tell anyone, Dear."

Chapter 26

MARGIE REPORTS

"We've come to look around."

Jane Collins and Mrs. Blodgett were standing at the back door.

"You want to look around?" asked Babs looking puzzled.

"After all the money we put into the wall paper, we want to see if the smoke ruined it," said Mrs. Blodgett walking around three over-flowing waste baskets, as they moved through the kitchen.

The women surveyed the plates stacked in the dish drainer, yesterday's dish of milk for the kittens on the floor, and on the dinette table, piles of stuff—note paper, pens, stamps, and a red address book.

"Doesn't look too bad in here," said Mrs. Collins. "How do the bedrooms look?"

"They got the least amount of smoke. The kitchen took the most," answered Babs.

"As long as we're here, let's look at the bedrooms," said Mrs. Collins.

Reluctantly the minister's wife led them into the bedroom area. As the women examined the walls, they observed the unmade bed. Babs breathed a prayer of thanks that, at least, the double bed in the guest room looked neat, though the closet was crammed with flannel graph materials, books, Babs' trunk, and Harry's battered suitcases.

"I see you have a couple of extra mouths to feed," remarked Mrs. Blodgett, watching the scampering kittens.

"Oh, you mean Nip and Tuck? They eat mostly scraps, and they are a lot of company for me," answered Babs defensively.

"I think we have a pretty good report on the state of the wallpaper for the Busy Bees," observed Mrs. Collins.

"You'll bring a hot dish to the next meeting, will you, Babs?" she asked. "It will be in the evening meeting, and husbands are invited."

"Yes. I understand a speaker from St. Michael's Hospital in Stevens Point will be speaking."

"That's right. And don't forget to bring your dishes and utensils. Did you ever find those glasses you left at Alberta's at the last meeting?"

"Yes, in another purse."

Refusing Babs' offer of a cup of tea, the women left by the front door.

"That's what I get for not making the bed right away! And they practically stumbled over those waste baskets at the back door!"

Unhappily, she scooped up the wastebaskets and dumped them before getting back to her thank-you notes. She was finishing a last note to the Young's for taking them in on that smoky morning, when she heard a rap at the back door.

"Who do you suppose that is?" she asked the kittens.

It was Margie.

"Here's that recipe for cupcakes from my Mom," she said, as she came in, her eyes taking in the draining dishes, the kitten's dish, the empty wastebaskets, and the pile of writing materials on the dining room table.

"Thanks so much for the recipe, Margie. Your mom sure makes good cake and pies, too."

"Oh, are those your glasses? Did you find them?"

"Yes, I found them."

"Have you seen Chester, the dog, lately?"

"No, I haven't. Has something happened to Chester?"

"Mr. Rennik, the postman, hates Chester. The dog bit him once. He told the Brown's, that if it happened again, he was going to take him to the pound. No one has seen the dog lately."

"What do the Browns say?"

"They're visiting Mrs. Brown's sister in Boscobel. When they get back, and they can't find Chester, watch out!"

Margie began pulling a string across the floor for the kittens to chase.

"Did you see Rev. Galvins' new Cadillac? It isn't new, but it's really fancy. My dad thinks it's funny that they got a black car when they live around here with so many dirt roads."

"It's a nice car. How are your sister and your baby brother?"

"Everyone but my daddy and me has colds. Daddy says he's going to take Mom and us kids and buy us some store-boughten clothes. I want a red dress."

"With your dark eyes and hair, Margie, you will look pretty in red."

"Do you think so? My daddy says if that's what I want, he'll buy it. Well, I'm going to see Mrs. Barker. Did you know, they're getting a new stove?"

"No, they are?"

"My mother wanted me to ask you, 'Why did Rev. Petersen borrow our pick-up?' He came by, Mom said, and told her he had to go to Saxville."

"You know more than I do. I didn't know he was going to Saxville. You have to leave? Tell your Mom thanks for the recipe."

"Bye, bye, Mrs. Petersen," said Margie, as she closed the door and started walking toward the Mac Barker's small house.

Half an hour later, Harry drove up in Tim's pick-up. Babs saw several large cardboard boxes in the back.

"What do you have there?"

"Watch and see."

Peeping noises came from the boxes. Aware that Harry's mom had canaries, she wondered if he planned to sell canaries. She followed him as he opened the wire pen and entered an enclosed area by the garage. On the rough floor, he set up, what looked to her, like a huge chandelier. He plugged it in. Peeping noises from the boxes grew louder. With a triumphant smile, he lifted the cover, revealing dozens of tiny chicks. The fluffy little creatures eagerly gobbled up the feed and water Harry gave them, and soon they were attracted to the warmth of the brooder. Only after they were all comfortable and satisfied, Harry closed the chicken coop, and came in the house.

"What's happening, Harry?"

"Honey, I saw an ad in the paper for free chicks. We have a chicken yard here, and I borrowed a brooder from Clara and Harvey Webber."

"Who's giving away chicks and why?"

"The hatchery in Saxville uses hens for laying. They wanted to get rid of the males."

"They're cute, but what are we going to do with them?"

"I plan to raise some to eat—we'll get a locker and freeze some, and I've made arrangements with a restaurant near Waupaca. The owner will pay me 60 cents a pound if I pluck and clean the fryers. This will help me to pay off our coal bill."

"Won't it be a lot of work, Harry?"

"I can handle it. This way I can bring in money we need, without holding a second job!"

Chapter 27

FOWL LUCK

"Your little chicks are growing so fast, Harry. You give them wonderful attention, even getting up in the middle of the night to check on them," said Babs, putting down her umbrella and settling into their Chevy.

"There's no use raising them if I don't give them what they need. Now the years I spent on the farm in northern Wisconsin are paying off. They're doing well, aren't they?" answered Harry.

"Yes they are. And you sure picked a stormy night to make a pastoral call in the country!" she answered.

As the raindrops pelted their car, the windshield wiper made a rhythmic accompaniment to their conversation.

"Selling off the chickens should make a good dent in our coal bill. It's so cold here in Wisconsin. Getting rid of all that debt'll be a relief, won't it?" he said, looking over at his wife beside him. "Babs, I'm glad you're coming with me to see these elderly people."

"Tell me about them, Harry," she said as lightning flashed nearby.

"Gary asked me to visit his wife's great-uncle Elmer who lives on a farm out of Rosebud. He's not expected to live through the week. Years ago, Elmer and Eunice attended the Rosebud Church, but they dropped out."

"They live in this desolate country? We're out in the middle of nowhere," remarked Babs.

At that moment, a cloudburst descended on the Chevy and the howling of the wind was punctuated by more lightning and violent rolls of thunder. Babs shivered.

Harry kept his eyes on the narrow highway, which after a while, became a one-lane dirt road. With jack pines on either side, and no settlements in sight, the road seemed to wander aimlessly through the dismal countryside.

"Are you sure this is the way to their place, Harry?" yelled Babs over the roar of the gale.

"Gary warned me it was five miles from the corner to their place," he answered.

"Haven't we gone ten miles already?"

The road made a sudden right turn. Tire tracks angled off to the left. On a fence post near the tracks, a homemade wooden sign, tossed in the wind and bearing the name "Brown," hung uncertainly on a rusty wire.

"Gary mentioned that sign," said Harry confidently, as he turned left, following the tire tracks. He squinted at the faint marks and sighed with relief when his headlights picked up a darkened farmhouse.

"Is anyone home?" asked Babs.

"See the vehicles? Some one is home," said Harry.

Parked in the yard were a rusty old Nash and a neglected-looking green Model A Ford pick-up. As they approached the building, they saw a faint light coming from the front room. An old woman with a lined face, her gray hair in an untidy bun, slowly opened the door.

"Are you Dorothy and Gary's pastor?" she asked.

Dressed in a faded house dress and a brown sweater with holes at the elbows, the stooped woman gave a crooked, welcoming smile as Babs and Harry mounted the creaky wooden steps.

"Yes, I'm Reverend Petersen, and this is my wife, Barbara."

"I'm Elmer's sister-in-law. Glad you came, Rev. Go on in the bedroom. Elmer's there, and Eunice is with him. Dearie," she said to Babs, "you and I'll stay in the parlor."

Babs' heart sank as Harry disappeared into a tiny bedroom from which came the moans of the dying man and the desperate prayers of his wife. Before taking a seat in the front room, Babs glimpsed a kerosene lantern in the bedroom, casting weird shadows on the walls and ceiling.

The old woman sat down next to Babs, her skin surprisingly white and transparent in the eerie, gloomy room. Solemnly fixing her large, watery eyes on the younger woman, the woman spoke in a cracked voice.

"My name is Mary. Years ago, I received the gift of the Holy Spirit. Oh, I have seen God working in many, many wonderful ways. God used me for His glory. Praise the Lord! And you, so young and pretty, have you received the gift of the Spirit?"

Babs felt as though she had stepped into an unreal world: the remote area, the darkness, a life-threatening illness, fearful cries from Elmer and Eunice, the wind whistling around the building, the smell of onions and stale grease coming from the kitchen, and the wrinkled woman beside her, talking strangely. She wished she were back home, or, at least, that she could see Harry.

"Yes, once I was beautiful, and God gave me many talents," continued the woman, her voice high and shaking with emotion. "Dear Jesus used me to help people, and I became a healer. *You* are young. What do you expect to do for God? Are you filled with God's Holy Spirit?"

Goaded, Babs responded, "I believe that when I became a Christian, I received the Holy Spirit."

Looking about, she observed that the room was sparsely furnished with straight wooden chairs, and lighted by a kerosene lamp set on a stark pine table.

"Oh, yes, Dearie," replied the woman condescendingly, "but I'm taking about sinless perfection. Have you received the Second Blessing, the gift of perfection?"

Mary leaned forward and looked at her closely, waiting for Babs' reply.

Babs could hear Harry's comforting voice reading the Twenty-Third Psalm, the moans of the patient and the anguished prayers of his wife quieted. The Psalm concluded, Harry turned to the fourteenth chapter of the Gospel of John:

"In my Father's house, are many mansions."

"Well, have you, Dearie?" demanded the woman.

"Oh, no, I haven't attained perfection, far from it."

"Ah," cackled the other, triumphantly, "you must continue to seek this gift. You need the Second Blessing."

While the lamp in the living room continued its doubtful glow, silence had fallen in the bedroom. The crone spoke again.

"Whenever anyone in Rosebud, even as far away as Stevens Point, got sick, I was called. They called me all the time. Many times, after I prayed, the sick person was healed."

Babs half listened, trying to follow what was happening in the bedroom. For a long time, Harry sat by the bed, apparently holding the invalid's hand, his presence comforting both Elmer and Eunice. After a while, he prayed with them, asking God for forgiveness and strength. As he started to recite the Lord's Prayer, Babs heard the man and his wife praying, also. The room fell silent.

"I am leaving now," said the young pastor, "but I'll be back tomorrow. Be sure that Elmer gets his medicine, Eunice, and I wish you both a restful night."

"Thank you, thank you, Rev. Petersen," answered Eunice. "God bless you for coming."

Emerging from the bedroom, Harry said good-bye to Mary, and he and Babs walked to the car.

As he drove home, Harry seemed deep in thought, while Babs reflected on the strange evening.

"Harry, you were so brave and helpful to Elmer and Eunice. You seemed to know exactly what to do."

His eyes were on the road.

"You've been so silent all the way home. Are you deciding what you're going to say to them tomorrow when you come back?"

When he didn't answer, she touched his arm.

"What you are thinking about, Dear?"

"I want to talk to Harvey and Clara Wells. They used to raise prize poultry. I wonder if the feed I'm giving the chicks is the best."

Chapter 28

CHESTER BUGS THE MAILMAN

"You'll never make it, Rev.," said Mac. "You'll never make it."

Mac was watching through the fence as Harry fed his chicks. The little fluffy, white leghorns were eagerly devouring the mash Harry put in the trough for them.

"Is that right, Mac?"

"You figure the amount you spent on that brooder, buying the chicks, the cost of the electricity, and paying for the mash—you'll never make it, Rev. You'll never make it."

"I'm giving it a try, Mac."

"You guys from the city don't realize how much it costs to raise livestock."

"We don't?"

"I've seen Chicago people come up here and buy a house. First thing they do is fix it up with a fancy bathroom and a new kitchen. Costs a fortune. After they've done that, there's no capital left to run the farm. They've spent it all. We see them selling out at a loss and going back to the city."

"You watched this happen often, Mac?"

"Yes, I have. Rev, you're going to end up with lots of chicken for Sunday dinners, but you won't come out. You'll never make it. You'll never make it."

Mac walked away, shaking his head over the follies of his greenhorn pastor.

As mailman Bob Rennik approached the parsonage from the opposite side of the street, he could hear Mac muttering to himself as he ambled home. Bob watched as the Rev. closed the gate to the chicken pen and went inside the house. Waiting by the mailbox he spied the pastor's missus.

"I have a whole stack of letters for you and the Rev. I don't see how you have time to answer so many letters," he said, handing a large bundle of mail to Babs.

"Do you have an extra heavy load today, Mr. Rennik?"

"Please call me, Bob. Everybody calls me Bob."

"Okay, Bob."

"Lots of these letters are from Illinois, I reckon."

"My husband is writing to his family and friends, so they'll will be here for his ordination."

"Ordination? What's that?"

"He will be officially a reverend."

"Doesn't he marry people and bury 'em and all that, now?"

"Yes, he does. But he will be recognized by this church and other churches."

"Recognized? We all recognize the Rev. Beats me."

"Are you early today, Bob?"

"I am. That damn—'cuse me, Mrs. Petersen—that darned dog, Chester, wasn't around to slow me up."

"Oh. What do you suppose happened to Chester?"

"Don't know. Don't care. Hope somebody got rid of him. The neighborhood's better off without that pest."

Bob moved down the street as Babs entered the house.

"You've heard from several people, Harry," she announced giving him the mail, keeping a blue-striped letter from California.

"Oh, good. Thanks, Dear," said Harry tearing open his first communication.

"Well, it looks like both Uncle Arnold and Marvin will be able to come."

"Your minister uncles, right? Didn't I see a note from your Mom?'

"Yes, she and Dad will be here. She said she'd be glad to sing a duet with Gary."

"Where will all the families stay?"

"Mom and Dad will stay here, and Lola Rankin and Thelma Young are arranging for the rest of the people to stay in homes in the area."

"That's great."

"The Busy Bees will serve three meals at the church: lunch and dinner on the day of ordination, and a potluck on Sunday after church. Tim Woods is the clerk, and he's written to all the churches in the association. He's invited the ministers and lay representatives."

"Sounds like a big crowd, doesn't it?"

"I think so. It isn't every day that a minister is ordained in Prairie Meadows."

"Oh, by the way, is that a candy wrapper I see by your chair?"

"Oh, I guess so."

"Honey, I'm concerned. You're putting on weight. You'd feel better and your feet wouldn't hurt so much if you would avoid eating between meals."

"Oh, I hardly ever have a candy bar. I just got hungry yesterday," he responded, looking away and studying a note from Dr. Miller, his Executive Secretary.

Babs had been finding empty chocolate milk cartons and peanut and candy wrappers around the house and car. That nibbling was a sure sign that he was feeling pressured.

"I'd better not say anything more," she thought to herself. "I'll try to fix nutritious meals and keep my mouth shut."

As she opened the letter from her mother, she mused silently,

"We are quite the pair! When I'm under pressure, I lose things. When Harry's tense, he eats. We have to encourage each other."

She went over and kissed him on both cheeks.

"Harry," she said, "I can practically see those little chicks grow. They sure gobble up the mash. I saw Mac out there talking to you. Is he as proud of what his pastor is doing as I am?"

Chapter 29

INTRODUCING THE REVEREND PETERSEN

The pews got harder by the minute, as he watched the ministers and laymen grilling the young man. They had questioned him at length about his conversion experience, his schooling, and his knowledge of the Bible. Jim Staley, pastor of the Stevens Point Church, like a smart alec, had asked the candidate to give a brief outline of the Bible. The would-be reverend had done surprisingly well on that—"Better than I could do," the man in the pew reflected. He had found Old Testament history rather uninspiring. Names like Hezekiah, Nehemiah, and Ezekiel, evoked vague responses in his mind.

He glanced at the candidate's parents. They seemed earnest, genuine people. The on-looker had heard that the father had attended Moody Bible Institute in Chicago, and for a while, served as a lay minister. He was an open-faced, tall, stout man. His weathered face and care-worn hands showed he belonged to the working class. Turning his attention to the mother, the man observed that she wore her long hair in a bun and had on a homemade, cotton dress. Like her son, she had high coloring and a ready smile. During the questioning, she appeared composed.

"She knows that he is going to win out in this time of testing," reflected the doctor. "She appears to have a great faith."

Deacon Jed Morris of Wild Rose, a short, intense young man, had been questioning the young man's theology. Now he was bearing down persistently on the subject of the Second Coming of Christ.

"When will Christ return? Will it be before the Great Tribulation or after?"

It was clear that the layman wanted the young minister to say, "before the Great Tribulation." But you had to admire the fledgling's courage. Stubbornly, he refused to be pinned down.

Breaking a silence, he replied,

"Jed, I don't really know what I believe regarding the Second Coming of Christ. I will have to give it more consideration, before I can give you a definite answer."

"He's taken a lot of punishment," pondered the on-looker. Glancing over at the young wife, also a seminary graduate, he saw that she looked tired and anxious.

"It's no wonder if she feels under a strain. She has a houseful of company, she is in the last trimester of her pregnancy, and she has endured this trial along with him."

"I guess we'll have to give you a little slack on the Second Coming, Brother Petersen," continued the layman from Wild Rose. "However, I have one more question for you. How do you like our Executive Secretary? Is he fair? Do you consider him a good boss?"

"Come on, Jed," remonstrated his red-headed pastor, Will Erickson. "What kind of a question is that?"

Suddenly, the layman's question had thrust the sometime-spectator in the pew into the role of full participant, and he saw that Harry's blue eyes, along with those of the whole company, were fixed upon him.

Harry replied, "Thanks, for that support, Will, but I'll answer the question. Since I'm employed by the churches of Prairie Meadows, Sterling, and Rosebud, I don't consider Dr. Miller, our

Executive Secretary, my boss. However, he has always been fair with me as well as kind and helpful."

Dr. Miller nodded and smiled at the aspirant, acknowledging the young man's trust, and thinking to himself: "I've been aware that Petersen is a little rough around the edges, but he has a lot going for him. He bears up well under pressure."

The Reverend Staley of Stevens Point was calling for a decision from the council.

"Mr. Chairman, I move that we proceed with the ordination," said Tim Woods, clerk of the proceedings.

"I have the honor of seconding the motion," said Rev. Marvin Petersen with a rare, proud smile.

Dr. Miller saw a relieved young Mrs. Petersen get up and leave as the business concluded. Harry's mother and Gary Lewis of Prairie Meadows, followed.

"They're practicing to sing a duet tonight," said Marvin to his brother, Arnold.

Some hours later, the ordination service completed, the Executive Secretary found himself in the parsonage, seated on a scuffed kitchen chair, holding a small tray with a piece of chocolate cake and a cup of weak coffee. There was a lot of laughing and talking. While Uncle Arnold and Harry reminisced about seminary days, Uncle Marvin warned people not to brush against the shelf in the dining room, and Babs showed off a spanking new baby crib from Harry's parents.

It had been a long day, interesting, but a long day. Dr. Miller had a busy schedule, and he was ready to hit the road and get back to his wife and home in Milwaukee. As he was congratulating Harry and expressing his thanks for their hospitality, Babs said,

"Harry and I have something to give you. . . "

"That's not necessary—"

"Jim Barry, the editor of our local paper, *The Banner*, printed the worship service for Harry's ordination. He got interested in the project and made up a few programs with the title at the front printed in gold lettering."

"We would like you one to have one of these programs," said Harry. "Thank you for coming, Dr. Miller."

As he drove away, the happy couple waved to him from the front porch.

"The beginnings of his ministry are humble indeed," thought the doctor, "but, with his courage and honesty, the sky's the limit."

Chapter 30

BABS COOKS UP A STORM

Babs beamed.

"I'm so excited and thrilled that your mom is coming to the banquet with me! I can hardly wait for your parents to get here. I'm glad they're coming up on Thursday and can stay all weekend. When do you think they'll arrive, Harry?"

"Oh, I think they'll make it by around three or four o'clock."

"Thanks for helping me get ready. I'm planning to make some of their favorite dishes. I want them to see how well I can cook. Harry, let me show you again how to make the bed with square corners."

She came around to his side of the double bed and demonstrated how she laid the corner of the sheet on top of the bed and carefully tucked in the side, smoothing it over, resulting in a perfectly made bed.

"I still don't get it," said Harry watching her.

Babs shrugged.

"Aren't you glad the people of Sterling gave us this colorful quilt for the guest bed? Too bad we don't have a dresser to go with it."

Putting a small arrangement of flowers on the window sill, she straightened the suitcases in the closet as best she could, and stood with her hands on her hips, surveying the room with its borrowed bed, the paper drapes, and the blond crib standing in the corner.

Her reverie was interrupted by the sight and sound of a wooden spool rolling on the bare floor, followed by an animated ball of black fur.

"Nip!" she said, stooping to pet the kitten. "What a character. Harry, I hope your parents will be comfortable."

"Of course they will, Honey."

"I'm so glad I'm over morning sickness. I must get busy. Will you run the carpet sweeper for me?"

After dusting the living room, she tackled the bathtub, her task lightened by remembering how Harry took a bath in the short tub. To wash his legs, Harry had to raise his feet high in the air. She laughed at the thought.

Entering their bedroom, she kicked the kittens' wooden spools under the bed and struggled to push in the reluctant drawers of the cast-off dresser, before leaving the room. After checking the front clothes closet, she walked through the living room where Harry was running the carpet sweeper, picking up a stray newspaper as she went. In the kitchen, she began to fix a gelatin salad for dinner.

All afternoon she kept watching for Louise and Mel's dark blue, 1940 Dodge, finally settling down on the davenport with the darning egg, to mend Harry's socks. Two sleepy kittens lay beside her. She must have fallen asleep, for suddenly she heard Mel and Louise's voices in the kitchen.

Rushing into the kitchen, she greeted her tall in-laws. Mel gave her a big hug, and Louise, a jar of home-made preserves.

"Oh, Dad, I'm so thrilled you two can be here! Thank you for the jam, Mother."

"We aren't wearing out our welcome then, coming here again so soon?" Mel asked, his blue eyes twinkling.

"No. We wish you lived closer," she said, giving Louise a hug.

Harry took their suitcases and put them in the bedroom, smiling as he did so, for his dad was putting on the coffee pot.

"My brother Lefty and Maxine been married for years, but Dad never felt free to put on the coffee at their house," he said to himself.

After dinner, they made plans for the next day. Louise and Babs decided to purchase material for Harry's shabby easy chair and ottoman, which Louise had volunteered to re-cover.

"While the women are working on the chair tomorrow, why don't we get busy and mend the fence around your chicken yard, son?" proposed Mel.

Friday morning, after finding flowered fabric in Stevens Point, Louise settled in the living room, to start her project, while Babs went to work on a roast beef dinner. Grateful for all that his parents were doing, and feeling especially brave, she decided to make a pie.

"I can use some of that lard Clara Wells gave me and fix Harry's favorite, pumpkin pie," she decided. "Everyone says that lard makes a wonderful pie crust."

The "boys," meanwhile, got a good start on the fence-mending. It was fun that afternoon to look out the kitchen window and see father and son together, working on the fence or running errands.

They assembled for a slightly late dinner.

Harry said grace, and Louise and Mel began to eat the individual, tossed salads Babs had put at each place. She passed small crackers to go with the first course. Unlike Uncle Marvin, Harry's parents made no comments about the serving arrangements, which they were becoming accustomed to.

"What do you think of Harry's raising chickens?" asked Babs.

"It's a good plan. Harry learned a lot in those years on the farm in northern Wisconsin," said Louise.

"It will take a lot of work. I hope he comes out well on the project," said Mel.

Following the first course, she brought in the dinner plates, putting them at Harry's place. Her sense of triumph, as she placed the platter with the roast and its accompanying vegetables in front of Harry, was somehow dashed at the polite silence of the "boys." As Harry started to serve, she brought in the gravy, setting it down on the table to pass.

"Babs," said Louise, "Your roast looks so good!"

Mel and Harry politely agreed. Babs relished her own serving, but couldn't help noticing Mel's and Harry's restraint. Most of the gravy was left untouched.

Following the main course, she cleared the table and set pie plates at her place. After pouring coffee for all, she brought in the pumpkin pie. It was the best she'd made yet, with a crust done to a "T", and the pumpkin filling, fragrant and inviting.

Still, as she began to cut the pieces, she sensed Harry's reserve. When both he and Mel asked for small helpings, she was demoralized. After she had served Louise and the men, she excused herself, went quickly to their room, closed the door, and lay on the bed, sobbing, dampening several of Harry's freshly-ironed, white hankies with her tears.

In a little while, Harry came into the room. He was puzzled and dismayed when he saw her lying on the bed, her face red and puffy.

"Darling, what's the matter? I love you."

"Oh. You do?"

The tears welled up in her eyes, and she turned away from him.

"Why are you crying? Did I do something wrong?"

"Harry, I tried so hard to fix a really special meal! You hardly touched it. I thought you'd, at least, like the pie."

"I loved the pie! The whole dinner was great!"

"Why did you just pick at it, then? Your Dad ate like a bird, too."

Harry turned away silently, studying his left shoe.

"Your mom enjoyed the food," she continued, "but you and Dad were bored with the whole meal! Here I knocked myself out trying to please you and your parents!"

"Of course, she liked it. Dad and I did, too."

"Well, if you liked it so much, why is there so much left?"

Harry looked at her, finally comprehending the measure of her frustration.

"Babs, I didn't want to tell you—"

"Tell me what?"

"About 5:00 o'clock, Dad and I ran out of nails and had to make another trip to the lumberyard. On the way back, we passed the malt shop."

Harry was hesitating. Within her, comprehension was beginning to replace despair.

"You didn't—"

"It's no reflection on your outstanding meal! We stopped in for coffee at Wilkerson's Drug and Malt Shop."

"At Wilkerson's?"

"Yes," confessed Harry. "We were hot and tired. Dad was getting hungry, and so was I. Honey, I'm sorry. We didn't think. To go with the coffee, Dad and I each ordered a double malted!"

133

Chapter 31

HOT AND HUMID

"It's hard to get up so early after all the excitement of your parents' visit."

"Did you enjoy having them here, Babs?"

"I sure did, except for Friday night dinner."

"We got a lot done with Mother covering the chair, and Dad and I mending the fence."

"Mother seemed to enjoy the Mother/Daughter Banquet on Saturday night."

"I know she did."

"Do you have time for another cup of coffee?" she asked, coffee pot poised in mid-air.

"Yes, good coffee, Hon."

"You'll miss your ottoman since Mother took it home to cover. Were you surprised when Clara and Harvey called you this morning to help them out on the farm?"

"Clara has mentioned her concern over Harvey's health more than once. I knew he was having a rough time."

"Do you think they'll stay in farming, or will they have to find some other work?"

"I think this is sort of a trial balloon. If I help with the cultivating, they will notice whether Harvey can manage the day-to-day operation. They want me to help with the harvesting."

"I hate to see you working so hard in this heat."

"I did it many times when I was younger."

"You said that about the time you were entering high school, your dad sold the house in Waukegan and bought land in northern Wisconsin"

"Yes, he did. Six months later, he was called back to the wire mill, and Mother and Lefty and I were left to run the farm."

"It amazes me that your dad and your mother were willing to let you drop out of school."

"I guess Dad had a romantic idea that he would leave the mill, buy a farm, and return to the soil."

"Your mom is a saint. Think of her! She let him sell the house she had inherited, in order to buy a bit of land, far from home. Then, when Dad got called back to the mill, he left her there, and her fourteen-year-old son had to drop out of school to operate the farm."

"Mother feels that it was the best thing that could have happened for their marriage."

"How's that?"

"Dad was lonely back in town. He stayed with Grandma Petersen, who'd never really liked my mother. While he was there, Grandma expected him to enjoy life, but instead, Dad moped around, missing his family and realizing how much he loved my mother."

"That's fascinating! Your mom put up with a lot."

Harry took another sip of coffee.

"Today will be a scorcher. I need to get an early start. Oh, look at those cats!"

In the early morning, Nip and Tuck were having a last morning caper before settling down to their morning nap.

"In this heat, you have your work cut out for you, Harry. Meanwhile, I'm feeling sorry for myself because I have to attend a special meeting of the Busy Bees."

"Will it be at the church?"

"No, for a change, it will be at Alberta's. The committee is going to plan Vacation Bible School which is coming up soon."

"You know that I will be coming home late."

"Yes. Vacation Bible School is a good cause, but I'm getting so big, I hate to stir out of the house—especially in this heat."

"Try to take it easy today, Honey. I'm not really looking forward to working in the fields," he said as he took a last gulp of coffee, "but they need the help, and we need the money."

Getting up, he gave her a hasty kiss, and left. She finished her second cup of coffee and tidied up the kitchen. Since it was early, she decided to settle down at the dining table to work on accounts. As she was considering whether they could possibly make a washing machine payment, the kitchen door opened, and in walked Mac and Henry.

Glad she was wearing her bathrobe, she greeted the old men. Henry answered with a smile, Mac grunted, and they walked through the living room, leaving by the front door.

"I'm ashamed of myself," she said as she locked the doors. "While Harry will be sweltering behind horses in the fields, all I have to do, is go to a meeting at a comfortable home. How can I complain!"

Deciding to pay ten dollars on the washing machine this month, she returned to the bedroom. With only two maternity dresses and the navy suit too warm for summer, she quickly slipped into the print, ready to go.

Usually meetings were held in the afternoon, but Alberta preferred to hold it in the cooler morning. Walking on the shady side of the streets, Babs arrived a trifle late. Since it was a small committee, all within walking distance, she was surprised to see several cars. She heard a buzz of conversation as she came up the steps. As Alberta opened the door, Babs was astonished to see about forty women seated in a circle around Alberta's living-dining room.

"Hi," she said to the women. "Are you all helping to plan Vacation Bible School?"

"Surprise!" they responded.

Each woman was in her Sunday best. She noticed lots of smiles and giggles and the smell of perfume. Alberta led her to a rocker in the circle. In her happy confusion, Babs saw Mrs. Galvin, the "milk lady"—Jane Carlson, Pamela's mother, Margaret, with her new baby, and some women from the Culture Club. Beside her was a parasol filled with beautifully wrapped gifts. Behind the parasol was a shining new high chair loaded with more colorful presents, large and small.

As she sat down among her friends and neighbors, Babs smiled and tears started down her cheeks. Alberta heard her say,

"My cup runneth over."

Chapter 32

FEVERISH

"Thank you, Mrs. Galvin, for bringing me and all the lovely gifts home. I'm glad you were at the shower, and it was fun riding in your beautiful, black Cadillac. Do you have time after I unload the car, to stop for a cup of tea?"

"I'd love a cup of tea. You couldn't walk home, carrying all the presents. Let me help you carry these things into the house."

The back seat of the car was filled with baby things: hand-embroidered nighties, rompers, knitted and crocheted blankets, booties, sweaters and caps, shirts, diapers, a baby book, and a plastic baby bowl and cup. It took Babs' breath away to see the sheer abundance of presents for little Judy.

As she unlocked the door, Nip and Tuck scampered outside.

"Let's lay these gifts on top of the double bed in the guest room."

"Now, will you call the room 'the nursery'?" asked Isabel.

"Oh, yes. It's the nursery! I can hardly wait to show all these lovely things to Harry."

In the kitchen, she bustled about making tea, while Mrs. Galvin seated herself in Harry's easy chair. In a few minutes, Babs carried in a tray with the teapot, cream and sugar, and two English bone china teacups. Pouring tea for Isabel and herself, Babs settled into the davenport.

"What a beautiful chair, Barbara, with the flowered slip cover. It's new, isn't it?

"Harry's Mom, Louise, re-covered it for us. Didn't she do a good job?"

"She surely did. And how are you and Harry these days? We haven't seen you since his ordination."

"We're fine. I'm getting heavy, but I guess that's to be expected."

"The last two months of pregnancy aren't fun."

"We are battling the budget. It's a struggle. Today, Harry is in Sterling, doing some farm work to help a family and working to reduce our fuel bill."

"Farm work is pretty strenuous in this heat, isn't it?"

"I think so, but Harry says, since he used to work in the fields when he was younger, he'll be all right."

"I hope so. By the way, I saw chickens in the pen outside. Are they for eggs, or are you raising poultry?"

"For poultry. It's Harry's project. You should see how devoted he is. At first, he'd get up in the middle of the night to check on them. He feeds them the finest grain, keeps the water coming, and really fusses over them."

Babs smiled indulgently at Harry's labor of love.

"What is Dr. Galvin doing these days?" asked Babs.

"He is concerned with lots of issues. He is very excited about the establishment of the nation of India. He is involved with the peace movement. On the local level, he is disturbed over the amount of drinking that goes on among Methodists in town. Sometimes, he uses the opening session of Sunday School to talk to the children about avoiding alcohol."

Babs was silent, picturing a Methodist family now attending their church. The father owned a tavern, and when his children came home from Methodist Sunday School, telling him that it was wicked to sell booze, he took them away from the Methodist influence, promptly enrolling them in the Prairie Meadows Community Sunday School.

"Thank you for the tea, Dear," remarked Isabel as she finished her cup. "Try not to overdo."

Babs went to the door with Mrs. Galvin, and waved good-bye, giving the kittens an opportunity to parade back into the house.

"You little guys are getting so big. Soon you'll be grown-up cats."

Taking them both in her arms, she poured another cup of tea for herself and sat in the easy chair with the kittens in her lap.

"What a lucky person I am, to have so many well-wishers and receive so many lovely things," she murmured.

She must have dozed off, for suddenly, Harry was home. He was red as beet, and walking very slowly. Following him into the bedroom, she helped him strip down to his underwear.

"You must be running a temperature," she cried.

Harry sank down into bed. Afraid that he'd catch cold, she tried to cover him up, but Harry threw off the blanket in a convulsive gesture.

"Oh, Harry," she said, "what happened to you?"

"It was hot in the field behind the horses," he said thickly. "I got so thirsty. . . . It took me forever. . . Finally I. . . finished. . . "

"I'd better call the doctor."

Harry became agitated.

"No, no, no, doctor costs too much!"

Babs gave him two aspirins and moistened a washcloth and put it on his burning forehead.

"Thanksh" murmured Harry, as he drifted off to sleep.

Throughout the evening, Harry lay there, perspiring and groaning. She kept applying the moist washcloth to his forehead and gently washed his tummy and neck. When he was alert, she supported him while he drank cold water. At midnight, when his fever seemed to have waned, she went into the nursery, moved all the "blessings" to the other side of the guest bed, and crawled in.

"What a day of ups and downs!" she said to herself before falling asleep. "I'd trade everything for Harry's good health."

Chapter 33

PLENTY AND WANT

He heard voices in the parsonage. The radio, perhaps? Harry opened a tentative eye. No, the radio beside his bed was silent. It was too much effort to find out who was talking. Yesterday was Sunday, and he had been absent from the pulpit. He wondered if his people had missed him. He drifted off. . . Awake again, he listened and sat up, fumbling for his slippers.

In the kitchen, Babs was fixing coffee, when Henry Perkins had appeared bright and early.

"How is the Rev. this morning?" he asked. "Sunday wasn't Sunday for us, without the Rev to welcome us to church and shake our hands."

"He slept better last night, Henry," Babs replied.

"Good," smiled the old man, as he passed through the living room and let himself out.

Babs went to the bedroom.

"Harry, would you like tea or coffee this morning?"

It was a big decision so early in the day. He hesitated, considering his choices.

"Coffee."

"Did you hear Nip last night?" she asked.

"No, what happened?"

"He caught a mouse. He wanted to show off, so he jumped up on the piano to wake me up," laughed Babs.

"Well, Nip is acting like a big cat now! Did you give him the attention he deserved?"

"I sure did. Last night he purred louder than Tuck."

"I think I'll get up today. I'm feeling better," said Harry.

"Good," answered Babs, returning to the kitchen, thankful that no weddings or funerals were scheduled for the next two days.

Hearing a knock on the door, and opening it, she saw Margie, wearing a new outfit and carrying two paper bags.

"Margie, you look so pretty in red!"

"My dad took us shopping yesterday, and Mom and us girls each picked out a boughten dress. My sister chose a green one, and Mom's is a blue print."

"That's exciting, Margie!"

"And today, Dad started to paint the house. It's gonna look really nice."

"Your dad is keeping busy, isn't he?"

"He sings a lot these days. I like to hear my daddy sing," she announced. "My mother wants Rev to have some of her apricot preserves."

"Thank you," replied Babs, receiving one of the bags from the child. "Oh, it looks so good! Harry will enjoy it a lot. Do I get a taste?"

"Of course. It's 8:30, and you're still in your bathrobe?"

Margie looked around the kitchen, her eyes falling on the window panes above the sink.

"Your kitchen windows are dirty, huh? Ours are, too, and Mrs. Pierce's windows are almost as dirty as yours."

As Babs put the preserves in the icebox, Margie continued,

"Boy, all the neighbors, except the Jarvises and the postman, Mr. Rennik, are worried about Chester."

"They are? Why?"

"Browns have been gone to Boscobel for a month. They've been visiting their new grandson. I'm supposed to feed the dog while they've been gone, but I haven't seen him."

"He isn't around?"

"No. Mr. Jarvis clams up when we ask about Chester. And Mr. Rennik says he doesn't know a thing about the dog. I think one of them knows where he is, but they won't say."

"That's a puzzle."

"So when Browns get home from Boscobel, and they can't find Chester, I don't know what's going to happen. Mr. Brown is mean, and my dad says that his neighbor, Mr. Jarvis, has a short fuse, too. I hope Mr. Brown isn't mad at me 'cause I didn't feed their dog. Well, I'm going over to Mrs. Blodgett's. My dad says for Mr. Petersen to get well soon. Bye."

As the young reporter left, Babs knew Mrs. Blodgett's windows would be inspected and a report made on those in the parsonage.

More important for the good of the neighborhood was the whereabouts of the black lab, Chester. Soon Babs saw Bob Rennik.

"I don't know a thing about that stupid dog, Chester," he said in answer to Babs' question. "But here's a bundle of mail. Lots of cards for the Rev. Hope he is feeling better," he said, walking purposefully down the street toward Mac's.

While Harry took note of an upcoming Red Cross meeting in Waupaca on Thursday and enjoyed his get-well cards, Babs opened a letter from home.

"Look, Honey," she said. "My dad and my brother, Al, both wrote a little note. Al enclosed a picture of his 1936 Chevy."

"Nice-looking car," commented Harry. "Nothing from your Mom?"

"Dad says the pears on our tree are ripe, and Mom is canning like mad."

"And I see some bills, huh?"

"Yes. I won't be able to pay off the entire gasoline bill from Standard Oil. It's twenty-five dollars. Our fuel bill, even with the money from your funerals and my music lessons, is three hundred and fifty dollars. Ray Gold sent us his usual monthly statement."

"I talked to Ray about it last week. He says not to worry."

"But we've got to get this paid during the summer. We will have to fill up the coal bin for next winter."

"Yes. You're right. I'll have to find some more work. What's that other note?"

"It's from Sterling. Claudia Morgan is having a shower for me at her home, and the men that night are getting together at John Waukowski's. Little Judy is getting so many lovely things! Oh, Hon, speaking of Sterling, I'm due at Mrs. Jones' for the meeting of their Women's Missionary Society. Will you manage lunch all right?"

"Fine. Run along," he said, settling comfortably into his big chair.

A sound from the kitchen made him look up. Mac, having noted dirty dishes in the sink and cups and saucers on the dinette table, strolled deliberately into the living room.

"You're up now, Rev.? The missus sent over some of her homemade relish. You'll like it. I left it on the kitchen counter."

"Thank you, Mac. Tell Mrs. Barker, thank you, for me."

Mac sat down on the edge of the sagging davenport.

"You know that retired Rev from Sterling who spoke for you, Sunday—"

"Reverend Jenson?"

"Yes. That Rev looks like his feet hurt. He and his wife—they sure scowl a lot."

"They do?"

"Sure do. He preached about the farmer who was going to Hell."

Mac got up and started walking to the door.

"He did?"

"Didn't have one smile for us, his wife neither."

"No smiles?"

"It was a different service, 'cause we expect the preacher to act cheerful."

Mac looked back at his pastor.

"You make us feel like Some One up there loves us."

Chapter 34

WHERE IS CHESTER?

"Boy, today is a hot one! Oh, Bob Rennik just put our mail in the box. He's early again," remarked Harry as he sat comfortably in the dinette, enjoying a second cup of coffee and stroking Nip and Tuck, who were contentedly purring in his lap.

"That means that Chester's still missing. Thelma Young, who knows the Browns really well, is worried. Lyle Brown is so attached to that lab! No one knows what he will do, if he returns home, and the dog is missing. According to Margie, their neighbor, Mr. Jarvis is mean."

"How does Will Jarvis figure in this?"

"Margie told me that Mrs. Jarvis gets her prized tulip bulbs from Holland."

"She does?" asks Harry, not comprehending.

"Chester likes to dig in Mrs. Jarvis' flower beds."

"The dog digs up her tulips?" asked Harry sympathetically.

"Yes. Will has threatened more than once to shoot Chester if the Browns don't keep him on a leash."

"No wonder Thelma is worried."

In the morning heat Babs had worked up a sweat, washing the breakfast dishes and sweeping the kitchen floor. Going to the mailbox, she picked up the mail and brought it in.

"Here's a note from Uncle Marvin, and one from my mother."

"What does she say?" asked Harry.

"She is pretty cheerful. She's worried because I've put on so little weight. And Dad has his vacation arranged for the middle of August. She will arrive by train on July twenty-first. Later Dad will be bringing a present for me and the baby."

"I can't use it?"

"Of course you can. You know Mother. What does Uncle Marvin have to say?" asked Babs, tactfully changing the subject.

"Aunt Luella is down in bed again. She's sick a lot. Uncle Marvin had a good time at my ordination, and he thanks you for the mug you got him on his first visit. "

"That's a surprise, to get a thank-you from Marvin. Harry, you're looking better. I've got to run. I'm due at Rosebud at 11:00. They asked me to prepare a flannelgraph lesson for their Daily Vacation Bible School. There's an egg salad sandwich for you in the cooler. Isn't it great that Prairie Meadows has ice delivery service in the summer time? Oh, Alberta tells me that Miss Hawk thinks our ice man is very handsome."

"Miss Hawk is smitten?"

"He's very muscular and goes around bare-chested on these hot days."

"Where do you hear all the gossip?"

"From Margie, Isabel Galvin, and Alberta."

"Getting back to the ice," said Harry, "I'm thankful we have an ice box in the kitchen so you aren't running up and down the stairs to the basement."

"Me, too. After Bible School, there's a picnic lunch, so I'll be gone a while, Dear."

She disappeared, returning in her familiar navy blue print dress, carrying her flannel board, the figures, and a wooden tripod.

"Oh, Harry I can't find my keys! Where do you suppose they are?" wailed Babs.

Harry began a methodical search, finally locating them under her stationery box on the davenport.

"Thanks, Harry. What would I do without you? Are you planning to work on your sermon today?"

"Right! In this heat, I'll work downstairs."

Harry settled into his chair to read. Nip pawed at his belt, while Tuck purred sleepily on his armrest. With this picture of domesticity in her mind, and, afraid she would be late, Babs hurried out to the car.

It was about three o'clock that afternoon when she returned, her arms full of packages, meeting Mac as he let himself out the kitchen door.

"Been shopping?" he asked, staring at all the bundles.

"Not shopping," she replied joyfully. "The Rosebud Ladies Aid gave me a shower!"

"Baby showers are a habit with you, aren't they?"

"Yes. And there's more in the car!"

"I'll help you, " said Mac.

Babs was surprised at the offer, as Mac went to the garage and emerged with several packages. They made short work of unloading the presents. As always, she was surprised at how quietly Mac walked across the room. Though he seemed inclined to linger, he refused her offer of a cup of tea, and headed out the back door toward his home.

Babs was smiling as she surveyed her blessings piled on top of the dinette table, when she heard the rattle of a wooden spool, rolling around on the kitchen linoleum, propelled by Nip. Peeking around the corner into the living room, she saw another black cat curled up in the lap of a tall man with a rounded figure, ruddy complexion, and wavy brown hair, slumbering in a colorful big easy chair.

Opening his eyes, Harry asked, "How did it go? Did the children enjoy the story of the Good Samaritan?"

"They did. And look what I have!"

Harry slowly got up, spilling Tuck onto the faded rug.

"Wow! What is all this?"

She put her arms around him, giving him a big hug.

"After the picnic, the women of Rosebud surprised me with a shower. Look at all the lovely things they gave us!"

A non-sewer, Babs was again surprised to receive many handmade baby garments. Picking up a tiny yellow nightgown, she was showing the intricate stitches to her husband when they heard a knock on the kitchen door. Answering it, Babs found Margie on the back porch, flushed and so excited her pigtails were lopsided.

"Come in Margie,"

"Guess what happened?" she cried, pausing as she noticed the pile of gifts on the table. "You didn't sew all those things, did you?"

"No."

"Well, you already had a shower from us and one from Sterling, I heard. Are these things from Rosebud? I'll bet Mrs. Eager was in charge, huh?"

"She was in on it," admitted Babs.

"Now your baby has all kinds of things!"

"Aren't they lovely?"

"Yes. Big news. The Browns just got home."

"Was Mr. Brown upset?"

"Yes, he looked mad. The first thing he saw was that part of their vegetable garden had dried up during that week with no rain. He was fussing about that. The Jarvises didn't come out of their house. But I saw them peeking around their curtains in the parlor."

"What did he say when he found out that Chester was gone?"

" When I told him I couldn't find the dog to feed, you know what he did?"

"No, what? asked Babs.

"He went over to the car and opened the door."

"Yes?"

"He laughed, and Chester jumped out! They forgot to tell me they were taking Chester to Boscobel!"

Babs, thankful a possibly ugly village squabble had been averted, said, "That's a relief!"

Margie retorted triumphantly, "Not to Mrs. Jarvis!"

"Why not for Mrs. Jarvis?"

"Chester headed straight for her tulip bed!"

Chapter 35

MOTHER ARRIVES

"Oh, Harry, your specially fitted shoes look terrible! What happened?'

"I was handling brine at pickle factory yesterday and some of it slopped over onto my shoes."

"We needed the money, but I'm glad that job is over with. You came home every night so tired."

"I admit it's hard to study at night after I'm on my feet all day."

"With my mother coming today, you need to look your best. Now your new forty-dollar shoes look all beat up. What a shame."

"I'll see what polishing will do for them."

"I have more bad news."

"What's that?" inquired Harry, getting out the shoe polish.

"Last month we were strapped, and the Standard Oil gasoline bill was huge, so I sent a money order for just part of what we owe. Today we got the notice that they've cancelled our credit card."

"We still have a Shell and a Texaco card, don't we?"

Babs got out the ironing board to deal with Harry's shirts. "Yes, but it bugs me to have our card cancelled."

She tested the iron, waiting as it warmed up.

Looking up from his shoes, he said,

"It bothers you a lot, doesn't it?"

"Yes, I try so hard to meet our obligations," she said earnestly, laying the first of his five white shirts on the ironing board.

"It won't be like this forever, Dear."

"I hope not," she said, brushing away a tear.

After she had finished ironing and putting away his shirts and handkerchiefs, she went into the nursery/guest room. Babs surveyed the bed neatly covered with the quilt from Sterling women, the windows with the paper drapes from Louise, and the flowers she'd arranged on the windowsill.

"It's the best I can do," she sighed.

Yesterday, she had thoroughly cleaned all the rooms, putting away the things which she and Harry had scattered throughout the house. Against doctor's orders, she had raked the lawn, and after that had swept the walks by the front and back doors. Neighbors dropped by to wish her well, but there was no word from the Collins family.

Returning to the living room where Harry had put on his freshly polished shoes, she said,

"Harry, it's a humble home, but it's never looked this neat and attractive. I hope Mother will be pleased."

"It looks nice, Honey. What are we having to eat tonight?" he asked.

"I'm splurging! Claudia and Mike gave us some apples. Tonight it's pork chops and applesauce. Applesauce is easy to make. With the lard from Clara Wells, I may fix an apple pie while Mother is here. According to Mrs. Blodgett, lard makes the best pie crust."

"Sounds good, Honey."

"Be sure to put away the shoe polish stuff," she said.

Harry wrinkled his nose, as he put the polish away.

Later, as they were driving toward Wisconsin Rapids to meet the train, Harry looked over at his wife. Her ankles were swollen, as was her stomach. Little Judy was growing bigger every day. Tears were rolling down her cheeks.

"What's the matter, Honey? Do you hurt somewhere?"

"No, I'm just so nervous about Mother's coming. I never do things well enough to suit her. It's impossible for me to reach the standards that she sets for me!"

"Babs, do you remember what your mother's friend, Mrs. Wolf, said?"

She wiped her eyes, and Harry could see a faint smile beginning to form.

"You mean about bragging?"

"Yes. Didn't she say once that she got tired of always hearing about how you are an accomplished pianist and organist, and you have a master's degree, and all that?"

"Oh, and she was always hearing about how pretty I am. And I married a professional man who took Greek and Hebrew in college."

"There you are. She is terribly proud of you."

"Only she is careful never to let me know."

Blowing her nose, she took a deep breath.

"I want to see her, but I'm afraid she'll be critical of our home and us. I never mention our financial struggles."

Harry drove on silently, angry at his mother-in-law who, he believed, occasioned a lot of Babs's suffering. He felt helpless to assuage her apprehension.

"She said that your Dad was bringing a gift for you and the baby?" Harry asked changing the subject.

"Yes. I wonder what it is. It must be pretty big, or she would have brought it in her suitcase. She said it was a practical item that I would use a lot."

"Hm-m-m. I wonder what it could be?"

"I'm intrigued, but we'll just have to wait. I see we're in Wisconsin Rapids. Do you know where the train station is?"

"Yes. We are almost there."

"Did you put in your camera, Harry? I want to get a picture of her."

"It's in the back seat."

Harry parked the car where they could watch for the train. Soon it puffed into sight, an old-fashioned steam engine with three passenger cars and one dining car behind it. They heard the blast as the engine rolled to a halt. Getting out of the automobile, Babs grabbed Harry's thirty-five millimeter camera, and went toward the train.

Soon, the porter in the second car stepped down, suitcase in hand, and placed the step-stool by the entrance to the railroad car. A rather tall-appearing, slender woman in navy blue with a wide white hat, trimmed with navy blue, came down the train steps carrying her purse and overnight bag. Her white hair was short and curling around her slender face. She had deep-set hazel eyes, a thin nose, and full lips. Pausing to tip porter, she looked up to see her daughter and Harry coming toward her.

"Babs, how are you?" she asked as she kissed her daughter.

"Fine, Mother. Harry wants to take your picture."

"Do I look all right?" she asked, posing in front of the train.

Greeting her, he deliberately took her picture, and picked up her bag.

"How was the trip, Mother?"

"Beautiful! I love traveling by train. I took the northern route, which was wonderful. In Minneapolis, I changed to this funny, old-fashioned steam train, part of the Soo Line. It's been an interesting experience."

An argument ensued as they got to the car, with Ruth insisting that she ride in the back seat, rather than the front.

"Babs, you won't deliver right away. The baby hasn't completely dropped. What does your doctor say?"

"He said I'd deliver around the twenty-first, which is tomorrow."

"I think it will be at least a week later than that. When I was head nurse in the delivery room at Merritt Hospital in Oakland, I saw a lot of women ready to deliver."

"How long ago did you work at the hospital?" asked Harry.

"Years ago, before I married, of course. Babs, are you taking care of yourself? You look tired to me. Do you let Harry do all the heavy work?"

"Harry helps a lot. I'm fine."

"I'm concerned. Al arranged his vacation, so that he could come after me when the baby is a month old. If the baby comes late, I'll have to leave you after only two and a half or three weeks. I don't see how you can manage. Of course, Harry can help out."

"Please don't worry, Mother. Let's just enjoy your visit. Are you excited about being a grandmother?"

"Oh, yes, I am."

"How about Dad?"

"Sandy says he doesn't mind being a grandpa, but he's not sure he wants to be married to a grandma."

"Sounds like Dad! What about Al?"

"Your brother is excited about becoming an uncle. He wishes he were close enough to get a cigar from Harry."

"Well, Mother, just think. Soon you'll get to hear Harry preach, and you'll get to hold your very own granddaughter."

"I can hardly wait," responded Ruth.

Chapter 36

FLIGHT OF THE STORK

"Harry," whispered Babs, "labor pains are coming every fifteen minutes."

"What?" he asked anxiously, turning over in bed to face her.

"I've been timing the labor pains," she repeated softly. "The pains are coming regularly."

"Maybe we ought to get up now. Are they bad, Honey?"

"No. They're faint. It's early, but I just wanted to tell you."

"Do you think we should get up yet?"

"No. It's three o'clock in the morning! Let's wait a little while."

Fully awake now, Harry looked ready for action.

"I don't want to have the baby here."

"Just cuddle me," she said.

"Shouldn't we get up? Shouldn't I call the doctor? It takes a half hour to get to St. Michael's."

"I shouldn't have awakened you. There's plenty of time.

Reluctantly, he settled back into bed.

They heard a faint knock at the bedroom door.

"Yes?" said Babs.

"I heard you talking in there. Have your pains started, Babs?"

"Just started, Mother."

Babs got up and put on her bathrobe, which no longer fully covered her figure. She opened the door and saw Ruth, fully alert, her robe half on.

"It's early. We are all awake, but the pains are very light. Let's go back to bed awhile and try to get some rest, Mother."

Sleep eluded them all. Lying in bed during the early morning, she watched Harry doze fitfully, the hours punctuated by light pains and the sounds of Ruth's restless footsteps in the hall, going back and forth from bathroom to guest room. Babs watched the sun come up.

"You and Mother have been wide awake for some time now," she commented.

"I'll put on a pot of coffee," said Harry getting out of bed.

By seven o'clock, the pains were coming every twelve minutes. After a bite of toast and a cup of extra strong coffee, Babs checked her overnight bag for the tenth time, and the trio set out for Stevens Point.

Arriving at the hospital, she wanted to pace. After walking around the hospital a number of times, she checked into her room. Putting on a hospital gown, she was examined by Sister Mary Martha, a nurse in a nun's habit, wearing large black spectacles and a severe expression. Afterwards, Ruth and Harry were allowed into her room. Watching her daughter, Ruth was plainly nervous about the approaching birth and the adequacy of the rural hospital. Harry, by turns, paced with Babs or stood around looking uncomfortable. With the pains still faint, Babs kept reassuring her spouse and mother.

When the lunch tray was delivered, Harry and Ruth left to get some lunch, while Babs tried to concentrate on a magazine article about using earth tones in home decoration.

"I notice that there is no mention of dirty gray-blue as a unifying color," she remarked to herself.

As she walked up and down the hall, she had observed a large, middle-aged woman arriving at 11:00 am in tremendous pain. Her husband, a tall, dark man with a slender mustache, hung around the maternity area in an ineffectual manner, while his wife prepared to deliver their fifth child. The nuns soon hustled the woman into the delivery room. By 2:15, the infant and arrived. Babs saw the husband, thrilled and happy, standing in the hall by the nursery window, admiring his youngest offspring.

"Now that he feels in charge again, he's lost that ineffectual air," she thought.

At 3:00 pm, Alice, a tiny, blond woman, and husband, Tom, an apprehensive redhead, settle into the room next door. Tom told her that they ran a dairy farm nearby. Soon, Alice was ushered into the nearby, delivery room.

In the midst of Alice's cries of pain, Babs watched a new roommate check in. The husband walked, chain smoking and clad in dirty jeans, with his wife behind, carrying a suitcase. She was thin and pale, and above her right eyebrow was a large, port-wine birthmark. As she deposited her ill-fitting, mustard-colored coat on the bed, the stern-looking Sister Mary Martha, arrived, reprimanding the husband.

"No smoking, and wait in the visitor's area, while we get your wife settled here."

Dropping his cigarette on the floor, he snuffed it out with the toe of his boot.

"A beer is what I need," he said as he left, "but I guess I'll grab me a cup of coffee."

Scooping up the cigarette butt with a tissue in silent distaste, the nun pulled the curtain around the woman's bed and instructed her to get into a hospital gown.

Next she turned to Babs. "When are you getting down to business to deliver this baby?"

"I'm not doing well, am I?" she asked apologetically.

"You've been here for hours and still haven't dilated much."

At that moment, Ruth and Harry returned from lunch.

"Are your pains getting more intense? Are they coming any faster?" asked Ruth.

"No, she's just fooling around," replied the nun.

"Fooling around!" Ruth cried. "She's doing her best!"

"Of course, but she hasn't made much progress." With that, Sister Mary Martha left.

Two hours dragged by, and the woman with the port-wine birthmark left for the delivery room, her gurney escorted by Sister Mary Martha and a gentle-appearing, Sister Mary Elizabeth.

At suppertime, Babs played with her food, while her family left to have dinner with the Rev. Staley and his wife, Charleen. The pains were more intense and coming every ten minutes. Sister Mary Elizabeth announced that she was beginning to dilate.

Dr. Sutherland came by and ordered some shots for her. Babs smiled at Harry, who had returned, and clutched his hand. People came and went. A curt nod from Sister Mary Martha told Babs that the nun now approved of her performance.

Babs was trying to place that woman with the port-wine birthmark. According to Sister Mary Elizabeth, her roommate had delivered a healthy baby with curly blond hair. Back in their room, the young mother slept. Why did her roommate seem familiar? Babs couldn't put her finger on it.

Ruth, sitting by her bed, was tight-lipped.

"I would have taken you to the delivery room long before this," she said as an intense pain gripped her daughter. Babs received more shots. Her water broke. Her bed began moving. Harry and Ruth were no longer with her, but she saw Dr. Sutherland. The woman with the dark birthmark . . . married four months ago . . . the bride with the mustard coat. . . the parsonage wedding with no joy . . .a shotgun wedding . . . no flowers . . . so sad . . . more pain . . . pain . . . .

It was morning.

"Please wake up now, Mrs. Petersen. You worked hard, and you should eat some breakfast," said Sister Black Spectacles.

Back in her room, Babs felt no pain.

"Did I have my baby?"

"You surely did, Mrs. Petersen. A fine, big baby boy."

"I did? Oh, may I see him?"

"We'll bring him in to nurse very soon. You do plan to nurse the baby?"

"Yes. Women in our family produce lots of milk."

"Good for you. Not many try to nurse these days."

Scowling no more, the nun left.

The door opened, and in walked Harry and Ruth, carrying an outlandishly large bouquet of gorgeous gladioli. Both had huge smiles.

"Have you seen my baby?'

"Yes, of course. We all saw him last night," said Ruth.

"Have you seen Dr. Sutherland?"

"Don't you remember Dr. Sutherland standing by your bed after the delivery? He said you were magnificent," said Harry with pride.

"I don't remember anything after they wheeled me into the delivery room. All those shots I guess."

"We have a little boy, Darling," said Harry. "Are you disappointed that it won't be Judy?"

"No. I thought you wanted a girl, Harry. I'm thankful for a healthy baby."

Sister Mary Martha entered the room.

"I must ask you two to leave. We are going to bring the baby in to be nursed."

"We want to see the baby up close!" said Ruth.

"Sorry. No visitors when the babies are in the room," stated the sister firmly.

"Goodbye for now," Harry smiled as he kissed her, and they left, Ruth looking back wistfully.

Babs was weary but exultant, and her arms fairly ached as she waited for her infant.

At that moment the door opened, and Sister Black Spectacles appeared, carrying the most beautiful new-borne in the world!

"Oh, Sister! Give me my baby!"

Chapter 37

GEORGE TAKES OVER

Babs was in tears. For several minutes, her infant had been trying to nurse, but her nipple kept slipping out of his mouth. He was beginning to whimper. At that moment, Sister Mary Martha came in to return the baby to the nursery.

"What's the trouble here?" she asked. "Are your nipples tender?"

"A little. But the real problem is that the little fellow is hungry, but he can't seem to keep the nipple in his mouth."

"Oh, I see now. You have inverted nipples."

"Does that mean I can't nurse him?" she asked fearfully.

"No. You seem to have plenty of milk. It means we have to be patient while the baby learns to pull. After a few times, he will straighten out the nipples. Let me help you."

Later in the day, while Ruth was down the hall at the nursery window admiring her first grandchild, Harry sat by Babs' bed, holding her hand.

"How are you feeling, Dear? That was a long, hard day for you."

"I'm tired but okay. The doctor said I have sixteen stitches, but I'm recovering nicely. What do you think about our baby?"

"He's wonderful. He is rather bald, but he'll get hair soon. His eyes are a deep blue, aren't they?

"Yes, He is beautiful. You know that Sister, Mary Martha, who was so crabby when I took so long to deliver?"

"She's the short, stout one, right?"

"Yes. Well, the baby is having trouble nursing because my nipples are inverted. He has to pull them out in order to nurse. Well, she worked with me for fifteen minutes, so that the little rascal could get his breakfast!"

"Good! She's not as cross as we thought?"

"No. She helped me when I needed it."

"Your Mom is a humdinger," whispered Harry.

"Oh?"

"While you were in labor pains, she was telling the nurses and doctor how to proceed. She wanted you in the delivery room a half hour earlier. She thought you needed shots for the pain earlier than they gave them. She insisted on peeking into the delivery room. She made such a fuss that Dr. Sutherland almost lost his temper. 'Take that woman down to the waiting room at the end of the hall,' he said. 'See that she doesn't get anywhere near the delivery room!' "

"He said that?"

"Yes. Your mom's a born manager!"

"I'm sorry you had that to worry about that along with everything else, Harry. I'm okay, and the baby's okay."

A light tap on the door, and Ruth walked in, her eyes sparkling.

"I've been looking over all the babies in the nursery. You have the prettiest one of all!"

"You like your new grandson?" asked Babs.

"Yes. He's a big fellow, too. Twenty-two inches long and eight pounds, fourteen ounces!"

Harry left to get a cup of coffee, and Ruth took the chair by the bed.

"How are you feeling now, after all that hard labor?"

"Tired and happy."

"Do you have plenty of milk?"

"Yes, I do, Mother," she said.

"Harry and I are painting the kitchen and bathroom, as you requested."

"Oh, that is kind of you, Mother! I hate that dirty blue. It was all through the parsonage before the Busy Bees decided to get wallpaper."

"Painting with Harry is different than painting with your father. Dad always said to paint lightly, just barely covering the surface. Harry says to put on plenty to cover the undercoat."

"Confusing, huh, Mother?"

"It sure is. But we're getting the job done. Harry is doing the ceiling, while I started on the wall behind the stove. That's a good place to begin as I'm learning the 'Petersen approach' to painting."

"Are you getting enough to eat?"

"Yes. I understand you don't get ice in the winter. How did you manage with no refrigerator?"

"We kept our food in the cool basement. Kept me slim, running up and down the stairs."

Just then, Harry entered, bringing a cup of coffee for his mother-in-law.

"Thank you, Harry," she said, rather surprised. "I don't usually drink coffee at this time of day, but it smells good."

"Mom prefers tea, Honey."

"This is fine, Harry," said Ruth.

"Did you tell Dad about the baby?"

"Yes. Your mother called your dad and brother, Al, and I phoned my folks. Kate Wells, Ed's spinster sister, is the phone operator in Prairie Meadows. After your mother and I told our families about the birth, she phoned all over Sterling telling them the news."

"I thought what operators hear is confidential," said Babs reprovingly.

"She had to tell everybody!"

"What are you children going to call the baby?" inquired Ruth. "*Judith* is not appropriate."

"No. We have decisions to make," said Babs.

At that moment, there was a knock, and all eyes turned toward the door as Sister Mary Elizabeth came in.

"Sorry, visiting hours are over. As soon as visitors leave, we'll be bringing the babies."

"I'd like to stay," remarked Ruth.

"You can come back for the evening hours," said the nurse. "It's the infants' needs that govern our procedures."

Ruth nodded.

"I agree. Babs, soon that baby will tell you when to get up and when you can go to sleep. He will change your life more than you can possibly imagine."

Chapter 38

GEORGE RECEIVES VISITORS

"The baby's crying, Harry."

"Wh-wh-wh what is it?" asked the sleepy father.

"Can't you hear him? The crib is only three feet away. I don't want Mother to hear and get up!"

"Oh," said Harry sitting up quickly and rubbing his eyes. "I'll get him."

Babs turned over in bed contentedly, as Harry picked up the infant and began to change him.

"Thanks, Hon," she said.

"Is the baby all right? Do you want me to help?" asked Ruth at the bedroom door.

"The baby's fine, Mother. I'm changing him, and he'll be nursing right away," answered Harry.

"Oh, he isn't hurting or anything then?" asked Ruth doubtfully.

"No, Mother, he's fine," said Harry, bringing his freshly changed son to Babs.

"Barbara, do you need anything?" persisted her mother.

Babs rolled her eyes at Harry, as he brought the hungry baby to their bed.

"No, thanks, Mother. He's about to have his breakfast now."

"All right, darling," said her mother sounding wistful as she went back to bed.

As Harry settled back comfortably in bed, he heard his first-borne smacking his lips over his milk.

"Isn't it great that George has straightened out my nipples? Dr Sutherland says that if we have any more children, they won't have any difficulty."

"Hm-m-m," affirmed Harry.

As Babs cuddled her baby, she felt happy, fulfilled, and sleepy. George emptied one breast and happily started on the second one. At last he was finished. He seemed most contented in the early hours of the morning after he drinking his fill and loading his diapers. Changing him, she noticed it was four-thirty when she put George in his crib.

"Harry doesn't believe me, but I'd swear that child smiled at me just now," she thought as she turned off the light and slipped back into bed. Welcome sleep came immediately.

She was dozing, when she heard her mother's voice.

"Babs, are you decent? May I come in?" asked Ruth.

"I guess I'm decent. I'm just waking up."

"You need your rest, Dear. I have a nice breakfast tray for you. Early this morning I sneaked in and got the Old Timer, so that you could stay in bed a while."

"Oh, Mother, what a lovely tray! You shouldn't have done all this. Where's the baby?"

Wearing a pair of Babs' yellow and brown shorts, Ruth looked trim and attractive in August's sultry heat.

"I've been holding him. Harry has him now. You know, mothers used to stay in bed two weeks after delivering a baby. I don't hold with this getting-mothers up the next day, as Dr. Sutherland advocates. I think a woman's figure suffers by not getting the necessary rest."

"I'm doing fine, Mother. We don't want you working so hard in this heat."

"There's so much to be done. I've hung out a load of washing and scrubbed the kitchen floor already."

"And fixed this beautiful tray for me!"

She was savored the bacon and scrambled eggs, juice, the hot coffee, and the buttered toast.

"This jam is delicious, Mother. Pear, isn't it? Where did you find it?"

"Oh, it's some I put up myself. Do you like it?"

"I sure do! I love these posies on the tray."

"I found your little rose bush. It's scrawny but puts out pretty blossoms."

"It was planted by the last pastor's wife who loved flowers. Don't I hear the baby crying?"

"Yes," answered Harry carrying in his son who was beginning to protest the delay of his second breakfast.

"Harry, I wanted Babs to enjoy her repast in peace."

"That's okay, Mother. I'm about finished, and George sounds hungry."

"You're putting him on a four-hour schedule, aren't you?" she asked as Babs got out of bed. "That's what I did with you and Al, and you turned out very well."

Babs took the baby from Harry.

"Dr. Sutherland tells me I should let George work out his own schedule. He says I'll have a much more contented baby if I let him feed when he's hungry."

"Oh, really? He advises that, does he?" responded her mother, watching her, as the baby began to nurse.

"I'd better get these breakfast dishes done. Do you know what?" Ruth asked as she gathered up the tray. "This morning, your elderly neighbor from across the street just walked right into the kitchen without a knock at the door. I was startled, and I told him that since this is your private home, he must knock."

Babs and Harry exchanged a look.

"What did he say then?" she asked.

"He wanted to see the baby, but I told him the baby was asleep. The baby wasn't asleep, but it isn't good to expose a tiny baby to all kinds of germs."

Ruth, carrying the tray, her head held high, left for the kitchen.

"As we were having coffee this morning, your mother told me we should get rid of the cats. She feels that they are unsanitary around a baby."

"She has been talking to me about Nip and Tuck, also. Do you think they're not good for a baby?"

"Cats spend a lot of their time washing themselves. When I was growing up, my family had cats. They caused no problems that I can recall."

162

George, having finished his meal, was sound asleep at his mother's breast. Babs put him tenderly in his bassinet, covered him with a light crib blanket, and turned toward Harry.

"How about a kiss, big boy?" she said.

After a hug and kiss from Harry, she stood before her clothes closet in her white slip, looking at the dresses and skirts that she had not worn for a while.

"Alberta told me not to be discouraged if I couldn't get into my things right away. I guess it takes a while for the feminine figure to get back to normal."

"Do you have something that fits loosely?" Harry asked.

"Yes. I think this blue and white wrap-around dress is just the thing," and she pulled it around herself, fastening the collar and tying the bow that held the dress in place.

"How do I look?" she demanded.

Before Harry could answer, they heard voices growing louder, apparently coming from the direction of the dinette.

"I said, 'The baby is sleeping right now.'"

"I won't disturb him long. I just want to see him."

"I'm sure you can come back at a more convenient time. His sleep was disturbed last night—"

"That's too bad. A little belly ache? Now which room is he in?"

The speakers suddenly appeared in the hallway outside the bedrooms. Ruth appeared to be trying to detain an animated woman. Mrs. Eager, from Rosebud, having sewn a lovely, pink nightie for "Judy," was determined to get acquainted with her preacher's new son.

Seeing Harry and Babs, she plunged into the room, followed by Ruth, wringing her hands in extreme agitation. Spying the bassinet, Mrs. Eager pulled the white baby blanket off the slumbering infant, and picked him up, kissing him on both cheeks.

"What a beautiful baby! I hope you'll let him wear the pink nightdress I made for him. Such a big boy!"

"He is a big boy all right, Mrs. Eager. Of course, he will wear the pink nightie. He doesn't worry about color."

The older woman smiled, revealing large, uneven, yellow teeth, and a gap in place of her upper left eyetooth.

"Your mom here didn't want me to disturb the baby, but my sister and me, we hardly ever get to Prairie Meadows. I didn't know how soon I'd get to see him," she said. "It's so exciting to

163

have a new-borne in the Prairie Meadows parsonage! My sister, Mae O'Reilly, is Catholic. She's out in the car. Can I take the baby—what's his name—out so she can see him?"

Ruth's anxious look was ignored by Mrs. Eager, who took Babs' hesitant smile for "Yes." She hurried out the front door with the baby at her shoulder, making straight for her old, black Dodge. Mae O'Reilly in the front seat of the dusty Dodge, held her arms out to take the baby. Holding him close, Mrs. O'Reilly smiled from ear to ear. At that very moment, Henry Perkins happened by, so that he got to hold the infant. As she was making her way towards the Collins, Mrs. Blodgett paused and crossed the street.

"It's my turn to have the baby," she said, grabbing George from Mr. Perkins and holding him against her ample bosom. Seeing her favorite rival coming up the street, Mrs. Blodgett held the baby up and cried:

"Nancy, look who I have here?"

Mrs. Addison, with great persistence, was able to persuade Mrs. Blodgett to surrender George to her for a moment. She held the baby's hands and kissed the wrinkles which made up his wrists. Finally, Mac joined the circle of admirers and insisted upon holding the little one himself. While the infant rested on his thin chest, Mac tried in vain to remember a lullaby that he had sung to his own son years ago.

Ruth watched the drama with mounting anger.

"Aren't you going to reclaim your baby? How can you let your helpless child pass from hand to hand like that? Suppose one of them has TB or some other disease?"

She looked from her daughter to her son-in-law as they stood quietly together in the living room, looking out at the scene before them.

"Haven't I heard that the new-borne possess an immunity for a while?" asked Harry mildly.

"Mother, the birth of our baby means a lot to the people of the communities we serve. They have watched me grow large. They showered us with hand-made gifts. Let them have their moment of joy. In a sense, he is theirs, too."

Ruth snorted. "Well, all I can say is, if he's theirs, they should take better care of him. Look what they're exposing him to!"

Chapter 39

GRANDPA MEETS THE OLDTIMER

"Mother, you're spoiling me! I insist on eating at the table with you."

"You might as well take advantage of my being here and get some rest. "

"Thanks, Mother. I have enjoyed taking it easy. I don't know why I'm feeling so tired," said Babs, stooping down to roll a wooden spool across the room for Nip.

"You said that, yesterday. You are suffering from post-partum depression."

"Depression?" she repeated finishing her second cup of coffee.

"Yes. A mild form of depression, which is so common among new mothers that it has a name, 'Post-partum Depression.'"

"I don't know about that, Mother. I just feel tired."

"No wonder, with all the people you let stream through your house."

The silence after Ruth's rebuke was interrupted, appropriately, by Mac walking in—quietly, as always.

"Good morning, Mac," said Babs.

"I see the Rev's chickens are getting big. They must be costing a fortune to feed. Hope he isn't running up a big feed bill."

"He's not. Thanks for your concern, Mac."

At the sound of the baby's cry, Babs left the room.

Ruth looked over her cup of coffee frostily at the early morning visitor who noted her outfit of yellow and brown shorts and seemed to feel unusually talkative.

"I have to warn young folks. Some young pastors have run up big bills here in town. When they moved, they left local merchants holding the bag," remarked Mac, his bald head glistening with sincerity.

"It's no wonder, with the low salary you apparently pay your pastors," retorted Ruth pulling at her shorts, trying in vain to cover her thighs adequately. "You keep them so poor!"

"Oh, it's not really a problem," said Mac as he edged toward the front door. "Ministers are used to being poor."

"Well, a pork chop costs them just as much as anyone else!" returned Ruth her voice rising as she heard the front door slam.

Fortunately, Ruth was distracted at the sight of George, in his mother's arms, holding his head up and gazing around in the bright morning sunshine.

"Give him to me! Oh, Grandma's beautiful grandson! What an adorable baby!"

Handing the baby to his eager grandmother, Babs began to clear the dishes.

"Why do these old men, Mac, you call him, and Mr. Perkins across the street, feel they can walk into your house any time?" asked Ruth, kissing George on the top of his head.

"They don't mean anything by it, Mother. We try to remember to lock the doors."

She filled the cats' saucers with milk and tuna.

"Why you don't just tell them that they must knock?"

"Harry reminds them, but they forget."

"Humph," sniffed Ruth.

"Mother, would you like to take care of the baby while I do a bit of shopping? Tonight I want to make a special dinner for you and Dad. He arrives today, right?

"Yes. I'd love to take charge of the Old-Timer. But why don't you let Harry do the shopping for you?"

"Harry left early to visit Claudia Morgan from Sterling, who's having an operation in the hospital at Waupaca. She and Mike, you know, lent us the piano. Harry likes to have prayer with people just before they go into surgery."

"He does?"

"He also has two meetings. No time for shopping."

"Aren't you resuming your activities too soon?"

"No, Mother."

"If you must," she said reprovingly.

After finishing her shopping list, Babs borrowed money from the encyclopedia and transportation bottles, and left.

Ruth held the baby kissing him and patting him until he fell asleep. Reluctantly, putting him down in his crib, she took the basket of washing outside and started to hang it up. As she hung the last diaper, a low, appreciative whistle came from behind her.

Startled, Ruth turned around and saw a tall man with a broad smile approaching her. His hair was sandy-colored, and he was wearing knickers and a green sports shirt.

"Oh, Sandy, you surprised me! I couldn't imagine who would be whistling at an old lady like me."

"Not so old—although you are a grandmother now, I hear," replied Al.

"Come on, we'll sneak in, and you can see our remarkable grandson for yourself."

Sandy and Ruth slipped quietly into the parsonage and stood at the door of the bedroom.

"Well, what do you think?" she asked him. "Isn't he absolutely beautiful?"

"Our little girl did a great job," he replied, taking a long look at his first grandchild. He reached for the smokes in his shirt pocket, as they sat down together in the living room.

"Where are the parents of the poor orphan?" he asked. "Are they off gallivanting while you attend to the baby and the laundry?"

"Hardly. Harry has people in the hospital and meetings to attend, while Babs went shopping. What about our gift? Did you remember it?"

"How could I forget with your reminding me all the time? It's in the car."

"Why don't we go out and bring it in? We can leave it in the guest room closet and give it to her after dinner."

"Okay. I'll finish my cigarette, and I'll bring it in."

"I'll help."

"No, it's too heavy for you."

Ruth opened her mouth to argue, but closed it.

"I've missed you, Sandy."

"Not enough to do?" he teased.

167

Later that evening, the four of them at dinner, Ruth noticed that Babs served cottage cheese and pineapple for the first course. No lettuce. She saw with approval that Harry was carving the roast and serving the potatoes and vegetables. While Babs forgot to warm the dinner plates, the flavor of the beef was good. While it took her daughter a while, she finally brought in dessert, a yellow cake with cooked icing, and served with rather weak coffee.

"Barbara is learning," thought her mother.

After George awakened, they retired to the living room where Babs nursed him.

Finally, Ruth could wait no longer.

"Sandy brought you something for you and the baby."

"And for Harry?"

"I doubt Harry will use it."

Al left the room, returning slowly pushing a rectangularly-shaped box on four wheels. One wheel squeaked.

"Dad, what do you have there?"

"See for yourself!"

"I can't imagine—" she murmured, handing the sleeping baby to Harry.

Deciding it must be an appliance, she removed the huge bow, carefully saving the paper, and opened up the box.

"Mother, you got me a mangle?"

"I did. You told me how a minister's wife has to iron a lot of white shirts. Now you'll be able to sit down to do them. Harry, too, will get some benefits, right?"

"My white shirts will look great."

"It's not just the shirts, Harry. On ironing day, your wife won't be worn out."

Babs smiled.

"Get ready to groan, dear family! From now on, thanks to Mother and Dad, I'll be in great shape when it comes to pressing matters!"

Chapter 40

CHICKENS

"Babs, they left!"

"My parents?"

"Yes. I didn't have a chance to say good-bye, or thank your mother for all she did!"

"You thanked them last night."

"Yes, but I thought I'd see them this morning. I feel so guilty that I didn't give them a good send-off or thank them adequately."

"Honey, don't worry," she said, kissing his wrinkled brow. "Mother and Dad like to get an early start. They know you appreciate what they did. I'll fix some coffee. That will make you feel better."

"I wonder what time they left," he mused, pacing the kitchen and dinette.

"George had his 3:30 am feeding. After nursing him, I put him down around quarter to four. I heard some one in the bathroom, just before I fell asleep. I'll bet they left around 5:30."

"Without a cup of coffee!"

"Oh, they made coffee and filled their thermos. They like to drive a hundred miles before stopping for breakfast."

"I'm glad they got some coffee. How could I sleep through that?"

"George got us up a couple of times last night. I hear him waking up. Get him, will you, while I fix breakfast?"

Shaking his head at the strange behavior of his in-laws, Harry returned and put George in his highchair.

"Remember I made an arrangement with a restaurant to deliver sixty dressed chickens at sixty cents a pound?" he asked eating his oatmeal.

"That's right! We can sure use the money," she said.

"Today's the day!"

"How will you handle sixty chickens, Harry?"

"I have it all planned. Right now, while we eat, I'm heating water in the canning kettle."

"I see you are."

About eight-thirty, Mac ambled by the parsonage. He looked on, as his energetic minister tied about a dozen squawking, young chickens upside down on the wire clothesline. Once secured, they were slashed at the throat, bloodying the ground beneath. Henry Perkins joined Mac and watched as Harry dumped the birds one by one into a large pot of hot water. Feathers flew as the chickens were plucked and placed in a gunnysack. Harry dumped out the water and took the empty container into the house. The men were curious about the next step, but, unfortunately, the doors to the parsonage were locked. Hanging around, they were joined by Mrs. Blodgett on an errand for the Busy Bees.

Their patience was rewarded by the re-appearance of the Reverend Petersen, clad in blood-stained pants, stalking purposefully toward the chicken coop. Mrs. Blodgett watched open-mouthed as her minister tied a dozen protesting leghorns to the wire clothes line. Her astonishment increased as he strolled down the line, expertly cutting the throat of each chicken.

"Pretty neat, huh?" observed Henry. "He must have done that before."

"Must have," agreed Mac, as Harry threw a second batch of bloody roosters into a plastic bag, and disappeared into the house. Soon, he emerged, carrying a large container of hot water, into which he dumped the chickens.

"I think it's disgusting!" declared Mrs. Blodgett. "And he, a man of the cloth. He shows no mercy."

"Chickens don't need mercy!" scoffed Henry. "Wonder what he's going to do with them?"

"Beats me," observed Mac.

"Well, I'm not going to stand around any longer watching this nauseating display. Jane and I have plans to make," and with that, Mrs. Blodgett gathered her purple skirts and walked off in a huff.

As Harry, for a third time, attached squawking white leghorns to the line, Babs noticed Margie standing next to Mac, staring fixedly at the procedure.

"She will have a lot to report," lamented Babs, herself astonished, at the speed and vigor of Harry's operation. "The way he cared for those chickens, I thought he was fond of them."

That evening, at dinner, she heard his account of the "slaughter of the innocents."

"I got all sixty plucked, cleaned, and delivered to the restaurant. Here's the check."

"What are we going to do with the money?"

"I was hoping to put all of it toward our fuel bill with Ray Gold. We'll soon have to order coal for next winter."

"But can we, when we owe so much?"

"No, and even though I'll be hauling sand next week, we'll still be in debt."

"You worked so hard. You're disappointed, aren't you?"

"Yes, but I must remember I'm lucky to have my work, my wife, and our baby!"

"And aren't you thankful that for dinner this evening you're having sauerkraut and wieners!"

"Yes, Dear, I've seen enough chicken for today."

Chapter 41

FINANCIAL DECISIONS

"Will, we appreciate your allowing us to come over and talk about our problems," said Harry as Will led them into his study.

"Glad if I can be of any help," he responded. "Isn't this what we pastors are about: helping other people?"

"Yes, but I'd much rather give counseling, than get it," said Harry ruefully.

"Look at it this way, this is an opportunity to know how your people feel when they come to you. Why don't you take that rocker, Mrs. Petersen. You have a beautiful baby. What's his name?"

"George. Please call me Babs."

"Thank you, Babs. Okay, Harry, are you comfortable in that chair?"

Harry nodded and remained silent, and Will sat in his office chair across the desk, his fingers folded across his stomach, his eyes on the baby, who was perched at his mother's shoulder and looking about.

Finding the silence unendurable, Babs spoke first,

"We don't know what to do. We owe three hundred dollars on last year's coal bill, and we're going to have to order more coal very soon."

She thought, surprisingly, that she saw relief flooding Will's face, as he responded,

"You feel really up against it, with fall coming, right?"

"We've been trying to get it paid off. I've worked in the fields and in a pickle factory, and raised chickens, and Babs has been giving piano lessons."

"I'm sure you've been doing all you can. It could be worse, though."

"Worse? What do you mean?" asked Harry resentfully.

"I know it's bad for you, but I was afraid that you were having marital difficulties. I thought maybe Babs and George were thinking of going back to Oregon, or something."

They exchanged a surprised look.

"Oh, no, Will. We have our arguments—"

"Like, why did you buy a set of encyclopedias?" she interrupted. "I'm from California, Will."

"Oh, California. Before we talk about the money problem, I'd like a cup of tea. Would you two like one?"

"Yes, thank you," said Babs relaxing. "I'd love a cup of tea!"

"Yes, thank you, Will," responded Harry.

In a few minutes, coming down the hall with tea service, Will glimpsed Harry and Babs kissing, and discreetly started whistling "The Old Rugged Cross," as he approached the open door.

"Already, you've shown us that being short of money is not an ultimate problem," she said, helping herself to tea and a lemon slice.

"We have a lot to be thankful for, Will. But we don't know just how to handle the situation."

Will took sugar and cream and stirred his cup thoughtfully.

"You don't feel free to go to either of your parents or relatives for a loan?"

"No," said Harry bluntly.

"Is your car paid for?"

"No, we have to make a car payment each month."

"Have you been able to meet the payments, Harry?"

"Yes, not easily, but we make it."

"Have you paid three hundred dollars on the principal?"

"Yes, more than that," answered Babs with excusable pride.

"I think your best bet would be to go to the bank, refinance your loan, and get an additional three hundred dollars."

Harry and Babs looked at each other.

"I never thought of that!" he exclaimed. "We could do that!"

"Yes, we could".

"Now, that's step one."

"Step one? What is step two?" asked the younger minister uneasily.

"Step two is to call a meeting of people from all three churches and tell them what you have done. Tell them that you simply can't live on—"

"Thirty-six dollars a week," finished Harry. "Do you think that will solve the problem, Will?"

"Look at it this way. The people want their church. To make it work, the minister and his family have to make sacrifices (as he spoke, Babs pictured the shabby baby buggy), and the people have to make sacrifices."

"I hate to be a burden. Our families don't have much money," said Harry.

"Yes, but if you and your wife make all the sacrifices, you may deprive the people of their opportunity to experience the discipline and the blessing of God. Do you think a sizable number of your people give a tenth of their income to the church?"

"No, very few, although I don't want to know what the individuals give."

"You are afraid you might tend to favor those who give more?"

"Not so much that, but I feel what a man gives is between him and God."

"Him and God and the financial secretary," laughed Will. "Without a budget, we can't plan."

"Well, yes, the people make pledges, we have a budget, but I don't want to know what individuals give."

"I don't know individual pledges," said Will. "But I have instructed our financial secretary to inform me when a family's giving suddenly changes—up or down."

"Why?" asked Babs, intrigued with the lesson in stewardship from the older man.

"I feel it's a spiritual barometer. People that love a lot, give a lot. If a family suddenly doubles its giving, some one has grown spiritually, and I want to know this. Or, if a family's giving goes down, it may be because of financial reverses, or it could be that some one is angry with God or the minister. I want to know this."

Harry remained unmoved.

"That works for you, Will."

"God does promise blessings to those who give, doesn't He?" asked Babs.

"Harry can quote Malachi 3:10: *Bring ye all the tithes into the storehouse, that there may meat in mine house, and prove me now herewith, saith the Lord of hosts, if I will not open you the windows of heaven, and pour you out a blessing, that there shall not be room enough to receive it.*"

Up to this time, George had been quiet, but now he was wet and hungry. Will directed Babs to a bedroom where she changed the baby. She returned as Harry was shaking hands with Will and thanking him for his counsel.

"We have to be running along, Will. I'll go out and start the car and get it warmed up."

"You've given us a lot to think about," she said as she waited. "Thank your kind wife for the tea, won't you, Will?"

In the car, Harry tucked a blanket around his wife and the fussy baby. As he eased the car into motion, suddenly, all was quiet.

Where there had been unmet needs and frustration, now the infant had not a care in the world. George was nursing.

Harry was thinking to himself as he guided the car on the snowy road,

"Babs and I have been feeling like George. We've been fussing. I wonder when and how the Comforter will meet our needs."

Chapter 42

STEP TWO

"I hope we are doing the right thing," said Harry, looking intently at the road ahead.

"We HAD to borrow some money from the bank last week to pay that fuel bill."

"I know that."

"You're glad we did it?"

"Yes," he said. "But I'm not so sure about the meeting tonight."

"You feel you're being a burden to the churches?"

"Yes, and I'm not sure how they are going to react. It may lessen my effectiveness as a minister."

"Owing a lot of money around town would also lessen your effectiveness as a pastor," she pointed out.

"You're right."

Harry kept his eyes on the road. Babs looked at George in her lap.

"We are getting home late. I had to wait so long in Dr. Sutherland's crowded office."

"Yes, but good news for your twelve-week check-up. Your stitches are healing nicely, and George is doing fine."

"Yes, the doctor teased me about our under-nourished baby! It's just that people will be coming at 7:30, and I'll be rushing to get dinner out of the way in time."

Her fears were confirmed at 7:15 as they were finishing dinner and they heard a knock on the door. She took a look at their dishes, and piled them into the greasy fry pan, trying to make as neat a stack as she could. She looked at the sink with disfavor, and suddenly piled everything into the dishpan, shoving it under the sink, and closing the cabinet door, hiding the mess.

Harry looked amused.

"I've never seen you do that!"

"I never have," she rationalized, "but this is an emergency! I can't stand the idea of receiving people with a stack of dirty dishes in the sink!"

Hurriedly, while Harry answered the door, she started the coffee and dashed into the bedroom, ran a comb through her hair, powdered her nose, and dabbed on her lipstick. As he greeted the arrivals, she returned to the kitchen, set out cups and saucers and small dishes for cake, assembled utensils, paper napkins, her serving trays, and sugar and cream.

Soon there was a noisy, friendly hubbub as people from Rosebud and Sterling came in by the front door, while those from Prairie Meadows used the back door. In the kitchen, she greeted shy Herb Dodds with Myrtle, a concerned-looking Tim Woods, who brought her a drawing from Margie, Mrs. Blodgett, solemn in her lavender and lace, and cheerful, neat Eben Morgan, in spotless overalls.

In the living room, she found Alberta and Lola Rankin talking to Clara Wells and her father-in-law, Ed, and Mrs. Eager in conversation with Mac and Henry Perkins. Mrs. Collins, out of character, was sitting quietly next to Fred and Thelma Young. Frank and Mary Waukowski, farmers from Sterling, were trying to make polite conversation with the Rosses, heavy-set farming couple from Rosebud.

Harry had brought a number of folding chairs from the church, which were put to good use. As Harry rose to speak, people gradually quieted down.

"Friends," began Harry, "I've asked you to come here tonight because I want to share with you a problem I, uh, we've, uh, been experiencing."

"Pastor," interrupted Mrs. Eager, "I hope that you and your family aren't suffering from an illness."

"We are not sick, thank you, Mrs. Eager."

"Praise the Lord for that!" she responded with relief.

"No, we are all well, but we have a concern we feel we must share with you."

The room became very quiet, and Tim Woods and Fred Young exchanged an anxious look, while Jane Collins and Mrs. Blodgett surreptiously glanced at one another.

"We recently went to the bank to refinance our car and secure a three hundred dollar loan."

"I suppose you had expenses in connection with the birth of your baby," said Mrs. Geraldine Ross, from Rosebud.

"No, Mrs. Ross, thanks to consideration from the hospital and doctor, we have met our obligations in that area."

"Oh, that's good," she said.

"We secured the loan in order to pay off last year's coal bill."

Harry hesitated, hating to go on.

"You see, Barbara and I have been trying to supplement our income without neglecting the parish work. The problem is that we find that we can't live on thirty-six dollars a week.'

"Well, Rev, I don't know what you expect. You live in the parsonage rent-free. Besides that, you don't pay taxes on the land like we do," said Charlie Ross.

"Charlie, we aren't here to criticize Rev. Petersen. We all know he gets a low wage," said Fred Young.

"We all have to watch our pennies," said Mrs. Blodgett smiling furtively at Jane Collins. "Sometimes we can't buy things that we'd like to have."

"You use a lot of gasoline in your calling, don't you, Rev.?" asked Mac, ignoring Mrs. Blodgett.

"Yes, Mac, I do."

"It might cut car expenses if you do what we do: buy a barrel of oil and add your own oil instead of buying it at a service station," remarked Charlie.

"That idea won't really help the Reverend," said Lola Rankin.

"Your remark about not buying new things, Mrs. Blodgett, what did you mean?" asked Alberta.

Doris Blodgett rolled her eyes, her voice dripping with sweetness.

"Haven't you all observed how nice Rev. Petersen's shirt collars look these days? Maybe you haven't you noticed the new mangle in the corner of the dinette. Our minister's wife can now sit down to do her ironing."

Babs flushed, as Alberta answered Mrs. Blodgett sharply,

"The mangle happens to be a gift to our minister's wife from her mother and father!"

Babs found her voice.

"Mrs. Blodgett, Harry and I are very much concerned over the twenty dollars we still owe on the washing machine you sold us. We certainly wouldn't go out and buy another appliance when we haven't paid for the washer."

"That's all right, Babs. You made a couple of payments recently," the older woman responded, obviously embarrassed to learn that the mangle was a gift.

"Let's get back to the reason why we're here," said Tim. "Each of the churches needs to look over its budget and see if we can make a bigger contribution to Harry's salary."

Babs hastily retired to the kitchen to slice the cake, as Harry concluded,

"The last thing we want is to be a burden to you. We just felt we had to share our situation with you."

"Harry, you should tell us about it. Each of us will think about what we can do," exclaimed Fred. The others in turn agreed.

Gradually people resumed their accustomed chatter. The front door slammed as Mrs. Collins and Mrs. Blodgett left. Lola, Alberta, and Mary Waukowski appeared in the kitchen to help serve refreshments.

"Babs, you shouldn't have done this!" said Alberta.

"You have enough to do with the baby and all," said Lola.

"I like to serve coffee when people come to the parsonage."

"It's not necessary at all," Mary reproved her.

People signed the guest book and all left except for the Waukowskis and the Wells.

"I hear the baby crying," said Mary. "Now you go and take care of him, and Clara and I will do up these dishes."

"Please, Mary, I'd rather you didn't."

"Nonsense. You work so hard. Is the dishpan under here?" Mary asked, flinging open the cupboard to reveal dirty dinner dishes, silverware, and a greasy frying pan piled in the dishpan. Mary stood frozen, in embarrassment.

"I had a late appointment at the doctor's," confessed Babs.

Reluctant to open any more drawers, Mary said, "Er, show Clara where the tea towels are, will you, Babs? Go ahead and see to George. We can do this."

As she left to change the baby, Mary began to wash the cups and saucers and Clara wiped them, while Ed Wells, Frank Waukowski, and Harry lingered in the living room talking about feed prices until the women were finished.

After they had left, Babs settled into their six-dollar rocker with the hungry baby at her breast.

"George, did you see those greasy dishes! Take my advice. Never try to deceive anybody! Just be yourself. If you're like your mother, you'll never be able to get by with anything, so you might as well be honest!"

Harry shrugged.

"And yes, George, I surely hope that our people will help us meet our expenses!"

Making contented sounds, George kept sucking.

Chapter 43

A TIME FOR THANKSGIVING

"Well, Tuck, hasn't anyone fed you today?" said Babs as she poured food into Tuck's bowl. "I'm really absent-minded, Kitty. Harry wants me to re-do the orange bit on his hunting jacket, and I can't locate my pincushion anywhere. Soon, George will wake up, and I won't be able to work on it."

"What's this?" asked Harry, appearing in the kitchen with his empty coffee cup. "What are you saying about me?"

"I've been trying to get at your hunting jacket. But I can't find my pin cushion."

Harry finished pouring his cup of coffee, set it on the dinette table, and started looking for the pincushion.

"Do you remember where you had it last?"

"I usually have it beside me on the davenport when I'm mending. Sometimes I sit in your chair to work, other times, I mend socks in bed."

Soon, Harry returned with the lost article.

"Oh, thanks, Dear. Where did you find it?"

"On the floor under the bed."

"Oh, thanks," she said, kissing him. "Now I have no excuse for not working on your jacket."

Pouring herself a cup of coffee, she brought it along with her workbasket and the jacket, and sat at the davenport to begin the project.

"The orange cloth is half off. I'm going to have to do a lot of stitching to make it right."

"Thank you, Honey. Oh, I got a phone call this morning from John Waukowski."

"You did?"

"He said that Sterling voted to give me a three-dollar raise."

"It's not much, but better than nothing."

"I guess Rosebud will stay the same."

"Do you think Prairie Meadows will do any more?"

"I don't know. Some people want to, but Bill Collins says that since they're providing the parsonage, they are doing more than their share."

"I suppose the expensive wall paper I chose came up."

"I doubt it."

Babs re-threaded her needle.

"By the way, when do you plan to go hunting?

"I'll go out Tuesday and Wednesday, and Thanksgiving morning if I haven't got a deer by then."

"Hope it won't be too cold."

"Don't worry about the cold. My jacket and boots are nice and warm," he said, closing the door and climbing the stairs to his study.

Babs tuned the radio to classical music, keeping it soft, so that she could hear George in the nursery. There was nothing much to see out the window. Bob Rennick went by, delivering their mail and walking down toward Mac's house. She spied Henry Perkins walking up the path to the front door.

"Hello, Mrs. Petersen," he said, as he walked in. "Are you working on Christmas presents?"

"No, this is Harry's hunting jacket."

"Wow! That's a big one. Takes lots of stitches, don't it?"

"Sure does. Do you hunt deer, Mr. Perkins?"

"No, I used to. Now I leave it to the younger guys, like the Rev."

"Will you be home for Thanksgiving?"

"Yes, my daughter Nell is roasting a goose. The whole family will be here. How about you?"

"Alberta has asked us to join them. I'm making pumpkin pies."

"Sounds good. Goodbye, Mrs. Petersen," and Henry walked through the dinette and kitchen, leaving by the back door.

At that moment, she heard George and brought him to the play pen next to the davenport, where he looked over his toys, rolling from his back to tummy.

She had stitched a few inches when Harry came down stairs, in time to answer the front door. A young high school boy stood at the front door holding a dilapidated Milwaukee Beer cardboard box.

"Are you Rev. Petersen?" the young man asked.

"Yes, I am," he answered. "May I help you?"

"No," he said. "Here's some stuff for you."

"Who are you, by the way?"

"James Barry, student body vice president of Prairie High."

"Your dad is the owner of *The Banner*?"

"Yes," he said abruptly.

"For us? What is it?"

"Oh, some cans and things that the high school kids collected for needy people. We do this at Thanksgiving. Here, take this."

Harry simply stood there, his mouth open, not comprehending the situation. Puzzled, Babs rose from her seat and joined him at the door. She saw an embarrassed youngster, trying to deliver a tattered Milwaukee Beer box.

"Are you Mrs. Petersen?" he asked.

"Yes."

"Take this, and have a nice Thanksgiving?"

The boy was fairly running down the walk to a green pick-up, parked at the curb.

"Oh, well, uh, thank you," began Harry.

The boy was gone.

"What is it?" Babs asked, looking into the box. "Let's put it on the dinette table, so we can see what's in it."

Harry carried the box to the dinette, and she began to empty it onto the table. A sack of navy beans, and cans of milk substitute, corn, chicken soup, tomato soup, tuna, sauerkraut, bottles of catsup and molasses, pancake mix, a pound of lard, and a bag of dog food had been collected. There was no card, no fruit, nor any sign of greetings or well-wishes.

Babs was devastated.

"Is this how the community feels about us?"

Harry was speechless. Putting the things back in the box, Babs stowed it in the corner.

"I guess I'll get dinner on," she said.

After dinner, Harry sat in his chair, holding his son. Coming out of his shock at receiving a "poor box," he tried to focus on preparing for deer hunting, as he watched his wife painstakingly re-sewing the orange cloth onto his hunting jacket.

"Why do you suppose they picked us to receive that miserable box of groceries?" he asked.

"I suppose they know we are poor."

"I still can't believe you and I got a charity box from the school. I grew up in a middle class family. We gave to others. We never received charity,"

"My family was the same, Harry. My parents would die if they found out that you and I got food collected for the poor."

"Do you think the high school children and grandchildren of the families in our church heard about the poverty of the minister's family?"

"I don't know. Maybe they got our name from some one. Maybe some one who wanted us to feel humiliated."

"Do you think so?"

"Could be, Harry. In a way, it's kind of funny."

"Funny?"

"You and I have always been on the giving end of things. Now we know how it feels to be on the receiving end."

"It's not so good, huh? Is that what it means: *It's more blessed to give than to receive*?"

Putting down her needle for a moment, she rested her chin in her hand.

"In my home church, if a family were down on their luck, they would be given things like ham, sweet potatoes, and fruit, and everything would be packaged attractively. I wonder if that made it any more palatable."

"Some day, Babs, we will probably be in a position to help some one. Maybe it's important that we know how it feels."

"Do you suppose this unfortunate, painful incident might bring us some understanding?"

"Don't know," he answered, as he watched George chewing on a wooden block.

"I have a serious question for you, Harry."

"What is it?"

"About that dog food, do you think Tuck will eat it?"

Chapter 44

LONELY AT CHRISTMAS

Entering the kitchen, Harry brought in a cold gust of air. Stamping his feet and removing his brown gloves, he vigorously rubbed his fingers together.

"You've been gone all morning," she said. "Come in, and get warm."

Harry took off his overcoat, earmuffs, and boots.

"Peter Wilkins passed away this morning."

"Oh, no. How did it happen?"

"Sudden heart attack. Elsie feels utterly forsaken. They had no children, and Peter took care of everything. A wealthy woman, she is alone. I must see her, this afternoon."

"Peter Wilkins died. I'm sorry. They were a lovely couple."

"I mailed your package of gifts to California!"

"Thanks, Honey," she said as he bent to kiss her and George. "That's a load off my mind."

"What are you feeding my son?" asked Harry, glancing at the small bottle of baby food.

"This is beef. He really likes it."

While his mother hesitated, George opened his mouth eagerly.

"George loves cereal the most, but meat comes in a close second."

"What else are you giving him?"

"I always give him vegetables along with the meat. Among the vegetables, he seems to like squash and green beans the best."

"Has he had cereal today?"

"No, remember? I give him that in the evening. I think it helps him to sleep longer during the night. By the way, how was the Businessmen's Association meeting?"

"Oh, very good. We had a guest, Fay Seevers."

"Oh, she runs the Express business. I got acquainted with her when that lovely, pink, china basket was broken enroute from California. She is a very attractive middle-aged woman, but she seems lonely."

"She doesn't seem to have any friends."

"Do you think some of the businessmen's wives will be jealous when they find out their husbands lunched with Fay?"

Harry shrugged as he sank into his chair.

"Harry," said Babs, following him into the living room, "It's starting to snow, the soft fluffy snow which makes everything so beautiful!"

He looked across to the davenport where George was nursing in his mother's arms, and beyond through the window behind them, where he could see the soft, white flakes slowly falling.

"It is beautiful," he acknowledged, opening the current issue of the magazine, *Pulpit Digest*.

That afternoon, while George was napping and Harry visiting the widow of Peter Wilkins, Babs worked on her hand-drawn Christmas cards. A small church in a snow scene was the subject. Because of the expense of three-cent stamps, she had resolved to make only fifty.

"You'd be smart to make a few extra," her husband had counseled.

"You're right," she acknowledged with a sigh.

The phone rang, and Mrs. Galvin was on the line.

"We haven't seen you for ages. Edgar and I are attending the Christmas concert at the college in Stevens Point next Friday night. We'd love to have you come with us. Do you think you could make it?"

"That sounds like fun. Let me think. I'll check with Harry and with Nell Perkins who gave me my Christmas present already—a pledge to baby sit George one night during the season. If both she and Harry have the night free, we'd love to go with you."

Later that afternoon, she was able to call and tell the Galvins they were free.

"We want you to come have dinner with us. Bring George along, and you can take him over to Nell's after dinner."

"Are you sure, Mrs. Galvin?"

"Certainly! Come at 6:00. We'll plan on that!"

"Thank you. It sounds festive."

That evening, Harry sat in his chair quietly, thinking about lonely people at Christmastide, like Fay Seevers, a successful business woman without friends, and Elsie Wilkins, a wealthy widow with no family. To Harry, it was ironic that at the time of year where the birth of the Christ Child was celebrated, many people felt sad, or even depressed. Silently, he began to pray:

"Eternal Father, I believe that Thou art loving and kind, that Thou art a Savior Who actively seeks all mankind for Thy heavenly family."

He looked over at his wife, who had laid aside the socks she was mending and was nursing their baby.

"As I visit the people, Heavenly Father, help me to be the instrument of Thy Peace and Love."

Looking out at a lone streetlight beside the church, he saw in the soft, gently falling flakes, a symbol of the grace of God covering ugliness, poverty, and loneliness.

"Bless us all, especially those who feel bereft at this season," was his silent prayer.

Chapter 45

WAUKEGAN HERE WE COME

"George looks flushed," said Harry's mother. "Is he running a fever?"

"Yes, but Harry insisted we come here to Grandma's," answered Babs, cuddling George on Grandma Petersen's sofa.

"I want to hold him, Babs," said her sister-in-law.

"Of course, Maxine. He's been cranky though," replied Babs handing the baby to his aunt.

George would have none of it, and cried until he was back in his mother's arms. Maxine shrugged and left the room to supervise her daughters.

"Louise, are you two still worrying about that baby?" asked Aunt Lila as she walked by on her way to the kitchen.

Babs said nothing. Harry's aunts, Lila, Beatrice, and Frances, had never had children. However, since they had cared for many nieces and nephews, they felt they knew how to manage a baby. Taking George into Frank and Frances' bedroom, she nursed him again, and he fell into a restless sleep.

Returning to the living room with George, she greeted Harry's cousin, Julie, and Harvey, who had visited them last year. The family were talking and laughing, and Harry was deep in conversation with his Uncle Arnold, eleven months his senior. As usual, Arnold was giving advice. This time, he was giving tips on how to manage uncooperative parishioners like Bill Collins. Arnold, who had vowed he would never take a church in a big city, at present, was pastor, of a church on the north side of Chicago.

On Christmas Eve, they sang Christmas carols with Aunt Frances at the piano, Uncle Marvin read the Christmas story, and the presents were distributed. Finally, Grandma and the "girls" repaired to the kitchen. With the large family, they served in shifts, starting with the youngest. Arnold and his family along with Roy and his family were served first.

Mel, being the oldest son, was served on the third shift. George began to fuss and cry. Babs and Louise left the table, trying to placate the baby, but George was inconsolable. Finally, as the baby continued to fuss, Arnold, passing through the dining room, took notice.

"Harry, your baby seems to be running a temperature. He needs a doctor."

"He does have a red face," responded Beatrice.

Lila felt the baby's forehead.

"I wonder if he has a fever," she said.

At that moment, Uncle Marvin, who had already eaten, came into the dining room. He saw his mother and sisters and Mel and Harry enjoying the feast, while Babs stood rocking George.

"What's up with that baby of yours, Harry?"

"He's been crying a lot, Marvin."

"He acts like he's sick, Harry," pronounced Uncle Marvin.

"Maybe you're right, Marvin," said Harry, reluctantly leaving his second piece of pumpkin pie. "I wonder if I could get a hold of my doctor friend, Don."

"Don will be at his aunt's here in town," said Grandma Petersen. "The family always gathers there on Christmas."

Harry phoned Don who came over immediately. The young physician hurriedly greeted the family and examined the fussing infant.

"He is definitely running a fever. I'll phone in a prescription for George. You will have to give him the medicine every four hours throughout the night," advised the doctor. "Although his fever is pretty high, with this medicine, he should be all right,

Babs. If there is any problem, call me. Here's the number where you can reach me."

Touched and relieved by Don's compassion, Babs's eyes filled with tears. With a last look at the baby, Don gave Babs a friendly squeeze of the hand and his card, and left to rejoin his own family celebration.

After Harry got the medicine, Mel and Louise, Harry, Babs, and George, left for Mel's home in Aurora.

"How is he?" asked Harry as he turned the car southwest toward Aurora.

"He quieter, but I'm worried, about him, Harry."

Mel and Louise had a surprise for them. When the mill had transferred Mel from Waukegan, he and Louise had rented a house. However, they had purchased land, and Mel had decided to build a house. They knew that he had laid the foundation and enclosed the house. The surprise was that he had already constructed the garage, and he and Louise were now living in it.

Arriving at the garage, made cozy with Louise's paintings and crocheting touches, they decided that the men would sleep in the house, and the women would sleep in the garage, taking turns getting up in the night to take care of the baby. And so it was.

The next morning, Mel and Harry entered the garage to find two tired but happy women, for George's fever had broken!

"I wouldn't have had George get sick for anything," observed Louise later. "But, in a way, it was a happy event, because I was there to help. George is my beloved grandson, and Babs is now indeed my daughter."

Chapter 46

ICY JANUARY

"Boy, it's cold," said Babs, hurrying back into the house.

"When it's clear and bright with full sunshine, you always get fooled, don't you?" he remarked.

"Yes. In California, when you look out the window at weather like this, it's warm. But, here, I can see my breath, and feel the chill in the air."

She shivered, poured another cup of coffee, and petted Tuck who began to purr loudly.

"You're a nice cat, but it's too bad you don't like dog food. I wonder what we should do with all the dog food that was in that charity box. Harry, what are you going to do today?" she asked.

"I'll be studying this morning. This afternoon, remember, I have a funeral, Dick James' father, Pete James."

"Oh, yes, he suffered with that cancer, didn't he?"

"Yes. He surely did."

"I'll never forget that evening we spent with Dick and Freda. You brought your violin, she played the cello, I, the piano, and Dick and Pete and the children sang. Dick's Dad enjoyed that. Maybe after a while, I'll invite them here for dinner."

"We'll see. Dick's pretty broken up right now."

"How about a kiss before you go upstairs? I won't be seeing much of you today."

After a hug and kiss, Harry opened the door and started up the stairs.

"You stepped over that mail and stuff I put on the stairs. Please take them up with you," she said.

Harry wrinkled his nose, but grabbed the "stuff" she handed him.

That afternoon she wrote thank-you notes for the Christmas gifts from their congregations. The thank-you's for California and Illinois had already been mailed. However, in the interest of economy, she decided to hand out her notes to local people, rather than mail them.

That evening, dinner was over early, and Harry settled into his chair with George.

"I wonder if George is going to have curly hair."

"He has so little yet, it's hard to tell."

Babs turned on the radio for classical music, got her work basket, took her customary place on the davenport, and started mending a sock for Harry. She loved to watch Harry as he cuddled the baby.

"Does your camera have film in it?" she asked.

"Yes. Why?"

"I'm enjoying this rare evening at home. I want to take a picture of you and George."

"My camera is in our clothes closet," he said.

Returning to the living room, Babs caught a moment of father/son delight on film.

"Do you see a light over at the church?" he asked.

"I'm not sure. Oh, there does seem to be a faint light."

"I wonder who's there."

Harry got up, brought George to his mother, and started putting on his jacket.

"I think I'll check that out," he said. "My flashlight is right here."

"Be careful, Dear," she said as he strode out the front door and down the walk to the church.

She watched him cross the road by the streetlight next to the church. It appeared that the storm doors to the cellar were open. She saw him following the flashlight into the basement. Twenty minutes passed, and she became increasingly anxious.

"I wonder who's over there and what they want. It's only an unfinished cellar with a furnace and kindling in the corner. Okay,

George, you want some cereal, huh? I'll fix it for you," and she brought him into the kitchen.

George was eagerly devouring his cereal when Harry returned. Dressed in a jacket with orange pieces half on and half off, his shoes muddy from the road, and wearing an expression of infinite sadness, he was a picture of dejection.

She looked at him sympathetically.

"Dear, who was there?"

"Bill Collins and his sons, Greg and Larry, and his son-in-law, Doug."

"Those young fellows never come to church. What are they doing over there?"

"Bill said he was tired of seeing no progress in our church. They are digging out the basement to use as a storage area."

"No one else is involved?"

"I guess not."

"Did they ask you to help?"

"They don't want my help. They were laughing, and acting superior."

"And you said Doug was there? He must be between sessions at seminary right now."

"Yes. He and Carrie are here in town."

"Last time they came to see us."

"Doug has changed. He isn't friendly any more. He even asked if we were using the budget book he and Carrie gave us for Christmas. Said they hadn't gotten a thank-you note from you. The guys all laughed when he said that."

"Oh, Honey, I'm sorry. They were poking fun at my custom of sending thank-you notes?"

He nodded.

"We know that Bill and his family aren't the only ones who care about the church, Harry."

"He is trying to shame the rest of the church, especially me."

Babs lifted George out of his high chair.

"Why don't we go back to the living room while George nurses. Pull down the shades in there, will you?" she asked.

Soon Harry was sitting in his chair, and George was in his mother's arms, nursing. Same room, same people, but a changed atmosphere.

Babs was silent. The only sound was the strains of Beethoven's Sixth Symphony from the radio. Finally, Harry spoke.

"The Collins' feel superior. They are so cold. Colder than the weather around here. With an attitude like that, how can anyone expect the church to grow?"

Beethoven's music filled the room.

"I don't know what to do. Nobody at seminary talked to us about how to handle a situation like this."

Babs' eyes filled with tears, as George fell asleep in her arms.

"I just don't know. What can I do?"

Harry sat in his chair a long time with his head in his hands.

Abruptly, he looked up, a faint smile on his face.

"You know what?"

She shook her head.

"I will call a meeting of the trustees!"

Chapter 47

FAREWELL TO FARMING

"What a nippy day! At least these stadium boots keep my feet warm!" thought Babs, walking briskly to town.

Ducking hastily into the Five and Dime Store on Main Street, she glimpsed owner Michael at his desk in the back room. His wife, Marion, was working on inventory.

"My, how do they have the patience to keep track of all these fussy, little things they sell?" she thought, selecting a box of paper clips and string for mailing.

"I always wondered why Mom always kept a ball of string in her kitchen. I should start saving string," she thought.

"Is this all you want today?" asked Marion as she rung up the sale.

"Yes. I'm mailing my brother's birthday package."

"Are you coming to the Culture Club, Babs?"

"I think so. What's the program?"

"We are having Brad Green show his slides from Alaska."

"Oh, that's right. Didn't he grow up around here?"

"Yes, he did. He claims it's colder around here in winter than in Anchorage. I hope you can make the meeting."

Babs smiled.

"I'll be there unless Harry is tied up and can't take care of the baby," she said as Marion put the money in the cash register.

"Let's hope your husband has a free evening," answered Marion, handing her the package.

Outside, Babs looked across the street at Bob Clark's Prairie Meadows Market. Through the window, she saw Margaret re-stocking shelves. She looked up and waved a greeting.

"People in town are friendly, and our parishioners are, too. But since Bill Collins walked out and his wife and her crony, Mrs. Blodgett, are against us, I feel there's a tug of war going on. Instead of our working together to build up the church and serve the community, people have to declare whether they're for or against Harry and me. I hate our becoming the issue," thought Babs as she walked into The Friendly Market.

"What can I do for you today, Babs?" asked Gary from behind the meat counter.

"Meat is expensive now. I think I'll get a can of Spam and fix it like you suggested with cloves and jam."

"Broccoli is a good buy today. Does Rev. like it?"

"Yes, he does. That's a good suggestion, Gary."

On the way home she greeted newspaperman, Jim Barry, Pat Riley of the IGA, and Pricilla Woods, who looked upbeat in a new jacket.

"Everybody acts friendly, but I feel alienated."

An old pick-up was parked in front of the house. As she walked into the kitchen, she heard people in the living room.

"You have definitely decided on an auction, Clara?" Harry was asking.

"We don't see what else we can do. Harvey isn't well enough to work the farm. Frank Waukowski would like to lease it. We'll sell all the equipment but live in the house. If we're careful, we ought to be able to manage. We'll keep a cow and some chickens, which I can handle."

"Here's, Babs," he said, as she came into the living room. "Clara has been telling me that Harvey has to give up farming."

"Pastor will tell you all about it. I have to go now."

"We just wanted to let you know about the sale. Bye," said Clara as she walked out to her pick-up.

"There goes a plucky woman," said Harry. "Farming has been their way of life.

The morning of Harvey and Clara's auction dawned bright and clear. Harry left early to attend.

"I'm not in a position to buy anything," he said. "But I want to be there for them."

"God bless you," she said, giving him a hug and a kiss.

"Let me hold George for a minute," he said. "He may be asleep when I get home tonight."

Sure enough, it was dark when Harry returned. He found Tuck waiting at the kitchen door to come in. Babs had set aside a plate of food for Harry. He kissed her and wearily took his place at the table, observing the cat, playing with a stray candy wrapper, which had just fallen out of his pocket.

"I had a sandwich, but your stew looks tasty."

"Was there a big crowd? Did it go well?" she asked.

"Pretty good. They got enough so they can buy a refrigerator, and a range to supplement their wood stove."

"Oh, they are planning to buy two appliances?"

"Yes they are. Clara said that some people are criticizing their purchases, but since they are never going to have that much money again, she feels this is their chance to get these things."

"Good for her. No matter what she and Harvey do, some one will criticize. She is doing what she thinks is best, regardless of what others say."

"H-m-m-m. Does that apply to ministers and their families?"

"I guess so, Harry. I need courage right now."

"What you need is a good hug. Come here."

He took her into his arms, and Babs leaned against him contentedly. Holding her away from him for a moment, Harry looked at her intently.

"I saw Father Kelly down town yesterday. He asked me when you were going to practice the Hammond Organ again."

"Maybe I could practice tomorrow. It would get my mind off things. What a great idea!"

Chapter 48

THE PRAIRIE MEADOWS TRUSTEES
MEET

Fred Young and Herb Dodds were first to arrive at the parsonage for the meeting. Fred set his huge, black umbrella to drip on the throw rug by the door. Herb Dodds, who had dashed across the street from his upstairs apartment, hung his raincoat in the hall closet. Mac arrived next, wearing an old, black coat, which Herb hung up for him. Last of all, Arthur Smith, recently baptized, came in with Tim.

"These ought to be dry by the time we need them," said Art as he carefully hung up Tim's and his jackets. "We don't expect rain like this in the middle of winter."

Fred, looked around the group, before taking up the business at hand.

"Pastor says that Bill Collins and the boys have started working evenings over in the church."

"What are they doing over there?" asked Tim.

"They decided to enlarge the basement," answered Harry.

"By themselves? They just started digging?" questioned Mac.

"Apparently," replied Harry.

"Well, probably 'cause I'm a new trustee I shouldn't say anything—"

"Go ahead, Art. What's on your mind?" replied Fred.

"When you asked me to become a trustee, Alberta, my wife, said that the trustees are in charge of the property. Is that correct?"

"Alberta told you right," rejoined Fred.

"If that's correct, why are they doing that when we are the ones in charge?" asked Art.

"That's a good question," said Tim. "Why are they digging, without checking with us?"

"I say they don't want our opinion!" said Mac shaking his bald head.

"What do you think, Pastor?" asked Fred.

"As trustees, you have been making improvements and operating on a business-like basis."

"We've been holding regular meetings and operating on a budget," said Fred.

"We opened a bank account, and Mrs. Rankin pays the bills in an orderly fashion," added Tim.

"We mended the front steps—" reminded Art.

"We fixed the leak in the baptistery," added Mac.

"We are getting the pews refinished. They really needed it!" said Fred.

"You talked things over, set goals, and carried them out," said Harry.

"So, maybe Bill Collins doesn't like what we are doing," mused Tim.

A silence settled over the group.

"The way it used to be, Bill Collins and his wife, Jane, always had their way around here," said Herb Dodds, speaking for the first time.

The men all turned to stare at Dodds, who reddened under their gaze.

"They did, didn't they?" said Fred. "They called the shots."

He paused.

"Well, what are we going to do about this basement business?"

"I guess we should decide whether it's a worth-while project or not," said Tim thoughtfully.

"Do we need the space?" Mac inquired.

"It would allow more room for storage of the long tables we use for potluck suppers," said Fred.

"We could get to the furnace easier if we have to," contributed Tim.

"We could store extra chairs there," added Dodds reluctantly, hating to endorse a Collins' idea.

"No use to turn down Bill's plan, if it's a good one," stated Fred.

"Fred, do you want to entertain a motion that the trustees adopt the basement project?" asked Harry.

"Who wants to make a motion?" asked Fred.

"I will. I move we take on digging out a basement under the church," said Tim.

"I second it," said Mac.

Though unskilled at parliamentary procedure, Fred was true to its spirit, recognizing that they were all in agreement.

"Well, that's decided," he said.

"Now, who's going to talk to Collins about this?" asked Tim.

"Since I'm the chairman of the trustees, it's my place," said Fred. "And before I see him, we need to decide when we want to get together to work. Tuesday nights or Saturdays are all right for me."

Unwilling to be bypassed by the Collins family, and fortified by the Babs' weak coffee, the trustees made up a work schedule, to be read during the announcement period at the next Sunday service.

Fred was the last to leave. He stood for a moment at the front door.

"Pastor," he said, "I feel good about what we decided. And it's good to see a young man like Art, taking an interest in the business of our church."

With a cordial handshake, Fred said good-by.

Harry shared with Babs his happiness at the response of the trustees, and began to hum *The Old Rugged Cross* as he got ready for bed. As she was slipping into her long flannel nightie, Harry came over to give her another hug.

"Tonight, you know what Fred called me, Honey?"

"Rev?"

"No, better than that," chuckled Harry. "He called me, 'Pastor!'"

Chapter 49

ZION VISIT

"Lord, for what we are about to partake, let us be truly grateful. Amen," said Frank.

"Pass the mashed potatoes and gravy to Harry, Beatrice," said Grandma Petersen from her place at the head of the large dining room table.

"Here you are, Harry," answered Beatrice with a smile. "It's so nice to have you and Barbara and the baby staying overnight with us. With Mel and Louise no longer living in town, we miss seeing the rest of our family."

Harry began to load his plate.

"Lefty still lives in Waukegan. He comes by sometimes, doesn't he?" he asked, passing the now lighter bowl of mashed potatoes to Babs.

"Oh, yes, your brother stops by," answered Lila. "Maxine and the girls and the new baby come, too. Lefty, though, is pretty quiet."

"You're going to let the baby have some of the dinner, aren't you, Barbara?" inquired Grandma.

"Yes, George can have mashed potatoes with a little gravy, and he can handle carrots if I mash them."

"Good," said Grandma approvingly. "He would like my stuffing, too."

"I'm sure he would, but I'd rather let him try one of your delicious rolls."

Grandma Petersen wrinkled her nose.

"My stuffing is not rich. He could eat it with no problem."

Babs said nothing but offered no stuffing to the baby.

"Are you still nursing George?" asked Frances.

"Yes, I am, Aunt Frances."

"The baby looks very healthy," said Beatrice. "You should feel proud of him."

"Thank you, Aunt Beatrice!" she returned, her face lighting up with appreciation.

Grandma had been staring at the baby for quite a while.

"Harry," she remarked, "your son appears to have an eye problem."

"An eye problem?" asked Harry. "What do you mean?"

Babs' expression darkened, as she turned, staring intently at the older woman.

"Haven't you observed that his eyes don't always track together? Sometimes one or the other pupil appears lazy."

"No, we haven't seen that, Grandma, and Dr. Sutherland has never mentioned such a thing, either!" returned his mother with spirit.

"Maybe he's waiting until George is a little older. Nothing can be done at this age, anyway."

Babs' eyes filled with tears.

"Please excuse me. I need to nurse the baby," she said, as she rose and took George upstairs to a bedroom.

"Now, Mother, see what you've done! She's all upset. The baby's eyes look fine to me!" exclaimed Lila.

"In time you'll see I'm right. Harry, you'll need to take that baby to a specialist, one of these days."

Later on in the evening as they were driving to see Harry's doctor friend, Don, Babs was crying in earnest.

"I'm running out of handkerchiefs!" she said, wiping her eyes. "Why did your grandmother say that about George's eyes? I don't see a problem, you don't see a problem, and neither does Dr. Sutherland! Probably Frank and Frances and Beatrice don't see it either. No one stands up to Grandma Petersen!"

"You may be right. But Grandma didn't mean anything by what she said."

"What do you mean? She was angry because I didn't give George any of her stuffing!"

"Babs, I don't think—"

"That's right! You don't think! Why do you always take the opposite side when I'm having a disagreement with anyone? Grandma is very bossy. She has no right to tell us how to bring up our baby!"

She blew her nose and wiped her eyes.

"Harry, do you have an extra hankie?"

"Yes, take this one," he said, handing her a white handkerchief.

As the tears flowed, Harry wisely said nothing. After a while, Babs stopped weeping and looked out the car window.

"Where are we? This looks like the country. Aren't we going to visit Don?"

"Yes, we're out of the city, and on our way to Zion, where Don's set up his practice."

"Zion? How far is that from Waukegan?"

"Not far at all. We're almost there."

"You sly dog! You didn't tell me that we were going out of town. I'm glad I insisted on bringing George."

"It's just a little way."

Soon Harry pulled up in front of a home in a modest neighborhood, and they got out of the car. Harry carried George, who had fallen asleep. The houses were lighted, and up and down the street, curtains were drawn.

"I had forgotten that city people like to close their drapes at night," she remarked, as they waited on the porch.

Don came to the door and welcomed them with quiet warmth into the living room where Gladys greeted them.

"Would you like to put George down in a bedroom?" she asked.

"Yes, I would," answered Babs.

"We are expecting in May. Why don't you put him down in our crib?"

"Thank you, Gladys," she replied, following the hostess.

Smiling, as she laid George in the crib, she said, "George will be comfortable here."

"Would you like a cup of coffee?" asked Gladys.

"I'd love one. May I help you?"

Soon the women rejoined the men in the living room.

"Where does your town get its name, Don?" asked Babs as she settled into the davenport, noticing that the sofa and chairs looked used, and remembering that she'd heard, some time ago, that Don's and Gladys' new furnishings had been reclaimed by the store, and they now had to get by with furniture borrowed from a relative.

"Zion refers to the heavenly city, spoken of in the Bible," said Gladys.

"Is it a religious city?"

"It was founded by a man named Volava, who called himself a prophet of God," stated Don.

"He took the Bible literally, and the colony lived by very strict rules," added Gladys.

"Didn't he teach that the Earth is flat, and Zion is the center of the universe?" asked Harry.

"That's right. You should hear some of the older people around here who can come up with lots of arguments against our earth being round," said Don.

"You asked if it were a religious city. Each spring the Zion Church puts on a passion play. It's a real production! But," said Gladys, "the city has become secular. They even have doctors, like Don, living in the town."

"That's right! The original colony did not believe in doctors, did they?" marveled Harry.

"No," answered Don. "They believed only in divine healing."

"To go to a doctor showed a lack of faith," remarked Gladys.

The evening went by quickly as Babs and Gladys got acquainted, and Harry and Don renewed their friendship. At ten o'clock, Harry glanced at his watch.

"We must get up early tomorrow to drive back to Wisconsin," he said, reluctantly finishing his third cup of coffee.

"Your day starts very early, doesn't it, Don?" inquired Babs.

"Yes, I have hospital rounds early and office hours until after five."

"Do you make house calls?" asked Harry.

"Very seldom. Doctors, these days, are too busy for that."

George was sleeping when Babs went to pick him up. He stirred but did not awaken.

"Thank you for a lovely evening," she said as they stood by the front door.

"Those cupcakes were delicious, Gladys," added Harry.

"They were from Don's favorite bakery," said Gladys. "I hate to cook."

"Goodbye, you two. Come see us when you come to Wisconsin," declared Babs.

"We may do that one of these days," answered Don.

On the way back to Grandma's, both were deep in thought. Babs was thinking about the people who settled Zion, who believed that the earth was flat, and that God healed only through faith.

Harry, on the other hand, was thinking about George, whose eyes looked normal to him. Was it possible that Grandma's sharp eyes saw something that they had missed? Putting that unpleasant thought aside, he said to himself, "Grandma must be seeing things."

Chapter 50

APRIL WEDDING PLANS

"Rev. Petersen, this is Harley Connors, my fiancé," said Emma Waukowski, blushing prettily, as they stood on the front porch of the parsonage. Harry surveyed the young couple. The red-headed young man looked uncomfortable in a starched white shirt, pulling nervously at his plaid tie. In contrast, Emma appeared calm.

"Hello, Emma. Glad to meet you, Harley," said Harry, shaking hands. "Won't you come in? I like to have a talk with young people before I marry them."

They seated themselves awkwardly on the shabby davenport as Harry had indicated.

"Emma's mother, Molly, tells me that you two plan to marry soon."

"That's right," replied Harley, his blue eyes resting tenderly on Emma, with her curving figure and long, brown hair, which fell in soft waves to her shoulder.

"Isn't Emma young to be marrying you?" asked Harry.

"No," stammered Harley, "she graduated from high school in January. We've been going together for a couple of years."

"How will you support her?" asked Harry.

"My folks have a farm near Rosebud. Dad is getting older, I help him, and some day the farm will be mine."

"Will you live with your folks?" asked the minister.

"No, I live in the old farm house. Dad and Mom built a new place about a half mile away some time ago, and I've been by myself for a while."

The phone rang, and Harry rose to answer it.

"Hello? . . . Oh, hello, Mother. How are you? . . . No, she's out shopping just now. . . . Oh, George is fine. He's taking a nap. . . . What does he do these days? He loves to eat, especially cereal and baby meat. . . . More active? Yes, he likes to crawl around the house. . . . He's got three teeth now and two more ready to come through. . . . Babs says nursing is sometimes uncomfortable. . . . Yes, we got that cartoon you sent about the bride's cooking. Babs cooks better all the time. . . . Do you want her to call you? . . . No? . . . Okay, let's see, this is Saturday. She will definitely be home by seven o'clock. . . . Yes, that would be five o'clock, California time. . . . Thanks for calling. Give our love to Dad and brother, Al. . . . Yes, she *will* be here at seven. . . . Bye."

Harry returned to his chair, to go ahead with his marital counseling.

"Emma and Harley, I always tell young people that when they marry, they marry the whole family."

Later on, Babs arrived home with her groceries, in time to see Emma and "her young man" leaving.

"How did the counseling go?" she asked.

"They seemed to listen well. She's very young—"

"But she's been preparing a long time to be married. When we were at her folk's home for the rib dinner, remember her lovely hope chest? For years, she's been laying away pillow cases, and table cloths and the like."

"Your mother phoned. She wants you to be here at seven o'clock tonight, so that she can talk to you."

"That's not a problem. We never go anywhere on Saturday nights. Oh, I hear George stirring. Did he sleep while I was gone?"

"Yes."

That night, as they prepared to retire, Babs, pink socks in hand, looked over at Harry.

"On the phone, Mom was begging us to come visit them this summer. Is there any way we could go?"

"Getting the time off may not be hard. Ministers often get a month off," replied Harry thoughtfully. "I would have to talk to each of the church boards about it."

"Mom said that they would take care of all expenses, while we are out there. But could we manage traveling back and forth from California?"

"We'd have to figure up to fifteen dollars a night at motels."

"I could make lunches along the way and could bring juice for the mornings. If we eat out along the way, we won't be able to afford desserts or drinks."

"We would have coffee in the morning. I can't get along without that."

"Okay. Your mother gave us a thermos. We could have that filled where we have breakfast."

"Good idea, Babs. Would you like to visit California?"

"Mother is really putting on the pressure. She wants to see us, and she wants to show George off to all her friends."

"But how do you feel?"

"I have mixed emotions. I'd love to be home and see the family and my high school and college chums. I'd like them to get acquainted with you."

"That would be nice."

"On the other hand, I'm concerned about our financial situation."

"Things have been a little better. Keeping the thermostat at 65 degrees helped keep the coal bill more in line."

"And I'm only serving coffee and no cake at meetings at the house, and not mailing thank-you notes but giving them out after church."

"I've been watching the gas consumption."

"And I have a few more piano pupils. We opened a bank account with the three hundred dollars people gave to George. Do you think we could put a couple of dollars aside each week and build up enough capital by the summer?"

"We can try."

Babs fumbled in her drawer and pulled out a handkerchief.

"I get nervous thinking about being home. Mother has high expectations for me. I can never be as good, or beautiful, or successful enough to please her."

She dabbed at her eyes, wiping away the tears.

"I get angry thinking about the way she treats you!"

"But she loves me! She just wants the best for me!"

"When she fusses at you, she is thinking of herself! She likes to complain to you. On the other hand, she loves to brag about all that you've done! She wants you to be perfect!"

"Harry, you're hard on Mother. She loves me a lot."

"Yes, but she wants you beside her, doing what she says!"

"That's true," she answered, blowing her nose. "But what she wants for me is good."

"What she wants is to dominate you. You have to learn to make your own decisions without feeling guilty if they are different from your Mother's plans!"

Babs sat on the bed. She had never thought of her mother in that light. She always felt, perhaps subconsciously, that her mother's opinions were right and hers were wrong. Whenever she had made a decision contrary to her mother's will, she suffered pangs of guilt. Didn't everybody feel guilty about "not minding your Mother?"

Two summers ago as she and her mother prepared for the wedding, Ruth emphasized that she and Al did not know Harry very well, nor did they entirely approve of him.

"After all your father and I have done for you, we deserve to have you near us, not two-thirds of a continent away. We are getting older, and we need you."

As they walked the streets of Oakland, selecting wedding invitations, planning the wardrobe for the wedding, consulting with the florist, selecting the wedding cake, and buying the trousseau, her mother talked and talked. While they made up the wedding list, selected a minister—Babs' pastor would be on vacation on the date of their wedding—and planned the wedding reception at the house, Ruth talked, and her daughter listened.

"Some day, not too soon I hope, you will have a family. Dad and I want to be able to drop by and see the children. If you are living in Wisconsin, how can we watch the children grow up? Parents want their only daughter living close by, so that they can be a part of her life and the lives of her children."

Babs began to wonder again if she were being selfish, first, to marry some one that her parents did not fully approve of, and, second, to settle two thousand miles away. She hated the thought that she was being selfish. She knew it was her duty to be kind. Yet, she had married a man her parents didn't know and had settled far away from them. The summer before she married, she had spent many sleepless nights, wondering if she should marry Harry.

When she was a child in Daily Vacation Bible School, one of the lessons was about JOY. To have <u>JOY</u>, you put <u>J</u>esus first, <u>O</u>thers second, and <u>Y</u>ourself last. That's <u>JOY</u>!

"Am I putting myself first?" she asked herself that summer. "Am I being self-centered? If I am, I will never have real joy! I'm so confused!"

There was one thing she knew, however. Harry really loved her. He wanted her by his side, to be his partner and his lover, while he answered the call to the ministry. In the end, the thought of Harry's love was stronger than all the arguments her mother could marshal, and she remained faithful to her commitment to marry him.

While she was, in her imagination, re-living the summer of 1947, Harry had been winding his watch, his final preparation before going to bed. He stared at her, as she was lost in thought. Suddenly, she smiled.

"You know, Harry, Emma is young in years, but, in a way, I think she is more prepared for marriage than I was. She knows how to cook and keep house, and, for quite a while, she has been making a lot of her own decisions."

"Yes, she has. And Harley has been living alone and making his own way. In spite of their youth, they are surprisingly mature. Emma, by the way, wants you to play the organ at their wedding."

"She does? I'd be thrilled! We'll have to find a babysitter for George. It will be a fun wedding, don't you think, Harry?"

Chapter 51

WISCONSIN IN THE SPRING

Since the middle of February, the letters from Babs' mother had been filled with glowing descriptions of fruit trees and bushes in full blossom. Crocuses and daffodils had bloomed and faded, and soon tulips would be out. Ruth wrote, "How I wish you were here with us to enjoy this beauty!"

Wisconsin! What a contrast! The white snow had given way to dirty slush and muddy streets. No flowering shrubs or plants of any kind. No green grass. Just mud, dirt, wind and chill. To Babs, accustomed to California's mild winter, the miserable weather seemed unnecessary. Not only ugly, cold weather was terribly expensive, though neither Harry nor George seemed to mind the elements. With the thermostat at 65 degrees, Babs wore warm underwear, drank hot tea, and kept busy.

Another blight on the season was hearing Mrs. Blodgett brag about her grandnephew, who was the same age as George. At nine months, her Paul was walking and talking, while George did neither.

"Harry," she said. "do you think George will be like my brother, Al, who didn't talk till he was almost three? Finally, when he spoke, we understood every word he said."

"Could be. George may be a little slow to start, but he's no dummy."

"More coffee?"

"Yes, thank you, dear," he said. "Good coffee this morning. Is it Hills Bros.?"

"Of course. Now, tell me about the board meetings," she said as she settled into the davenport. "Will the churches give you time off, so that we can go to California this summer?"

"Yes. Sterling and Prairie Meadows will give me a month of paid vacation."

"Oh, good! What about Rosebud?"

"Rosebud had a difference of opinion. The Jameses and Mrs. Eager wanted to give us the vacation, but Charlie and Geraldine Ross were opposed. Charlie reminded me that farmers never get a paid vacation. So, they released me, but without my $7.00 a week pay."

"Honey, do you think we can make it? I've been putting a couple of dollars aside each week."

"I hope so."

"Oh, I'm so excited! It seems like years since I've seen California!"

Harry rose from his chair and took her in his arms.

"Dearest, I know you've missed living in California, but your being here has meant everything to your lover."

"Harry, I love you with all my heart!"

In their tender intimate embrace, time stood still.

Suddenly, Babs saw a movement at the window. A man, his face pressed against the glass, was staring at them. Springing away, she saw it was Bill Collins!

He had seen their naked expression of love and desire! Feeling vulnerable, she fled to the bedroom, slamming the door. Working furiously, she made the bed and tidied up the room.

In the living room Bill's voice was loud and abrupt. Suddenly, it was quiet.

Soon, she heard a gentle knock. Babs opened the door and went straight into Harry's waiting arms. In the hall, no one could see them. She began to cry.

"What is it, Honey?" asked Harry.

"Didn't you see him at the window? It looked like he'd been spying on us for a long time."

"No, I didn't. Is that why you ran out of the room?"

"Yes," she said, wiping her eyes. "He is a mean, small man. I feel sorry for him. And we have to deal with him!"

"We've thwarted his plans. He can't stand it."

"Why did he come here?"

"Fred Young talked to him about the basement project. He said since it's a church project we all have to work together, and he showed Bill the work schedule from the trustees."

"Fred did that?"

"Yes, and Bill didn't like it. He is hitting me where it hurts!"

"What do you mean?"

"He told me that the Red Cross would no longer need my services in the Blood Bank program. I can bill them for mileage for this last month, and that's it!"

"He *is* a small, mean man," she repeated. "What do you think brought this on?"

"Evidently, he blames me for the action taken by the trustees."

"He's right about that. You have been pinpointing their duties and encouraging them to take charge, haven't you?"

"Yes, I have," he admitted.

"And so?"

Harry brightened.

"This is the first time Bill Collins has failed to get his way in the Prairie Meadows Church."

Chapter 52

EMMA GETS MARRIED

Harry had presided at many weddings. Most were small and held at a home, at the church, or in the parsonage. The Waukowski wedding, however, would be different. It promised to be the most elaborate wedding Harry had ever conducted.

Coming from a large family of aunts and uncles, Emma was marrying a Connors, another big family from Rosebud. Her attendants would include a maid of honor, five bridesmaids, a flower girl, and a ring bearer. Harley would have a best man and five ushers, including Emma's two brothers, John, Jr. and young Marvin.

After the wedding practice, fifty friends and relatives gathered with good-natural talk and laughter for the rehearsal dinner at the popular Augiers Restaurant in Wild Rose. Emma had sewn a satin slip for each of her attendants, and the groom gave tie clasps to his best man and the ushers. Marvin came to show his clasp to Babs, his piano teacher. She and Harry were seated at the head table with the bride and groom, their parents, and grandparents. Emma was flushed with excitement, while Babs observed that her mother, Molly, looked pale.

"Molly feels uncomfortable," whispered Babs to Harry. "but she loves Emma enough to go along with these elaborate plans. Harley's mom, however, is in her element. Isn't she pretty?"

Harry looked down the table at Mary Connors, with her short, strawberry blond hair, green eyes, and a sprinkle of freckles across her nose. She was laughing at a remark made by John Jr.— Emma's elder brother.

"Mary's having a good time."

The next day dawned clear and bright. Most of the slush had melted from the streets. The wedding was to be at 2:00 pm in the large Lutheran Church in Waupaca. Harry would have felt more at home with the wedding in Sterling, but the Sterling Church was too small. Emma not only wanted ample room for all the family and friends, but also craved a church with a center aisle as well.

On the day of the wedding at 12:30, at the parsonage, Harry was dressed and ready to go. He paced, as Babs finished nursing the baby and donned her familiar grey wedding suit.

"Harry, would you take George across to Nell Perkins? The diaper bag and baby food are on the dinette table. I'm almost ready."

Taking George over, he greeted Henry and Nell briefly. As he re-entered their home, Babs called out,

"Are you back, Honey? I forgot to send along George's toys— they're on the davenport."

"Does he really need them?"

"He'll be more contented if he has them."

Harry silently groaned but took the toys to the Perkins. Returning, he found her ready at last.

"I don't want to be late," he said as he eased the car onto the highway to Waupaca. "I've only been to that church once."

"Oh, John, Jr. drew a map for us. I forgot it. It's on the dinette table, dear."

Harry's face was grim as he turned the car around and returned to the house. As she raced to the back door, Babs almost stumbled over Mac, who was peeking into the kitchen. Unlocking the door, she rushed into the house, re-appearing five minutes later.

"I'm sorry I left the map. Lucky we came back. I'd left the wedding music on the piano."

"Have you forgotten anything else? Do you have your reading glasses?"

"Oh, dear, let me see," she answered, fumbling through her purse. "Yes, my glasses are here. Thanks, Honey."

Again they departed. To Harry's surprise, they arrived on time at the large, frame Lutheran Church. The parking lot was already half full. Babs found her way to the organ and selected the organ registration she'd chosen for the prelude. Harry went to the small room off the sanctuary where he found a jittery Harley with his brother, Allen, the best man. Allen was looking at the ring, entrusted to his care, while Harley, who'd just broken a shoelace, was tying his shoe.

"Are the girls here?" inquired Harry.

"Yes, they've been upstairs for hours," said Allen.

"I wish I could have seen Emma."

"Never mind, Harley. You'll see her every day from now on."

"Why won't they let a guy see his bride on the wedding day?"

"It's just a custom," said Harry, opening the door a crack and noting that the church by now was packed with excited wedding guests.

Organ music came from the sanctuary. Harley began silently pacing up and down the small room. Harry was tempted to join him, but concentrated on the recognizing some of the organ numbers—"Because," "I Love You Truly," and "Oh, Perfect Love." Following that, they heard Emma's cousin, Louise, sing "Bless this House."

Suddenly, the trumpet sounding from the organ announced the beginning of the "Wedding March."

"Follow me," said Harry shaking inside as he made his way to the front the sanctuary.

Looking back, he saw the best man behind him and said,

"The groom is supposed to follow me, and then the best man."

The brothers changed places, and they marched in.

The men watched as the ushers came to join them. Next, five young girls in pale blue dresses marched one by one down the aisle, followed by a tiny girl in pink and a boy in blue and a young woman in pale pink. The children stood uncertainly until the maid of honor held out her hand, and they came and stood by her. The trumpet announced the bridal procession. As the bride and her father appeared at the back of the sanctuary, Harley's eyes were fixed on Emma who smiled as she walked down the aisle on her father's arm,

The bridal party was at the altar, and all were looking at Harry. "Be seated," he said. "Dearly beloved—"

All were silent as he reverently began to read the Episcopalian marriage service. Suddenly, Harry panicked. He had forgotten their names!

"Do you, (What's your name?)--" he whispered to the groom.

Quiet titters were heard across the front of the church.

"Harley," the groom answered.

"Do you, Harley, take thee, (What's your name?)--" he whispered to the bride.

More titters extending back a way into the church.

"Emma," said the bride.

"Do you, Harley, take thee, Emma, to be thy lawfully wedded wife?"

Beads of perspiration formed on Harry's forehead and upper lip. He struggled on, through the preliminary vows.

"Who giveth this bride?" he asked.

John answered, "I do," and he handed his daughter to Harley and sat with his wife, as the circle of attendants and ushers came together.

The pastor continued to read, coming to the sacred vows.

"Say after me," he read to the groom, his mind again going blank, "I, (What's your name? he whispered)--"

The groom's jaw dropped as he repeated, "Harley."

The congregation was chuckling.

"I, Harley, take thee, (What's your name?)--"

"Emma," she responded.

By now, even those at the back of the church were aware of the situation and were smiling.

The young couple said their vows, reverently exchanging rings. Finally, Harry pronounced them man and wife.

Emma's cousin, Louise, stood up to sing "The Lord's Prayer." When she was finished, the couple looked at Harry expectantly.

Harry said to Harley, "You may kiss the bride."

Harley and Emma exchanged a nuptial kiss, and the organ trumpeted the joyful recessional. The congregation burst into loud talk, congratulations and good wishes, as the bride and groom marched triumphantly down the center aisle.

Harry stood at the front of the sanctuary, his smile belying his embarrassment. Concluding the organ recessional, the minister's wife, came down and stood beside him.

"It's awful! I messed up, sweetheart," he sighed.

"It wasn't awful. You did your best, they recited their vows, and everyone enjoyed the service."

"Do you think so?"

"Yes. Listen to that happy conversation from the narthex. People have already forgotten it."

He held her tight in the empty sanctuary.

"Do you know what I'm going to do next time?"

"Memorize their names?"

"Better than that. I can't trust my memory when I'm scared. I'll write their names in my wedding book!"

Chapter 53

ONE OF THOSE DAYS

Babs had given George his daily bath, dressed him, and settled him into his high chair.

"Oh, George, m-m-m-Abdec!" said his mother, getting out his vitamin drops.

George opened his mouth, ready to enjoy his delicious vitamins. Babs put the spoon with Abdec to his lips as she made sucking noises. As always, anticipating the delightful taste, George gulped down the drops. Having tasted Abdec, his mother felt a bit guilty at her pretence, but decided that the end justified the means. George always took his vitamins with alacrity, and he was a healthy baby.

She put some dry cereal flakes on his tray and started to heat water, placing his jars of baby beef and baby carrots in the water to warm. George carefully picked up one tiny flake and put it in his mouth.

"M-m-m--," he said.

"Oh, you want some more flakes?" asked his mother.

"M-m-m."

"Here you are."

George polished off the flakes and started to eat his baby food. With a random wave of his arms, his baby beef and spinach toppled over onto the floor. George surveyed the mess of brown and green on the floor.

"Ehr, ehr," he said.

Suppressing a sigh, Babs found a rag and wiped the food off the floor, and opened two more jars of food. After a while, George nursed, and settled into his crib for his morning nap.

As she returned to the kitchen to mop the floor, put away the baby things, and do the breakfast dishes, she heard Harry on the phone in the dinette, talking to a number of Red Cross volunteers in the county, explaining that he would no longer be directing the blood bank project.

Before tackling the dishes, she went down in the basement to get two frozen squirrels, which Harry had brought home from their frozen locker earlier.

"Squirrel for dinner tonight will be tasty," she said to herself, "and also a saving."

In her zeal to save money for the trip to California, Babs had served Spam twice last week. In the view of her husband's complaints, she was happy when he brought squirrels home from the locker.

"I'll surprise him," she said to herself, "and fix it with vegetables and serve it with brown sauce. He loves that!"

Soon she finished preparing the game and put it in the slow cooker in the stove.

"I wonder where my dear husband is going?" she said to herself, as she watched him back the car out of the garage and head toward town.

Returning to the bedroom, she glanced in the mirror. Still in her nightgown, her hair was wild and limp and with no make-up, she was pale. She had started to make the bed, when she saw her mother's last letter lying on the box beside their bed.

"She's really putting on the pressure to have us come to California. I'd better sit down this minute and tell her that we're coming," she thought.

After a diligent search, she located her pen and stationery. Finding the pen out of ink, she was rummaging through their closet for the jar of ink, when she heard a knock at the front door.

"Oh, who's that?" she groaned. "I look a fright!"

Quickly, she threw on her bathrobe and ran a comb through her hair, in a vain attempt to smooth it. Pinching her cheeks to make them a bit rosy, she reluctantly answered the knock.

At the front door stood the principal's wife, Adrianne Downing, striking in her black wool suit (at just the right length!) complete with a black and pink accessories.

"Babs," she said, "you're not feeling well. I should have called first."

"That's all right, Adrianne. I'm glad to see you. Would you like to come in?"

"Oh, thanks, another time. You missed the last meeting of the Culture Club, and I wanted you to have this information about our annual card party."

"Oh," said Babs hesitantly.

"The theme this year is May flowers. I see you have a rose bush. Roses would be lovely to decorate your card table."

"Adrianne, I'm sorry I won't be able to attend the card party. I explained my situation to Miss Hawk."

"Oh, I hadn't heard. She and I are co-chairmen this year. I'm sorry to have disturbed you this morning. Phil and I are on the way to a wedding, and I thought I might as well drop this off."

"Adrianne, it was thoughtful of you."

"You look so pale."

Adrianne turned and walked down the steps toward their immaculate, sky-blue Cadillac.

"I hope you'll be feeling better soon," she said, as she got into the car beside her husband.

Babs watched as the handsome couple drove off.

As she walked through the living room, she noticed the overflowing darning basket on the davenport, three pairs of shoes scattered about, and an untidy cluster of newspapers around Harry's chair.

"There's my jar of ink on the floor!" she said, as she stooped to pick it up.

"This should teach me to get myself dressed and the house in order before this time of day! I'm thankful she didn't accept my invitation to come in!"

After checking on George, who was still sleeping peacefully in his crib, Babs went quickly to the bedroom and began to dress. As she started to apply her make-up, another knock came at the front door. Putting down her eyebrow pencil, she tried to straighten her bath robe. As she approached the front door. she saw that the caller wore a purple lilac hat with fuchsia bows set firmly on iron-gray hair. It was Doris Blodgett.

"Hello, Mrs. Blodgett," she said, opening the door.

"Hello. I'm running some errands, and I wanted to ask Rev. Petersen if he could come by and pick up my propane tank and get it filled again for me."

"I'll tell him you stopped by, Mrs. Blodgett."

"Are you sick, Babs? You're white as a sheet."

"I'm all right, Mrs. Blodgett."

"Take care of yourself. Spring weather can be treacherous," she scolded, as she walked down the steps on her way to the Collins.'

The minister's wife sighed.

"Harry has been so busy. He won't like to hear he's supposed to get Mrs. Blodgett's fuel tank refilled."

She dressed, George woke up, and Harry still had not returned. Babs straightened up the living room, answered her mother's letter, and fixed a couple of tuna sandwiches.

She was adding carrots and potatoes to the squirrel, cooking in the kettle, when Harry, followed by Tuck, came into the kitchen. His brow was wrinkled, and he looked tired as he gave her a kiss.

"Are you hungry?"

"I guess so."

"Did something happen?"

"Oh, I was calling on Mrs. Rigby, Clara Wells' sister, the one I baptized in the river last year. She's been sick."

"I'm sorry."

"Then, I stopped by to see Clara and Harvey. He's still not doing well."

"Even with giving up farming?"

"That's right."

Harry paused, lost in thought.

"What happened, Dear? Come and sit down and have some lunch."

"I was on my way home when I had a blow-out," said Harry, seating himself at the table. "I had to change the left back tire. Stopped by at Collins' service station. He told me the tire wasn't worth fixing. Said we needed four new ones."

"Oh, dear."

Harry looked at his sandwich with disfavor.

"I said we couldn't handle that, so he put two new ones on the front and rotated the back tires. Before we leave, I'll have to buy a couple more tires."

"You charged them?"

"I charged one. I paid for one. Mrs. Rigby insisted on giving me some money for gasoline."

"That was fortunate, Harry."

"After lunch, I'll have to study."

As he mounted the stairs, she cleared the table.

"I know he doesn't like tuna sandwiches, but I'll make it up to him tonight with my special dinner," she thought. "Dinner in the slow kettle smells so good! I can hardly wait."

At 5:30, the table set, the meal ready, she called him to dinner. After he said grace, she served grapefruit for the first course. Clearing the table, she brought in her "piece de resistance" on a platter. Harry smiled as he began to carve.

"This is done to a T," he said, as he sliced the meat, and put the vegetables on her plate. She waited as he prepared his own serving. Her mouth was watering, as she watched him take the first bite.

Harry took a generous portion. He choked, scowled, and gulped down some milk.

"Do you have a piece of bread or anything?" he asked.

"Why? What's the matter?" she asked as she got up. "Don't you like it?"

"No, taste it! The game taste is strong and horrible!"

Babs took a taste and spit it out.

"Harry, I thought I was so smart about cooking game. I forgot to soak it overnight in salt! That game taste is all through the potatoes and vegetables! It's no good!"

She took the two plates and emptied the ruined food into the garbage pail under the sink.

"Babs, I'm sorry your dinner turned out bad."

"It's a big disappointment to me as well as to you."

Reaching into the shelf under the counter, she drew out the frying pan Louise had given her for Christmas.

"It's been a dreadful day! The dinner was the last straw! Will you settle for scrambled eggs?"

Chapter 54

SMILING THROUGH

"Pastor, with our national convention being held in Milwaukee, I feel that you and your wife should attend."

"Tim, I hadn't even given it a thought."

"Would you like to go?" asked Fred Young.

"I'm sure I'd receive a lot of inspiration and information about what our church is doing in home and foreign missions," answered Harry.

"Is that a 'yes'?" inquired Gary with a twinkle in his eye.

Tim looked at the rest of the trustees.

"I'd call that, a 'yes.'"

"I can't afford to go just now, and I don't want to be a burden on the church."

"However, if we paid your way, you could attend, right?"

"I guess so, Tim."

"We've been talking it over, and we are willing to put up $75 for you and Babs to go," said Fred.

"You are?"

"I like to go to Grange meetings once in a while. I find out about new gadgets, different crops, and I get to see farmers like myself. It's encouraging," said Eben.

"I see," said Harry.

"A minister, like a farmer, needs some encouragement and new ideas, according to Dr. Miller," said Tim.

"We have to admit it wasn't entirely our idea," said Fred.

Harry looked puzzled.

"Tim got a letter from Dr. Miller, our Executive Supervisor in Milwaukee."

Every man was watching Harry closely.

"A letter from Dr. Miller?".

"Did you know about the letter, Pastor?" inquired Herb Dodds.

"No," said Harry.

"See, I told you he didn't," said Art.

"What are you talking about?" asked Harry bluntly.

"When Tim got this letter from Dr. Miller, Collins said that you put him up to it!" said Fred.

"Put him up to what?"

"Dr. Miller suggested that since the National Convention will be so close, we should see to it that our pastor and a lay person attend."

"And that we pay their way!" added Art.

"He thinks we're made of money," said Mac, shaking his head.

"I polled the trustees, Pastor, and everyone but Mac here is willing to send you."

"That's wonderful," said Harry.

"We haven't found a lay person who wants to go."

"Like I said, Dr. Miller thinks we're made of money," said Mac.

"Even if I don't go, I'm glad you want to send me," said Harry.

"Now it's settled. You make your arrangements. The Rev. Jensen from Sterling said he'd be willing to preach here on the Sunday you're gone," said Tim.

"Oh, oh," muttered Mac, "isn't he the preacher who always looks like his feet hurt?"

"What's that, Mac?" asked Fred.

"He's been here before. He preached about some man on his way to Hell. That Rev. Jensen has forgotten how to smile."

"Well, Mac," said Art, mischievously, "now it's up to you to give him something to smile about."

Chapter 55

SNOW IN JUNE

"Your mom and dad's place looks so beautiful! Did you notice the beautifully scalloped flower beds?" asked Babs as they drove up to his parent's home.

"No. I had my mind on going to the convention. The gardens look nice, don't they?"

"After living in the garage, I'll bet the house feels spacious. Honey, I can hardly wait to see George. Do you think he'll remember us?"

"Of course he'll remember us! We've only been away four days!"

Harry pulled up into the driveway, and his excited wife jumped out of the car and ran to the back door. Finding it unlocked, she knocked vigorously and disappeared into the house. Harry followed her at a more leisurely pace. He found his mother seated by the teeter-babe where she had been feeding George. George had stopped eating and was staring at his mother. Tears filled his eyes, he opened his mouth, and began to cry.

"What's the matter, Baby? Did you miss your daddy and mommy?" asked Babs.

"Mah mah," said George holding his arms up.

"Oh, George, I missed you so! Mother, was George good while we were gone?"

As she spoke, she lifted him out of his teeter-babe, holding him close. Normally not a cuddler, George, in a rare moment, permitted hugging and kissing from his mother.

"He surely was all right," replied Louise. "We didn't hear a peep out of him. I don't know why he is crying now."

George looked over at his father and started to cry again.

"Come here to your daddy, boy," said Harry, taking his son from Babs' arms, and lifting him high, so that he touched the ceiling.

George began to laugh.

"Oh, you like your daddy, do you?"

That evening when Mel got home from the mill, he was surprised to find George in a tearful mood. However, after the baby had been put to bed and the house was quiet, Mel began to think back.

"Remember Lefty's children, Louise? When we took care of little Louise or Katie, the babies were always good when we had them. But, when Lefty and Maxine came to get the girls, they were always fussy."

"I remember, Mel. You're right. Lefty would be so apologetic because he thought that the babies had been difficult when they were gone."

"And we'd always tell him that the girls slept well and got along fine."

"Thanks for telling us. I was feeling guilty, too, afraid that George had been a bother," said Babs.

"By the way, one morning, I gave George a soft boiled egg," said Louise.

"How did he like it?" asked Babs.

"He ate it after making a face or two. Have you given him eggs before?"

"Not yet. The doctor said that some babies don't digest eggs too well at first. But it's time he had one."

Louise got up from her chair.

"Wait here. I know you're going to have to leave the first thing in the morning. I have something I want to give you," and she left the room.

Harry and Babs looked at each other wide-eyed, in anticipation. Mel smiled. Soon, Louise returned with a large, rectangularly-shaped package wrapped in white tissue paper and tied with an teal blue bow.

"This is for both of you," she said, tactfully handing it to Babs.

"Mother, how nice of you. I can't imagine—"

She opened the package deliberately, having been taught to save gift-wrapping paper. Harry watched her with increasing impatience.

"Let me help you with that," he said as he held out his hand to take it.

"I have it now," she said, as she removed the last of the tissue paper, revealing a lovely water color painting of a mountain lake with a pine tree in the foreground, framed in blond wood.

"Oh, it's Lake Tahoe, isn't it? How lovely, Mother!" she said.

"You painted this, Mother?" asked Harry as he looked at it carefully.

"Yes. With our two sons raised, I decided I'd get back into water colors and painting. Do you like it, Son?"

"It's beautiful! But where did you get the idea of Tahoe?"

"Do you remember that big postcard you sent us on your honeymoon?"

Harry looked blank, but Babs' eyes lighted up.

"I know you both love Lake Tahoe, so after you sent us that card, I decided it would be a suitable subject."

Handing the picture to Harry, Babs gave Louise a hug.

"You couldn't have chosen a better gift, Mother. When George gets older, it will be very precious to him, also."

Babs kissed Mel, too.

"In my opinion," said Harry, "this painting is one of the best you've ever done. Thanks, Mother," he said simply.

"She worked hard on that," said Mel. "I think she did a great job!"

"I wondered about it when I was painting it. After all, you have both seen it, but I never have. I hoped that you'd like it."

"We love it, Mom," said Harry.

The next morning, after offering their thanks and goodbyes they left for home, arriving at Prairie Meadows in the afternoon. Harry found a lot of mail and messages to attend to, George was inspecting his play pen and toys, while Babs surveyed the week's accumulation of dust, considered where the Tahoe picture should be hung, and started the washer.

"I'm having wieners tonight," she told Harry. "Will you do the dinner dishes, Sweetheart?"

Harry wrinkled his nose.

"Are you feeling pushed?" he said. "And if so, why?"

"I'm swamped. Daily Vacation Bible School starts tomorrow, and Nell Perkins asked me to give a flannel-graph story to the whole school at 11:00 pm each day. I have to finish preparing. And, oh, Honey," she said, "remember you said you'd take care of George at 11:00 each day."

"Did I say that? Suppose I have a funeral or something?"

"In that case, we'll have to make other arrangements. But if you could arrange to do your work downstairs during that time, it will be a help."

"Oh," said Harry reluctantly. "I wonder how Vacation Bible School will go. Here it is June, but over the radio the weatherman made a forecast of a cold snap tomorrow."

The alarm clock went off bright and early the next morning, continuing its raucous noise until Harry grabbed it, and shut it off.

"What a relief! I hate that alarm!" cried Babs, as she bounced out of bed and opened the shades to a white world.

"Harry, it looks like we got at least three inches of snow!"

Harry blinked, closed his eyes, and rolled over. "That right?" he mumbled, his voice muffled by the covers.

"At least, recess at Vacation Bible School is taken care of. The kids can play in the snow. Isn't this amazing? Snow in June!"

Chapter 56

OFF TO CALIFORNIA

"Pass the mustard, please, Harry."

"Yes, I always forget you prefer mustard to ketchup with hash," he said sprinkling a liberal amount of ketchup on his plate.

"Do you think we'll be ready to leave by morning?"

"I think so. I've lined up speakers for the Sundays I'll be gone."

"You stopped the mail, I gave notice to the 'milk lady', and you got the travelers checks, right?"

"Yes, and Gary found some boxes at the store which you can use for packing."

"Thanks, Dear. I've notified all my piano pupils, you took Nip and Tuck over to Margie's, and I stopped ice delivery. What about the lawn?"

Babs was crossing off items on her list.

"Gil Perkins, across the street, will mow it for us."

"Both Henry Perkins and Mac breezed in yesterday to see how much of the packing I have left to do. I hate packing!"

"You aren't going to insist that we take George's playpen, are you?" asked Harry in his most patient tone.

"Harry, remember, George is used to the playpen. At motels, he can sleep in it. When we get to Mother's, I can set him in there and not worry about his getting into things."

"That pen is too big and bulky! We can watch him at your Mother's."

"That's easy for you to say. We need the pen. Where will he sleep in motels? He's outgrown his bassinet."

Harry wrinkled his nose and appeared ready to leave the table.

"Honey, where did you put the boxes?"

"I left them in the car. I'll get them."

"Great! I have a couple of favors to ask."

His face assumed a guarded look that she'd learned to recognize.

"After you bring in the boxes, will you get George to bed and do the dishes for me, so that I can finish the packing?"

"I guess so," he said without enthusiasm.

Harry hurried out to the car, almost stumbling over Mac on the back porch.

"'Scuse me, Mac."

Mac recognized his pastor's state of mind, as the younger man plunged out the back door toward the car, shaking his head and muttering softly, but with great emotion,

"Women! Women!"

As Harry dashed back into the house carrying a large assortment of cardboard boxes, Mac smiled sympathetically, recalling when he and Rita had packed to visit their son in South Dakota.

With the boxes in hand, Babs quickly filled one with baby things, including disposable diapers, which she had never used before. Another was for her clothes, and a third for Harry's. Harry was finishing the dishes when she came in with the fourth box.

"You don't need that one?" he asked delightedly.

"Oh, I'm using it for food and gifts."

"Food and gifts?"

"I'm bringing Wisconsin cheese for my Mom and Dad, and some of our canned tomatoes and green beans for people who entertain us."

"But food? Aren't we eating out?"

"Yes, but I'm bringing baby food, morning juice for us, and the ice box for sandwich makings and fresh fruit."

"The ice won't last too long, will it?"

"We can get fresh ice."

Harry looked discouraged.

"You always load us down with so many things."

The following morning, Mac saw a light go on at the parsonage at 5:30. Pastor drove the car close to the back door and began bringing out over-flowing boxes to the car. He appeared increasingly agitated, as he tried, in vain, to stuff a large item into the trunk. Finally, as Mac drew closer, he saw that it was a baby's playpen.

"No wonder he's upset," said Mac to himself.

There was no sign yet of either Babs or the baby.

At 7:14, the missus came out carrying a number of paper bags, followed by the Rev, carrying the baby. The missus and the baby settled into the front seat. The pastor locked the door and got in. As Mac was turning away, he saw the door on the passenger's side open, and the missus getting out. She fumbled a long time unlocking the back door and disappeared into the house. Five minutes later she emerged with a triumphal look, carrying another large, paper bag, a big, brown purse, and a diaper bag.

Seeing Mac, she smiled, waved, and they left for the West.

"Boy, two thousand miles to California," said Mac. "Young people have a lot of get-up-and-go. I wonder if they turned off the water heater. I don't think I can see from the outside."

He walked up to the back porch, waving to Henry Perkins across the street, out for his morning stroll.

"Hi there, Mac! Did the young folks get off all right this morning?" he asked.

"Guess so."

Mac decided that he could not tell whether the water heater had been turned off or not.

Henry called out,

"Wait! What do I hear?"

It was the pastor's car, loaded to the gills, and returning to stop once more by the back door. The missus got out and walked up the back stoop.

"Did you forget something?" asked Mac.

"Yes, I can't find my glasses."

She fumbled again with the key, finally letting herself in. Mac glanced at his pastor who was stoically watching as a robin on the lawn, diligently scratched for a worm.

At seven twenty-four, she came out, again locking the door.

"Goodbye, Mac," she said. "You and Henry keep an eye on the place for us, won't you?"

"That we will, ma'm. That we will."

After they left, the two old men stood for quite a while at the back door. Everything was quiet.

"Oh, I guess this is it, Mac," said Henry. "I think they're finally on their way to California!"

"Reckon you're right, Henry. And it's too bad. I forgot to ask him if he'd shut off the water heater."

232

Chapter 57

HIGHWAY FORTY

As their 1941 four-door Chevy sedan with Harry at the wheel made its way into southern Wisconsin, Babs broke a long silence.

"Honey, I would like to drive."

"That's okay. I like to drive, and I'm not tired."

"You may not think you're tired, but you are. You've been at it a long time. But that's not my only concern. Since I married you, I almost never drive, and I need to keep up my driving skills."

Silently he considered what she said. While he felt it was a man's place to drive, her request was reasonable. He noticed that they were on the outskirts of Madison.

"I prefer to drive, but I agree we should share the driving. Why don't you take over, after we get out of Madison?"

"Thank you, Harry. Meanwhile, I'll enjoy the scenery. Madison is such a pretty city with its lakes. It's the home of University of Wisconsin, isn't it? It's where we saw the Cal-Wisconsin game."

"Right. That seems like a long time ago. By the way, how is George doing?"

"He is watching the scenery, too."

About twenty minutes later, as homes and businesses were giving way to picturesque, green farms, Harry drew over to the side of the road and parked. While Babs got into the driver's seat, Harry put George in the back seat, which he'd built up with boxes and blankets. His son settled, Harry got into the passenger side.

"What is all this stuff piled around my feet?"

"I have toys and snacks for George, my purse—"

"You have two purses."

"Well, I don't need to carry two purses. When we stop for the night, remind me to put one of them in the trunk. Can you put it in the back seat for now?"

"Yes," said Harry as he tossed one of the purses in the back, where it landed with the sound of broken glass.

"Oh, I hope you didn't break a mirror," she said, driving carefully.

At Dodgeville, they found a small, attractive city park, with tables and swings. She parked and spread out a tablecloth, and they lunched on egg-salad sandwiches, coffee, and apples.

"Are you glad we have the thermos, Harry?"

"Yes, the coffee stayed nice and hot. Thanks, Dear."

While Harry disposed of the garbage, Babs pushed George in the swing, before resuming their trip. Harry drove through Dubuque, never dreaming that before long, he would attend school there.

In Iowa, the roads were narrow and curving among the rolling plains. Suddenly, they heard a loud explosion, and Babs at the wheel could scarcely keep the Chevy on the road.

"It's a blow-out, Honey! Get over to the right as soon as you can!" Checking the rear-view mirror, Babs saw no vehicles behind her. Slowing down, she pulled over and stopped in the narrow parkway.

Harry got out.

"The left rear tire blew. I'll have to change it."

George was screwing up his face, ready to cry. Babs got out of the car, taking the baby in her arms.

"It's all right, George. Daddy will take care of us."

Suddenly, a large shining truck and rig slowed, passed, and stopped in front of them. The trucker alighted and came toward them.

"Let me help you," said the rangy young man with red hair, freckles, and a friendly smile. "I have high-powered equipment that will get you on the way in no time. Every one, please get off the highway. We're in a dangerous spot here."

Bringing his jack, he had the car up, the tire off, and the spare in place and secured, in five minutes. Lowering the jack, he put the used tire in the trunk and returned to his vehicle. Waving and smiling, he drove off before they could thank him.

Babs felt shaky, as she got behind the wheel again.

"That man's an angel, isn't he, Harry?"

"Yes, and I didn't even thank him."

"He didn't want your thanks, Harry. He wanted you and your family safe."

"And he's right about the danger. Changing a left tire on a narrow highway is scary. I didn't recognize how dangerous. We'll have to stop a little early and get the tire replaced this afternoon before the garages close."

They found a garage in Des Moines where the tire was replaced with a used tire for only a dollar. "This will be our spare tire now," said Harry. Leaving the garage, they selected a clean motel on the western edge of the city. As they were getting settled, Babs noticed a broken mirror in her brown purse.

"Some people would say we were going to have seven years of bad luck," she said.

"You don't believe that, do you?"

She hesitated. "I guess not. I just have to buy a new mirror, huh? Oh, I'm going to put this purse in the trunk. I only need the black one."

"That's right."

"You know, I was kind of discouraged at the late start we made this morning. I was hoping to leave by 6:30 at the latest."

"That early?"

"Yes. And then, I forgot the diaper bag, and we had to go back again for my glasses. Sometimes, I act like I don't have a brain in my head."

"Don't berate yourself. We had some delays, but we'll get there. Tell me why you wanted to leave so early."

"It's the way my family traveled. Mother and Dad liked to get out of the cities before the morning traffic. And they liked to drive in the cool, early morning, rather than the hot afternoons."

"It's May. The afternoons aren't too hot yet, and I can manage the traffic."

"You're right, Harry. We'll get there, even if we don't leave early in the morning. I must remember that."

Harry looked over at his wife getting ready for bed and George, sleeping contentedly on soft blankets in his playpen.

"I can see now why you insisted on bringing the pen."

That night as they bedded down, they were grateful for a safe journey thus far, and thankful to the Good Samaritan, a red-headed trucker, who helped them in their hour of peril.

Harry said, "I must remember God answers prayer through thoughtful people. I need to be sensitive to the needs of those around me. I may be close to some one who, like me today, who needs a Good Samaritan. I must alert to my opportunities."

"Harry, you are a Good Samaritan."

"Why do you say that?"

"Well, today, for example, you never reproached me for my forgetfulness. And when I asked for a turn at the wheel, you gave it to me. Actually, you help all the time. And, by the way, have I told you lately that I love you?"

Chapter 58

BABS FORGETS

"Iowa seems to go on forever," sighed Babs.

"Yes, and it's slow-going on these narrow roads."

"In that field, are all those little plants corn?'

"Right."

"They have a lot of growing to do, don't they?"

"Sure do. I'm going to let you take over," said Harry, pulling off the road onto the entrance to a farm.

"Oh, good. George needs changing, and I need to stretch my legs."

George smiled as his mother changed his diapers.

"Sometimes these paper diapers leak. I prefer the cloth ones," said Babs.

Soon, they were on their way, and Babs was making pretty good time, when they saw highway signs warning of "Men At Work."

"Better slow down," advised Harry.

As they came around a curve, they saw about a dozen cars and trucks waiting behind a stop sign, held by a highway construction crewman.

"It looks like they're re-surfacing the highway."

"A slow day," she sighed.

"We might as well be patient," said Harry.

"H-m-m."

"Look, we're lucky. There's the pilot car coming our way, leading the cars through."

They watched as a long line of vehicles approached, continuing east, while the dusty, black pilot pickup made a turn and got ready to lead the westbound group of cars.

"That's a break. Harry, would you give me my dark glasses?"

Babs started the engine as the lead car began its trip, followed by three blue sedans, four pick-ups, three large rigs, a green coupe, and their Chevy.

"Where are the glasses, Babs?"

"They should be in my purse."

"I don't see them."

"Look in George's diaper bag."

"Not there," responded Harry as he searched the bag. "I'll look on the floor and between the door and the passenger seat."

By the time they got through the area of roadwork, Harry had looked everywhere.

"Did you check the glove compartment?"

"Not there."

"I just had them. I was wearing them while we were eating lunch in that city park."

"Did you take them off?"

"I don't think so--Harry, do you suppose I took them off and left them somewhere?"

"It's possible."

"Oh, I hate to lose those prescription glasses that Mom and Dad gave me."

"We can turn around and go back after them. It's only seventy miles or so."

Babs groaned, pulled off to the right, and waited for the cars behind to pass. After they went by, she crossed to the opposite side of the road, and took her place among the line of cars waiting to go eastward through the re-surfacing area.

"Once more into the breach, dear friends, once more," quoted Babs in an exaggerated tone, to George's delight.

Returning to the city park seemed to take ages, but she finally drew up to the picnic table where they had recently eaten lunch. Seeing no glasses around the table, she walked to the rest room, shuddering again at the dirt she saw. One at a time, she inspected each of the five toilet cubicles, searching in vain.

"Could I have left them at the motel?"

With not a sign of them by the basins or on the shelf nearby, she had turned to leave, when she noticed something on the floor by the wastebasket. Walking over and bending down, she spied her precious glasses!

"Harry," she called as she ran back to the car, "I found them!"

"Good," he said. "Shall I drive for a while?"

"Go ahead," she said, thankfully settling into the passenger side of the car. "Onward and upward! And seventy miles westward, you, too, shall have the chance to follow the lead car!"

Chapter 59

TRAVELERS

"I'm glad I was able to persuade that woman in Rawlins tocash a check for me."

"Yes, we have this expensive habit of eating," Babs said, as she took over the driver's seat. "I thought travelers checks would be accepted everywhere."

"Everywhere but Rawlins."

Having changed George's diapers and made a comfortable bed in the back seat for him, Babs focused on driving. Harry soon fell asleep. As they approached the Continental Divide, Babs welcomed the opportunity to do some mountain driving. For an hour, she made good progress. However, as she drew nearer to Rock Springs, and the two-lane highway became curvier, she found herself following a red sports car trailing an old Dodge pickup traveling at 40 miles per hour. She fretted, for the on-coming traffic was just heavy enough to keep her from passing. She began to sing *When Irish Eyes Are Smiling*. After that, knowing that George was listening, she broke into a few bars of *Danny Boy*.

Unexpectedly, there was a break in the traffic, and the little sports car darted around the pickup. Babs followed, making it just before they got to a curve. Sighing with relief, she slowed up. The relief was short-lived, however, for she heard the unsettling sound of a siren.

"I wonder if that's a fire truck, ambulance, or the police," she thought.

Looking in the rear-view mirror, she saw a highway patrol car right behind her. Harry awoke, and George, startled by the siren, began to cry.

"Is he after us?" asked Harry, blinking, and trying to rouse himself.

"I'm not sure."

"Better stop and see what he wants."

Babs drew over to the right. Getting out of the car, she opened the back door, and took George in her arms.

"It's all right, baby," she said as she kissed him.

A tall policeman came forward.

"May I see your driver's license ma'm?"

"Oh, yes," she said, giving George to Harry. "It's in my purse."

After a quick search, she found her purse on the floor on the passenger side. She opened it.

"Is something wrong?" she asked.

"Ma'm, I've been following you for two hours. You did everything right until just a few minutes ago."

"A few minutes ago?"

"Yes. The driver of the red car took a chance when he passed the 1935 Dodge pickup. He was close to the curve. And you followed!"

Babs paused in her rummaging through her handbag.

"I was taking a chance?"

"You sure were. All you needed to wipe out your whole family, was a fast vehicle coming around that curve!"

The young man's eyes were stern yet kind.

"Oh."

"Your license?"

"Officer, it must be in my other purse. I put it in back in one of the boxes. "

Harry went round and opened the trunk.

"I think I know which box it's in," she said. "Officer, do you mind holding the baby a minute? The siren scared him."

The man looked surprised but took the baby who eyed him with curiosity. George immediately became intrigued with the patrolman's shiny badge. Harry began to remove boxes from the back. Babs scanned the contents of each one as it emerged from the depths. In a few minutes, all the worldly possessions they had with them were out of the trunk and lined up on the side of the road.

"That's it," said Harry.

She began to dig through the box holding her clothes again. Finally, she found it in the ample pocket of her winter coat.

"Here it is," she said triumphantly, and she began to rummage through the brown purse.

The policeman gave Harry a look of sympathy, and handed George to him.

"Here you are, officer, " she said as she passed him the license.

The patrolman studied it carefully.

"Did you know that it expired two months ago?" he asked.

"No. You see, since the baby came, I haven't been driving much, and I didn't realize it had expired."

"I'm going to let you go with a warning. Get this license renewed, keep it with you when you drive, and be careful when you start to pass. Make sure you don't follow a bad example and pass on a curve."

"Thank you, officer," said Harry.

"Yes, thank you for your patience," added Babs.

"I'm a new father myself. Not only do you not want an accident," he said, "but you don't want your baby scared again by the sound of a siren!"

With a final, faint smile, he turned and went back to his car. As the patrolman drove off, Harry began loading the boxes back into the trunk. Babs, holding George, felt shaky.

Noticing how pale and anxious she looked, Harry said, "I think you'd better let me drive for a while."

"You know, when I passed that pick-up, I didn't realize I was so close to that curve. The good Lord and the kind policeman have given me a second chance. Harry, I'd love it if you would drive. I want to simply hold George for a while."

Chapter 60

HOME COMING

"Oh, Babs, it's so good to see you! Sandy, look at the Old Timer! Come to Grandma, sweetheart!"

George clung to his mother and began to whimper.

"Mother, he just woke up. To him, this is a new place. Give him a little time."

Sandy gave his daughter a welcome hug and kiss and went to the car to help Harry unload the car. Soon the hall was filled with overflowing boxes. Ruth viewed them with distaste.

"Sandy, you and Harry please take these things up to Babs's old room. Babs, I borrowed a crib and a high chair from the church. George is going to be very comfortable here. George, come and give your grandma a kiss."

George said nothing but turned to look at his grandpa who was busy with boxes and not paying any attention to him.

"Are you hungry, Babs? Do you want a bite to eat?"

"No, thanks, Mother. It was hot in Sacramento. We stopped and each had an ice cream cone. You should have seen George trying to eat his. He got some on his shirt."

"Yes, I see," said Ruth. "His shirt is dirty. Would you like a glass of ice tea?"

"I'd love a glass of ice tea, Mother. We need to cool off. Harry, did you bring in the playpen?"

"No, it's still in the car."

"Would you bring it in, please? Mother, I'd like to set up the play pen. Where should we put it?"

"I'll bring the ice tea into the living room. Why not put it here?" she said, indicating a spot near the fireplace.

While Ruth left for the kitchen, Harry went after the playpen. Sandy settled into his favorite chair, while Babs sat on the edge of the davenport, holding her baby, concerned that George might soil, move, or break something.

"How was the trip, my daughter?" asked Sandy, lighting a cigarette.

"Oh, it was pretty good. The trip through Nevada was terribly hot."

"Yes," said Harry as he brought in the playpen. "On the way home, I want to drive through Nevada at night."

"Dad, the sweat was just pouring off of all of us, as we came through the desert. Harry, would you hold George? Let me set up the pen, okay?"

Harry sat down, while Babs placed the baby in his arms. Ruth entered, as Babs was getting the pen in place. Since the playpen was next to the coffee table, Babs picked up a glass bird from Austria and a marble bear, souvenir of Yosemite Park, and put them on the mantel above the fireplace.

"I don't want George to break anything," she explained.

"Babs, please don't move our things. This is our house. Leave things where they are," directed Ruth.

"George has to learn to leave things alone, daughter. Teaching him that lesson is part of your job as a parent," added Sandy, as he replaced the two animals on the coffee table.

"It's hard to teach a child in a three-generational setting, Dad. We are trying to teach him, but he is very curious and investigative, and it's not easy."

"No, it's not easy," said Harry.

"Well, you two must recognize that he needs to be trained from the beginning," said Ruth. "No one ever said that being a parent would be easy."

The sparkling bird intrigued George, and he reached for it.

"No, George. That's Grandma Ruth's birdie," said Babs, moving the pen away from the coffee table and searching for a change of subject. "By the way, where's my dear brother, Al?"

"Oh, he's at work at the Ford plant, of course. Your dad took the day off to welcome you. George, don't you want to come to Grandma?" asked Ruth, holding out her arms.

George said nothing but looked at his grandpa, smoking in his arm chair.

"Grandma loves you, Old Timer. Babs you don't have a very friendly baby, does she, Sandy?" said Ruth, looking for support.

That night as they were settling down for the night, Harry was concerned about his wife's anxiety.

"I can see why you insisted on bringing the playpen," he said. "They expect George to act like a well-behaved adult. No compromises."

"That's right. Remember, when they're by themselves, mother and dad spend their free time in the breakfast nook in the kitchen, or the little sun room back of the living room. They never use the living room except to entertain company. That's why it always looks so nice: there's no wear on the furniture, and nobody touches anything"

"Is that the way you were brought up?"

"Right."

"Did it seem strange to you that the "parlor" was off limits?"

"No, that was the way it was. Sometimes I went in to get a book to read off the shelves. But, in the main, I went into the living room to practice the piano, to help Mother do the dusting, or to entertain company."

"That's all?"

"Well, when we were kids, and it was raining, sometimes Al and I brought his little cars into the living room. Dad's chair, the other easy chair, and the piano bench were homes for Al's cars, and the davenport was an apartment house where my families of cars lived."

"Sounds like quite a game."

"It was. Every little car was named for a fruit. The toy locomotive was Cantaloupe. Of course, he eloped with his girlfriend, Banana. My favorite little car was named Orange, and Al's favorite was Apple."

"How do you remember all that?"

"Every family had a large car or truck which they used to transport the family—like when they went camping."

"It was kind of like playing dolls."

"Al wouldn't play dolls. However, on a rainy day, he'd play "family cars" with me. But, if one of his friends came over, he stopped playing."

"I enjoyed seeing Al tonight at dinner. He has a full-time job at the Ford plant where your Dad works, right?"

"Yes. He is training as a machinist."

"Boy, your mom is sure frustrated that George won't come to her, yet."

"Dad doesn't pay any attention to him, so George is making up to him already. Of course, I try to tell her: 'Just ignore the baby, and he'll come around.'"

Both were tired after their long trip from Wisconsin to California, and Babs promptly fell asleep in the bed that was hers as a child. Harry lay awake beside her, thinking about the family that he was now a part of.

Al had talked about going camping. He assured his brother-in-law that it was a lot of fun. Having never in his life gone camping, Harry was skeptical. When he finally dropped off to sleep, he dreamed that he was camping in Yosemite. He sat in a camp-chair, which collapsed, and he landed on the ground. During the night, a bear entered their camp and devoured all the food. In his dream, he was wondering why some people thought camping was fun.

In the morning, he told her about his dream.

"I had a bad dream, too," she said.

"What happened in your dream?"

"While you and I went shopping, George stayed here with my parents."

"What's bad about that?"

"He broke Mother's crystal bird."

Chapter 61

HARRY HELPS OUT

"Look at all the lovely things the ladies in our church gave you, Babs!"

"I'm so surprised, Mother! After all, we've been married two years. I certainly didn't expect them to give me a shower."

Babs picked up a red and gray paisley scarf from the bed, where she'd laid all the gifts.

"Well, Geraldine said that they intended to have one for you before you were married, and since the time slipped by, they wanted to remember you now. You have a lot of thank-you notes to write, don't you?"

Babs began to put the gifts in one of their boxes, which she'd lined with paper.

"Yes. I'll have to write from Wisconsin. I need to get all the addresses."

"I have most of them in my address book."

"I will get a lot of use out of these lovely blouses. And look at this lovely lace slip! Oh, by the way, did you know that your pastor had asked Harry to read the Scripture in the morning service, and preach at the evening service?"

"No, I didn't. That's kind of Dr. Kramer, isn't it?"

"Yes. Harry is glad that he brought some of his sermons with him. He'll probably want to spend the morning preparing."

"Babs, did I hear your brother ask you and Harry to go for a ride in his 1936 Chevy?"

"Yes, he said to be ready when he comes home from work tonight."

"I hope that he will drive very carefully."

"He's never had a moving violation, has he?"

"No, but—"

"I'm sure he will drive very carefully. He's proud of that car of his."

Babs paused in her task of folding George's diapers.

"This visit has gone by so fast! Al has his crowd of friends, and we've kept busy with my friends and the family. You know, Al and I really haven't had an opportunity for a good talk. He hasn't settled on one girl yet? Still playing the field, right?"

"Right. He has his job at the Ford plant, and he and his buddy, Pete, enjoy going up to Clear Lake for water skiing. Al works on his car, and he goes to youth fellowship at church. He keeps pretty busy."

That evening, Ruth and Sandy took care of George. Al took Babs and Harry on a drive through the Arlington and over to Point Richmond.

Babs was impressed with how bright and shiny the car looked.

"Lots of spit and polish went into making this car look so great!" she said.

"Yes. Try not to put your hands on the dashboard, Harry. That leaves a mark."

"Oh, sorry, Al."

"I'm taking you where my friends and I liked to drive in high school."

"Lots of hills," said Harry.

"Yes, and when I think how fast we drove in those days, it scares me to death."

"You're more mature now, Al. By the way, Dr. Kramer asked Harry to help out during morning worship, and preach on Sunday night."

"That's great. I've never heard Harry preach. What are you going to talk about?"

"I'm not sure. I'm thinking about it."

"I always like it when Harry talks about people in the Bible. He has some fine sermons, for example, on Peter and Nehemiah."

"My sister is your greatest booster, isn't she, Harry?"

"She sure is. I don't know what I'd do without her," answered Harry turning to give Babs a kiss.

Upon their return, they discovered that Ruth had decided, since it was a rare warm summer evening in the Bay Area, to have a picnic in the back yard. Babs was home in time to set the table, and Harry helped his father-in-law bring out the chairs.

When they were seated, Ruth asked Harry to say grace.

All bowed their heads.

"Rub-a-dub-dub," said Harry. "Thanks for the grub!"

The younger Al laughed.

"You went to the same summer church camp that I did, Harry!"

"Oh, they taught you that, did they?"

"They sure did."

"It doesn't sound very reverent, does it, Dad?" asked Babs.

"Takes all kinds," he responded, as he passed the potato salad.

"This chicken is delicious," said Harry.

"What are you feeding the Old Timer?" asked Ruth.

"Tonight he gets squash, beef, and applesauce."

"He seems to like everything."

"Yes, Mother. He has a healthy appetite. His favorites are oatmeal and strained beef. As you've noticed, I feed him a variety of foods."

"It's so wonderful to have the whole family here. We are going to miss you so much when you have to leave on Monday," sighed Ruth.

"It's been fun here, Mother, but we have to get back. Harry will be preaching next Sunday in Wisconsin."

"Couldn't you stay just a little longer?"

"It will take us at least five days to get across the country. We are pushing it to stay this weekend," said Harry.

Ruth's face clouded.

"You wouldn't have deprived us of this last weekend, would you, Harry?'

"No. We were going to leave on Saturday, but when Dr. Kramer asked me to speak, I felt I should. Yes, we are staying, but I'm concerned about getting home. Hope we get back by Friday night. I need time to prepare for the following Sunday."

Ruth frowned, but said nothing.

Sunday was exciting for Babs. She was pleased that Dr. Kramer had asked her to play the piano along with the organist for the hymns. To be In her large home church, and hearing Harry reading the Scriptures was a delight. Hoping to hear Harry preach that night, she was grateful when her father offered to take care of George, so that she could go with her mother and brother to the evening service. Harry preached on Thomas, the doubter.

At the close of the Sunday evening service, Harry stood at the back of the sanctuary with Dr. Kramer and greeted the people. He heard a lot of encouraging words about his sermon. A number of the people spoke of their appreciation of Babs, who, before she married, had taught Sunday School, sponsored the high school youth, taught Vacation Bible School, and played the organ and piano when requested.

One of the last parishioners to greet Dr. Kramer and Harry was Ruth Walker, proud to be walking with both her daughter and son at her side.

"I appreciate your asking my daughter and her husband to participate in the services today, Dr. Kramer," she said as she shook hands with him.

"I need to thank you, Mrs. Walker. When you suggested my asking your son-in-law to have a part in the service, I had no idea he was such a fine preacher. Thank you."

Babs and Harry stared at Ruth.

"Mother, it was your idea for Harry to preach?"

"I thought it would be nice."

"You knew we were planning to leave Saturday?"

"Something was said. I really didn't know. There was nothing definite. The way it worked out, Daddy and I got to see you and the Old Timer for a couple of more days."

Babs's mouth opened in surprise.

Harry frowned but said nothing.

Al laughed.

"Mom, you're really something!"

"I don't know what to say," said Babs.

Dr. Kramer looked surprised that his words evoked such a response.

Ruth looked from one to the other.

"Well, now, you have to admit, hasn't this weekend been a wonderful treat for all of us?"

Chapter 62

SUMMERTIME IN PRAIRIE MEADOWS

"Wow, our grass is up a mile!" she said, as she poured his morning coffee. "Didn't you ask Gil Perkins to mow it for us?"

"H-m-m."

"Honey, could you stop by at Margie's, this morning, and pick up the cats?

Harry was engrossed in looking over the mail, which had accumulated in their absence.

"H-m-m."

The sun was streaming into the dinette, and George looked contented in his high chair, carefully picking up corn flakes off the tray and putting them in his mouth.

Babs brought Harry's bowl of oatmeal, moving magazines and papers to make room.

"Any interesting mail?" she asked, as she put a couple of slices of bread into the toaster.

"Here's a birthday package for you," he answered, handing it to her.

"It's from Uncle Marvin," she said, as she began to open the package.

"Oh, look, Honey, he sent us a couple of mugs!"

"Well, that's nice of him. Does he say anything?"

"He and Aunt Luella wish me a happy birthday, and send greetings to you and the people of Sterling. I never expected your uncle to mug us."

"Mug us?" he answered with a groan. "I guess you made a hit with him. He and Aunt Luella never remember my birthday!"

Babs looked over at the small white shelf, which Uncle Marvin had accidentally brushed against on his visit some time ago, resulting in broken china.

"Here's some more birthday cards for you," he said, passing them over to her.

"Thank you. Oh, I suppose we have a lot of bills," she said, glancing at the cards before beginning on her cereal.

"Utility bills, coal, milk, car payment, Collins' service station, Texaco, and Shell."

"Oh, you charged gas at Collins' before we left?"

"I had to."

"Oh, dear. Tell me, how does the oatmeal taste?"

"Let me put the mail aside, and I'll tell you," answered Harry as he put the mail on the floor beside him. "It's good! You added apples?"

"Yes. My brother, Al, said he likes apples in his oatmeal. Is there a letter from the state office?"

"Pass the sugar and milk. Yes, Dr. Miller will be speaking at the Stevens Point church in two weeks and wants to stop by and see me."

"If you want to invite him for dinner, that would be fine."

"He may be tied up."

The phone rang, and Harry answered it. Babs fed George his baby cereal, snatching a bite of oatmeal for herself from time to time. Soon, George had polished off the cereal and happily accepted the cracker his mother offered him. As Harry put down the receiver, his eyes were moist.

"What is it, Dear?" she asked.

"That was Fred Young."

"Something wrong? Is Thelma all right?"

"Thelma is all right. But Fred is concerned."

"About what?"

"The church. Bill Collins."

"What about Bill?"

"It seems as though, in my absence, he recalled that this year is the seventy-fifth anniversary of the founding of our church. He's been writing to all the former pastors and inviting them to be here the third Sunday in July to help us celebrate."

"He's doing this all on his own?"

"Yes. Up till now he hadn't talked to the deacons or the trustees."

"He hadn't?"

"Not until last week. Jane Collins talked to the Busy Bees a couple of weeks ago. She's got Mrs. Blodgett and Rita Barker and some of the ladies working on a big dinner for that Sunday."

"It sounds like a wonderful idea, Harry. Why has Bill been keeping it all to himself?"

"Fred thinks he's trying to embarrass the pastor and the rest of the church. A big anniversary is coming up, and no one but Bill Collins is doing anything about it!"

"Fred is pretty upset?"

"Yes, he is, and he's anxious about the reaction of some of the people."

"He is?"

"Yes. Bill Collins has been spending a lot of time over at Eben Morgan's. He asked Eben, as senior deacon, to sign some of the invitations, which he and Jane composed, and invite the Rev. and Mrs. Abbott to stay with them during the anniversary celebration. He asked Eben to introduce him at the service when Abbot comes to speak."

"There's no harm in that, is there?"

"According to Fred, Eben now says we're all 'back numbers' because we didn't get the celebration going. Eben feels it's up to Bill and Jane to do everything."

"I'm surprised that Tim Woods didn't mention the anniversary. Wasn't his Dad a pastor of this church years ago?"

"Yes, he was. It must have slipped his mind."

"Oh, how many former ministers will be coming?"

"Five have been invited. So far, only Rev. and Mrs. Abbott have accepted the invitation."

"I'm curious to meet—"

The phone rang again, and Harry went to answer it. Babs quickly piled up the dishes and prepared to bathe George in the sink. As always, George enjoyed playing in the water and getting his bath. Babs was drying him off, when the kitchen door opened, and Mac walked in.

"You're back, huh?"

"Yes, Mac," she said.

"The baby has grown, and you have a tan. Enjoyed that California sunshine, did you?" he asked as he made his way toward the dining alcove.

"Yes, we had a nice visit, but I'm glad to be home."

Mac turned and gave her a rare smile.

"Have you heard about our big celebration coming up? The ladies are going to cook up a storm."

He turned the corner to the living room, and she knew he'd left when she heard the front door close. She wrapped George in a towel and went to lock both the front and back doors.

"I'm not ready to receive unexpected guests. I need to finish unpacking," she told George.

"Honey," she called upstairs, "would you get the playpen out of the car for me?"

"Yes, as soon as I'm off the phone," he answered.

"What now?" she wondered, as she dressed the baby.

"George, let's go into Mommy's bedroom, and you can watch me unpack."

In a few minutes, Harry appeared at the bedroom door.

"I've set up the playpen in the living room."

"Thanks, Dear. Who was that on the phone so long?"

"It was Tim, talking about the program coming up. He and I agree that we should take part in the celebration."

"Oh, I do, too."

"It may not be a lot of fun for us. If the Rev. Paul Baker comes, Collins will be elated. Baker is a humorous speaker. Tim thinks Collins will try to arrange things, so that the former ministers speak, and I'll be sort of left out."

"Oh, Honey," she said, giving him a hug.

"I'm *glad* to see the others get the recognition they deserve, but I've done my best here, and the attendance at Prairie Meadows is up 30%, and Rosebud's is up 100%."

"You've done well, Honey."

"Do you think so?"

"I sure do. The people here love you."

"Sounds like Eben and Marcia have been alienated."

"Do you think that's going to last?"

"I hope not. I can't understand why Bill is acting this way."

"Do you think he'd act this way if things were going poorly?"

"I don't know."

"Remember the question I asked you the night of our welcome party?"

"No. What did you ask me?"

"I asked you why Jane Collins scolded me."

"That's easy! She was jealous of you."

"That's right. The people In the Prairie Meadows Church are pulling together and things are going well. Tell me, does that give you a clue why Bill Collins is acting like an S.O.B.?"

Chapter 63

DVBS

"Will this be enough fish, Alberta?" asked Rita.

The Busy Bees were gathered around the table at Alberta's, preparing for Vacation Bible School.

"I ran off fifteen sheets, and there's eighteen fish on each sheet. That ought to be enough, don't you think, Jane?"

"No. We have forty-five kids signed up from our church, and they are working hard at inviting other kids. Every time they bring a friend, they get a fish. The one who earns the most fish gets a new baseball mitt," answered Jane, proudly tossing her head.

"You see, Babs," said Mrs. Blodgett who was cutting out fish almost as fast as Babs could color them, "you and Pastor weren't here to manage the publicity for our Daily Vacation Bible School, DVBS, but Jane, here, has been doing a wonderful job."

Babs added a touch of red to the fish she was coloring.

"Each child who comes gets one of these paper fish. And everyone who brings some one gets another fish. If Margie, for example, brings a neighbor, she gets a fish for every day he comes. We'll need a lot of fish," advised Jane.

"I see," answered Babs, applying the final bit of orange to the fish she was working on and putting it in the box next to Alberta at the table.

"Not only that," added Marcia, Eben's wife, who was also coloring fish, "the kids get a fish for every Bible verse they memorize."

"Any Bible verse?" asked Babs.

"No. We have a list of Bible verses, or they can get their choice approved," laughed Alberta. "Otherwise, every child will memorize verses like *Jesus wept*."

"The theme for our Daily Vacation Bible School this year is courage," said Jane.

"That's why, at your 10:00 am spot on the schedule, we want you to tell flannelgraph stories like David and Goliath," said Alberta.

"I'll be glad to do that," answered Babs.

"I'm almost finished lettering the chart that will hold their names," said Rita.

"Oh, Jane, guess what?" asked Marcia.

"What is it, Marcia?"

"We got a note from Rev. Abbott. He and his wife definitely plan to attend our church anniversary celebration

"That's wonderful. Will they stay with you?"

"Yes. We are so excited. We just love the Abbotts. Their kids are the same age as our kids. All our kids are grown, but we remember a lot of good times together."

"He has a wonderful singing voice—" said Rita.

"And she is the most accomplished pianist we've ever had," interrupted Jane, looking at Babs. "Maybe she'll play for the morning worship."

"That would be very nice," said Babs.

"I'm so glad that you all could come over and help get ready for Daily Vacation Bible School. I think we'll have a great time this year. We have so many new families to draw from."

"Of course we would help you, Alberta," answered Rita Barker.

"Is anyone ready for a refill of coffee or tea?" asked Alberta, circling the room with the coffee pot.

"No, thanks, none for me, Alberta. I'd better leave for home. Harry said he had an appointment at 11:00, so I need to go home and take care of George."

"Next time, maybe you can bring George," said Mrs. Blodgett. "Then you can stay longer and help us more."

"I'll see you all later. Thank you for the coffee, Alberta," said Babs as she left.

Walking briskly back to the parsonage, she saw Bob Rennik approaching, carrying a heavy load of mail. His left hand was bandaged.

"Hello, Bob, I haven't seen you for a long time. Did you hurt yourself?"

"It's not a matter of hurting myself. That damn—excuse me, ma'm—darn dog bit me."

"Chester bit you?"

"That's the one. Bit my left hand, and I'm left-handed. Mrs. Jarvis wrapped my hand. I'm about ready to sue the dog's owner. Three months ago, I refused to deliver mail to the Brown's house. They have a post office box now."

"Oh."

"But now, that damn--, er, darned dog goes after me when I deliver the mail to Woods or Jarvises. He's a vicious dog and should be put down. Well, thanks to him, I'm running late again. Bye."

She watched as the mailman walked on quickly. Babs had a lot of sympathy for a man trying to do his job in the midst of harassment. Harry, on the other hand, had pointed out that the dog in question was around children of the village all the time, and no one had ever reported a bite or even a snarl from Chester. Puzzling situation.

That evening over scrambled eggs (scrambled eggs because the gasoline bills were intruding into their food budget), they talked things over.

"I need to get busy on the flannelgraph work. Alberta asked me to prepare a Bible story about courage for each day of Daily Vacation Bible School."

"Courage, huh?"

"Besides David and Goliath, I'm thinking about Joshua and the Battle of Jericho, Sampson and Delilah, and Daniel in the lion's den."

"That's four."

"Yes, I need another story."

"Do you want to stick with the Old Testament?"

"Not necessarily."

"What about Peter walking on the water?"

"That's a good one! You relate so well to the Apostle Peter, Harry."

Harry smiled and took another bite of Italian squash.

"You know, I feel very uncomfortable about this coming seventy-fifth anniversary, Harry. I usually enjoy celebrating and meeting other pastors and their wives. Somehow, I seem to dread this one, " she said, as she cleared the main dish.

"Is it because you realize that Collins is doing this all on his own?"

"Maybe."

"Lots of guests are being invited, older people will be asked to talk about the 'old days,' and the ladies will put on a big spread. But I agree, something is lacking".

"Harry, did you know that Dr. Galvin has been invited?"

"No."

"I was talking to Mrs. Galvin on the phone, and she told me. You know, I wonder if Father Kelly will be here. And I wonder if Bill Collins invited people like Jim Staley of Stevens Point and Will Erickson of Wild Rose."

Harry shook his head.

"I wonder if he remembered to invite our Executive Secretary, Dr. Miller."

"Oh, he should be invited."

"Well, I'm going to go over and talk to Bill Collins this evening. Whether he likes it or not, I'm the pastor, and I need to know what's going on around here."

"Oh, Harry, you're wonderful! I really love you! And while you're talking to Bill, and George is down for the night, I can prepare for DVBS."

Chapter 64

BROODING STORM

Harry knocked on the door of the one-story bungalow where Collins' lived. A light was on in the living room, and also in the front room, which served as Bill's Red Cross office. Hearing a radio on in the living room, Harry was certain that Jane was there. It was Bill, however, who answered the door, his shirtsleeves rolled up and his rimless glasses pushed up on his balding head.

"Harry," said Collins, looking surprised.

"Hello, Bill," said Harry. "May I come in? I feel we need to talk."

"I'm tied up. You and I have covered everything. You can see I'm busy."

"Are you working on church business or Red Cross?"

"Both."

Tall Harry pushed a rebellious strand of light brown hair back from his forehead, fixing his large blue eyes on his host's pale face. In spite of his casual manner, the young minister seemed to be planted on Collins' front porch for the evening. It was obvious that Harry was determined to talk.

"After I made it plain that I receive neither help nor inspiration from your sermons or your style of leadership, I hardly expected you to come here again."

"Bill, we have to put our personal considerations aside for the good of the church."

"Oh, come in, if you must," said Bill opening the screen door. "I'm working on personnel matters in regard to the Red Cross," and he took his place behind his large, flat desk, which was covered with letters and papers.

Bill did not invite Harry to sit down, but Harry found a chair and drew closer. The young minister felt, that his opponent had, perhaps unconsciously, taken refuge behind his desk, which was a rather formidable antique. Idly, Harry wondered how often Bill had holed up there during confrontations with his wife Jane.

"We need to talk about the church's anniversary celebration," said Harry.

"Oh, I think not. I've got the services lined up, and Jane and the women are taking care of the food."

"You forget that I'm the minister here. I am responsible for the worship services in this parish."

"Unfortunately, you do have that responsibility. However, since you and every other officer in this church were ready to ignore the seventy-fifth anniversary here in Prairie, *I* came to the rescue and got the wheels in motion.

"Who did you invite?"

"That's 'Whom did I invite?,' Harry. Oh, I'm sorry. I forgot that, since neither of your parents attended high school, you never learned to speak the King's English correctly."

"Let's leave my father and mother out of this discussion, Bill. Who's coming and taking part?"

Bill shrugged his shoulders.

"Fourteen ministers have served this church. Seven of them are still living. I wrote to six of them. Was unable to find the address of Josiah Goodrich, who moved to California fifteen years ago."

"Lola Rankin, might be able to help us. She mentioned once that Rev. Goodrich had married her and her husband."

"That's right! I never thought of that. I'll ask her."

"How many of the six answered?"

"I still haven't heard from Donald Charles. The other five replied."

261

"Who will be coming then?"

"The Rev. Abbott, Oscar Lewis, and Eric Pierce are coming. Baker and Johnson sent greetings."

"Do you want to read their greetings? Since you did all this correspondence, you should get this recognition, Bill. I'll preside at the services, of course. Do you have a schedule of events? I'd like to look it over."

Bill squirmed in his chair, taken aback by the poise and strength of the young man before him.

"That's what I was doing just now—setting up the activities for the weekend of celebration."

"Two heads are better than one. We can work together on this. And you are better acquainted with these ministers than I am."

Bill surprised himself by handing Harry the unfinished program he was working on and pointing to the first day.

"Friday night we can call 'Homecoming,' and it will be potluck at the church, with host families bringing extra for the visitors."

"What about a program, Bill?"

"I hadn't got to that yet."

"Maybe we could get Freda James from Rosebud to play the cello. She does well. Will any of the ministers be there?"

"The Rev. and Mrs. Abbott are coming for the whole time."

"Well, Bill, after I heard about this, I knew the deacons would want to help, so I phoned Morgans. Eben told me that Pete Abbott does magic tricks. Maybe he would perform for us."

"That's a possibility," answered Bill slowly, reluctant to agree his pastor.

"I see you have another potluck for Saturday night. Would we want two potlucks in a row at the church?"

"What would you suggest?" asked Bill defensively.

"A picnic in our local Veteran's Memorial Park might be a nice change for Saturday. We could always move to the church if it rains."

"Possibly."

"I talked to Tim Woods. He has some old slides regarding the church. He said he'd be willing to be responsible for a short slide show about the history and people of the church. We can also ask him to tell something about his father's pastorate here."

"I have some slides that might be amusing."

"Good. Fred Young does too, and Eben has some good ones of the Abbott children along with his own kids, taken in Sunday School years ago. I have some recent slides."

"Well, I guess after the picnic, we could come back to the church for a slide show then."

"It would be good to sing some songs and read some Scripture. I was wondering if the children's choir would sing a couple of songs. People love to hear the children."

"Jane is tied up with the Sunday church banquet. I don't know if she'll have time to work with the children's choir."

"I see. Now, for the Sunday morning service, we want to involve all the ministers. I'll preside. Have you heard any of them preach?"

"I've heard Rev. Pierce. You've met him. Baker's a great speaker, but, unfortunately, he can't make it."

"Abbott will be doing the magic. How about Oscar Lewis?"

"It was my intention to invite Lewis to speak on Sunday morning," answered Collins stiffly.

"That's fine. We'll work together on this after we receive word from Lewis, Donald Charles, and Josiah Goodrich. By the way, I'm sure you have a part in mind in the service for Dr. Miller, our Executive Secreatary."

Bill looked blank.

"Uh, well, uh, yes, I guess he should be invited."

"I knew you'd want him. Since you tell me you're so busy, I'll be glad to get in touch with Dr. Miller. And let me see about Josiah Goodrich."

"All right," said Collins uneasily.

"Bill, it's wonderful to have an intelligent man like you, dedicated to the work of the church. I'm sorry to interrupt you when you're busy. Give my greetings to Mrs. Collins, will you?"

Harry rose to his full height, extended his long arm across the wide antique desk, grabbed Bill's right hand, and shook it. Standing there for a moment, he seemed to fill the small room. Suddenly, he was gone.

Bill sat at his desk for a long time contemplating the revised program for the anniversary week. After a while, he took out a small cloth and began to clean his bifocals.

"That Harry! He never does what I expect him to do!"

Bill tipped his chair back, screwed up his mouth, and began to imitate Harry's voice:

"'You should get this recognition!' 'I'm sure you have a part in mind for Dr. Miller!' 'Wonderful to have an intelligent man like you!'"

Bill shook his head. He cupped his mouth and called out to his wife,

"Jane, what about having the children's choir sing during the church anniversary celebration?"

There was no answer. She must be listening to her favorite radio program, "Amos and Andy." She hated to miss a single episode.

As Bill rose from his chair to go to speak to his wife, he muttered,

"That Harry! The man doesn't know enough to come in out of the rain! He doesn't even recognize an enemy when he sees one!"

Chapter 65

MINISTERS GALORE

"Rita, you haven't lost your touch at the griddle," said the Reverend Donald Charles as he pushed his plate away, sipping his cup of coffee.

"Yes, Rita, you're spoiling my husband," said Dorothy Charles. "Now, he'll expect waffles and sausage and eggs for breakfast at home."

"Here's another waffle coming up, hot off the iron. Can't you eat just a half more, Rev. Charles?"

"I'd love to, Rita. But no more room."

"I bet he could use some more coffee," observed Mac from his place at the table.

"Dorothy, won't you have this waffle? You've hardly eaten a thing!"

"I shouldn't, but I'll take half," replied Dorothy.

"This coffee hits the spot, Rita. Unfortunately, I'll have to be excused in a few minutes," said the minister. "Harry asked us all to come over early, before he goes to the Rosebud service, to make sure every minister knows what he's to do in the worship service this morning."

Dorothy buttered her waffle.

"Pass the syrup, please, Mac," she said.

"Good maple syrup, isn't it?" he said as he passed it. "We had to pay five dollars for that little pail."

"I'll take a drop or two," replied Dorothy. "Babs invited us wives to come, too. Wait for me, Donald. I must finish Rita's delicious waffle."

Rita smiled indulgently.

"Glad you're enjoying the breakfast. Rev. Charles, you and your wife look so young. You both stay slim."

"Besides that, Mrs. Charles doesn't have gray hair," said Mac.

"We take a two-mile hike three times a week, and we swim in the summertime. Are you about ready, Dorothy?"

Dorothy finished the last bite of waffle, wiped her mouth, and hurriedly applied lipstick.

"Yes, I'm ready, Donald. Rita, I hate to leave you with all these dishes. Mac, do you help with dishes?"

"No, but I'm pretty good at taking out the garbage, huh, Rita?" he asked.

"Yes, Mac. And you take care of the money."

"That's no trouble. Taking care of money is fun, isn't it, Rev. Charles?"

"If I had any, I'd agree," laughed Donald, signaling his wife to hurry.

Mac watched his former minister and wife as they made their way down the block toward the parsonage, two slim figures, about the same height. He thought the blond Mrs. Charles looked pretty sharp, dressed all in blue. She was tugging at her hat, which wasn't at the angle to suit her.

Mac returned to the kitchen where Rita was eating her breakfast.

"They look so young! Did you notice, Rita? That minister's wife doesn't have a gray hair!"

"Mac, you're so naive," Rita replied as she cleared the dishes and prepared to wash them.

As the Charles' approached the manse, they saw a tall gaunt figure of a man emerging from the house next door. Dressed in a shiny brown suit with his rebellious white hair standing out in all directions, he was carrying a large, black Bible. As they approached, they saw coffee stains on his red tie. The three met at the cement sidewalk, leading to the parsonage door.

"I'm Reverend Eric Pierce," said the tall man, changing his Bible to the other hand, so that he could shake hands with Charles.

"Glad to meet you," answered the other man as they continued toward the front door. "We are Donald and Dorothy Charles. You served this parish before we came to the Prairie Meadows Church. Aren't you the man who loves to fish?"

"Right you are. You've heard of me then?"

Donald knocked, and Harry answered, as a black cat escaped out the door.

"Welcome, Eric," said the host to his sometime neighbor, and turning to the others, "I'm Harry Petersen. Come in. Are you the Charles,' by any chance?"

"We sure are, Donald and Dorothy."

Donald looked around and saw a roomful of animated people, seated on the sofa and window seat. A tall woman with dark hair approached, carrying a tray with a coffee pot and cups and saucers. She indicated an easy chair and a kitchen chair next to it.

"I'm Babs Petersen. Won't you sit there? Would you like a cup of coffee?"

"No, thanks," answered Donald, taking the wooden chair.

"I'd love a cup of coffee," said Dorothy as she appropriated the easy chair, and watched her hostess pour a cup of weak coffee. "Donald rushed me through breakfast."

"Donald," said a red-haired man, from his place on the window seat, "you must be the Charles'. I'm Pete Abbott, and this is my wife, Opal," pointing to his plump freckled-faced wife beside him.

"You can remember us because we both have red hair," answered Opal.

"And I'm Oscar Lewis," said the man next to them on the window seat. "My claim to fame is that I love Dalmatians."

Everyone laughed.

"Do you all know Eric Pierce, who's wandering over there to the sofa? His daughter is our neighbor," said Babs.

"We just met him. He's famous for fishing," said Donald.

"Also, over on the sofa are Joan and Josiah Goodrich. I believe they came the farthest, from Los Angeles," said Harry.

"You can remember me, by my great height and this fine head of black hair," acknowledged Josiah rubbing his bald head.

"And we brought each of you an avocado from our own back yard," said Joan.

They thanked her as she passed around the bag of avocados.

"What are they? A vegetable, a fruit?" asked Eric.

"Do you eat the skin?" asked Opal.

"We serve them with fruit in a salad. You don't eat the rind."

"Would Dalmatians like them?" inquired Oscar.

Everyone laughed again.

"I'd like to go over the service," said Harry. "Maybe we should go upstairs."

"Why don't we girls adjourn to the dining alcove, and let the men have the living room?" suggested Babs.

Opal and Joan left their places and came to sit down at the dinette table, but Dorothy Charles lingered, comfortable in the easy chair. Finally, she rose.

"Donald," asked Babs, "may I take the kitchen chair you're sitting on? Why don't you try the easy chair?"

With a triumphant glance at his wife, Donald settled into Harry's chair, as the ministers began to go over the final plans for the morning worship service.

"Gentlemen," said Harry, "I'd like to arrange the service as follows: Pete Abbott, lead songs; Eric Pierce, read Scripture; Josiah Goodrich, give pastoral prayer; Oscar Lewis, preach; and Donald Charles, give benediction. I've asked Dr. Galvin, the Methodist minister in town, to give the invocation, and then he will leave for his own service. I'll preside at the service, and Donald, I'd like to ask you for a bit of extra help."

"What is that, Harry?"

"Bill Collins was going to read the greetings from the absent ministers and from Dr. Miller, our Executive Superintendent. However, his wife phoned me this morning to tell me that he, unfortunately, will be tied up today in Stevens Point on emergency Red Cross business."

"Yes," contributed Oscar Lewis, "I'm staying with him and Jane. There was a bad fire at St. Michael's Hospital in Stevens Point. He got the message early this morning."

"That's too bad, Harry. He is the one that got this celebration underway, isn't he?" asked Pete Abbott.

"Yes. Too bad."

"You want me to read the greetings?"

"Yes, Donald."

"I'll be glad to do it, Harry."

The Rev. Josiah Goodrich, having heard about the situation from Lola Rankin's viewpoint, commented with irony,

"Isn't it a shame, Harry, that the fellow who worked so hard to bring the anniversary celebration to pass, cannot be present to enjoy it with us?"

"Yes, Josiah," agreed Harry. "Bill Collins won't be with us. A real shame."

Chapter 66

LET'S SLEEP IN

"It was as wonderful celebration, wasn't it?"

"It really was, Babs. I didn't expect to see so many lay people as well as ministers here."

"Everybody had such a good time at the Homecoming, Friday night."

"Freda's cello solo was well-received, and you did a fine job of accompanying her."

"It was fun. Thanks for taking care of George while she and I practiced."

"Pete Abbott is really good at magic tricks," said Harry.

"He sure is. Did you see how big Mac's eyes got when Pete made his five dollar bill disappear?"

"And how excited Mrs. Blodgett got, when he 'found' the bill in her purse," chuckled the pastor.

"Pete and Opal Abbott are nice people to know, Harry. I'm so glad they came."

"People enjoyed the picnic in the War Memorial Park on Saturday, don't you think?"

"Yes, I'm glad you suggested that picnic, so that we didn't have two pot-lucks in a row. Just a minute, I'm running the bath water."

Babs disappeared into the bathroom, and Harry took off one shoe and sat idly on the edge of the bed, thinking about the past weekend, a time he'd been dreading. Instead, it had turned out to be a delightful experience! On Sunday, Oscar Lewis had delivered an outstanding message on differing gifts, his homely illustrations involving Dalmatians enjoyed by all.

The only hitch in the morning worship had occurred when Eric Pierce stood up to read the Scripture. The passage concerned the weakness that St. Paul had, and his prayers that God would remove his "thorn in the flesh." As Eric read, Harry was wondering at the appropriateness of that particular passage of Scripture. Suddenly, Eric recognized that he had made a mistake— reading from II Corinthians, rather than from I Corinthians, as requested by Oscar. With an apology, the Reverend Pierce, with great deliberation, searched, and found the correct Scripture, and read the passage, regarding gifts of the Spirit.

As Harry sat with one shoe on and one shoe off, he was thinking about Eric's "talent" for getting mixed up. Babs, rosy and relaxed from her bath, re-entered their bedroom and perceived that Harry was deep in thought. She went to check on George, who, as usual, was sleeping on his tummy with his head turned to the left. She kissed him, smoothed his blanket, and returned to their bedroom. Concluding her evening ritual of brushing her dark hair and putting it up in pink socks, she climbed into bed. After arranging the pillows behind her, she sat cross-legged, regarding Harry thoughtfully.

"Hello there," she said to her motionless husband. "I can see that you're far away. Are you coming to bed?"

"What's that?" he asked.

"Day dreaming, are you?"

"Oh," he said, starting to pull off his left shoe, "I was just thinking about the ministry. Every minister has his gifts, and every

270

lay person, also. Look at Eric Pierce. He blunders along, but he makes a contribution. Everyone likes him."

"Yes, they do. When he officiated at the wedding when you were so sick, he got all mixed up, but he married the couple, and the relatives accepted his efforts. No one became resentful. They all chuckled."

"I'm like Eric. I just blunder along. I'm not smooth like Donald Charles, or humorous like Oscar Lewis, or comfortable and friendly like Pete Abbott, or deep, like Josiah Goodrich."

"You feel that of all the ministers here, you're most like Eric?"

"Guess so," muttered Harry dropping his shoe on the floor.

"Come here, you big lug! You're wonderful and successful. You've done very well here, against a lot of indifference and opposition!"

"I have? Do you think I've done a good job?"

"You certainly have," she said putting her arms around him. They cuddled close.

"I'm so wound up, I can't settle down," he said.

"We've been so busy. If George will let us, why don't we sleep in tomorrow morning?"

"That sounds good to me," he said. "I'll put you on hold while I go brush my teeth, okay?"

"Okay," she said, stretching out on the bed.

Slumber came much later.

Harry was watching Fred Young and Bill Collins as they put on boxing gloves and prepared to fight. Mrs. Blodgett, in a large, orchid hat, was in Bill's corner, while Myrtle Dodds, wearing a small, black cap, was in Fred's. Myrtle kept yelling, "Kill him, Fred! Kill him!"

The floor was rolling, and, suddenly, a baby, in a ring-side seat, was crying. Harry rolled about convulsively as the baby continued to cry.

"Harry, it's all right! George is crying. He wants to get up," said Babs as she scrambled out of bed.

"Wh-wh-what's that?" mumbled Harry.

"Go back to sleep, Dear. I'll take care of him."

"Ah," said Harry, turning over and immediately falling asleep.

Harry was a teen-ager, back on the farm in northern Wisconsin, now in charge, since his father had been recalled to the mill. Their neighbor was on his way to help him butcher a pig. Harry had never butchered a pig before. But he couldn't get out of

271

his chair. His neighbor was knocking on the door. He couldn't get up. He heard voices. People in the living room were talking.

"Oh, hello, Mac."

"Hello, Ma'm. The missus lent you a casserole dish—"

"That's right. I fixed scalloped potatoes for the Sunday banquet. It's in the kitchen—"

The voices drifted off.

Back on the farm, he and his brother, Lefty, were milking cows. Lefty kept teasing him about a neighbor's daughter. Harry picked up a forkful of manure to throw at his brother. He tossed hard, and it landed in the pail of milk next to Lefty.

"Now you're in trouble," said Lefty triumphantly.

"I don't want to cause you any trouble," said a woman's voice. "Pastor told me, I was to let him know if Harvey needed help with the farm. Today Harvey's in bed with a fever."

"Won't you sit down, Clara? I'll be just a moment."

Harry's eyes were open, as Babs, in her flowered housecoat, came into the room.

"It's Clara. She needs your help."

Harry was struggling to wake up.

"They borrowed Frank Waukowski's tractor for today. Harvey was planning to cut early rye, but he can't manage it."

Harry grabbed his pants and started to put them on.

"Honey, you'll need to wear work pants—not your best suit."

Babs was looking through the closet. Finding his overalls, she brought them to him.

"Tell her I'll be out in a minute."

"Harry, you'll need to eat breakfast. You can't work out in the fields without."

"I don't have time," he said, vainly trying to button the overalls.

"I've already told Clara that you were sleeping in this morning, and you haven't had breakfast."

"Oh, what a mistake that was, trying to sleep in."

"Take your time. I'll fix your oatmeal."

She was gone. Harry heard some loud purring as Tuck paraded into the room.

"Where's my socks?" he asked himself, as Tuck brushed against his legs.

He heard a knock at the front door. To his relief, some one answered it.

"It's Mrs. Blodgett, isn't it? I'm here to get some help from Harry. Can I help you?" Clara Wells said.

"You're from Sterling, aren't you?" asked Mrs. Blodgett.

"Yes, I am. What a pretty hat you're wearing, Mrs. Blodgett."

"Thank you. I came to see the minister. I know you're from Sterling, but I don't know your name."

"I'm Clara Wells. Come in."

"I need to see the pastor. Oh, there you are, Rev. Petersen," said Mrs. Blodgett, as Harry came into the living room.

"Good morning, both of you," said Harry.

"My propane tank is empty, Rev. Petersen. I'd like you to get it filled."

"He's going to help Harvey and me with cutting the early rye today. Maybe I could pick it up for you," said Clara.

"It's pretty heavy."

"There's probably some man who could help us."

Harry moved toward the kitchen, where he found George playing with the measuring cups and his wife, cooking his oatmeal. She poured him a cup of coffee.

"This is Grand Central Station this morning," he said, as the door opened and Henry Perkins came in, carrying the quart of milk left on the back steps.

"Good morning," said Henry handing the milk to Babs who put it in the icebox. "How's that big boy doing today?"

"Good morning, Henry. George is doing fine. Your cereal is ready, Dear."

"Getting a late start are you, Pastor?"

"Yes, Henry, but I'm making up for it now," replied Harry as he sat down at the table and poured milk on his oatmeal.

Henry walked on toward the living room.

"You missed Margie, Harry. She came by a while ago and took George for a buggy ride."

By the time Harry had finished his oatmeal and eaten a couple of pieces of toast, Clara came into the dinette.

"Pastor, I arranged for Mr. Perkins to take care of getting Mrs. Blodgett's propane tank filled."

"Thank you, Clara. Now I can concentrate on the rye crop. I'll get the car."

"No, Pastor. I'll take you and bring you back. That way, Babs will have the car available in case she needs it."

"I'm packing him a lunch," said Babs.

"Babs, we'll take care of Harry's meals. I'm so thankful that Pastor can help us."

"Remember to wear a hat out in the field, Dear. You sunburn so easily."

"I don't know where it is," he replied, as he and Clara walked toward the door.

"Wait a minute!" she called, as she dashed into their bedroom. "I saw it on the closet shelf!"

Clara had started the car, when Babs, with George in her arms, ran out to deliver the hat. Since Harry's mind was on the task ahead, he grabbed the hat absentmindedly as they drove away. Mother and son watched Clara's 1940 green Dodge pick-up, as it gathered speed and drove out of sight.

"George, your Daddy has a busy day ahead of him, and your Mommy has to get dressed!"

George looked down the road in the direction of the pickup. He pointed and said, "Da da."

"Yes, Daddy's riding in the truck. He's going to work. So much for sleeping in!"

Chapter 67

I DON'T WANT TO COMPLAIN

Harry sat at his desk in the study upstairs. As usual, he had tipped the wooden, kitchen chair against the wall, so that all his weight was on the back legs of the chair. He loved stretching his legs this comfortable way, a habit which scared Babs.

"Honey," she would say, "please don't do that. You look so precarious. I'd hate to have to rush you to the hospital."

While Harry indulged himself, his wife, with George, was attending Culture Club at Miss Hawk's. The librarian was hosting a garden party especially for mothers and young babies. The speaker for the afternoon was a woman from The Boston Store in Milwaukee. Her topic was "Using Accessories to Make a Fashion Statement."

This morning, over breakfast, Babs told Harry that she was looking forward to the Culture Club meeting.

Harry looked at his wife quizzically.

"Is this the woman who told you to eat pudding with tablespoons?"

Babs laughed.

"She told us to use our cream soup spoons for desserts."

"Is the speaker that same lady?"

"I don't know."

"Well, if it is, I can expect you to leave your purse home and henceforth carry your compact, hanky, and comb in a loaf pan, right?"

"She is also going to talk about baby fashions."

"Oh, poor George!"

George looked at his father and said, "Da da!"

At that instant, Harry looked at George's eyes, and wondered silently, "Was one pupil 'lazy'? Did the left eye go slightly inward? Oh, I guess not."

The painful moment passed.

"Harry, I'm really looking forward to seeing the members. I've had to miss so many meetings."

"I'm glad you can go. I have an appointment with Dr. Miller as well as lots of studying to do."

Babs had left the house in a happy mood for George had on a new mint green outfit from his Grandma Ruth, and Babs was dressed in a flowered skirt and one of the new nylon blouses that the ladies of her home church had given her.

Harry had watched her drive away, slowly so that George did not lose his balance in the front seat.

"I'm so lucky! The girl I married is beautiful, and our baby is so alert. Standing up by the car window, he doesn't want to miss a thing!"

With the house quiet, Harry had a golden opportunity to study, but his mind was in a whirl. The seventy-fifth celebration had gone very well. Everyone had enjoyed the fellowship of former pastors and their wives, along with former members, who had attended the homecoming. The programs were interesting, and the women had outdone themselves preparing the banquet held after the Sunday service. However, Jane Collins was becoming increasingly abrupt and critical, while Bill would barely speak to him. Harry felt himself grieving over the disunity in the Prairie Meadows Church.

"What can I do to improve this situation?" Harry asked himself.

Hearing a knock at the front door, Harry let the front legs of the chair down with a thump.

"That must be my Executive Secretary," he said, quickly descending the stairs to answer the front door, almost stumbling over Tuck who was dozing at the foot of the stairs. Tuck retired to the piano bench with wounded dignity.

"Come in, Dr. Miller," Harry said, as he opened the door. "I'm so glad to see you."

"Thank you, Harry," responded the older man as they shook hands. He sat on the sofa Harry had indicated. "How are your wife and that fine baby of yours?"

"They're fine, Dr. Miller. George has a great appetite and is growing like a weed. Babs and the baby are at a garden party right now. She sends you her greetings."

Tuck made his move and jumped up on the sofa at the opposite end from their guest.

"So kind of you to ask me to dinner. I'll take a rain check on that, thank you. But, frankly, I'm happy that we have an opportunity to talk privately. Tell me, how is the work going here?"

"Well, there's a lot to be thankful for. Rosebud has a full house now at every service. The people are inviting their friends."

"Have they mentioned raising their financial support? As I recall, they give only ten dollars a week or so."

"They contribute seven dollars toward my salary, but did not pay me during my month's vacation."

"They are enjoying the work of the church, but are chary of paying for it, right?"

"I guess that's so," answered Harry reluctantly. "Rosebud is a pretty rough community. They're limited in their perceptions, and they tend to be suspicious of outsiders as well as each other. But, you know, they sure do love to sing the Gospel songs, especially with Babs at the piano."

"Sounds like you're enjoying them. How about Sterling?"

"The congregation is a mass of contradictions. There are some outstanding people there, like Mrs. Jones and her family and Clara and Harvey Wells. I see signs of spiritual growth among some people like Frank and John Waukowski and their wives. Even old Ed Wells has come around and been easier to live with."

"But their numbers are about the same, aren't they?"

"Yes, there are some unresolved resentments and jealousies that people are reluctant to give up. I don't see numerical growth coming until they talk things out and forgive one another."

"As I recall, they're quite strict, are they not?"

"Yes. A pastor years ago convinced them that they should never put on a dinner—not even for fellowship. As a result, they have few opportunities to work together. Furthermore, I've been disappointed that I haven't been able to start a weekly Bible study group there. They could be good givers, but they worry about their mission dollars going to the denomination, afraid that the money won't be used to bring people to Christ."

"H-m-m-m."

"There's a retired minister and his wife, Rev. and Mrs. Jenson."

"Oh, yes, I met them once."

"I expected that a retired minister would be supportive. However, old Jenson scowls all the time, and his wife always looks grumpy."

"No encouragement, from them?"

"Right. But Dr. Miller, I don't want to complain. We've had some wonderful times with many of our people here."

"Tell me about Prairie Meadows."

"The church and Sunday School attendance is up by thirty per cent. A number of young couples have been attending our services. Financial giving has increased. We've had a number of baptisms, including Alberta Smith's husband, who is now a trustee."

"I remember her, that pretty blond lady," said Dr. Miller with a smile.

"Some old timers who had dropped out, now attend."

"How are Bill Collins and his wife responding?"

"There's a problem. He's temperamental. Doesn't come to church very often."

"Would you characterize them as supportive?" asked Dr. Miller, leaning forward.

"Supportive? I don't know. She runs the Busy Bees, that's the women's society, and leads the children's choir."

"But they're not helping you."

"No, they don't help me. In fact, he likes to give me a bad time."

"Like trying to humiliate you through a church anniversary celebration?"

"Yes," answered Harry looking startled. "You heard about that?"

"One of your parishioners told me about it."

"One of my parishioners?"

"Yes. The fellow I'm thinking of is on our state Commission for Evangelism. At a recent Commission meeting, he shared his concern with me, over the unfair treatment Bill Collins has been giving you."

"Who are you talking about?" asked Harry, raising his voice. "Is it Fred Young? I didn't know he was on a state commission."

"No. Not Fred Young. It's Woods, Ted Woods, I think."

"Tim Woods?"

"Yes, Tim Woods."

"Well, I'll be," mused Harry as he rose from his chair.

"Say, Dr. Miller, Babs made some coffee and cupcakes. Would you like some?"

"Coffee would be fine. I'll skip the cupcake. Have to watch myself, attending so many dinners and potlucks."

"Gotcha," answered Harry as he went to get the coffee.

Tuck, who had been inching closer to the visitor, began to purr loudly, as the executive supervisor got up to look over the rich assortment of sheet music on the rack of the piano.

"This young couple have had a rude initiation," he said to himself, "but they are plucky."

Harry appeared with a tray, complete with coffee in English bone china teacups, silver teaspoons, a silver cream and sugar set, and cupcakes on a silver dish.

"Babs prepared this tray for us before she left."

The older man was struck by the contrast between the elegant tray and the signs of poverty apparent in the threadbare rug, the scuffed wooden chairs, and the sagging sofa.

"I take a little cream in my coffee, thank you," he said, as he helped himself from the silver creamer.

Harry set the tray on the piano stool and served himself.

"Thank you, Harry. By the way, had you considered the idea of moving on to a new parish?"

Harry paused, his teacup in midair.

"No, I hadn't, Dr. Miller. "I've been here only two and a half years, and there's a lot still to be done."

"These are not the only people who need the Good News."

"That's true, but I know these people. People like the Dodds, the Youngs, the Woods—"

"You love these people, don't you?"

"Yes, I do. And their needs are so great. Harvey Wells from Sterling, for example, has had to virtually get out of farming, and we have a number of widows of limited means who need help and encouragement."

"Do you get discouraged when you see your plans thwarted by unfriendly people—people with knowledge and experience who could help you, if they were willing?"

Harry was silent. Only the purring from the black cat could be heard. Finally, the young minister said,

"When I read the Old and New Testaments, I see that spiritual leaders, who set out to bring peace and good news to others, often found themselves embroiled in conflicts with people who somehow became enemies. To my surprise, I have discovered enemies here. I'm beginning to recognize that making enemies is part of the life of a minister."

Harry paused and looked out the window at the church across the street.

"But, I have to admit, I get discouraged sometimes."

"You have learned a lot, quickly. And your loyalty and regard for your people is commendable. However, I would like to tell you about a group of people who need an energetic pastor—people, I believe, who would support you."

Harry laid his half-eaten cupcake on his saucer and fixed his eyes on the supervisor.

"There's a town south of here where there's a substantial congregation. The people are largely of British stock—including successful farmers, small businessmen, and schoolteachers. It's a prosperous community—you can buy any kind of car, right there in the town. A few years ago, a wealthy, Congregational Church dissolved; most of the members chose the church I'm thinking of as their home church. Since the Congregationalists are getting along in years, they need a lot of pastoring."

"Sounds interesting," replied the younger man.

"As I said, they are a substantial people. The two-story parsonage is well-kept. They just remodeled the kitchen area. There are brand new cupboards in the kitchen, with a nice pantry off the kitchen. One of the men is a good carpenter."

"I wonder if they have a refrigerator," mused Harry.

"I'm sure they do."

"Babs would love that. Without a fridge, food spoils. She gets tired of running up and down stairs in the winter to put things away, and having to use an ice box in the summer."

"Of course, she would enjoy the conveniences."

"That's not the important matter."

"No, but your wife's comfort is a matter to consider."

Harry sat motionless in his chair, looking out in space.

"This is like a bolt out of the blue to me, Dr. Miller. I had never even considered a transfer."

"I understand, Harry. Sometimes the Lord pulls us, sometimes He pushes us. We have to be open to His leading. Now, I have another appointment to keep, but I want you to talk it over with Babs and think it through. The church has a speaker lined up for Sunday, but they are expecting me to send a candidate for the following Sunday. Call me in my office on Tuesday morning to let me know if you are willing to preach there. I would recommend that you go and look over the situation. Remember, I feel that they are a deserving group who would profit from your leadership."

"Wow, what you say is exciting! What is the name of the community you are talking about?"

"It's Springvale, a lovely spot," said Dr. Miller as he got up and put his teacup on the tray. "They grow a lot of corn, produce butter and cheese, as well as sell cars. Two of the fellows in the church are car dealers, by the way."

"I wish Babs were here to ask questions," said Harry as he walked to the door with the older man.

"Give her my greetings. Babs plays the piano, I know," replied the supervisor, as he walked out down the steps toward his car. "By the way, does she play the Hammond Organ? I believe the Springvale church has a Hammond."

Chapter 68

CANDIDATE?

"Harry, do you think that we've packed everything we'll need?"

"I hope so. We packed a lot of things last night. It's amazing to me, the amount of stuff you always insist on bringing!"

"I'm sorry, Honey," she said as she settled into the front seat of the car, "but since we're going to visit your folks after spending Sunday in Springvale, I had to pack with that in mind."

"Okay," he said, looking at her. "We don't want to be late. Can we get started?"

"I guess so," she replied, doubtfully.

Harry turned the key in the ignition and started the car.

"See Mac and Henry across the street? They are wondering where we're going," he remarked as he pulled away from the house.

Halfway around the block, Babs laid her hand on Harry's arm.

"Oh, oh, what did you forget this time?" he asked in a resigned tone.

"I left a pint of our canned string beans, that I want to give your mom. It's on the dinette table."

"On this one trip, can't we just forget about it?"

"Honey, please turn back. I feel as though I've forgotten something else."

282

Soon, the two slight old men were rewarded by the sight of their pastor's car pulling up by the back door. Henry dug his elbow into Mac's side.

"I told you, Mac. They're back."

"All right, Henry. I'll bet it's a two-return trip today."

"I'll bet it will take them three returns this time. Look at that back seat all piled with stuff!"

The men watched with interest, as Babs got out of the car, unlocked the back door, and vanished inside. Turning their attention to Harry, waiting in the driver's seat, they saw no movement out of him, but noticed that the baby, standing in his father's lap, was watching Chester, the black lab, chase a calico cat headed past the parsonage. Finally, the minister's wife opened the back door, set two parcels on the steps, and locked the door behind her.

Pausing a moment, she unlocked the door once again, and reentered the parsonage. A moment later, she emerged with a paper bag, locked the door, picked up the other two parcels, smiled and waved at the old men, and got into the car. As the car pulled away, the men could see her leaning over the back seat, placing the bundles there.

With one accord, the men crossed the street and stood by the back porch, waiting.

"She went back into the house twice, Henry. That's a two-return trip, for sure."

"No," responded Henry, "that was a one-return trip. Neither of us won."

"Well, I was closer," replied Mac, putting his nose against the window in the back door. "Can't see nothin'."

Meanwhile, as Harry turned the car south, he relaxed a bit, his attention on the road.

"Harry, what did Dr. Miller say when you told him that you would consider the Springvale Church?"

"He said that I wouldn't regret it. He said that the church is substantial and stable. I told him I wasn't sure about it, and he said, 'Take your time. Look over the situation, and then make up your mind.'"

"Who did you get to preach for you?"

"Rev. Jenson said he'd preach in Sterling and Rosebud. But he didn't want to speak at Prairie Meadows."

"I guess P.M. doesn't enjoy his messages! So, who will preach at P.M.?"

"I called Pastor Will Erickson at Wild Rose, and he got me in touch with Jed Morris. Jed is preparing to become a lay minister, and he'll be coming."

"Is Jed the layman at your ordination who gave you such a bad time about your beliefs in connection with the Second Coming of Christ?"

"He's the one!"

"I wonder if Prairie Meadows will like him. Did you tell Will what you're doing this Sunday?"

"Yes, and he said that he was glad that I was looking around. According to him, some pastors get tunnel vision."

"Your mom and dad sounded excited about our coming to see them after visiting Springvale and the possibility of our moving closer to them."

"It's been a long time since we've had a visit. With Dad working extra hours at the steel mill, they couldn't come up."

George alternately sat in his mother's lap or stood up by the window, to view the passing landscape. He was fascinated by the tall silos located near the barns. Pointing to a silo he said, "Da da?" and Babs responded, "Silo. That's where the farmer keeps the grain for his cows."

Throughout the trip, George noticed and pointed at silos, repeating, "Da da," with his mother replying, "Silo."

"Honey," asked Harry, settling into a comfortable position at the wheel, "Am I a good preacher?"

"You certainly are. Your sermons are always interesting. I learn a lot from them."

"I'm wondering if the people in Springvale will like what I have to say."

"Of course, they will! What is your subject today?"

"I'm preaching on commitment. Remember the story of the rich, young ruler who went away sorrowful because he had a lot of this world's goods and didn't want to sacrifice his wealth to follow Jesus?"

"It sounds challenging, Dear."

They lapsed into silence. Babs found herself thinking about the possibility of moving, and the happy prospect of living in a well-maintained parsonage, and even having a refrigerator! She was intrigued with the thought of occasionally playing a Hammond Organ.

"If we are transferred to Springvale, won't I feel lucky that Father Kelly showed me how to play the Hammond and work the drawbars to create sounds like clarinet, flute, violin, and diapason?"

Harry, on the other hand, at the wheel of the car was wrestling alternately with the scary prospect of preaching to a different congregation today, and feelings of guilt for even considering leaving people he loved.

"If I decide to move on," he asked himself, "am I quitting just because the going is rough?"

He found Will Erickson's comment about pastors with tunnel vision arresting.

"But don't the people of my parish need me?" he asked himself.

He recalled Dr. Miller's word about being open to God's leading.

"The Springvale parish needs an energetic pastor, and they are people who will support the man in the pulpit!"

"I don't really know what I should do," said Harry aloud.

"If you're asking the Lord for guidance, don't you think He will give it?" asked the minister's wife.

"I don't know. I hope so."

After a couple of hours of driving, they arrived in Madison and stopped at a cafe for breakfast.

"What a wonderful treat, going out for breakfast!" said Babs as she settled George into a high chair, and, with the help of their cheerful, red-headed waitress, pulled him close to their booth. She gave him a soda cracker.

"Stopping here breaks up our trip," answered Harry. "You had hoped we'd get out early enough not to be observed, right?"

"No chance of that, was there? The people of Prairie Meadows get up with the birds."

"Would you like coffee, and are you ready to order?" asked the waitress.

"Two coffees, please, and I'd like two eggs over easy with bacon and wheat toast."

Babs was considering the menu.

"What do you have for babies?"

"Some mothers order scrambled eggs or corn flakes.'

"You don't have oatmeal?"

"Sorry."

"I'll have scrambled eggs with wheat toast for me, and corn flakes for George," she decided.

"Coming right up!"

"Oh, I hope I do all right," said Harry, sipping the hot brew.

"You'll do fine. Dr. Miller and George and I have a lot of confidence in you."

An hour and a half later, Harry was on Library Street, driving past the Springvale Memorial Church. As Dr. Miller had told him, it was a half block from Main Street, an attractive, stuccoed building with broad steps leading up toward a rather imposing entrance of double doors. Along the wall fronting the street was the sanctuary decorated with four, tall, stained glass windows. The area behind the front entrance was two stories—possibly containing the educational unit.

"The building looks well-kept, doesn't it?" remarked Babs.

"Yes," replied her husband, cautiously.

"Tall trees beside the church."

They craned their necks as Harry drove slowly by.

"There's a two-story Victorian right next to the church," she said.

"It's probably the parsonage."

"No flowers," she remarked. "I suppose the last minister's wife wasn't interested in tending a garden."

"Dr. Miller told me that the former pastor was close to retirement. Maybe they didn't have the pep to take care of a yard."

Harry looked in the rear-view mirror and saw a blue Chevrolet behind him.

"I'm slowing people up," he said. "I'll go around the block."

He turned left, drove up the hill, past other Victorians with attractive gardens, and made another left. They saw a school on the right, and a park on the left.

"H-m-m, that blue sedan is still behind me," he noted as he made a third left turn onto Upper Main Street, going past beautiful, two-story homes on the right, and the city park on the left. A final left turn landed them on Library Street once again. Harry slowed and stopped in front of the church. The driver of the sedan followed suit.

"The church is on a hill with a pretty park beside it!" exclaimed Babs.

As they were getting out of the car, a tall couple from the sedan behind them approached. The man, wearing a three-piece navy blue suit, had a trim mustache, large brown eyes and a smooth complexion, while the woman had a rangy look with short blond hair and an open smile.

The man smiled and extended his hand.

"Are you Rev. and Mrs. Petersen from Prairie Meadows?" he asked.

"Yes, we are," answered Harry shaking hands.

"We are Norman and Sally Churchill from the Springvale Memorial congregation," he answered, taking Babs's hand.

"What a charming man!" said she to herself. "My mother would say, 'He wears his clothes with an air.'"

"We are here to welcome you and make you feel at home," announced Sally.

"Thank you," answered Babs. "Harry, would you carry George?"

"I'll take him.," he answered reaching for his son. "There's a rest room at the church, isn't there?"

"Yes, but we can do better than that. I have the key to the parsonage, and you can make yourselves at home there," responded Norman, brushing back a stray wisp of his dark hair.

"Fine," replied Harry.

"I laid out towels and soap for you," said Sally. "Dr. Miller told us you were tall like us, and you surely are!"

Harry locked the car, and the four walked up the street to the two-story Victorian beside the church.

"Did you have a good trip down?"

"Very pleasant, Mr. Churchill."

"Please call us Norman and Sally. If some one says, 'Mr. Churchill,' I think I must be in trouble," he answered with a twinkle in his eye.

As she climbed the steps to the parsonage, Babs wondered if one of these days she would walk up the steps many times. The house was large, with high ceilings and shiny blond wooden floors. The living room was bare, except for a maroon rug on the floor.

"If the minister's wife doesn't like the rug, we can get rid of it," announced Sally.

"Personally, I like it," said Babs.

"We'll wait here in the living room," said Norman. "You can look around and freshen up. The bathroom is off the kitchen."

Harry and Babs walked through the bare, spacious dining room located behind the living room, and entered the kitchen.

"Oh, I love these brand new metal, kitchen cupboards, Harry! And look, there's a refrigerator!"

The door to the bath was open, and they saw it contained a large washbasin and medicine cabinet, ample towel racks, and a large, old-fashioned tub with claws.

"Harry, you could really stretch out in that tub!"

"I could, couldn't I?"

He set George down.

"Here's the new pantry that Dr. Miller mentioned. Nice. Let's look around."

Walking through the swinging door, followed by George who was creeping along the floor, Babs found herself in a large room with six doors leading off to all parts of the house. The first door disclosed a large clothes closet.

"How nice, to have closet with a door!" she gloated.

Harry joined her as she explored.

"Look, Honey," she said, "this door goes to the basement, this to the hall, one to a small front room, and others to a closet, and the kitchen."

Opening the last door, they found themselves looking into the dining room.

"I must get over to the church to orient myself," declared Harry.

"There will be time after church to see the whole parsonage," said Norman. "Why don't we go over to the church now?"

The men left together.

"George needs a fresh diaper," said Babs, picking up the baby.

"Would you like to change him in the kitchen?" asked Sally.

"Yes, I would," returned Babs laying George on the counter.

"Our congregation is all excited about the prospect of a new pastor," remarked Sally as they locked the parsonage door and walked toward the church. "Dr. Miller told us that we can expect a meaningful worship service and a good sermon from the Rev. Petersen."

"It's a good thing that Harry has gone ahead and didn't hear about the expectations of the people," said the pastor's wife to herself. "He's feeling enough pressure as it is!"

Chapter 69

OPPORTUNITIES FOR SERVICE

In May, when the Petersens left for California, Babs had seven piano pupils: four little girls including Pamela, plus Marvin Waukowski of Sterling, Pat Riley's grandson, Peter, and her adult pupil, Pat Rice. As far as she knew, all were planning to resume lessons in the fall. Babs took her responsibilities as piano teacher very seriously.

Take Pamela Clark, for example. She had been taking lessons for over a year and a half. Yet, she had made almost no progress.

While shopping one day at Clark's Market, Pamela's mother, from behind the meat counter, greeted Babs cordially as she looked over the selections of meat and fish.

"Today," Margaret said, "I recommend the lamb chops." Finding that she was the only customer in the shop, Babs decided to broach the subject of Pamela's music lessons.

"She hasn't made much progress, is she?" replied Margaret.

"No, she hasn't. She always does what I tell her to, but I don't think she is interested in the piano. But Pamela has shown me pictures that she has drawn. Sometimes she gives me a picture."

"She's quite a little artist, isn't she?" laughed Margaret.

"Yes. I put her drawing of her cat, Cherry, on my ice box." Margaret smiled, and Babs hesitated and then pressed on.

"I'm wondering if perhaps Pamela would enjoy taking art lessons."

"Art lessons? Oh, I heard there's a teacher in Stevens Point who gives them."

"Pamela is a very dear child and very talented, but I'm not sure that her area is piano music."

"Bob and I have talked about her piano playing. Peter Riley, on the neighboring farm, hasn't been taking as long as Pam, but he loves to play little pieces for anyone who will listen. Not Pamela! Perhaps we are putting too much pressure on her. Maybe we should maybe give her rest from the piano."

Babs nodded.

"I think you may be wise."

At that moment, two women walked into the market.

"I'll take three lamb chops, Margaret," said Babs.

"Here you are, Mrs. Petersen," answered Margaret as she weighed and packaged the chops. "Thank you. I appreciate what you said."

On the way home, Babs was thinking about her other pupils. Pat Rice was doing so well; she hated not to be able to continue to help her with her music.

Another responsibility, dear to her heart, was the Sunday School at Rosebud. Attendance was up. They all seemed to enjoy her stories from the Bible, told in flannelgraph. These times were precious, and she was thinking about them as she walked to the Woods' house where she'd left George.

She knocked, and Pricilla answered. As she entered, she saw George, Margie, and her little sister building a high tower with blocks. How George laughed when the tower fell down!

"Does George have to go home?" asked Margie.

"I'm afraid so," answered Babs. "But he can come again if you want."

"The girls enjoyed him so much, Babs," said Priscilla. "Tim Sr. and Tom went to Wisconsin Rapids."

"Ma ma ma da da," said George, creeping over to his mother.

"You had a good time, didn't you, George," said his mother, picking him up, "but now we have to go home."

"I'll get the teeter-babe," volunteered Margie.

"Goodbye, and thank you for having George over," said Babs as they left.

After lunch, George went down for his nap, and Babs turned on the public radio station for classical music, settling into the sofa with Tuck, the darning egg, and three pairs of Harry's socks. After a while, she heard footsteps, and Harry entered the living room.

"You look tired! Did the Prairie Meadows Businessmen's Association have a good meeting?"

"Yes, we had election of officers."

"Who's the new president?"

"Jim Barry, of *The Banner*."

Babs thought that, under his air of cool nonchalance, Harry looked excited.

"Who else was elected?"

"Ray Gold, owner of the fuel company, came to the meeting for the first time. They elected him secretary."

"Oh, do you have an office now?"

"No. As soon as I get the minutes typed, I'll turn the secretary's book over to Ray Gold. I'll go up and get started."

"By the way, you got a phone call."

"A phone call?"

"Yes, it was Clara Wells. She said that Harley's nephew, Tom, is taking over the farm next to theirs. She thought that you'd like to know that Tom said that he'd be glad to help them out."

"That's interesting," mused Harry. "Two of my responsibilities in Prairie Meadows and Sterling, are being taken over by other people."

Chapter 70

DECISION

A week passed with no word from either Dr. Miller or the Springvale Church. In the midst of calling on prospective members and the sick or working at sermons, Harry caught himself daydreaming about a church located in a prosperous country town. During the first week after his visit, Harry truly believed that he was about to receive a call from the church, the "substantial church," which Dr. Miller had led him to believe would welcome his leadership.

Every time the phone rang, he jumped, and each day he watched eagerly for the arrival of Bob Rennik with the mail. However, as the week wore on, he felt less and less certain about his chances of being called.

During the second week, he became moody. He decided that he'd been presumptuous even to preach at Springvale. Evidently, he had not lived up to the expectations of the people. He had failed to challenge them. The congregation would find a more gifted and competent minister. And the man they chose would take his place in the community as a servant and a leader. Yes, the church had a great future, but he would not figure in it. He had failed.

Sitting at his desk upstairs Harry found himself, thinking and praying about his life. What about Babs and George and himself? What kind of future lay ahead of them? He reluctantly admitted to himself that he had become excited at the thought of moving, and that he truly wanted to serve where he had candidated.

"However," he said to himself sternly, "I must remain in Prairie Meadows until the work to which I have been called, is completed."

He sighed.

"Heavenly Father, I confess that the excitement of a possible change distracted me from my duties in Prairie Meadows, Sterling, and Rosebud. In putting distance between myself and our friends and neighbors here, I have tasted discontent—it's bitter fruit. I ask Thy blessing on my ministry here."

Harry shook his head, exasperated at the longings that tugged at him. By the close of the second week, the young pastor had to acknowledge that he was going about his duties with a sad heart. Facing a third week, he had to share his feeling with Babs.

"You know, it's like I'm hanging between two worlds and am part of neither," he said as he sat in his chair and perused *The Pulpit Digest.*

George had been creeping around the living room, and now was occupied with putting variously shaped objects into his plastic ball.

Babs looked up from the sofa where she was folding diapers.

"What do you mean, 'two worlds'?" she asked.

"Well, we had a glimpse of Springvale, with its lovely people and a beautiful church in a prosperous town.

He paused.

"By the way, I sure enjoyed talking with Jerry Jones, the car dealer. He told me I'd be needing another car soon, and he'd be glad to keep an eye out for one for me."

"I thought Jerry was captivating. Do you think he'd give us a break on a used car?" asked Babs.

"Maybe he would have."

"Norman Churchill was charming, too, and Sally, so generous."

Harry sighed. Babs looked at him thoughtfully.

"And this parish is the other world?"

Harry nodded.

293

"I see Bob Rennik out there, putting our mail in the box," she said, getting up and walking out the front door.

Harry saw her talking with the mailman before coming back into the house. She came in with some letters and sat on the sofa.

"Had you heard, Harry, that Chester got hit by a car?"

"Chester, the dog?"

"Yes. It's ironical—"

"Why ironical?"

"Fay Seevers is a loner, you remember."

"A loner, except that time she was determined to join the Prairie Meadows Businessmen's Association."

"Yes, Dear," answered Babs sweetly. "It's ironical because she doesn't like people, but she really loves dogs—especially her collie, Eric. Well, she was driving down Fifth Street and looked over at Eric in the front seat. Just then, Chester dashed out in the street, chasing a calico cat, and Fay didn't see him and ran into the dog."

"Was it serious?"

"Bob said that Chester's left leg was broken, and he'll will be out of commission for a while."

"I'll bet Bob's relieved."

Babs nodded.

"Bob doesn't like to see a dog hurt, but he's glad that Chester won't be bothering him for a while."

"What's in the mail? Any letters from Springvale or Milwaukee?"

"No. Letters from your mom and mine."

She passed the mail to Harry except for the letter from her mother.

"According to this notice, my subscription to *The Pulpit Digest* is expiring. I guess I'll renew it."

"Should you wait, in case of a possible change of address?"

"No, if the Springvale Church wanted to call me, I would have heard by now. I might as well face it, the good Lord knows that I have unfinished business here, and if I'd been offered the chance, I would have moved."

He marked the renewal card and marched out to the mailbox.

She glanced up as he returned and sat down in his chair again.

"I guess you're right. You have large responsibilities here, and my piano pupils need lessons, and the Rosebud Sunday School needs my teaching."

Harry sat motionless, staring out into space.

"Oh, in this letter, Mother wants to know whether we'll be moving or not. She says she has to know because she and Dad are picking up a new Nash in Racine, Wisconsin the last of August, and they want to visit us before driving home. She wants to hear all about George, of course."

The phone rang, and Babs went to answer it, with Nip and Tuck following. After a brief phone call, she went to the icebox, took out a quart of milk, and poured some into the cats' dish. They eagerly drank.

"You two were thirsty, weren't you?" asked their mistress.

Returning to the living room, Babs resumed folding the diapers.

"Who was that on the phone?"

"Alberta, about Culture Club. She wants me to be co-hostess with her in January. I said I would."

"Might as well."

"Life has to go on. What does your Mother say, Harry?"

"They liked the jar of green beans that you brought, and Dad says 'Hello" to George. She and Dad are praying for guidance for us."

"No problem. Since I won't even have a chance to turn down the Springvale assignment, I'll have no trouble detecting God's will, that's for sure," he frowned.

Another week passed. When the pump in the Prairie Meadows Church gave out, Fred Young called a meeting of the trustees. Vainly, Harry tried to focus his attention on the problem before them.

Both Fred and Tim noticed his absent-minded responses. Lingering a bit after the others had left, Tim asked Harry if anything was wrong.

"I hope that you and the missus and the baby are fine."

Fred stood silent on the front porch, cocking his head in concern.

"Thank you, Tim, Fred. We, uh, the family, are fine. I guess I'm a little tired."

"Are you taking your day off, Pastor?" asked Fred. "We know that Sunday is not a day of rest for you."

"Fred, you sound like my wife. I guess I should take some time off, once in a while."

"Yes, we know you need it," said Tim, as he and Fred began to walk down the front steps.

Closing the door, Harry went to the bedroom.

"Honey, Fred said I ought to take a day off."

"Yes, you should."

"Well, I have to go to Wisconsin Rapids tomorrow to get my shoes fixed. Why don't you come along?"

"Yes, I could pack a lunch, and we could eat in the park. George likes the swings. Oh, dear—"

"What's the matter?"

"Tomorrow is the day the Busy Bees meet. They expect me to be there."

"Well, I expect you to be with me."

"I made a Jell-O salad. I'll take it over to Rita. She's hosting the meeting."

Harry smiled.

"It will be good to get away for a few hours."

The following evening, after Harry and Babs had finished dinner and George had been tucked into bed, she carried a tray with her engagement teacups, coffee pot, and cookies, into the living room. Pouring his coffee, she passed him the cookies.

"Well, the coffee tastes very good in these pretty cups," remarked Harry. "How come you're using them?"

"This is my way of saying 'thank you' for taking a few hours off. George and I enjoyed having you all to ourselves."

Harry looked at his wife tenderly, watching as she worked on her needlepoint.

"I don't take time off very often, do I?"

"That's right, you don't."

The phone rang, and Harry rose to answer it.

"That's my mother, Harry. She said she'd phone tonight."

Harry picked up the phone.

"Good evening, Harry," said a familiar voice.

"Oh, hello. How are you?"

"Fine, but Harry, I owe you an apology."

"Apology? For what?"

"I just got back from a three-week vacation," answered Dr. Miller. "Normally, I should have been in touch with you, much sooner than this."

"That's all right, Dr. Miller."

"I'm afraid I kept you dangling."

"Not really. I can accept the fact that the people of Springvale are looking for a really good preacher."

"Yes, they want a good preacher."

"I realize that I haven't completed my work here."

"What?"

"I confess that I was attracted to the Springvale Church, but I realize that I'm not yet ready for a challenge like that."

"Harry, you are drawing all the wrong conclusions. When I returned I found three letters and five phone messages from Springvale people, including the Churchills, a persuasive fellow named Jerry Jones, and a cranky woman, Mrs. Snodgrass."

"Eight messages?"

"Yes. The people loved you and your wife and your baby. They are extending a call you to serve as their pastor."

"Oh?"

"You will accept their call, won't you, Harry? It involves a lot more responsibility and a substantial raise."

"Dr. Miller, I can't take this in. Do they really want me? When I didn't hear, I figured that it was all off."

"It's not off. It's definitely on. The people are unanimous in their desire to have you as their minister. Talk it over with your wife, and call me back tomorrow morning, if possible."

"All right. Thank you, Dr. Miller," said Harry looking dazed, as he hung up the phone.

He turned and saw Babs standing beside him, her color heightened, her eyes bright.

"Do they want us?" she whispered.

"Yes, they want us."

"What are we going to do?" she asked, holding her arms out to him.

"Right now, I feel like celebrating, don't you?" he said, drawing her close.

"Yes, my darling, let's celebrate! It's wonderful that we're going to serve in Springvale!"

His kisses were hot on her neck.

"Well, tomorrow, I guess I'll call Dr. Miller and tell him we accept."

"Great," she sighed. "Anything else?"

"Well, you'll have to call your mother and tell her we'll be moving."

"Oh," she said, between kisses, "Do you think I should cancel helping Alberta in January?"

"H-m-m, unless you want to come back here next winter, " answered Harry, as he picked her up and carried her to their bedroom. "My darling, I love you so."

"Sweetheart!"

Later on, resting in his warm embrace, Babs traced his full lips with her index finger.

"I just thought of something, Harry."

"Is it important, my love?"

"To a minister, yes. "

Running his hand though her dark locks, he asked,

"What important matter concerns my lover?"

"Gorgeous, that notice you put in our mail box? Do you want to send our new address to the *Pulpit Digest*?"

An English teacher, a pastor's wife and a journalist, Betty Rae McCormack came to rural Wisconsin as a young bride. A Californian, she was intrigued with the midwestern point of view which she encountered. Religion, jealousy, people unexpectedly kind or cruel, were part of her experience. *To Cook A Squirrel,* reveals the problems, dilemmas, joys and frustrations facing an inexperienced minister and his family.

How to Cook A Squirrel
A recipe from Betty Rae McCormack's files

Gut and skin the squirrel as soon as possible.

Soak overnight in cold salt water.

Rinse thoroughly.

Coat in flour and quick-fry, using bacon fat in very hot pot until browned.

Add a handful of coarsely chopped onion, a handful of chopped celery and a spoonful of finely chopped garlic about a minute before the browning is complete.

Drain any extra fat, but leave bits of flour, seasonings and squirrel in the pot.

Add chopped vegetables and salt and pepper to the pot.

Include enough water to just cover the squirrel. Simmer on low heat until the meat is just falling off the bones.

Serve with chilled fresh fruit and biscuits.

Your kitchen will smell like heaven!

Breinigsville, PA USA
26 October 2010
248094BV00002B/1/P

9 780615 382913